The Last Prophet

Michael J. Hallisey, M.D.

D1415954

Praise for
THE LAST PROPHET

"A delicious mix of mystery, medicine and masterpiece artist Caravaggio."
--Jeffrey J. Fox. Author of the international best seller,
How to Become a Rainmaker.

"Captivating, intelligent, and delightful. I was hooked from the first paragraph. A true Thriller!"
--Brian Wilson, Lifestar Flight Nurse

"Murder, mystery, science, art, and literature intertwined to produce a thriller blurring the lines between history and fiction. With each turn of the page travel back in time and around the globe in pursuit of the solution to a deadly puzzle. An intricate and interesting story."
--Stuart K. Markowitz, M.D.
President, Hartford Hospital
Senior VP, Hartford Healthcare

"International intrigue...underlying sexual tension between Genevieve and Jake...unravel clues involving Caravaggio paintings, Shakespeare passages and the shadowy world of the Knights Templar—a first novel on par with Dan Brown's finest."
--Jean Kelly Cummings, esq.

"Twists and turns, incredibly suspenseful, thrilling nonstop action. This thriller skillfully intrigues the reader with art history, medical mystery and adventure."
--Erin Kirby

"From the first sentence, THE LAST PROPHET immerses the reader in heart-racing suspense that you never see coming. You can't put it down!"
--Greg Frani, M.B.A. LifeStar Flight Respiratory
Therapist

For the boys

ACKNOWLEDGMENTS

The origins of this book start with my four boys. It was a tradition in my home to tell bed time stories. And, I loved history. My four sons would climb into their bunk beds, the lights would go out and I'd do my best to weave an historical story of art, literature, religion, travel. I'd make up a new chapter every night. Unfortunately, I'd usually fall asleep in mid sentence then awakening to them screaming, "more Dad, more!" When they went off to college I went off with them—but to a public library where I could research, to a hospital helideck where I could interview Lifestar nurses and pilots, to an ER where I could watch great trauma doctors on the front lines and to some great museums to see firsthand the shock and awe of a Caravaggio painting. You should try it sometime . . . after you read this book.

Along the way my wife's patience was worn, her criticism invaluable and her love undying. I was extremely grateful to have the advice, support and editing of Helen Whall, Ph.D., the Rock Star of Shakespeare scholars and my former Professor at the College of the Holy Cross. Tiffany Yates at FoxPrint was extremely helpful and brutally honest. Jean Cumming's advice was timely and helped pull the project into focus. Finally, Richard Marek, the legendary editor, took me under his wing and guided me with advice on how to write with passion. To all, I am deeply grateful.

Prologue

2100 hours
June, 2012
Connecticut General Hospital

The Lifestar MedEvac helicopter punched into the turbulence and plunged downward like a jumper on a bungee cord.

Doctor Riley McKee looked up from her patient. Her stomach plummeted and she gasped a quick breath. Grabbing her shoulder harness with one hand she pushed down with the other on the cushioned cargo seat. She stiffened momentarily when a burst of adrenaline sent a cold tingle down her spine. The air ambulance continued to race at 140 miles per hour 2000 feet above the moonlit skyline toward Connecticut General Hospital.

A column door slid open and two intravenous fluid bags sloshed onto the seat next to Greg Wilson, the flight nurse. From across the cabin he flipped up his night vision goggles, NVGs, and his dark eyes glared out from beneath his flight helmet. He threw one palm up at Riley, speaking into his voice activated microphone, "Some choppy air over the Connecticut River. Different temperature, you know." He smiled, turned back to check the patient's heart monitor, all the while rocking back and forth.

Riley rolled her eyes in mock approval. She loved her career as a trauma surgeon. But she didn't like the occasional flying. *Or, whatever I'm doing inside this contraption,* she thought.

Looking up and down the narrow medical bay, Riley assessed the dying patient on the stretcher. He'd been shot point blank in the groin, likely slicing open the femoral artery. The blood loss had slowed beneath the compression pants. Drops of blood now congealed on the floor, turning purple-black in the blue-lit cabin. Leaning forward, Riley lifted the patient's upper eyelids and waved a penlight into his eyes. *Still no response. His head must have hit the pavement after he was shot.* She instinctively placed her stethoscope on his chest and checked for his rhythmic breathing, quickly realizing that listening was impossible over the sound of the engines. She put her hand on his chest. His breathing and heart rate were regular.

An Andrew Jackson gunshot injury, Riley pondered. A "Jackson" still made plain to emergency trauma surgeons the barbarian hopelessness on the city streets.

The seventh president was now part of the evil of inner city America. Andrew Jackson was enraged when the fastest duelist in the United States, with twenty-six confirmed kills, called his wife a prostitute. Jackson challenged him at twenty paces and even allowed the sharpshooter to fire his pistol first. When the bullet hit him, he only grimaced at his chest wound two inches from his heart. He then casually lowered his gun and intentionally shot the man in the scrotum. The duelist died a slow, miserable death. On the street, shooters still invoke the president during a groin shot of execution or retribution. It was a harsh warning to the survivors. In the Emergency Room, doctors shudder at the idea of another Andrew Jackson gunshot. *Twenty paces,* Riley thought. *The Prez earned his face on the twenty dollar bill alright.*

Not wearing NVGs, Riley reached through the eerie shadows of the medical bay and dialed back the saline infusions swinging from the clanging steel hooks. Her head felt warm and light inside her flight helmet. She tried to distract herself from her fear of flying. She glared forward over the central console and orange drug pack, studying the glimmer of LCD screens in the cockpit.

She glanced back again at the flight nurse. Wilson's flight suit was adorned with a small American flag, its pockets revealing a bulky claw nose scissors for cutting clothing, a large bore needle and syringe for collapsed lungs and a survival knife in the event of a jungle crash. *The jungle in Connecticut?* She thought. He stared at the two inch silk tape stuck to his thigh that he was using to record the patient's vital signs. His shoulders pulsed like a rapper to the pitch, roll and yaw of the aircraft while she felt more like a ping pong ball shaking in a tennis can.

The helicopter thumped into another air pocket and leaped upward. The patient shifted on the stretcher, pushing against her knees in the tight cabin. Riley turned to look out the window in the side door. *Ugh. Long way down. Nothing between me and a pavement pancake.* She flashed a rapid sign of the cross. Wilson blasted back into his mic, "The patients make you atheist but the flight makes you religious." Smiling, he pointed upward with his index finger. "Don't worry . . . those thwacking rotors can beat back gravity."

"Gravity?" She murmured, knowing that he couldn't hear her whisper over the 90 growling decibels of the Arriel engines and beating rotors. When the Code Red call exploded across the radio earlier, her stomach knotted up. The routine flight had become a gunshot trauma and they'd turned back to dash to the scene.

Riley gazed back at her patient. Her focus was drawn to the bullet wound. The rapid shift in the stretcher position had displaced the artery compression device, exposing the bleeding site again. Unlatching her harness, Riley instinctively reached over to stanch the bleeding.

Wilson screamed out at Riley, "Get your harness back on!"

"But he's bleeding again." Riley mouthed the words, unhooking her communication cord.

His face flushed red. "Your harness!" He yelled, pointing to Riley to sit back. She couldn't hear him over the howl of the rotors.

The pilot partially turned inward to look back from the cockpit. He bellowed, "Riley, get back in your seat. We're a half mile out!"

The air ambulance weaved past the Traveler's Insurance Tower then banked back before whirling into a steep arc. The tail boom was a bug-like shadow across the moon above the Hartford skyline when they approached the largest, and only, helipad that could accept Marine One in New England. Steel red frames extended up, out and around the hospital helideck holding the thick perimeter safety netting.

Drawing closer, the helicopter started to slow its airspeed. Descending through 500 feet the rotating blades sliced the darkness.

"His wound is opening up. He's bleeding out. His blood pressure is dropping." Riley screeched angrily. Lunging across the stretcher from her seat to get better compression, she grasped for the patient's right groin. She threw her hands out over the wound and applied deep pressure. The blood spurted up between her neoprene-gloved fingers. *I got this,* she said to herself.

Reaching across the patient from his harness, Wilson grasped the dangling black cord and hooked up Riley's comm. His shoulders cast a passing shadow over the supine patient. He placed his hand on Riley's arm trying to rotate her to look at him. Then, he leaned back with shock exploding across his face. Without warning, the patient had turned, snapping a gun up like a cobra from his side and pointing it into Riley's face.

"Riley, I thought you did a full exposure of the patient?"

Riley fixed her stare at the front gun sight, the cold muzzle stuck against her nose. She froze. She could hardly speak. The man's eyes were so dark he seemed dead. Yet his stained teeth clenched in terror and sweat poured down his face.

"You cut his trousers north to south. You did it." She stammered.

She felt her heart thump in her chest, skipping a beat. She tried to swallow but her tongue was dry. *What should I do?* Her eyes shifted back and forth.

She felt the spreading chill of icy tension. The roar of engines grew louder in her head.

Wafting from the barrel she could smell gunpowder burning through her nostrils. She felt a bead of sweat balancing on her forehead.

The green LED beacons radiated from the hospital into her peripheral vision and glimmered across the cabin. This meant they were near "short final," in their landing approach. Spot lights flooded the deck and reflected through the night sky. The large blue H for the Connecticut General Hospital floated into view through the side door window. The helicopter shuddered as their forward movement slowed.

"Riley, I've got faith between my teeth." Wilson calmly garbled over the comm link.

The patient swung his gun back and forth from Riley to Wilson, his face filled with rage. Wilson raised both his hands in a surrender pose to the gunman.

She looked up to see a syringe in the nurse's mouth and

recognized the drug succinylcholine locked and loaded in the shaft. It would bring instant paralysis. He nodded to her. She knew what he wanted to do. "Just give me two seconds, Riley."

In one swift motion he squeezed the needle cap between his teeth, grabbing the syringe with his thumb extended. He slammed the needle into the patient's arm, compressing the paralytic drug into his body tissues.

The patient let out a piercing scream. The man flinched and squeezed the trigger. The gun flashed and a round whizzed overhead into the cockpit avionics. Then a second hiss of gunfire. The bullet sliced through the pilot's seat. Wilson fumbled forward and grabbed the gun from the slumping patient.

The helicopter suddenly wobbled and pitched sideways in the evening sky. It paused momentarily then picked up speed. The nose dipped downward.

A loud grunt came across the radio. Wilson and Riley looked at each other and then the cockpit. The nose pulled back up, froze, and suddenly plunged again. The unconscious pilot slumped forward in his harness slamming on the cyclic stick.

Riley gasped. She was thrown forward and blindly clenched the side door handle. She felt like she was in an elevator dropping in a high rise. Then stopping abruptly. Throwing out her arms, Riley was tossed like a sack over the top of the patient.

Wilson jumped up but his harness yanked him back. He yelled but Riley could not hear him, "May Day!" Smoke billowed through the compartment and the smell of melting plastic on metal choked the cabin.

Riley felt burning in her chest as the adrenaline flooded her veins.

The chopper vibrated, stalled, crashing thunderously on the edge of the helideck, hopping and sliding sidelong like a drunken college student.

Riley yanked on the side door which slid open. The machine tilted. She rolled forward, hitting the outside door. The rolling movement threw her back into the cabin then out again. Riley tasted a liquid in her mouth, blood. It was her blood. Clutching the side handle, her legs swinging out over the side of the skids, she felt her body vibrating from the rapid movements, the echoes of the rotors shaking her muscles. She was then thrown into the air and through the open door, her body caught and dangling alone through the helideck's perimeter safety net.

The engines violently belched out smoke, the copter turning onto its side, splintering the titanium rotors. Impotent, the lifeless machine rolled off the side of the building and disappeared behind the trail of smoke. The helicopter tumbled 130 feet and exploded in a ball of fire.

Suddenly, complete silence.

Chapter 1

Two years later

0600 hours
June, 2014
Connecticut General Hospital

Dr. Jenny Neugold bolted through the Emergency Room doors, the tail of her white coat fluttering in her wake.

"Where's Riley? Dr. Riley McKee?" Jenny shouted to the startled nurses at the station desk.

"She's . . . she's in Trauma Room two." A nurse sputtered.

Jenny planted one foot onto the wheel plate of a stainless steel intravenous pole and skip paddled with her other foot, skating down the hallway.

"Watch out Dr. Neugold!" The nurse shrieked. Jenny hastily turned the corner and picked up speed. "Dr. McKee's working on a gunshot patient."

Jenny ignored her.

Her unsteady carriage teetered and rattled on the linoleum floors. She briefly lost her balance then switched her feet, leaned forward and centered herself on the plate, careening down the narrow corridor between the stretchers and frightened orderlies. Jenny then picked up speed on the straightaway, moving like a white coat tornado. She felt the electrical sting of adrenaline racing down her back and the urgency to find her friend and fellow surgeon.

Turning another corner she scooted through the pillared foyer, sailing past the internal medicine cubicles toward the Trauma rooms. Pushing one hand off the wall she spun the wheels into the middle of the hallway.

Ahead, Jenny saw Riley emerge from the Trauma Room

removing her surgical gloves, her gaze transfixed in shock back toward the exam room. Riley partially turned. Her back slammed into an empty gurney.

Jenny's makeshift sailboat raced past Riley and she skidded to a stop. Jenny waved two silver rings in one hand.

Riley snapped her head down the hallway and raised her hands. "Jenny? What are you doing?"

"I solved the puzzle," Jenny said breathlessly. She tossed the two metallic bangles into the air, launching herself off the intravenous pole. Like most sanitized Emergency Rooms there were no paintings or pictures in the hallways of Connecticut General Hospital. The sky blue walls funneled a soothing optical illusion through the windowless tunnels of trauma rooms that regularly welcomed the night's faithlessness. Long oak railings split the walls like fallen medieval lances and, on occasion, were used to handcuff cantankerous patients. Despite the mirage, this area of the ER was the final stop for many of the city's depraved gangbangers. The vision and structure were sterile, utilitarian . . . awaiting their last cries of defeat.

"You didn't hear me. I figured out your puzzle." Jenny's eyes widened. Twirling the two silver rings, her voice wheezed slightly, her breathing strained from racing through the hallways. Her ponytail waved through the air like a red flag. Holding out her hands she shared her excitement. "I love the prize."

"Jenny, not now." Dr. Riley McKee gaped, the muscles around her eyes contracting to a rare look of fear.

Jenny beamed, ignoring her. "But I figured out the riddle. Setting a clue in Gregorian chant? At first I studied the EKG printout." She spoke at staccato cadence. Her head pivoted side-to-side with her hands explaining the discovery. "I analyzed the rhythm and . . . the grid markings. But then I realized it wasn't a common arrhythmia. And the tiny squares were notes. Notes! Very clever of you. But then the clue 'pneumonia' finally clicked. I recognized that they weren't notes at all . . . but neumes—from the Greek word for pneumonia."

"Jenny?" Riley's voice grew serious. "Stop…" She paused for effect. "It was a shot to the upper thigh. I just finished pulling out a nine-millimeter slug from that patient." Her eyes signaled back into the room at the supine patient.

Riley's urgency still didn't register with Jenny. Jenny lobbed the rings into the air.

"Another *Andrew Jackson* gun shot." Riley's stern voice sliced the air.

Jenny's body suddenly tensed. She turned. Her pulse accelerated.

The silver rings hit the floor and rolled back toward Riley standing in the doorway in front of her trauma patient. The words blazed through Jenny's mind like a muzzle flash. *Another groin shot?! An* Andrew Jackson. *The last time that happened . . . was two years ago . . . she'll relive the nightmare of that horrific helicopter crash.* Jenny shook from her trance and fixed her stare on her fellow surgeon.

"A warning shot?" Riley's cheeks went pale and she squeezed her eyes tightly. "Another gang war?"

She's trying to shake it off. Jenny put both hands up to her mouth.

"Okay. Is he stable?" Jenny asked.

"Yes. He'll live . . . for now."

Only true emergencies made an ER doctor's heart race. The most horrifying emergency for a surgeon. . .the *Andrew Jackson* meant more trauma patients were coming soon.

"I don't think he shot himself. He didn't have a pistol in his pants." Riley moved her fingers into a star pattern. "The angle of entry." Gritting her teeth, her voice elevated several octaves. She locked her fingers. "Classic star-shaped powder burn from a close-contact shot. Tissue melt caused by the propellant."

Jenny sensed the conflict in her tone. Fear churning with anger.

It was anger directed outside the hospital at the boulevard of crime, an endless B movie of depravity where neon lights sold night for day. Nothing more than a rubbled street of yesterday's promises, the broken Jersey barriers standing much like gravestones.

Jenny scrutinized the patient without seeming to do so. Her look was likely perceived as resentment. She knew he'd live. . .this time because of Riley. The ashen patient on the stretcher grimaced back at Jenny, his steel handcuffs flashing beneath the large array of operative lights. He shook his head back at her. A little attitude from the man was expected . . . it was the deterrent he took back from the streets. Jenny understood the moment. It was rare that the "shot" patient was the one wearing the handcuffs. *This gunshot burned deep into Riley's memory. She can see the helicopter exploding.* Jenny thought.

Jenny studied Riley. Shuffling her feet, Riley's simple blue surgical scrub pants shook like pajama bottoms. Her blond tresses covered much of the V-neck opening on her shirt. But a blush of red was visible on her freckled chest. She hiked her eyebrows, let out a long breath of frustration and spun her claddagh ring, the crown disappearing into her palm. *Some wounds carried a dangerous scar.* Jenny thought.

Jenny walked slowly toward Riley, spread her hands outward on the door frame and looked deeper as if into a gaping chest wound. Pulling back, Jenny combed her hand through her hair, staring back and forth from Riley to the patient. *That projectile was the harshest of warnings.*

Chapter 2

Emergency Room
Connecticut General Hospital

Fresh blood trickled down from the wounded patient's stretcher. Jenny motioned toward the patient and tried to speak. No sound came. She closed her eyes and absorbed the silence.

How did she treat him so quickly? Jenny wondered. She was always impressed with Riley's diagnostic skills, her ability to piece together subtle physical signs other doctors overlooked or discarded prematurely. *Is that why Riley was so brilliant with her puzzles?* Why she constantly challenged Jenny with her brain teasers—both medical and historical.

The bloody surgical towels dressed the steel bin on the floor. The polished Mayo Stand drooped like a waiter holding up the crimson-stained gauze, steel clamps and half-used sutures. The patient on the gurney turned and faced away from them. Jenny fired an expression of dread toward Riley.

The two trauma surgeons drifted closer together. Jenny grasped Riley's anxiety. Hanging lifeless from the perimeter netting of the helideck two years earlier, Riley had narrowly escaped death. *The groin shot brought the memory back.* Grinding through the hours of work, thousands of vulnerable patients and years of friendship—they knew each other. Jenny felt her fear.

Riley stepped back and gestured for Jenny to walk a few steps out into the hallway with her. Jenny glared at the rings on the floor. She reached back and snatched the silver bracelets. The jubilation over solving that puzzle had to wait.

"I need to talk to you." Riley said haltingly. She glimpsed at the clock on her iPhone. "I've got less than thirty minutes to finish up. Can you help me with this patient before I call the police to take his statement?"

In her mind Jenny heard the words "shot himself" again. She saw a black and white image of her younger brother sitting on the couch, waving her father's gun. He looked so happy. A Glock

17. Black like their Labrador. She followed the intimidating red laser light on the pistol around the room. Then there was a flash. Suddenly, he was lying flat, lifeless. The image of losing her brother hung like a fog in front of her. The sirens coming closer. Adults closing in around her. *Where was Dad?* More sirens closing in. Jenny shook herself back to the present. She felt herself sweating, her ears getting warmer. She took a deep breath. Riley had taught her to control her emotion. She blew the air out. The rush of heat subsided.

"Sure. I can help." Jenny said, her voice drifting off.

"The quicker I get done . . . well." Riley stopped. Jenny squinted one eye, sensing something was rushing in Riley's throat. Then Riley made a snapping noise, forcing air out. No words. She put her hand up to her head and spun one eyebrow between her thumb and forefinger. Jenny knew the sign. Riley was holding back.

"You're making that face again, Riley."

"What?"

"What's wrong?" Jenny asked and she swallowed hard. She wagged her head, coaxing Riley to elaborate. "I'm your best friend. What is it?"

"Later. When we get done with this patient. I don't want to be late."

"Riley? This patient can't get far with that wound." Jenny pleaded. "He'll be limp for months. The whole street must be on fire right now with that hit. Besides, someone's more likely to finish him off right here if you don't get the police here quickly." Jenny figured there was one angry shooter lurking in the city.

"I've wanted to tell you." Riley's voice was serious, her look focused. "I think there's someone following me. I noticed him last night when I walked home from work. He was outside our apartment house."

Jenny was startled. *It's more than the painful memory of the helicopter.* She sensed it from the urgency in Riley's voice. "Who?" She knew her fellow trauma surgeon didn't scare easily. Her fearless heart could tame an armed gangbanger.

"Something I thought I saw. It was eerie. It was late but he had dark glasses." Riley started slowly then hurried her words. "Shoes shuffling on a sandy sidewalk in the darkness. A man on the sidewalk behind me . . . so I crossed—then he crossed. I stopped—then he stopped. I . . . I waited a moment until I saw a hospital security car coming toward me. I turned and he was gone. Then I . . . I . . . I ran into the apartment and locked the door." Her face flushed red and her eyes opened wide.

Jenny steadied herself against the wall and considered Riley's uneasy tone. "You're flustered because you're in a rush. To get things done before your trip to Ireland."

"Maybe . . ." An overhead page echoed through the ER. Riley shifted awkwardly. Jenny felt a growing heaviness in her own chest.

"You've always told me . . . take a few deep breaths, focus. Don't let panic creep in." Jenny said.

Riley waved her hand at Jenny. "Listen. I've been looking into a secret that relates to some old knights. It might be why someone was following me."

"What secret?" Jenny replied.

"History. Medieval and medical history. Medical doctor knights."

"I love it. That sounds great." Jenny encouraged Riley. "That's a great puzzle. Let me help." Jenny said. "Tell me about it. I just solved your Gregorian chant hidden in an EKG strip. I should be able to do Medieval history."

Riley stared coldly. "I wasn't intending to drag you in."

Jenny shot back a look of betrayal. It was her nature to help. "Do you have any idea of what you're looking for?"

"I have scattered clues. Puzzle pieces. Supposedly the mystery behind the knights' power was a miraculous healing source. It made them rich and celebrated. Powerful yet discreet. Imagine the command of patient's lives? Imagine a secret cure for cancer?" Riley's tone filled the words with reverence. "How'd you like to have a miracle cure in your black bag?"

The gears in Jenny's scientific mind cranked steel on steel, then froze. Riley's query didn't fit any equation she knew. She felt skepticism crawling in. "All through history there's been claims of witches' brews, herbal cures, phony snake oil salesmen and miracle healers. They were all imposters. Charlatans, quacks."

"Maybe so. It might be nothing." Riley's voice dropped a key with each word. "But this one's intriguing. I'm surprised that no one has discovered the power of these knights—their wealth and influence. I thought maybe I'd hit on something. Like I cracked open an ancient vault. And the air sucked me in. Like I turned a key and the knob clicked. Then . . . I thought someone was following me."

"Let's turn your patient back over to the police and we can talk about it." Jenny said.

Together they turned and looked into the room for Riley's patient. The stretcher was empty. Jenny stepped forward and snapped her arm around the side curtains. No one there. She stepped deeper into the Trauma Room. Crimson drops of blood speckled a path toward an adjoining bathroom. The small window over the sink was open. Steel hand cuffs dangled from the window sill.

Jenny turned back around while pointing toward the window. "Riley, your patient disappeared."

"Jenny, call Security stat."

Chapter 3

Emergency Room
Connecticut General Hospital

Riley spun around the Trauma Room, her hands fanned out by her side. Finally, she threw up her arms. "Do you think he heard us?" Riley asked Jenny.

Jenny waved her hand. "I don't know."

Two security guards quietly surveyed the Trauma Room. Suddenly, their walkie-talkies crackled.

The taller guard turned to Riley. "Doctor, the police are here. We'll take it from here. You can leave."

Jenny continued. "I doubt that patient is afraid of the police. But he's certainly afraid of who's hunting him out on the boulevard."

Reaching down to pick up her computer bag Riley shook her head. Then she moved toward the sink. She stopped and dropped the bag, staring at the faucet.

Jenny noticed Riley's rare indecision. Her friend was rattled. *It's that Knights' medical secret that's scaring her,* Jenny thought.

Riley washed her hands twice before tossing her bag over her shoulder.

Jenny twirled the two bangles around her right index finger again. "Don't you think your treasure hunts are getting a bit elaborate?"

Riley squinted and smiled. She flapped her index finger close to Jenny's cheek. "Now you know what a Gregorian chant looks like. It's all about the rhythm. Just like a patient's EKG."

"I love the bangles. Great reward."

"They're going to look good on you."

Riley's love of mind-bending puzzle games was famous at the inner city hospital and yet, many fellow doctors had given up participating. While family life and holidays evaporated for both patients and staff at the hospital, Riley made them come alive again daily with her brainteasers. While some doctors relieved their stress with the *New York Times* crossword puzzle or *ESPN* sports, Riley and Jenny enjoyed testing their minds with art and literature. Jenny knew the treasure hunts had a deeper meaning to both of them. *Or, maybe that she'd always won the contests made others quit?* Jenny thought. *It probably prevents Alzheimer's.* They both loved the challenge, the stimulation and sometimes, the rewards.

Jenny pulled the card with the musical clues from her lab coat. She realized that the puzzles were also symbols of their friendship: she couldn't recall when it happened but their rhythms were synced like an EKG. Jenny knew Riley could tell when she was hungry, when she needed sleep and, of course, when they both needed a martini. Sometimes "both patients and patience was tested," she'd say. Jenny felt confident with her long-time friend and fellow physician who could diagnose her feelings.

Though Jenny was laid bare by Riley's innate personal insight, she sensed the warm camaraderie that protected them from loneliness. Riley didn't abuse her inner knowledge of Jenny's feelings, her crush on a local golf professional, or her passion for art history. She looked fondly toward Riley and realized that their trust was in each other more than anyone else.

Now she was happy for Riley. She was soon off duty and heading to Ireland on vacation while Jenny went off to Bermuda.

Riley glared at her iPhone again. "You began yesterday's treasure hunt at eight o'clock, which means you've set a personal best. This past year you've hunted down art history clues, music mysteries, Shakespeare secrets and even learned about ciphers."

"Of course," Jenny groaned. "I could have been doing something important instead…like sleeping." Jenny didn't mean it. She loved the contest and the battle of wits. *I know. It keeps us sane in this hospital ward.* And she knew that Riley spent sizeable time and research conceiving the puzzles.

"Let's walk." Riley said. "There's more about that secret."

"The secret about the knights?" Jenny asked. Her heart thumped against her chest.

"Yes. Remember when I went to Ireland to see that Caravaggio painting years ago? While I was there in the museum I met an old obstetrician. He took a liking to me. I stayed in touch with him."

"Is this where you get your puzzle clues?"

"Yes, some. The obstetrician has been gradually sharing some fascinating Medieval and medical history. He writes letters the old fashioned way. Sometimes scrawling off the page."

"Tell me more. Remember, I solved your brainteaser about the only artist ever mentioned in a Shakespeare play."

"He claims that there were many doctors during that era who experimented with miracle healing."

"If you could call them doctors, yes. But they never wrote down what they did." Jenny said.

"He claims they did. He writes how scientists, artists and writers hid clues within their work. Codes and mysteries that they wanted to preserve yet conceal. He scared me."

"And the knights protected the medical secrets?" Jenny asked.

"Exactly."

"Why the knights?"

"Because healing powers were invaluable to keep them alive. To protect their ability to return to fight for the kingdom."

"Did he say what the medical secret is?" Jenny asked. She grabbed her long red ponytail and repositioned the elastic band. Her bright blue eyes opened wide with anticipation.

"No. He skirted around the actual secret. It's as if he doesn't know what or where it is. But yet he wants to pass it on. To me. Testing me. Trusting me."

"I love it. Maybe he's the white knight we've all been looking for." Jenny beamed. "You could be a knight." Jenny felt the intrigue. Riley had taught her friend well.

"You mean a Dame." Riley replied.

"Yes, Dame Riley! Either way, that's a great treasure hunt. Let me help." Jenny said.

"Listen." Riley squinted. "There's a clue I discovered about a missing Caravaggio masterpiece. I found a document that referred to a 'Last Prophet.' I shared the document with him. It seemed to upset him. The obstetrician then said to lay low until I met him Ireland."

"So, this isn't just a vacation? I thought you were just touring around alone?"

"Not really."

"Throw me some of those clues." Jenny felt the urge building. Knowing that Riley was holding back.

"I'm not sure. Because of the strange things in the last few days . . . I'm worried something menacing is going on. You know . . . the creepy guy that followed me the other night. Now this *Jackson*." Riley said

Jenny stopped walking. She felt betrayed. *Not sure?* Jenny didn't know if Riley was rejecting her or if she was unclear about what she'd found. She knew saying less would be better. She tried to control her anxiety but she felt the warm blood rush into her face and she instinctively squeezed her upper lip. "Do you want to sit down and talk about it?"

"No. I told you all I know. I think I need to explore this mystery with Jake." Riley said.

Jenny felt the floor drop beneath her feet. "Jake?" Her eyes darted back and forth.

"Jake . . . Jake Bolton." Riley said.

"Jake Bolton? You're going with someone? I've never heard of him."

"I didn't know when it was best to tell you . . . but he's meeting me shortly."

Jenny was frustrated. Angry. *She's going to solve this puzzle with someone I've never met?* "Wait . . ." Jenny searched her thoughts for a response. Nothing came to her.

"Hey. You look upset."

"What . . ." Jenny started then reconsidered. "What does he do? Who is he? Where's he from?" Jenny asked.

"He's someone who can protect me."

Jenny kept pushing the thought of rejection to the back of her mind. "Someone to protect you? Like a serious boyfriend?" *Why didn't I know?* Jenny thought.

"It's not like that with Jake. I was just worried when that man followed me the other night so I called him."

"And he can help you solve this puzzle too?" Jenny added reluctantly.

"Yes. You can meet him. He's here."

"Where?"

"He's meeting me on the Skywalk."

Jenny waited, hoping for more information. She wanted to be the best at solving puzzles. Her competitive juices were flowing. *To keep my reigning title. At least throw some holy water on me. To know that Riley believed in my abilities.* Riley didn't budge. Instead, she began to walk again. "Wait." Jenny said. *I don't like the idea of this guy Jake.* She thought. Then she paused. She thought about the best way to ask the question. She decided not to ask for anything. "Never mind." *Maybe it was the right time for Riley to move on?* She thought.

"Hey. Jenny you'd be great with Jake." She shuddered. "If, for some reason . . ."

Jenny grabbed her shoulder and turned her. "Whoa. Now you're scaring me!"

Chapter 4

Connecticut General Hospital

"If there's a secret cure that could save patients . . . that would rock the world." Riley said, nodding slowly.

"Of course. Like the Chamberlen Secret. That Renaissance doctor hid his delivery device for 200 years. Can you imagine how many Moms and babies could have been saved if treasure hunters had found that secret a hundred years earlier?"

Riley smiled. "Yes. Exactly."

"There are still other medical mysteries out there to solve. One hundred years ago the life expectancy was 41 years of age. Now it's 80! That longevity improved by hunting for medical clues. We just need to keep looking and I might be able to help."

"Like finding penicillin in moldy bread. Or, the Polio vaccine."

"They were all laying right there on the path waiting for scientists to pick them up." Jenny said.

"I hear you. But, I've got my big gun Jake coming in. Just in case though—I left a key for you in my room. And that obstetrician's name is Dr. McGrath." Riley replied.

"Another puzzle? Count me in."

"Like I said. You love the challenge. And you caught on faster than anyone I've ever played with."

Jenny hugged her friend. "This is what we do. While playing games is exhilarating, motivating . . . medicine is art and science." *This is a real life crossword puzzle. The artist in the doctor brings life to the science.* Jenny thought.

Jenny admired Riley's diagnostic skill but knew that she herself was catching up. Then what? Then she knew she'd want more. *I guess then I'd know how Riley felt around the rest of us mere humans,* she thought. *Then I'll need my own Jake. Maybe I'll understand my own feelings for a man. And I'll need my own Ireland trip.* "Off to Ireland now with your boyfriend?" She wanted to tease Riley.

"I told you, he's a special friend. Not my 'boy' friend."

"I can't wait to see him." Jenny imagined a handsome Ivy Leaguer sauntering in with a huge smile and a dozen red roses. *But why not take me?*

Riley marshaled her friend with a "no trespassing" stare. "I know what you're thinking. No. It was a weird week . . . and it ended with that *Andrew Jackson.*"

"So you do have a boyfriend," Jenny said.

Riley shook her head and a half smile appeared.

Riley and Jenny passed the new residents arriving for their first day of training. With pressed white coats and Starbucks in hand, they wore their shiny new stethoscopes like prayer shawls. Jenny wondered if they knew what the two women now knew, would they still enter the gates? Would they work without sleep or food or encouragement to save people whose lives were quarantined by tow zones and cement barriers? Would they willingly stitch the flesh of those who spent more time in jail than in church? Would they pull a knife blade out of a dying man? Probably. But never again with so much hope.

The two women walked through an administrative hallway toward the Hudson Street Skywalk overpass that connected the second floor to a hospital-owned apartment complex. The glassed skywalk was known to many as the "Bridge of Sighs," after the Ponte dei Sospiri in Venice. That famous Italian bridge connected the prison cells to the Doge's Palace, where those under arrest would be interrogated. According to legend, the condemned would look out over the water and sigh at their fate. Jenny looked down on the city of Hartford and wondered, *Who were the lovers, who were the prisoners of a city that had grown so harsh and unsentimental?*

At the intersection to the overpass, Jake appeared and Riley burst into a run. She jumped up and threw her arms around his shoulders.

Jenny stood back and admired. There was a glow of warmth between Riley and Jake. *Who was this guy? Another riddle?* Jenny knew this was as far as she would go. They would walk across the glass Skywalk while she would take the intersecting hallway down to her office. Folding her hands, Jenny looked down and waited. She glanced up when their embrace ended.

Jake wore pressed Wrangler jeans, a sharp white cotton shirt and a black Calvin Klein blazer. He had a cleanly shaven square jaw, a bona fide cleft chin, deep blue eyes and a jet-black crew cut. *The guy was enough to get a girl drunk without drinking.* Jenny swallowed and felt the blood rushing to her head.

"Genevieve Neugold, this is Jake . . . Jake Bolton," Riley said.

His handshake was firm. Warm like his smile. "Nice to meet you. I wish it'd been sooner."

"The pleasure's all mine. Genevieve. That's a beautiful name. You doctors are getting more beautiful and smarter all the time. That must be why you all wear those blue scrub uniforms, right? To intimidate men?"

Jenny felt the warmth of her blush. She liked this guy. Smooth. Working the girlfriend's girlfriend. Just enough but not over the top. "Thank you, Jake. They're just easier to clean." She turned and hissed toward Riley, "Why didn't you tell me?"

"Are you joining us for the trip?" he asked, smiling back and forth at Riley.

Jenny saw the surprise on Riley's face. "It's Jenny, and I'd love to join you, but I'll be swimming in Bermuda. Have fun, you two." She hugged Riley, whispering, "What is going on? Who is this guy Jake?"

"Jenny." Riley paused, looking back and forth at Jake. "Jake is my brother."

Jenny spun back to Jake. Jake nodded with a smile. She swallowed deeply. "But . . . I thought . . . I don't know what to say." She waited. "But I thought you were . . . working in Africa. On some . . . some" She heard herself stammering. "In some volunteer group . . . or something."

"Yes. Something like that." He smiled.

Jenny felt a rush of heat. *Whoa, this guy is hot.*

"I called him when I got a little nervous. Everything is fine now."

"Okay. But you had me stunned there for a moment.' Jenny said.

Jenny hugged Riley again and spoke softly. "Girlfriend, I never would have made it without you. The quips, quotes . . . those treasure hunts. . . the puzzles. See you on the other side of July. I feel better that he's your brother."

"Don't forget. Just in case. The key." Riley squared Jenny's shoulders and nodded.

Chapter 5

Outside Connecticut General Hospital

Five hundred meters down Hudson Street, a black spider of a man crawled across the apartment building rooftop. Moving along the slate in a practiced crouch, he was a hunting cat in a field.

A car horn blew. He froze momentarily. He waited and listened. Then he restarted his steady but quick movements in surgical precision. His long, camouflaged rifle bag dangled over his shoulder. Like a round loading into the chamber he glided toward the four-foot parapet protecting the south side of the building.

He wore a thin wool cap and a black Lycra running suit. His skin was gaunt yet tanned. His flat face accentuated his bushy red eyebrows. He knew that his prey, though now invisible, would cross perpendicular to his final firing position. Tasting the cool morning air, his senses were keen to the temperature and humidity effects on a kill shot. His focused mind slowed the rush of adrenaline racing through his bloodstream that fired his synapses. It slowly calmed his "buck fever" that can throw off the shot.

He was without his spotter. But he moved with confidence . . . and ruthlessness.

He dropped his bag at the edge of the brick wall, knowing that he had a clear sight line down the two lanes of Hudson Street. Positioning himself, he held up an anemometer to check the wind velocity and direction. Unfolding his M40A3 sniper rifle, he placed the swivel bipod on the roof, and removed his favorite Marksman II scope to check his target point.

Locking his scope back into place, the shooter searched up and down the streets. Dialing the black knob, he "doped his scope" to get his distance to the target. He knew the average person was 36 inches from waist to the crown of the head. Like a veteran quarterback he studied all the movements of his opponents on the field. A chaotic waltz unfolded in front of him: red brake lights flickering across the boulevard like fireflies, white coat merciful men and women hustling in and out of the hospital. It was not unlike the commotion on the city streets of Fallujah.

The sniper took slow, deep breaths and focused first on the Twain Street back entrance of the hospital that led to the Cancer Center and ER. He knew this was where his "special" patient would choose to exit, through the hospital area known as "the Colonnade," a column of narrow white brick buildings surrounding the semicircular entrance to the Cancer Center. The nearby side door doubled as the loading dock for the necropsy room and was called the "Lion's Mouth," because it was reminiscent of where defeated warriors left the Roman Coliseum. The patient would soon be limping out the door from the groin shot he'd delivered. Then the man would give his handkerchief signal that the mark was coming.

Anticipating the thrill, the shooter briefly emptied his lungs. He briefly scanned for his target location. His mark wasn't necessarily guilty. Nor innocent. No identity. Just far enough away that the eye could only see black on white. Just another target. One that was moving through his time and space. The wrong time and space. And needed to be eliminated.

Gauging the distance and angle, he focused, gradually slanting his head. Supine now, the assassin corrected for the wind speed and, through his scope tracked his patient limping toward a blue Corolla. He knew the feel of the three pound pressure to the trigger pull. Racing at twice the speed of sound, the bullet would make 200,000 revolutions a minute propelling into his target in one half second. Ripping through them, the person would be dead before they heard the shot.

The patient deftly tied a red handkerchief on the door handle to alert the shooter that his target was coming. The "signal." He continued following the patient with his scope while the man staggered into the car and drove toward the Hudson Street intersection beneath the skywalk.

Chapter 6

Skywalk
Connecticut General Hospital

Riley grabbed Jake's hand. She glanced back at Jenny then froze . . . like she'd seen her own ghost.

Jenny gave a thumbs-up and turned down the perpendicular glass corridor that made up the Skywalk.

Riley returned a comforting smile, twirled sideways toward the twenty-foot glass windows, and pondered the moment. Jake kept walking forward, extending his long arm backward, and pulling her down the skywalk.

"She's a swimmer?" Jake asked.

"Yes. A very good one. All American."

Riley exhaled. Jenny was a tall soft shadow moving away like a time lapse image.

Riley swiveled back to Jake and her demeanor changed. She squeezed his hand. Her face was taut, serious. "There's something wrong. I sense it. I swear last night I saw someone following me near my apartment."

Jake opened his hand. "Are you sure?"

"It was dark. But I saw the shadow of a man in the glare of the street lights."

"It could have been anyone, Riley. A passing pedestrian."

"This was the second time I've seen him. The first time he stopped at my house and stared at me when I ran in. That's when I texted you" Riley's legs stiffened. She felt frozen on the walkway.

"I'm sure it was . . . nothing," he said, rolling his upper teeth across his lower lip. Riley recognized that he sensed she was right. But he wasn't saying anything that would fuel her anxiety.

She quickly looked away. Her eyes stared through the glass tangentially back toward the adjoining building. Sunlight poured in. She saw Jenny watching them through a side window. Within the window frame Jenny looked like a fleeting and mysterious character; much like an historic black and white porthole-style portrait whose familiar gaze follows you throughout the room. Riley willed herself to keep going but her legs wouldn't move. *I can't stop staring. Get away from Jenny,* she thought. *Just in case. Not to scare her. But to protect her.* Jake clutched her hand again.

"Do you remember when we'd play chess all afternoon at the beach?" She asked. "All those pawns, rooks and knights? Life was all black and white."

"Yeah. Why?"

"Do you remember what you always told me? When you always beat me?" Riley continued to watch Jenny's shape in the window. Much more like a tronie-style painting, her friend projected an expression of enduring emotion and faraway gaze. Jenny's soft ocean blue eyes were lost over the distance to her. Riley felt the urge to fill in her colors.

Jake laughed and broke Riley's trance. "Not always. What did I say?" He asked.

"'Don't ever give up your queen—she's the smartest, most powerful player on the board.'" A rush of cool air blew down the skywalk. She turned and felt it hit her face. A door had opened at the other end. She moved her legs slightly. Then she turned tangentially again at Jenny in the window. "You were right. The queen is so important in chess. Before the Medieval era she could only move one block at a time." Riley folded her arms protectively against her chest.

Jake shot an alarmed glare at her, pausing to stare. "What happened?" he asked.

"Around that time queens became important to motivating their soldiers. The queen could move through the kingdom and find secrets others overlooked. So they changed her role in chess— as in life—making her less restricted. High level chess players rarely attack early with their queen. They wait. The Queen waits. She's most powerful when the board is open or when the enemy king isn't well-defended. Now . . . you need to protect your woman. Protect the queen." Riley shot Jake a dour glare. "Keep the queen safe and from being exposed . . . Jake, I know I found something that others have overlooked. The secret of these knights is profound AND well-hidden. We need to get moving."

#

Jenny paused at a crosswise window so she could watch the Skywalk rise up and over the city street, making Riley and Jake seem regal as they walked away from the hospital.

Jake was pointing to the treetops rustling in the early summer breeze just below the 30-foot height of the Skywalk. His commanding physical pose reminded her of a Rodin sculpture. His chiseled frame and handsome smile had radiated the heat that had briefly dissolved her into a blushing and stammering puddle in the hallway.

The entering sunlight reflected off the steel window supports—creating a hologram effect around Jake and Riley. An ornate crown molding at the end of the corridor was shaped like an inverted and endless staircase, bathing them in the glimmer. *My God*, Jenny thought, *they are walking through an Escher drawing!*

Jenny was happy for Riley. *Her brother?* Jenny sighed.

A sudden crash, metal hitting metal, broke her reverie. Her head snapped toward the street. Car horns blared below the Skywalk. Jenny awoke from her trance.

Her training as a trauma surgeon made her instinctively run toward the crash—back toward the Skywalk overpass entrance. Then she saw Riley and Jake hesitate halfway across the bridge. Another crack. The Skywalk glass exploded, blasting Riley and Jake across the walkway.

Riley spun backward, her head slamming into Jake. Jenny saw her friend fall, her arms outstretched like one crucified.

Jenny reached for her friend though she was fifty yards away. "Riley!" Jenny screamed. Jake's head slammed against the opposite glass wall, his arms closing on Riley. Their bodies landed on the floor facing each other, shards of glass raining down on them.

Jenny raced toward them. She tried to scream again. Nothing came. Her legs churned across the Skywalk like they were in hip-deep water. Jenny slid to her knees next to them. She saw Riley lying across from Jake, Riley's crimson blood emptying between them.

Chapter 7

Step-down Unit
Connecticut General Hospital

Dr. Jenny Neugold lightly touched the enigmatic scar on Jake's ankle. She studied his face, anticipating a pained response. None came. The large man remained supine, tranquilized.

She brushed her tongue over her dry lips and continued her methodical survey down his body.

The wide circumferential blemish was unlike any wound she'd seen during her trauma surgery career. She was intrigued by the acuteness of the injury and moved closer to the examining table, bringing the surgical lights down over the wound. The color was pink—the sign of freshly-healing hypervascular skin. It blanched white when the tuft of her finger pressed the crusted scar. She released—then bright red. She pulled her shoulders back.

She adjusted her surgical loupes, tilted her head toward his toes, and felt the speed of her pulse in her chest. The foreshortened nail plate on his great toe was black—a sign of old trauma. The exposed nail bed was red and raw. There were mutilations on the remaining toes. She calculated: the black nail plate, the length of free edge—at least six months ago.

The trauma surgeon looked back over her loupes at his blank face. Dried crimson blood was painted at the corner of his nose. She listened to the steady ping of his heart beat. His respirations, though shallow in his massive chest, were steady, saturating his blood stream with oxygen. When Jenny placed her stethoscope and listened to his heart, no reaction registered in her patient. There was no flutter in the waveforms of his vital signs when she scrutinized his injuries.

She sat back and thought about the wounds. Both ankles. Narrow markings. Partial healing. No infection. This wasn't from the Skywalk shooting. It was circumferential. Like . . . ? Her chest tightened. Then she felt the rush of nausea that came with the answer. *Like shackles.*

She recalled her work with Doctors Without Borders in Syria. There were patients arriving who'd been subjected to a form of torture called the German Chair, a cruel technique dating back to the Medieval era. The prisoners had been tied down onto the frame of a metal chair with their legs secured to the seat. When the frame was bent back into a flat piece of metal the victim was slowly pulled apart. Her gloved hands instinctively moved up toward her mouth but she stopped herself. Swiveling aimlessly on the stool she sensed her heart racing, the moisture beading on her forehead, clamminess. Her blood pressure was dropping, her heart rate slowing. The signs were all locking in on her. Engulfing her.

Shackled. She thought. *Who would do such a thing? Where was Riley's brother from? What kind of work was he doing in Africa?*

She tried to fight back by breathing deeply. It wasn't working. She'd seen thousands of traumas but nothing like this in many years. The room was closing in and she shut her eyes. She braced her feet on the floor, leaned forward on the stool, put her head between her knees, quickly exhaled and reached up with her forearm to wipe her head. The queasiness subsided. Grabbing the side of the stretcher she stared upward and steadied herself.

She turned back to the sleeping Jake Bolton, noting the colorful tattoo covering his bulging deltoid muscle. She'd seen plenty of "tatts" in the ER gangbangers. *This doesn't look like a gang tattoo. Nor is it a military symbol.* The skin was embossed in a red-and-white fleurs-de-lys surrounding a large white sculpted stone—like an altar. Beneath the stone, two angels leaned over a lion with anchors bisecting its body. The lion rested on top of a small cave. She wondered if this was a mistake from his teenage years. She made a note to check him for hepatitis.

Jenny moved her inspection lower, detecting a familiar pockmark: the indentation of a gunshot entry on the anterior tibia. The bone was deformed. The thin skin was dusky but healed. She reached around with her gloved hand to rotate his leg, looking for the exit wound.   Her patient groaned and lifted his head.

"What are you doing? Who are you?" Jake sputtered. His eyes were red and moist, waking from narcosis. He reached out with both hands toward his ankles, pushing the sheet downward. He searched under the shoulder of his hospital gown for something. His biceps tensed.

"It's okay Jake." Jenny said.

"Riley!" Jake shouted. He rolled across the hospital bed and hit the floor on all fours, groaning at the impact. His monitoring wires flew off him like chains rattling onto the floor.

"Jake, it's okay." Jenny repeated. "You're going to be a bit groggy."

He jumped up, and drove Jenny across the room. He grabbed her arms, pinning her against the wall. She let out a whimper of pain. Cabinets emptied, surgical instruments hit the metal sink. "Don't move or I'll snap your neck. Who are you?"

She went cold with fear.

Jenny peered around Jake's chest and saw flat lines racing across the cardiac monitor. *Maybe someone will see the monitor and come running? No. This is a restricted and secure area of the hospital!*

"It's Jenny, Riley's friend. You're in the step-down unit."

"Huh? What?"

"The hospital. Riley was shot . . . I can't breathe." She heard the name "Riley" echo through her head. It started with a high pitched sound deep in her brain, and then gradually grew louder as if someone had screamed the words inside her skull. Then it washed over her.

She saw herself sprinting down the Skywalk again, screaming for her friend. Hoping for some sort of reaction. *Move Riley. Move! Show me you're alive.* Jenny dove onto her knees beside her friend. She put her hands out to cradle the motionless body. *She lay there like a lifeless doll. Her big open eyes staring through me. Like someone had thrown their toy on the floor.*

Jenny slowly turned her over—Riley's blood spilling onto her white coat. She groaned at the weight of Riley's body in her arms. Lifting Riley's limp shoulders she rolled her back into a sitting position. Riley's heart was shot and Jenny's life was shattered.

Jenny felt the tears on her face and she snapped back to hear Jake talking.

"Where's my bag? Where's my gun?" Jake's neck muscles were taut, his face red.

"You're in the ICU. The hospital. Let go of me."

There was a knock on the door. The door shot open and the nurse appeared. "Is everything okay, Dr. Neugold?"

Jake slightly loosened his tense grasp on her blue scrubs.

"Yes. We're fine. I'm fine."

The nurse looked up and down at Jake. "Do you need some water?"

Jake shook his head. He seemed stunned, disoriented.

"We're fine here. I'm going to finish examining him." Jenny said.

The nurse closed the door.

Jenny sensed he was remembering: the Skywalk, the glass shattering, now her. He would come around. Sensory overload while his central nervous system was recovering from the concussive effects of the trauma. She knew the feeling from years in the emergency trauma service: patients out cold one moment then waking to a drastically changed world. She detected the hollowness in his mind. She needed to be calm—to get him to calm down.

"Riley?" He asked.

Jenny closed her eyes. "She died. A gunshot to the chest. I'm sorry. I couldn't save her."

Jenny paused. Rarely did she let her emotion enter the trauma room. She tried to stop but could not.

This man was not just another patient. He was family to Riley. *And, this is personal to me. He'll understand my feelings.* "Horrific. She was my best friend. Seeing her lying there—I hurt. I bled." She said.

Jake released her, raised his hands in surrender and stepped back from the wall. "Forgive me."

Jenny sat back down on the stool and rubbed her arms, watching Jake move swiftly around the room. He was looking for his belongings. *He was packing like he was leaving. This was her patient and her hospital. His sister was shot and he's leaving? Didn't he hear me say that Riley was killed? She said he was her brother. Is he really? So now he's going to run away?* She reflected on his movements. His indifference angered her.

He stopped moving. Then he squeezed his eyes shut and rubbed the back of his head. She spied an opening. *He's feeling the rebound effects of the trauma.* "Jake, you have a significant concussion."

He opened his eyes. Staring silently back at her he appeared to struggle to digest the words. "That's why I hear a freight train running through my head." He gave a momentary look up and down at her scrubs then spun back to packing.

He tossed his civilian clothes from the cabinet onto the bed, yanked off the cloth ties on the back of his hospital gown and pulled it over his head. He grunted in pain. He kept moving like he was exiting a plane. Occasionally he stopped to rub his head again. *He'll feel the concussion for awhile,* she thought. *This isn't my typical trauma patient—scared and unable to face himself alone again.*

He ripped the intravenous line from his arm and began to dress. His blood slowly oozed down his arm. She watched in wonder. Waited. "We don't have a lot of time and we're not safe here." He said. "I came back for Riley. She warned me. She was afraid for her life."

"Listen." Jenny said. The fire in her eyes was building. "You're in a post-traumatic stress meltdown. Stop. Let me give you a sedative. You're upset and angry, but you need to slow down." The *post-trauma stress* hit her. She felt the fresh wounds in her own chest. *My own trauma.* She wished to herself that she'd listened to Riley about the man following her. *Maybe I could have done something? Maybe I should've called the police for her?*

"'Riley's life was in danger. I didn't see it coming. Now I need my gun. I can still move in all directions and get out of here. You don't understand. That gunshot was meant for me."

Chapter 8

Step-down Unit
Connecticut General Hospital

The surgeon's alarm in Jenny's mind startled her.

It was like the sudden awareness that an operation was going awry. The thought of someone invading the sanctity of her hospital to shoot Riley was a nightmare. It would be further tragedy to now lose Jake Bolton. She needed to reassure her patient . . . and herself.

"Jake, you're safe in this area of the hospital. It's a secure, isolation unit. We use this only for special circumstances like this. You need to slow down. There's an armed guard outside to protect you." She silently hoped the guard was skilled enough to stop a shooter . . . but now the guard might need to stop her patient from escaping. She shivered at the thought.

Jake snorted and shook his head. She felt he was only partially listening to her. "He won't stop a sniper shot like the one that got Riley." He said.

"Listen. Let me help. Let's start with 'who are you?' The hospital has Jake Bolton—and that's from me. You have no ID's. No history. No previous records."

"You don't need to know." He threw his hospital gown on the bed then tied on his boots.

"I'll call the police."

"Go ahead. I'll be gone. Then you'll be in danger." He stood and put her head in his hands and stared deeply into her eyes.

Jenny sensed a warm touch. He wasn't going to hurt her. He was still searching for answers.

He snapped his head upward. "Go ahead. You won't call. I'm your only hope to find Riley's killer. You can't do it."

He must've felt that, she thought. *There was a spiritual reverence in the way he spoke, like his words and voice were meant to comfort me.* He wasn't threatening. *I need to gain the upper hand here.* "Then you should stay to help Riley. To find her killer here." She said. "Are you really her brother?"

He sat back on the bed, turned his face down and buttoned his shirt.

That got him. She thought.

He stopped abruptly. "Older, right?" He glanced over at her feet, like he couldn't face her.

"What?"

"Older brother? Right?"

Jenny realized that he was still confused, and she was conflicted. She'd seen hundreds of people die in the hospital trauma rooms. Veritable shreds of protoplasm twisted, blown apart or bleeding from hellacious trauma. Mere objects on the cold slab of the trauma table. They weren't a person or a family member. Just a blob of cells. Her mental process was to compartmentalize. To make them objects. Riley died in her arms and she was fighting back the tears with mental tricks. But the horror couldn't be stopped. It felt different when it was someone she knew. Someone she loved. Someone she knew loved her.

"Let's start again. I'm Dr. Genevieve Neugold. Riley was my only true friend. My family."

Jake appeared to move back further on the bed. She sensed he was calculating her words. Something deeper was registering with him. Jenny stared at him, waiting for a reply. Nothing came.

"I'm part of this. I'm not detached. All I've been doing since she died in my arms . . . was cry. I don't know what else I'm supposed to be doing right now but cry. This isn't me. It's like I was dropped out of the sky but, when I landed, the world around me was upside down. I'm a doctor. It doesn't make sense. This isn't what I do." The saliva in her mouth grew thicker as she spoke. Her sadness was turning painful. "I felt like running. Running away. Instead . . . I'm here. You've been out cold. And I've been crying."

"Genevieve is one of my favorite names." His tone changed. He turned and stared at her with his big blue eyes. She froze. The penetrating gaze was distinctly familiar to her. Calm. Persuasive. She studied him for his sincerity. "She was a great Medieval princess, the patron saint of Paris."

"Huh? I . . . I didn't." She stuttered when her heart skipped a beat.

"You know? Attila the Hun was preparing to attack Paris? The beautiful princess gathered the French citizens and told them to pray for God's protection. Surprisingly, Attila redirected his troops and Paris was saved." He grinned and nodded. "Genevieve."

Stunned, she stared back at him. She'd seen his smile before. He was inside her head. But not like her trauma patients. *I need to gather myself and be strong.* She thought.

"Crying's not going to get us anywhere," he said, standing and putting his hand on her shoulder. She sensed an unnerving familiarity to him.

"Riley and I had a plan to make the world a better place." Jenny felt like she was spitting out the words. "This isn't a third world desert with some gunman perched on top of a pickup truck shooting through the streets. I shouldn't have to stand in my own doorway with a rifle in my hands."

"If I leave . . . you won't have to. We're running out of time. I need to get out of here. I need your help." Jake said.

"And, if I'm going to help you I need to know more about you. We can start with those scars on your legs."

Jake sat down on the stretcher. "How do you know that?" She realized that he was slowing down. Adjusting to a confusing new reality. The adrenaline surges were keeping him going.

"I'm your trauma surgeon. Until she was shot and killed, I was also Riley's best friend—so it seems we have something in common."

Her own words reverberated through her. *She was shot and killed.* She knew it was difficult to be a compassionate doctor in the face of such lawlessness. She slammed her fist on an IV solution bag for effect.

But there was no satisfaction. She was still in pain. Jake was speaking to her. But there was no sound. Her mind wandered and blanked out his words. *What kind of society do we live in when a woman devoted to caring for the sickest of sick is gunned down in broad daylight with this . . . this man by her side? Her work as a trauma surgeon meant nothing? I couldn't save my friend.*

"I need to get out of here." Jake said. He sat down and put his elbows on his knees, folded his hands, pointing his thumbs upward and resting his forehead on them. Jenny couldn't tell if he was praying or meditating. He was likely still suffering from his traumatic brain injury. She stepped back, realizing he was just as angry as she was.

"Right now you're locked in here with me. That cop outside won't let you leave. What did you mean when you said that gunshot was meant for you?"

He didn't look up. "Is there someone you consider an enemy? Someone so vengeful they just don't stop coming after you?" he asked.

Jenny started to answer, and then decided there was no answer.

Chapter 9

Step-down Unit
Connecticut General Hospital

Jake and Jenny settled back like two boxers staring out from their corners. No bell was going to bring them out.

His hypnotic stare reminded her of a woman practicing Lamaze classes. All focus . . . no talking. Determined stares. Eye to eye. She swallowed deeply.

Frustrated, Jenny wanted to try something different. She reached into her lab coat pocket and felt the three-inch molded plastic. She squeezed her fist then rolled her fingers open to him. "You're hand was clenched down on this when we brought you in here."

He stared at the white chess queen lying sideways on her hand like it was sleeping. A small pink splotch was on the queen's dress, likely Riley's blood. A scratch in the plastic at the base made it uneven. He tilted his head several times studying the piece like it had a face hiding beneath the crown. He raised his arm and palmed the black stubble on his head.

Jenny detected faint dark rings encircling his piercing blue eyes, enhancing their appearance. His hands were large but symmetrical. His shoulders—although hunched—were broad and sculpted. Slowly, a faint smile finally appeared on his face, like recognition of a long lost childhood story had come to mind or a hollowness was suddenly filled with joy. He reached forward and gently grasped the queen and closed his eyes.

Jenny felt like she'd handed him a fifty pound weight—her hand rose when he took the piece. He opened his eyes and stared at her for a lingering warm moment. They were bewitching and penetrating, yet hauntingly familiar like they'd pulled an intimate message from her soul. She leaned back and rubbed her moist hands.

"You start."

"Dr. Genevieve Neugold." Jenny knew that repetition with

trauma patients was common. Productive. The stress hormones heightened the amygdala activity in the brain that recorded exciting events like a DVD writer. Sudden drops in brain activity were still possible for days and would result in confusion, somnolence, questions.

He was challenging her now, she knew. *He wanted to trust me. Looking for more than my qualifications.*

Jake blotted the blood leaking into the forearm of his shirt. "Listen." Jenny said, "Continuous steady pressure stops that bleeding. I know. Fresh blood will coagulate."

Jake looked at his arm again. "Yes. She's my younger sister. Riley contacted me. It was urgent. She wanted my help. She thought she was in danger. Someone was following her. Strange clicks on her cell phone like someone was there. She said she'd received a clue to a 400-year-old mystery hidden in a series of Caravaggio paintings."

"Caravaggio," she murmured.

"Yes." She said she'd discovered some clues to a painting called The Last Prophet. Then someone made a threatening phone call to her. I came right away."

"She told me she was scared," Jenny added. "Very unlike her. It worried me." *Caravaggio?* She thought. He was that wild master painter from the Baroque. Because of the way he lived, more of his paintings were lost, stolen or scattered all over the world than any other painter. *Clues in a painting were nothing new.* "She mentioned Knights with a secret power. You know, like kings, queens, chivalry."

Chapter 10

Step-down Unit
Connecticut General Hospital

"The gun, knives? The tool kits, some electronic gizmos I found in your backpack?" Jenny asked.

"You went through my bag?" Jake shouted. He spun on one foot toward her.

"When you come through my door I get to search everything." Jenny stepped forward to challenge him—a lesson she learned from her stepfather, the part-time umpire. *The batter's more likely not to argue if you confront him,* she thought. "There's one thing I don't understand." They were inches apart now. Jenny raised a clear plastic bag in front of his face and shook three brown oval rock-like objects.

"My peach pits." Jake said.

"Peach pits?" She squinted at him.

"I chew on them. Like tobacco chaw."

"All three at one time?"

"No. One in my cheek. Suck on it all day, keeps my mouth moist. The lips won't dry out in the desert." He smiled. "If my day goes badly I can eat the center and kill myself like Steve McQueen."

Jenny recognized the reference to the Laetrile chemotherapy agent in peach pits that acted like cyanide. The famous actor had increased the visibility of the schlock treatment by going to Mexico in his attempt to find a cure for his lung cancer. "I hope it doesn't get that bad."

"It can." He grabbed the bag and tossed it onto the stretcher.

"Tell me about those wounds on your leg." Jenny replied, pointing downward.

"You said you'd help me." His tone was beseeching now. "For Riley."

"I can't promise . . ."

"Promise." Jake didn't wait for a reply. "I was in jail. This guy was trying to extract information from me. His cigarette was his weapon of choice. Over and over again on my knees. After awhile I couldn't feel anything, so I was becoming useless to him. No information. No response from me. He was going to kill me . . . or use me in a hostage trade. And then I broke free."

"Tell me about your tattoo." She raised a finger.

He turned to look at his right arm. "I got that for Riley."

Jenny leaned back, surprised.

"Sort of. She sent me a picture a few months ago. She asked me to hold on to it for her. I liked it so much I put it here." He patted his deltoid.

"Do you know where it's from?"

"No idea. I never got the chance to ask her."

It's likely a clue, knowing Riley.

"I like the lion. That's why I keep this lion's tooth." He pulled a leather string from his pocket and strung it around his neck. The ivory colored tooth looked like a miniature boomerang. "Killed him in Nigeria years ago."

"Killed a lion? That doesn't sound right."

"It was either me and the village or him."

"Huh?"

"I wasn't hunting him. I was assigned to live in this community in Nigeria. Young men and women were disappearing from their village every week. The agency I worked for thought Boko Haram was dragging them away to make them slaves."

Interesting. So, this guy worked for a human rights agency in Africa? That would explain some things in his backpack.

"Late one night, I'm patrolling the village and I hear a rustling sound. Then a short scream. At the edge of the woods a lion is dragging a young girl by the leg from her tent. I run after her and dive on to the lion. The beast was enraged. I was taking his dinner. I got to keep his tooth and these scratches." He lifted his shirt and turned, exposing the large, pink, swath-like scars on his back. "The lion went the way of Mufasa and we won over the village."

"I thought that lions rarely attack villages."

"True. They're scavengers. But when they lose their natural prey they can become man-eaters. Like the Tsavo River massacre."

This is too sophisticated to make up. She thought. *I believe him.*

"You need rest. And darkness. You've suffered a significant head injury and you've been unconscious for fifteen hours. We can get your gun later. I'm calling the attending neurologist because he'll want to examine you."

"I'm not staying trapped in here . . . I'm leaving. I need to get my gun and get into Riley's apartment." His expression was cold, his tone defiant.

"I can't let you leave. The guard outside has orders to contact the police when you wake up. The police want to talk to you. Any shooting brings a policeman. Questions. Paperwork. They want to know how you're involved. Let me get them. Let me get the neurologist."

"No! You're my doctor now. You watch me." Jake paused. "As a doctor, you can't divulge my information, correct?"

"Yes. Everything is confidential."

"This is the crossroads of my personal and professional life. I'm CIA. I know what I'm doing."

Jenny's shoulders snapped back. "CIA? Don't be ridiculous." Jenny turned away. *CIA?* She had a vision of a man in a tuxedo; gun in hand, racing through the streets of Florence and diving into Neptune's fountain to stop some international crime. *Instead, he looks like he's been tortured in some dungeon beneath Venice.*

He fixed a numb expression. It made her uneasy. *I can't tell anyone.* She opened a nearby drawer, pulling out the surgical instruments. It was something she did when she was confused; sorting the clamps, scalpels, scissors. Finally, she just threw them all together and put both palms down on the counter.

What was Riley into? Riley said that Jake could protect her. Her "big gun." She focused on his face. Not like a physician. Like an angry girlfriend. His eyes were deep blue with thick black eyelashes. He blinked a few times. *Was it intentional?* His face was tanned with scattered cheek freckles surrounding a symmetrical nose. His mouth was open—much like he wanted to speak but couldn't. She saw conviction. She saw Riley's brother.

"You have to trust me. And if you can't trust me, trust Riley. Trust my sister. She wanted me here for a reason. You see this tattoo?" He patted his arm.

"Yes."

"The lion, the altar, the grave stone? You know I'm a walking clue from Riley. You know that. Deep down. Help me."

She wanted to ask him about the CIA. She kept hearing the words: *help me. What am I to do? I've checked his wounds. He's awake now. My job is done. I can go now. But where am I to go? Just run? He's a patient. But, he's my connection to Riley. Before Riley left the hallway she said, "Just in case." This man is all that I have left* just in case.

There was a loud thud outside the door, like a bag hitting the floor. Both their heads snapped toward it.

"What was that?" Jenny asked.

Jake slid Jenny against the wall. He reached under his shoulder. "Crap," he said. "No gun." He moved closer to the doors and peered into the space between them. "I can see the hallway floor. There's your cop's hat, turned on its side, empty."

Chapter 11

Step-down Unit
Connecticut General Hospital

"Your cop is dead." Jake turned toward Jenny. "I also see a man across the hallway with a gun. He's crouching behind the nursing desk. Now it's just the two of us here. Where's my gun?"

"In that desk."

Jake's face contorted. "Great."

"You can have it when you're discharged." She said.

"This discharge isn't going to happen the usual way. That thug out there knows where we are."

Jenny started toward the door. "Don't move." Jake snarled, and shoved her against the wall.

"I can't. . . ." Jenny sputtered. She shoved him back.

He shot her a surprised look. "I'm sorry. I won't do that again."

"We're both a little testy right now. Let's focus on getting out safely," she said.

He swept his long arm across the cabinet shelves, emptying boxes of gauze, stainless steel operating instruments and bottles of iodine onto the stretcher. He stared at the mess, shaking his head. "What's this?" he asked, pointing at a large red steel cart.

"The anesthesia cart." Jenny felt a sudden wariness.

"Get over here. I need your help." He paused. "Please."

Jenny started toward him. "CIA? CIA. I meet all kinds of con men in the ER . . . but CIA? Riley called in the CIA for her latest treasure hunt? I thought you were her brother?"

"I'm both. Brother and CIA. Because of the CIA, Riley and I couldn't be together too often. I have unique skills. And she wanted me to help. The fact that she was killed means a lot to me too. Put the two together? I'm going after her killer. So, let's try to find out what she was up to."

Jenny thought about the key that Riley left for her. She was worried she was being followed. *This doesn't make sense for me . .*

. or her. Yet Riley said the key was in her room. The obstetrician. What was the name . . . ? McGrath. I would be great with Jake. *She wanted me to have those clues, just in case.* Jenny stood motionless.

"All right." She said, "Let's do this together."

He turned and sliced open several brown boxes with his knife. Long plastic anesthesia accordion tubes fell onto the floor. He tossed the materials aside. "What I would give for a bottle of alcohol and a match right now."

"I've got a better idea," Jenny said. She moved to another wall cabinet and pulled out a large glass bottle from under the cabinet, holding it up to his flashlight. "This is called a vacutainer. If you ever drop one of these, and, I have, they—"

"Explode?"

"Implode! There's a one-liter volume of suction in this bottle. It's under enormous negative pressure. When it shatters, the implosion scatters it into thousands of minute needles of glass."

He locked eyes on her. "I like it. What else?"

"Two hundred-microgram doses of dexmedetomidine are in this drawer. It's a powerful sedative agent. Instant paralysis."

"Get me several vials." He said.

"I just need to dilute the liquid first." She took a syringe, filled the pharmaceutical bottle with saline, shook it, and withdrew the concoction back into the syringe, repeating the maneuver on two more vials. She plunged the needles into the rubber top of the vacutainer bottle, which sucked the fluid inside, spreading it over the inside glass.

"Here." She handed him the bottle like she was passing a newborn baby to a father. "Hold this bottle very carefully."

She shifted past him to look through the fissure between the closed wooden ICU doors. The gunman was partially exposed behind the desk. She noted a metal fire door directly behind him. His dark eyes frozen, the gun was intently focused on the ICU door. She turned to Jake. "How's your arm?"

"Pretty accurate when it has to be." Jake wind milled his free arm and moved toward the door. "He's waiting for us to open the door. Then he'll start shooting."

"Okay. When you open the door—throw that bottle against that wall behind him."

"He doesn't realize he's camped on top of my gun. Otherwise, he'd just come in here and shoot us." Jake ran his hand across the sink. "I want you to crouch behind that cabinet until I say, 'clear.'"

"Test your arm again. You're going to be a bit groggy for awhile because of your head injury. Physically you're fine except for those leg wounds."

"I'm just getting used to the sound of that freight train in my head. Adrenaline keeps me going."

"That works with a lot of patients." She nodded at him, liking his grit.

Jake looked through the crack between the doors. "That's not Riley's killer. A marksman, who tried to hit me or her, wouldn't expose himself like that. But I still need to take him out."

Jake thrust open the door and underhanded the bottle like a rugby ball down the hallway. Then he jumped back behind the doors. The hissing sound of suppressed gunfire echoed down the corridor. He braced himself in front of Jenny, protecting her.

Wood splinters flew across the ICU room, shredded plaster fell from the ceiling, and glass exploded onto the wall.

Jenny screeched. Jake lowered her behind the floor sink and shards of debris fell on them. The door swung open and bounced off the jam.

Suddenly, silence. Nothing. The gunfire stopped.

Chapter 12

Step-down Unit
Connecticut General Hospital

Jenny moved aside while Jake leaned back and surveyed the corridor.

Jenny looked down the hallway, and then moved aside. The gunman was lying across the floor, lifeless. His gun impotent by his side.

"Let's go. Now!" he yelled. His long legs carried him down the hall in a quick second, kicking the man's gun away.

Jenny trailed behind, knelt down and instinctively palpated the gunman's neck. Jake grabbed the gun and went for a kill shot. She grabbed his wrist. "No. He's out. That's enough."

He was dark skinned with dark hair and a heavy beard. "Middle Eastern. Couldn't be more than 30 years old." Jake murmured. Then he moved to the desk nearby and yanked the large drawer open.

Jenny glared at him, still catching her breath. She could believe in him. *Riley must've been right about Jake.*

Jake sighed without looking up. "You're right. Give me that IV tubing and I'll tie him up." Jake pointed to the policeman's radio. "Pick it up. Say Ten-Double-Zero and then give this location in the hospital."

Jake pulled up his backpack and gun. "Jenny, I need more help."

"What can I do?" She felt her heart stop beating briefly then momentarily pounding out of her chest.

"Get me into Riley's apartment. Please."

"I can do that." She said, still reeling from the excitement.

Jake ran back into the ICU room, finished dressing, and pitched his backpack onto his shoulder. Jenny followed, watching him curiously.

His fingers suddenly caught on a jagged hole in the back pack. He reached under the cabinets and flipped on the fluorescent lights. The canvas had been torn. He unzipped the bag and upended it onto the bed table, pulling out a loop of rope, a large folding knife, a pair of green binoculars, and several electronic devices. With two fingers he pulled up a small metal, blood-tinged object. He rolled the bullet in his hands. "A .308," he muttered.

"What is it?" Jenny eyed his hand inquisitively.

"A 308-caliber bullet. It must've gone through Riley and then hit my bag. It spun me around on the bridge."

She studied the bloody metal and he rolled it over in his muscular fingers. "The police are going to want that."

"They can't have it yet. I need to return it to its owner. This was a highly trained and specialized sniper shot."

"But the 'highly specialized sniper' missed the shot if he was after you. And who would shoot Riley? Listen, we have random drive-by shootings in this city all the time. We once had a shooter chase a wounded guy through the ER. And the guy he was after was already half-dead."

"You don't understand. I've got my enemies and at the same time Riley stuck her finger into something dangerous. This was a 308-caliber rifle shot. Had to come from a quarter mile out. That's a professional. The sniper club is a small group, and the number of those who could make that shot is even smaller. The wind, a miscalculation, maybe a mil dot reticle may have caused him to miss me."

"So, you don't think he meant to hit Riley? She told me she was worried." Jenny felt her muscles tighten. The words racked her with guilt.

"No. No, it was me. It had to be." Jake strode around the room. "But the whole thing makes no sense. Why here? Unless they killed her to stop me. That must be it."

Jenny searched Jake's eyes. "I feel the way I do after a thirty-six-hour shift—none of this seems real."

"If they were after Riley they might come after you. If they're after me, I need your help."

Jenny nodded. She couldn't look at him. She didn't want his face to influence her. It was decision time. A chill ran down her back. She put her finger through the button hole of her lab coat and twisted. It helped her think. She searched her memory for Riley. In that darkness on the edge of her mind she saw the barest of her feelings. The choice was clear. "I believe you. I think I know what

Riley would do."

"I do too. She'd come with me."

She felt conflicted. Then her eyes scanned his serious face. "How much older?"

"Huh?"

"How much older than Riley are you?"

"Eight years. You can trust me. We need to leave together." He said.

There was a momentary pause. "You're right. She was so quick on her feet. You're so much like her. I believe you." Jenny could rattle off protocols she learned in medical school, but Riley could improvise on the run, dropping famous quotes with ease in the face of incredible stress. "What can we do?"

"Make the ten-double-zero call on that radio now. Can you tell me how we get out of here without being seen?"

Jenny looked at the unconscious man. "He's anesthetized. The drug paralyzed him but he's not asleep. He may remember everything we just said. He'll start moving any second. I'm sorry. I should've warned you."

Jake reached over to a wooden placard that said, "Give the Gift of Life. Give Blood." He wound up like a cricket batsman and snapped the board across the thug's head.

"That'll work." Jenny nodded. "The best place to get out unseen is through the autopsy room. From there we can get to Riley's apartment."

"The autopsy room? I almost went out that way earlier."

Chapter 13

Riley's Apartment Building

Jenny gawked at Jake's black pistol grip hanging beneath the pit of his arm.

She looked past him when he moved through the outside archway cut from the brownstone wall surrounding the apartment building. She sensed he was analyzing the entryways and exits, the shadows, the eerie silence. She no longer felt conflicted about her decision to stay with him. He was her patient.

He focused like her surgical colleagues looking for a cancer inside a patient's abdomen. He'd warned her that the apartment could be the scene of a fire fight. The thought of urban warfare slowed him down, he told her.

Every sound was magnified. *I don't need a stethoscope to hear his breathing.* She thought.

"I remember going through a house in Afghanistan three years ago." His voice was taut and measured with a cool, steady cadence. "Room to room. You need keen peripheral vision and lots of adrenaline. Booby-traps. Blue burkas mixing in the darkness. Quick decisions; insurgent or friend? Hand-to-hand combat or the gift of a piece of fruit. Then suddenly an entire wall explodes and we're in a firefight. A peach pit right now would be ideal."

Jenny laughed nervously. She felt her own pit—in her stomach. The thought of another shooting scared her. Everywhere she turned on the street the shadows moved. They climbed the front steps of the grand wraparound porch and entered the large and imposing Victorian-style home that housed Riley and Jenny's apartments. While yellow security lights bathed the exterior in an artificial daytime glow, the interior of the Victorian two story house on Washington Street had long ago been converted to apartment living for four young doctors.

Once in the lobby, it was obvious the other doctors in the building had already cleared out their belongings, having completed the academic year. Jake groaned while he inspected the complex architecture of windowed bays and bright vibrant colors, typical of what was the richest city in America during the Victorian era. Garbage containers overflowed with papers and bags, broken furniture fallen nearby. He led the way across the main entrance which gave way to two elongated, paired, and expansive parabolic staircases that met on the second floor. Jake pointed to every window and doorway along the hall, and kept his back to the outside wall, then cautiously crept along the stairs. She could hear his breathing holding steady.

Jake grabbed her hand and pulled her up the stairs. She noticed that he studied the ceiling lights and the hallway rugs. He glanced out the window from the staircase to the street, looking for any suspicious movements. He looked down the center between the wooden staircases, apparently scanning for anyone who might be flanking them. Jake continued to lead until the couple reached the landing a few steps below the second-floor corridor.

He crouched down like a cat and motioned to her.

"I can see only two doors at the end of the hallway," he whispered.

"Mine is on the left. Riley's apartment is on the right," she replied.

"What do you call those horizontal railings on the staircase? You know, where you put your hands?" he turned and asked.

"Banisters."

"How about the vertical support things?"

"Balusters," she responded. "Why?"

"I was just thinking. Before I blacked out, I thought I heard Riley say, 'look for the barrister . . . the barrister.'"

He quickly turned back to the corridor. They were eye level with the second-floor hallway and needed only three more steps to reach it. The walls were covered with flaking flowery paper that looked a hundred years old, but the hallway seemed clear of anything threatening. "Jake. It's so quiet. I don't think anyone's here."

"That's what bothers me."

"Riley lived across the hall but we often shared dinner," Jenny said. "She mentioned her 'brother' occasionally and how she missed seeing you." She felt her heart racing again.

"I need you to whisper right now," Jake said in a soft but

stern admonishment. "Was there anything else unusual going on with Riley at work? When she texted me about the Ireland trip I realized it had been a while since I'd seen her. I travel a lot and we couldn't get together too often. Even for a text, she sounded stressed."

"No," Jenny answered. "Where in Ireland were you going?"

Jake didn't respond. He lay flat on his stomach glaring at Riley's doorway. "Was there anything she told you, anything more that sticks out in your mind?"

Jenny froze momentarily. "Riley had said she was going to see the man who would marry her." Emotion creeped into her question. "There was a moment that I thought that was you."

Her comments didn't seem to register with him. Jake appeared focused like the lion at the edge of the woods. Black and yellow police tape criss-crossed Riley's closed door. "This is far enough. I want you to stay here on the landing. Wait for me. If I don't come out in five minutes, then run to the nearest police car or station."

Jenny felt him release her hand. She wondered how Jake could do this for a living. How could he tolerate the reach into the unknown? He rose like a tower on to the landing, grasping for the last staircase. "Do you have a roommate?" He suddenly stopped, turned and barely mouthed the words.

"No."

"Or a dog? Did you leave your radio on?" He asked.

"I love dogs but . . ."

The hallway suddenly exploded in a fusillade of bullets. "Stay down," Jake yelled.

Bullets blasted through the walls. The floorboards shook beneath them. Plaster shards and wood splinters flew at them like a tornado while the glass from the ceiling lights exploded. Jake buckled backward and covered Jenny's head, pinning her below the landing tread. Lunging forward on his knees onto the top stair, the pistol appeared magically in his right hand. He disappeared down the hallway. Jenny threw her hands over her head and muffled a scream.

Chapter 14

Riley's Apartment Building

Jenny heard Jake's footsteps bounding down the hallway. Then a crack like a door jam shattering.

Voices and footsteps reverberating through Riley's apartment. She shivered when sweat beaded down her back.

She wondered if she should run. She turned. Started crabbing down . . . then froze on the edge of the staircase. She dug her fingers into the carpet on the bull nose stair above her. *I'm staying.*

There was a sudden loud yell . . . then a gunshot. A jolt of adrenaline pumped through her. She pinned herself against the top stair, her heart pounding like a hammer on her sternum.

Was Jake shot? What am I going to do? I need to call the police. She heard ringing in her ears. It was not anything she'd experienced in the pressure cooker of the trauma room. Exhaling, she willed herself back. Then she evened her breathing and felt her heart slow its anxious beat. She felt a wave of guilt rush over her. *I'm staying*, she thought. *For Riley.*

She rolled on to her back and curled up against the runner on the staircase. She closed her eyes and prayed. Seconds raced like minutes. Suddenly, she felt a hand reach into hers and pull her up. She opened her eyes. Hoping. "Jake. What happened?" She rolled over, shaking from the pounding stream of adrenaline. Standing was an effort.

"Jenny. It's all clear. Come on."

"What was that?" Jenny asked breathlessly.

"We need to hurry. Someone must've heard that gunshot and the police are gonna be here in minutes."

Jake pulled her steadily down the hallway. She stepped gingerly around the broken glass and shards of plaster. They pushed through the debris on Riley's doorstep and stepped over broken police tape.

Jenny spied a body lying between the living room and the bathroom. Jake stepped toward the man then glanced out the window into the darkness on the south side of the building.

"What was this guy looking for?" Jenny asked.

The man gripped a pistol in his lifeless hand. Jake rummaged through the man's clothing, still scanning the room for movement. He kicked the gun away. Then he clutched a curved metal object and held it up to Jenny.

"What's that?" she asked.

"This is what shot up that hallway. Notice the semi-circular shape. His buddy got out the window. It's from his AK-47."

Jenny was bewildered. She spun around and murmured, "AK-47?"

Jake sprinted into the bathroom and disappeared. He came back out. "Nothing."

"What are you looking for?" She stared at the body on the floor and wondered if she'd made a mistake staying with Jake.

"We don't have much time," he warned. "We need to search!"

A cyclone had blown the room into a pile of puzzle pieces. Jenny saw that the couch cushions were overturned, the upholstery slashed from twelve to six. The fish tank had been shattered; the television lay on its screen. Books were thrown from their cases, and dishes from the kitchen littered the floor. *This guy did a lot of damage.*

Jake ran his hands along the walls then kicked the debris on the floor. Jenny stood passively near the ransacked bathroom. Chaos and destruction filled the room. Jake shouted quickly. "Listen. We've only got a few minutes. The police will be here shortly."

"Why can't we just wait for the police?" Jenny pleaded, her hands outstretched. She felt that she had a good rapport with the police from the ER patients they'd brought in over the years.

"Because of that AK-47. That tells me Riley unearthed something ominous. She's touched something sinister."

Jenny stared at him. *Even if he's in the CIA, can he protect me?* She thought. *Maybe he's Riley's brother but I don't want to die.*

"I don't know about all this, Jake." She moaned.

Jake stopped rummaging through the room. "I understand what you're thinking. I show up and Riley is killed. Yeah, maybe they were after me. I don't think so anymore. If they were here with AK-47's, they were after something that Riley had or has. And, because of the clues she shared with you? You're in danger."

It felt logical to Jenny. She wondered if Riley had ever seen him in action like this. "This is all rather chaotic and exciting in a strange way. What should I look for?" Her scientific mind was clicking.

"Look at me. Trust me. I will protect you. Is there anything you see that isn't Riley's?"

Not waiting for an answer, Jake rushed to Riley's bedroom. Jenny felt the pull of his gaze and followed. She opened a few drawers, finding nothing unusual.

He began pulling apart the bed, turning over the cabinets, flipping open books, emptying her jewelry box.

Jenny spotted Riley's passport on the floor and handed it to Jake. He slid it into his jacket. She sensed that he didn't want to look. *He doesn't want to see Riley's face. The reminder must be too harsh.* But then he picked up Riley's Canon pocket camera, and opened the photo folder to find a picture of Riley dated from the week before.

Jenny looked around his flank. The image reminded her not just of a woman now gone forever but a friendship that had been strong in spirit. She remembered Riley's blue eyes and thick lashes. She paused. *Just like Jake's.* Always beaming. She felt her neck heat up. A primitive anger was overtaking her. She needed to turn it into action. *She was always there for me. And I wasn't there when she needed me.*

Jake was still staring at the camera. Riley was standing with a small boy in the doorway of a building, her arm around his shoulders. The boy had a small but very round face, a narrow chin, a wide space between his eyes, a flat nose, and a short neck. Jenny knew she'd recognize him if she'd ever seen him. She hadn't. Jake closed the file and pocketed the camera.

He scanned around the bedroom at the empty bookcases, the drawers and the overturned mattress.

Something must be so obvious I'm not seeing it. Riley wanted to pick something up in this apartment. What? Why? She thought. *Where's the key? Riley said there was a key!*

"Targeting her means they're on the offensive right now," Jake said. "We need to turn the tables on them. And quickly."

Jenny moved into the bathroom, where she methodically emptied the medicine cabinet. Nothing. Stuck in the corner of the mirror was a photo, an aging Polaroid. It showed a young boy and much younger girl holding fishing poles by the side of a pond. The two were beaming and had their arms around each other. Jake appeared in the bathroom, startling her. He grabbed the photo. She squinted when she saw him smile. "That's us." Then he slid the print into his jacket and continued his search.

His confidence warmed her. She lifted the flower vase. "Nothing."

"There must have been something here," he said, returning to the bedroom. Jenny raced past him to help. She studied layers of shattered glass and chess pieces jumbled around the carpet. "I must've been too late. Maybe they found whatever it was they were looking for. They were just waiting to take us out."

He pulled Jenny behind him toward the exit. "Let's go!" But he quickly turned back. "Wait one second."

"Of course. Whatever you say."

"Go fish, Riley," he said, taking the Polaroid from his coat.

"Go fish?"

Jake hurdled the couch—racing back into the debris-filled living room.

Chapter 15

Riley's Apartment Building

"Look at the smashed fish tank. There's no water dripping down the side?" Jake turned his gaze to Jenny. "I didn't appreciate at first that my hand was dry when I passed it through the gravel."

"So . . . ?" She was mystified.

"So . . . where are the fish and why isn't there water dripping down on the chest? They didn't drain the tank first before destroying it. How many fish did she have?"

"Just two goldfish, Mac and Cheese." *This must be one of Riley's puzzles!* "They were there just last week. Cheese is the yellower one. Mac has a black mark on his face that looks like a tiny cigar."

Jake shook his head. "Mac and Cheese? Oh, Riley!"

Jenny shrugged. "I don't know where they are. But Jake . . ." She hesitated, trying to calculate her words. "She told me more. She said she left a key here for me."

He put his hand on her shoulder and waited. His eyes were calm blue oceans. His stare was genuine concern. Like he was the actor with gravitas within a thriller movie. Her pulse thumped out of her chest. He waited. He wanted more information. Then he looked at his watch. "We need to clear this place in less than five minutes."

"There's more. His name is Dr. McGrath. She met this old obstetrician when we were junior year abroad in college ten years ago. She was in London again a few years ago and Father Landry took her for a side trip over to Dublin to see a Caravaggio painting. She said that she renewed the friendship with Dr. McGrath." *I feel like I'm handing Jake what Riley called whimsies—a stack of those unconnected serpiginous-shaped puzzle pieces.*

"Landry?" He asked.

"Yes. He's a Jesuit priest. Taught us Renaissance art." She said.

"You doctors like your distractions."

"It takes the stress away."

"McGrath?"

"She said Dr. McGrath was still teaching her secrets. She said he was 'testing her.' And she tested me all the time. That's why she said she left a key in here for me."

"I know she was worried. I can't see the reason to kill her. I don't know why I was left behind." Jake said solemnly.

"What was she like growing up?" She wanted to know about their relationship.

"Awesome. She was my balance. She'd forgive me for my mistakes because she understood me."

Jenny jumped back. His emotion touched her between her shoulders. *Was he playing me? He did feel what Riley had felt for him? Interesting . . . a brother and . . . a man with warm feelings.* She sighed. Then she nodded.

"She watched. She listened. She knew. Right?" Jake added.

"Yes. Yes . . ."

"You know what I'm talking about."

"She could see things that no one else saw. That's why she was so gifted at creating puzzles. She saw the world moving so slowly she anticipated every move around her. She deciphered medical mysteries."

"She would have been great in the CIA."

"She was the best in the ER." She said.

"I know. Long before you knew her. Long before she started saving the lives of the many casualties of society—she was a girl. A girl growing up like any girl. She fixed others' bones and muscles . . ." He paused. "But to put her all back together now is impossible."

She stepped back, feeling herself nod repeatedly, hoping he wasn't lying to her. "This is personal."

"You're right. When it comes to someone you know who dies—it's . . . it's very different. I've also seen a lot of people die. But I'm on the other side of the gun. This is more than protecting your queen in chess. This is personal for you and me."

"We . . ." She started to say, and then stared. "Riley is owed more." She felt that was the best she could do for the moment.

"Riley wanted you to go with me. She told you about the key in the event that she couldn't make the Ireland trip," Jake said. "You seem skeptical."

"I've just seen too many liars in the Emergency Room."

"She was my sister. And she prepared you to help me. You need to trust me."

"That would be Riley."

"Think." He said.

"I am."

"She hid the fish with the key. Just in case someone came along." He added in a rush. "Wait! Stop. Where would you keep the fish where no one would look?" Jake sprinted into the bathroom with Jenny in tow, lifting the toilet seat. There was nothing. He lifted the tank top. Nothing.

"Let's work it out the way she'd want us to do it." Jenny felt the rush of the hunt. "Come on, Riley; talk to me." She said. "Look." A few wilted roses and a pair of scissors rested on the bathroom counter. She pointed at the vase of yellow roses, as if waiting to be refreshed.

"From you?" she asked.

"Yes." He lifted out the flowers; they'd been stripped of all their thorns. Looking into the vase, he saw two yellow fish swimming in circles. "Jenny!"

Jenny leaned in to look. "That's Mac and Cheese, all right." He put the vase down on the sink.

A slender, transparent piece of fishing line hung down from the stems. He drew it up and grasped a short silver key. "I'm sure this is what they were after." Jake said.

"That's got to be it. It's just like her to take elaborate steps to hide it." Jenny said. She grabbed his arm. He looked down and smiled at her. She bit her lip, sensing that the game was changing.

Jenny wondered what Riley's plan for her had been this time, what reward would have awaited her at the end of this game. Intricate engravings on the tiny handle suggested the key was ancient. The teeth were jagged and irregularly spaced. It was too small to be a door key and too old to be a car key. "Now . . . what kind of door does this key open?" She asked.

Jake shook his head.

Jenny touched his hand. "I'm realizing how important all this was to Riley."

"I agree. But how? Tell me what you're thinking." Jake asked.

"One of the last things Riley said to me on shift was that she left a key in her apartment for me. A clue. Just in case. This is the 'just in case.' I know she wanted me to take up this puzzle. It was if she sensed someone might kill her."

"I think Riley practically ordered you to come to Ireland with me. I need to know what else she said."

"I've told you everything." Jenny replied. She sensed where he was going. She thought. *He'll get us through this. His confidence is Riley's confidence. My best friend has been killed but this was the last thing she wanted for us.*

"I'm convinced you possess more clues than you realize."

Jenny's temperature rose. She was caught up in the thrill. "I'm going with you. She wanted me to have this key. She wanted me to go with you." Jenny felt the rush of confidence in her own voice. She knew he was right. *My best friend was killed and she wanted me to do this . . . just in case. This is my time. My medical skills might also help him.*

"It's not going to be easy," he said. "But I want you there."

"You know it looks like a . . . what do they call it . . . a cigar box key?" She ignored him. "My dad had one of those little cigar boxes. It had a tiny keyhole."

"You mean a humidor. I don't think this is a humidor key, but I like your thinking. We need some help. We need to find out what Riley was up to before we leave for Ireland. We need to find Digger." He waved the key in front of her.

"Who?"

"Digger Walsh. An old friend. I haven't seen him in years, but he worked in Hartford after he got out of the CIA. Paranoid. Hates everybody. Mean, he lives like he'd been thrown into hell. He drinks like a fiend but we can trust him. And he always knows what's going on. He watched after Riley."

She heard the sound of approaching sirens. Jenny shot Jake a look that said she hoped it was time to stop and talk to the police. Jake shook his head. "You're not as safe with the police as you are with me. You need to come with me until we figure out the rest of what Riley wanted me to see. She left more clues, I'm sure of it. We get Digger."

"What about Riley's funeral and wake?"

"There's no time for that. It wouldn't be safe to stay here

for you or me. Listen, it hurts me that she's gone. More than you know. She'd want us to do everything to stay alive and solve her last brainteaser. Solving this puzzle will lead us to her killer."

"I can do this." She said.

"I can tell you right now." She heard a subtle but momentary change in his voice, something that caught him off guard. "She left both of us a message. 'Just in case.'" He held out the key in the palm of his hand. "Splitting up the clues was her way of bringing the two of us together."

"I always teased Riley about being too good for this world." Jenny said. "Riley dragged me to the chapel most Sundays. I slept while she sang the hymns and prayed. But there was one time Father Landry had given this sermon. He was angry about something. I don't remember what. But I remember him closing the sermon with fire in his voice warning, 'All it takes for evil to succeed is for good men to do nothing,' He looked over at Riley and me. 'Or women.'"

"Riley. That's Riley. She wouldn't stand down. I won't either!"

"I need to get my medical bag across the hall, and then let's go," Jenny said with sudden decisiveness.

"Good. Give me your cell phone. I need to replace the SIM card so that we can't be tracked." He turned on the tap to put more water into the vase for Mac and Cheese.

Chapter 16

Huldra Oil Field
North Sea, Norway

The Sikorsky S-76 fought, and then abruptly plunged through the thunderstorm's downdraft. Beads of rain exploded across the cabin window, shifting in direction.

The twin turbo shaft engines perched above the passenger cabin swallowed the water while the lone cabin passenger grabbed his fallen black Stetson and jammed it back down on his head. Charles Pratt no longer feared the sudden plummet over the Huldra Oil Field in the North Sea. He gave a thousand-yard stare across the ten-foot cabin. His pilots were in control.

The helicopter bounced upward from the landing platform on his expansive oil rig. It hopped once then settled across the yellow circle. The pilot slowed the engines and turned. The anxious passenger tossed his headphones onto the seat and exited before he could hear the instructions. Pratt moved toward the gathering crew standing beneath the derrick and next to the metal booms, drilling draw works and mud pumps.

The pilot yelled but Pratt either couldn't or wouldn't hear him. The pilot turned to the copilot. "He'd rather have his head cut off."

Pratt took in the splattering rain, the growling engines of the helicopter and the clanging drill pumps on the oil rig. The chaos was comforting in a cruel way. His tortured body was wet and cold but his numbness was sustained by his anger and determination. His bulging abdomen sloshed when he moved across the deck. His doctor had called it "Lennox Disease" or . . . some strange name. Like everything else about his body—he didn't care about the name and, suspected his doctor was too afraid to tell him the truth anyway.

A contractor strode out from under the derrick to greet Pratt. He wiped his hand with a large red rag and then extended it.

Pratt screamed over the sound of the storm and the helicopter, "Listen, your job is to carry out my time lines and budget. They need to be my specs." Rain hit his face and he spit the water out with the words.

"Mr. Pratt, I am."

"No, you're not."

"I thought I was."

"I told you no women on the rig!"

"I thought you meant no women visitors, no family, no prostitutes."

"You're an idiot. No women. None. Period."

"Sir, you'd best speak to your brother. I work for the drilling contractor. He's the company man for your exploration outfit, and we're just following his lead."

"My brother did this? Where's he?" Pratt screamed.

Stephen Pratt pushed his way through the small crowd of workers that had gathered. He shot out his hand to greet his brother. Charles Pratt looked at him, wild-eyed with anger. With the discipline of years spent in boardrooms, he counted down to neutral. He walked a few feet away, jammed his wet hat on a mud pump, and then combed his hand through his soaking hair. He faced his brother. "I've got a bunch of Alhambra thugs and some Italian Mafia with millions of dollars rough necking all over Europe and Asia looking for the Caravaggio painting, and I don't have time for you or the crew to be disobeying my orders."

"Charles, we're doing great out here with the drilling."

"And I shouldn't be on this oil rig. I don't need to be distracted by your screw-up. I need to be looking for that painting."

"Charles. I don't understand. We're doing what were supposed to be doing."

"I only have so much time to find this . . . this Last Prophet painting by Caravaggio. And, you know that I've had to neutralize some people along the way Stephen."

"I understand," Stephen replied.

"She's a bitch, ain't she?"

"Huh?" Stephen said, opening the palm of his hands to signal his confusion.

"You brought a damn bitch on board? I told you 'no.' And you brought one here."

"Yeah, she's one of the roughnecks. A damn good driller. She runs one of the machinery crews."

"I said no women. None. It distracts the men and reduces productivity."

"I assure you she's not interfering with our work."

"I don't have time to argue. I've seen too many oil jobs screwed up because you brought a woman on board. I need to focus on retrieving this Last Prophet painting or else I won't be running this company anymore."

One of the men stepped forward. But he was brushed aside by another worker, who then stepped directly in front of Charles. "I'm Beth Breyer." She stuffed her gloves into her oily overalls, and extended one hand.

"I don't care about your name." Charles Pratt grabbed the boom hook, rammed it into her belt and yanked her up, swinging above him. Her helmet flew off, her hair falling down her back. She swung her arms wildly, trying to push back but her hands flailed across his wet coat. He wound the winch swiftly into position.

"What are you doing?" Stephen Pratt roared. The men moved forward.

Pratt pulled a small handgun out from under his shoulder and pointed it at the crowd of men. He cranked the wheel with his free hand; the winch jerked the woman upwards. He spun the wheel and dangled her out over the raging ocean.

"Charles. No. Stop!" Stephen howled.

Pratt swung his pistol back and forth from the crowd of men to the woman oscillating over the North Sea. He yelled, spitting the rainstorm back from his mouth, "Now carry out my time lines and budget on my specifications. And that means no women." He let go of the brake on the winch and turned back toward the helicopter. The chain released and the woman plunged downward. Stephen Pratt grabbed the spinning wheel before it sent Breyer into the sea.

Pratt took his hat and strode decisively toward the helicopter. The pilot was still tying down the front landing gear. Pratt kicked him in the backside. "What are you doing? Let's go."

Pratt disappeared into the helicopter and out into the storm.

Chapter 17

College of the Holy Cross
Worcester, Massachusetts, U.S.A.

"There is no passing lane on a tightrope," Father Landry said with a clever smile, "and you don't know life until you've been on that tightrope—two hundred feet in the air—during that vanishing second when you lose your balance and start to run, knowing you've lost control and must risk it all to get to the other side. Do you stop, release your fear, or go back?"

The congregation gathered in St. Joseph's chapel for the wedding of college classmates murmured when Father Landry finished his sermon. "Remember this: Trust each other and always look for the best in each of you. I ask you to turn around and face your witnesses. And now . . . I pronounce you husband and wife. Go forth." Applause broke out to receive the newlyweds. A short while later he followed the crowd out of the church and closed the large steel doors behind him.

Aware that both this day and his academic year were now complete, Reverend John Landry, S.J., turned back to the narthex and marched alone back through the nave. The wedding of two former students capped it all. Landry always looked for a way to smile through *tristesse*, the mellow sadness that typically washed over him at the school year's end. But summer also brought him time to travel and pursue his post-doctoral research as an art historian, a privilege he embraced with joy.

The sudden sound of metal scrapping metal broke his meditation.

His legs tensed at the steps of the chancel and he glared back into the fading chiaroscuro of the church.

His heart raced.

"Hello? Anyone still here?" He called out, only to hear the echoes pinging off the stone walls and high ceiling.

He waited. He snapped his head left, then right. Nothing.

He felt his heart thump; the sound of his breathing grew louder. He started moving again. At the sanctuary, the priest picked up the wedding couple's missals at the prie-dieu, stacked them neatly on the corner of the high altar, and looked out again on the rows of pews. So many young men had worshiped here, especially before 1972, when mandatory daily mass was abolished and the school became co-ed. Now, he supposed, the few men and, yes, women who attended services voluntarily must be genuinely pious. But still delightfully impious, too.

An abrupt shuffling sound from the left transept shattered Landry's thoughts. He heard a click, like a key turning in a lock, to his right. He felt a sudden thump in his chest, as though his heart had skipped a beat. "Hello?" He stammered. "Is there someone there?"

Landry swallowed deeply and waited quietly for a few moments in the growing darkness, staring in the direction of the sound. Still nothing. He decided his hearing was deceiving him. He glanced at his watch. Dinnertime. He needed to get up to the residence.

He saw a figure like a shade suddenly breaking through the darkness. A middle-aged man dressed in a tweed suit jacket, black pant, and a rumpled white shirt crossed between the pews to enter the center aisle. He had bushy red eyebrows that glowed in the fading light. He clutched a large black metal briefcase hung from his shoulder.

"You startled me," Father Landry said.

No answer came back from the strange man.

Chapter 18

College of the Holy Cross
Worcester, Massachusetts, U.S.A.

"Are you with the wedding party?" Father Landry asked, waving toward the church entrance.

"Good evening, Father Landry," the man replied in a cold, gravelly voice.

"Are you lost, young man?"

"Father, I'm from the Art Crimes Team of the FBI." With his free hand he awkwardly raised a gold and blue badge upward toward the steps of the chancel.

Father Landry squinted back and pondered. *Art Crimes Team?* He fumbled his index finger under his roman collar and felt his pulse race. He stammered, "Art . . ."

"I've a few questions for you." The man reached out and rapped his knuckles on the briefcase. "Why don't we go back into the sacristy and have a glass of wine?"

Landry pulled his chin back. His eyes hardened on the strange man. The reference to altar wine irritated the elderly priest. It made him suspect his visitor was mocking him. "Thank you, but I'm running late for dinner."

The man climbed the first step. "I need fifteen minutes of your time and I'll be on my way. I need help with some pictures." He lifted the briefcase. Father Landry noted his round eyes, a flat face, and a large mouth. His skin was moist and glowed in the candlelight like a toad's.

After a few tense moments, the priest directed his mysterious guest to precede him. He declined, allowing the priest to lead the way into the sacristy.

The last glint of evening sun refracted through small stained-glass windows into the sacristy room. An eerie swath of dust rotated through the light cutting across dressing table. Father Landry slid into a chair behind the table in the center of the room. The man sat impassively across from him, gazing at the cabinets and polished wood appointments, then back at Landry.

Toad placed his briefcase on top of the table, clicked open the locks, and lifted the top half. "Father, you've been hard to find."

"I went to New York City for two weeks right after exams."

"Have you ever heard of seven works of mercy?" Toad asked

"Of course. You've come on a Saturday night to ask me that?" Landry sighed.

"I mean, have you heard of the painting *The Seven Works of Mercy*?"

"You ask that question but don't know of my work on the painters who attempted the subject? The Master of Alkmaar, or Frans Francken, or Caravaggio?"

"Car-a-vag-gio." The strange man seemed to blow out the syllables like bubbles of air. "Yes. That one. Tell me about Caravaggio."

The scholar exhaled and probed the strange Toad eyes, instinctively tugging again on his collar. *Caravaggio should be easily recognizable to the Art Crimes Team. He was a master painter. Too many people turned up dead when Caravaggio and his paintings were involved. And why was Toad sweating so much?* He hoped stretching out the time would bring help. *Surely someone would miss me soon?*

"There's much to talk about with Caravaggio," he said. "You could call him the Baroque Bad Boy. He was quite the rebel, you know, a rambunctious fellow who had many swordfights and was wanted for murder, then painted the people from the streets and bars he frequented, turning those heartless scenes into spiritual paintings. He was very popular at the turn of the seventeenth century, but he was labeled an artist who had one hand on the devil and the other on the brush."

Toad sighed. "Are the acts of mercy the same as the works of mercy?"

"Yes. It's a Catholic belief that there are acts that should be undertaken by true believers to help others. They are actually recognized by Eastern Rite churches, Roman Catholics, Orthodox Christians, and Lutherans. They originate from the Beatitudes. You know, 'Blessed are the merciful, for they shall obtain mercy,' et cetera. These works were germane to Caravaggio's time in sixteenth- and seventeenth-century Italy. A severe plague had ravaged the continent and there were sick and dying people all over the streets. Why do you ask?"

"I'll ask you the questions." Toad pulled out a black pistol and planted it on top of the table.

Father Landry sat back quickly.

He felt adrenaline tingling up and down his back but he didn't know whether it was the surprise of being admonished by the stranger or his fear of guns. "You're not going to shoot a priest inside his own church?"

Toad took off his glasses and pinched the bridge of his nose. "What's so special about this man Caravaggio that you've spent the last six summers tracking his work around the globe?"

Landry stood. Even his brother Jesuits didn't know about his unpublished work on Caravaggio. Barely breathing, he stared a long moment at the man, and then gradually at the gun.

"He was an exciting fellow." Father Landry ran his index finger across his dry lips. "The Catholic Church had a love-hate relationship with Caravaggio. He was such an explosive figure. The Church preferred artists like Raphael, who painted glorious cardinals and popes. Or Michelangelo. He gave them some trouble about payments, but painted celestial mystical places. Those two were great artists but relatively controllable. Things changed in the sixteenth century. The plague took its toll on the faithful. Martin Luther challenged the excesses and hypocrisies of Rome. He called for reform. He got schisms."

Landry lifted the wide sleeve of his alb and glanced at his watch. Good. *By now my absence at dinner would have been noted. I must keep talking until someone comes.*

He plowed on, hoping to calm himself . . . and slow his strange guest. "The Council of Trent addressed the needs for Catholic Church reform and developed a counterstrategy to meet the threats of Protestantism. The Council admonished the Catholic bishops and cardinals who had abused their privileges at the expense of the Church, expressly pushing the clergy to live modestly and frugally and attending to the poor. Trent reemphasized the importance of the seven sacraments but asked the clergy to focus more on salvation through faith and the active performance of good works. Remember, there were no newspapers, no Internet, no nightly news broadcasts, no public schools. The Church taught the masses through art. Rome sought out someone to communicate their message to the suffering masses. Art was power."

"What about Caravaggio?"

"While Michelangelo and Raphael were a cool drink on a hot day, Caravaggio was a blunt weapon in the counterattack on Protestantism. His paintings ignited fires in the masses. His images burnt the souls of the wayward Catholics. By the way, the method was wildly successful. Over the course of the next hundred years, fifty percent of Protestants converted back to Catholicism."

"What do you know about a painting called, The Lost Prophet?"

Father Landry hesitated momentarily. He didn't want to betray his oath to provide the truth but felt that the man had given him an escape. *It's the Last Prophet. Caravaggio's Last Prophet! Maybe someone stumbled upon it!* He thought. *This man got the name wrong!* He said, "I've never heard of any painting with that name."

Toad splayed his hand out on the table and stared at the priest like a lion that was about to pounce. The priest sensed the peculiar man had enough of his lecture. Father Landry licked his lips when he thought the man's hand moved toward the pistol grip.

"Father, do you recall Riley McKee as a student here?"

"Yes. She graduated many years ago."

"Is there any reason that her name would be mentioned along with *The Nativity* and *The Seven Acts of Mercy* in a communication out of Syria?"

"Syria? No . . . Is Riley okay?"

Toad ignored his question. "*The Nativity* is the most coveted painting on the FBI's top-ten art crimes list. I looked up its background. It seems to have disappeared years ago."

Father Landry sat back down. He swallowed deeply, aware that he was helpless to defend himself. *This man is a fraud. I'd better try something.* He thought.

"You'd know that already if you were truly from the FBI. You'd also use the word 'provenance,' not 'background,' if you were from art crimes. Who are you?"

Toad tilted his head toward the gun, like an agreement had been reached. "Father, I'm sorry to tell you that Riley McKee was killed earlier today."

Father Landry blessed himself, stood and walked over to the cabinet of vestments, turning his back on the imposter, and fighting back tears. *She must've deciphered the final clues to the Last Prophet painting. No one knows exactly what or where it is. It's the stuff of legends . . . and people always end up dead. I warned her so.* He thought. "She was an exceptional student, a beautiful young woman inside and out, a brilliant, caring doctor."

He stood there quietly, motionless, praying.

A closing door in the church echoed into the room. *Good news, I hope,* Landry thought. He continued on. "We humans can never know the providential reason for tragedy. . . ." The priest raised his voice, hoping to alert someone. "But there is no reason for what you're telling me. Explain your purpose here." He spun on his heel to confront the man. The Toad was gone.

He veered out into the church to find the narthex and transepts empty. He paused, looking at the altar. *If he killed Riley McKee why didn't he kill me? She must have figured out the cipher I sent her. He's planning to follow me and what I know. She must've figured out the mystery of The Last Prophet. She warned me to drop out of sight if this happened.*

Landry quickly changed out of his vestments and exited the church through the transept. The sun was now blocked on the east side of the church, and shadows were deepening. He headed toward the hill beyond the portico.

#

The bride and groom had returned to the portico for some last pictures, taking advantage of the sun's new angle. The bride saw Father Landry walk up the road to the Jesuit cemetery tucked behind the hedges. Delighted that her day had gone so perfectly, she ignored both her mother and the photographer's requests to stand still, lifted her train over her arm, and raced to hug her favorite priest one more time.

When she reached the cemetery, she looked down the rows of simple white headstones, searching for Landry. At the only other exit stood a solitary man in a black suit holding a briefcase. The bride waved to him shyly, mistaking him for another Jesuit.

"Young lady, did Father Landry go that way?" He asked her pleasantly.

"No. He went your way."

The man shot her a puzzled look. He looked inside the cemetery at the limestone markers and the looming chrome crucifix, abruptly turned and strode up the hill.

The bride stood alone considering the mystery of the priest who'd disappeared.

Chapter 19

CIA Headquarters
Langley, Virginia

Karen Smith closed her eyes and tossed her Yankees cap onto the enormous walnut table.

She rubbed her eyes with one hand and propped her briefcase on top of her chair with the other, absorbing the silence alone in the large room. She admired the colorful maps on the walls then turned face-to-face with the windows of the fifth-floor conference room. Finally, she released a deep, tired breath, fogging the reinforced window of the CIA building.

As station chief out of Amman, Smith knew the importance of an immediate download for the hotel operation gone badly. Her hurried drive out of Damascus across the highway of Route M5 to Amman left her with little sleep. There, she caught a deafening Air America flight to Incirlik Air Base in Turkey. She stole a shower and washed away the sand from the Gariyah desert that had filtered in from the open windows of the beat-up Toyota. The 39th Air Base wing then hopped her back to Dulles. Deputy Director Kevin Felice was waiting for an explanation. Given that today was Sunday, he wouldn't be happy.

Two of her best CIA operatives, Jason Williams and Willie Park, had traveled back with her to the Special Activities Division, sometimes called the Special Operations Group in order to avoid the unpleasant acronym "SAD." The group was composed of crack paramilitary operations officers, veterans of the Marine Force Recon. The SOG was the most talented group of paramilitary specialists in hostage rescue, material recovery, sabotage, and counterterrorism.

Smith was expecting nothing less than a public colonoscopy from the Deputy Director for the fiasco in a delicate city where hatred of America ran deep. She'd been a devoted friend to Felice's wife during her Georgetown Hospital treatments but, that emotion was checked at the CIA door and she knew he was all business in the office. Because Williams and Park were fiercely loyal to Smith and appreciated the decisions she made in the field they would speak up for her. The two men knocked, entered and sat quietly at the conference table.

Leading up to the operation she'd had reliable Intel that the insurgent Syrians were trading some religious art for cash from the Italians. Her two experienced teams had cased the hotel for a week; its setup was perfect: There were only two entrances to the twelfth-floor rendezvous point. She'd set up a control center down the street, with cameras in each of the hotel passageways and a bug in the room. She'd inserted one of her covert men into the room for the exchange. The Italians had the cash—twenty million Euros as a down payment on the artwork. The most notorious arms dealer in Syria was to be there, and she wanted him alive.

But someone had tipped off the operation. Or someone had ratted them out. In a country where no one could be trusted, even if they were bought, she knew the assets were as shifty as desert sand and it was difficult to operate on either side of the law.

Deputy Director Felice entered the room with two people Smith did not recognize. The woman was tall, wore a navy blue pants suit, and had her silver hair twisted into a French knot. The man was taller, also wore a navy blue suit, and was balding. Felice was dressed in a bright green Lacoste golf shirt that revealed his well-tanned arms and neck. His black slacks covered what Smith knew were skinny legs that graced the patio of his Virginia country home. His wire-rimmed glasses made him look like he was ready to read the Sunday newspaper while sipping a Bloody Mary. *That's what he's probably been doing*, Smith thought.

She'd come to befriend Felice and his wife outside the agency and, the bond still held. Nancy Felice had suffered terribly from pancreatic cancer. Felice had kicked himself with guilt for the months that he and her doctor had ignored the early warning signs that might have saved her. Despite the hideous pain, Nancy died with grit and grace. But Smith knew that the events of her death changed Felice as a man, a father, and a spook.

He had one dislike: excuses. He didn't want to hear or see them. From the head of the table, Felice gestured for his guests to sit opposite Smith and her two operatives. It was customary not to introduce someone unless it was necessary. And it was totally unnecessary to identify almost any agent by bureau or name.

"Smith, what happened?"

"We were set up, sir. We had actionable intelligence that a buy was going down that involved one of Syria's most notorious arms dealers, Malik Nogabyeh. He was there in Damascus, in the hotel, in room twelve. We'd followed procedure to the last detail; all of our information was accurate. But we didn't know there'd be a third party there who'd shoot up the place, take the money and the evidence of the art."

"Is there any way you could've done this differently?"

"No, sir. I've been going over it in my head. No sleep. Sorry. Strike that," she said, not wanting to create a pretext that would anger Director Felice. "All of our Intel said that this was a drop and trade."

"What were you thinking, getting involved in an art buy?" the male agent fired across at her.

Smith glanced over at Director Felice, who nodded his head to allow her to answer. "We weren't there for the art. In fact, we don't believe any artworks were there either. This was about a bag man for Assad."

"Did you think that the size of your teams might have tipped them off?"

"No." Smith stopped. Then her shoulders slumped as she gave her answer more thought. She felt the cold rush of elements piecing together. "You're from the FBI, aren't you? The reason you're here is the art? Is that what this is about?"

"You should be reminded, Ms. Smith, that the FBI has jurisdiction over art crimes theft, even in international territory!" the FBI man snapped back.

"This operation was to go after the thugs funding Assad in the Middle East, nothing more."

The female agent sighed loudly and looked straight at Karen Smith. "Did you ever consider that this was the FBI's responsibility? Missing relics and art?"

"I know the protocols perfectly well." The Art Crimes Team had been established in 2004 to stop cultural property crime, and the FBI division had recovered millions of dollars in stolen art. Smith didn't like the idea of weighing art against a terrorist. "But this was not about the art, ma'am." She struggled to stay polite, but Smith's voice kept rising. Her two operatives shifted their positions in their chairs.

The woman spoke again. "You may have lost our one chance at recovering *The Nativity*, likely one of the most valued missing paintings in the world."

"Lost? Excuse me." Smith felt like spitting the remaining desert sand at her. "I just lost— No . . . I just had one of my best men shot center mass in a hotel room in some godforsaken sand dune in the middle of nowhere while chasing down the meanest SOB in all freaking Mesopotamia, and you're worried about art? The art that wasn't there?"

"Enough!" Felice's response echoed. Huddled in the Virginia countryside, she felt the empty building shake on a Sunday morning.

In the ensuing silence, Smith thought about FBI director Robert Mueller, who'd been on the job for just one week when 19 terrorists fired four Boeing jets up America's butt to shatter America's peace. In the days and years that followed, Mueller had made counterterrorism his greatest priority. A joint counterterrorism center had been established at Langley to share FBI and CIA data on potential threats. But the two agencies had no experience sharing, and cooperation was stressful. A shared office accentuated the tension. Both agencies generally agreed that "Fidelity, Bravery, and Integrity" covered the U.S. mainland, and the CIA had the rest of the world. But since 9/11, all boundaries were, at best, a matter of debate.

The CIA never shook off its frustration and frequently reminded the FBI that the CIA had sent them a report that some Arabs were planning, as early as 1998, to fly multiple planes into the World Trade Center. Part of the problem was that the FBI lived in a world of specificity, like targets, dates, mug shots, while the CIA reported on trends and movements. With all the media talk of excuses, blame, and recrimination, the CIA and FBI weren't getting anywhere. Maybe it was the experience of watching his wife in her waning days, maybe not, but Smith could sense Felice looking for her to speak. "Well, Kevin, where we do we move on from here?"

Felice pulled down his glasses and folded them into his case, which he flipped over and over on the tabletop. "There's more information from the FBI," he said, turning to his colleague from the bureau.

The FBI man stared down at the table. After a long moment he looked up. "Last week we picked up a communication that came out of Damascus regarding *The Nativity*. We were just gathering our team and consulting experts when you set your Op in motion. We had no idea that you were there, mind you."

"So much for interagency intelligence sharing," Smith said dryly. "Elaborate. What is *The Nativity*?"

"It's a painting we've been trying to recover for forty years—a masterpiece stolen from Sicily in 1969."

"And you think that the Syrians were selling that painting back to the Italians at the hotel."

"We were hoping." The silver-haired woman paused conspicuously, looking up and to the right.

Smith noticed that the woman was biting her lip. *Either she didn't recognize her own signs of lying, or this gal was far greener than her distinguished looks promised.* Smith knew what was wrong. *This woman has never been in the field.*

"There's something else you're not telling me," she said to the woman. Before the agent could answer, Smith looked over at Felice, who was frowning, a signal that there was a problem.

The director took the ball. "What? What else is it that bothers you about the Syrian fiasco?"

"Jake Bolton." The FBI woman responded.

"Jake Bolton?" Smith demanded.

"Yes, you're Jake Bolton." The FBI woman continued. "The communiqué out of Syria mentioned a young doctor named Riley McKee. Someone we had no record on. Yesterday, Riley McKee was shot from long range by a sniper in broad daylight as she left her hospital shift in Hartford, Connecticut . . . walking side by side with . . . Jake Bolton. But there's more. We found a dead Syrian national in McKee's living room last night with a .45-caliber bullet in his forehead. Her apartment had been ransacked. Jake Bolton has now disappeared and my men are searching for him."

Smith struggled to control her own personal tics. She could not let the federal agents see her agitation. "You assume that Jake Bolton was involved in this buy in Syria? He wouldn't be involved in anything that would hurt the United States."

Felice waved his hand toward Smith, taking command of

the table. "We do know that Bolton took leave three days ago and flew from Kabul, to Rome, and then on to Boston. Jake is a captain in the MARSOC. And yes, he worked for Smith from time to time."

"What is MARSOC?" the male agent asked from across the table.

"Marine Special Operations Command." Smith said. "He'd be in the 2nd Marine Special Operations Battalion, or MSOB, that engages in direct action and special reconnaissance in Afghanistan. If I know Jake Bolton, he was in the meanest, harshest areas of that war. He's an expert in unconventional warfare and foreign internal defense. He was part of our first group to go into Afghanistan along with SOG as part of Jawbreaker, the special operation that was in country two weeks after nine/eleven. They were intensely brave men, flying from Uzbekistan into the al Qaeda–infested Panjshir Valley with GPS mapping equipment, satellite communication gear, and millions of dollars in cash to meet with the Northern Alliance, then quickly build a force to fight bin Laden and the Taliban."

Karen Smith stood up and turned away from the conference table. *Jake hadn't been in Syria for years. He'd been in Iraq and now Afghanistan. He was the best special operative I've ever worked with—cunning and brilliant, creative and confident, and he always carried out a mission with attention to detail. He was a great Marine. He was the most honest guy I've ever met, and he didn't as much as yawn without having it planned in advance. He was not involved in her operation going bad. Jake Bolton? Not possible.*

Chapter 20

Digger's Apartment Building
Hartford, CT

Jake threw the car into park and thumped the steering wheel. Then he threw out his middle finger at the three-story building topped with an array of antennas and dishes.

"What's the matter, Jake?" Jenny asked.

"Just a bad memory."

"Of?" Jenny rotated sideways, sensing pain in Jake's voice.

He leaned forward over the driver's wheel, twisted his head upward and glared at Digger's house. "An awful memory of an operation in Amman, Jordan, in 2001."

His voice elevated several octaves and Jenny sensed his anxiety. She gulped for air as he spoke.

"I was headed alone into an al Qaeda safe house. It was an empty street at the wrong hour in a hostile neighborhood. Circumstances had dictated no prior surveillance. I hesitated just a few seconds and lost any element of surprise. A bullet to my leg stopped me before I got to the door. I was evac'ed out."

Jenny's thoughts wandered while he painted the scene.

She surveyed his body and instinctively looked down at his leg, feeling the pain he experienced. She'd felt his trauma directly. His wasn't the painful fiction of one of her forsaken ER patients. *This suffering was for me. His life matters personally now. And . . . to my survival. He remembers the pain—unlike my patients. It's a response that's intriguing. Likeable. But I don't know how he holds himself together after having his sister shot?* She looked up at his face.

Jake continued, "On the flight home a military officer returning to his job as a veterinarian told me that the moment he opened a door to an exam room, he could tell whether growling Fido was going to bite him or if he was just staking out his territory. The veterinarian warned me that no matter where, when or what, he had to enter that room with confidence so the dog would know who was boss."

Jenny turned back toward the traffic circle, "Why that memory now?"

"We took too much time. We hesitated. It's a trap. The FBI knows we're looking for Digger's help."

She gaped at the array of antennas studding the roof of Digger's hideout. How do you know?"

She watched him scan across the intersecting streets and added up the evidence for her. "Do you know how an old-fashioned clock works? Twelve, one, two, three," he said, dialing below the dashboard. "Now, three o'clock: The guy at the gas station in the overalls. He looks too clean and, there's only self serve there. There, nine o'clock: the mailman parked in his truck. He's got an earpiece. Federal employees are not allowed to listen to music while driving. Then, twelve o'clock front and center: the two guys by the open manhole wearing the orange vests. They have black leather shoes on. Italian leather? At least two fifty. Would you go into that sewer?"

"If they're FBI, why don't we talk to them?" Jenny asked. "Aren't they on our side?"

"It's not like chess where the pieces are black and white."

"Isn't there someone in the FBI we can trust?"

"No."

She shot him a quizzical look.

"For two reasons: One, because we won't know for sure who they are. And two, even if they're ours, we don't know when or where we can trust them."

"But you're CIA. If you can't trust them, why should I trust you?"

Jake turned. "One word: Riley. She trusted me. You know that. And I know you trusted her."

She felt a rush of excitement. "How? How do you know that?" *I want to know more about who you are.* She thought.

"Because she was my best friend in the world." Jake answered.

Jenny's eyes scrutinized him like an operative exam. She'd heard so many lies in the ER, seen too many bad actors believing their tragedies—but in their dying moments confessing to the truth they've denied themselves. *It's like they find God or something. And yet, this likeable guy, he's got scars from being shackled. By what and whom?*

"You still have doubts, I can see it. She protected my identity for a reason."

"Because?"

"Because . . ." Jenny noticed that he was slow to answer, sensing a truth he deeply felt. ". . . She loved me. And for that reason you should trust me. Regardless if they were trying to kill me or Riley, this is a much bigger crisis than we know. Someone along the chain of command is crooked. No one should have known about my visit to Riley. No one. We need to find a way around the government for now. Just give me more time."

"I loved Riley. Never steered me wrong."

"Put aside your desire to call family or friends right now. They'll track us or them and, they can get hurt."

"I want to find out who killed her." She squeezed her lips with her hand, wondering if she should say more. *I like him. There's a chance here.* She stared back at the red triple-decker house at the corner of Bond Street with disgust. Jake probably knew Digger was in there waiting for them. She watched Jake tap his hands on the steering wheel, calculating.

"I'm looking at those ornate cornices for signs of Digger's own surveillance. See that flash of steel at the corner of the building? That glint is a high-powered telescope." Jake said.

"Is he looking at us now?"

Jake didn't answer. Instead his finger drifted to the third floor of Digger's house, where a clothesline extended from the porch to the nearest telephone pole. "What a cheap son of a bitch." Jake's big blue eyes opened wide in recognition of the ruse.

"What do you see?" Jenny asked.

"Digger is a conniving old spook, and I'm sure that those sheets hanging from that clothesline are just camouflage for a line that's tapping into the passing telephone lines and stealing electricity."

Jenny eyed the building. From the roof, four antennas pointed off in different directions and likely downloaded data from agency satellites.

"See the yellow-orange construction container on the side of the house? Looks like a refuse tube extending from a third-floor window to the Dumpster at the corner of the empty yard? A perfect escape route. Digger has everything covered."

While Jake dissected the house, Jenny looked over at the sidewalk where a folding signboard was covered with red-and-white lettering. "I have an idea." The sign was for the Company 32 Fire Department spaghetti supper. She looked back at Digger's house. "Jake, go back up the street. I think I know someone who can get us out of this. Let's get some spaghetti!"

Jake shot her a perplexed glance, "I trust you too."

Jenny froze. She instinctively rubbed her palms on her pants. *Like he's reading my mind. He knew my next move.*

#

Arriving at the firehouse, Jenny instructed Jake to stay behind her while she strolled up the driveway to the open doors. The red brick firehouse was adorned in patriotic flags. A warm breeze was not enough to reduce the feel of the humidity. Outside, several topless fireman scrambled around the building stacking hoses. Standing between two heavy rescue trucks baking out on the asphalt, she was promptly greeted by a well-tanned fireman washing his tiller ladder and wearing just his suspendered pants. He looked only too pleased to see an attractive red head on a hot summer day.

"Is Webb Landis here?" she asked. He kneaded his towel like it was a lump of pasta dough while he looked her up and down. She ignored the ogling. "Can you let him know that Dr. Jenny Neugold is here to see him?"

The fireman yelled toward the garage, "Wow! Webber! There's one hot babe out here to see you!" He turned back to his work.

A yell shot back from the darkness of the garage: "I told you not to call me that. It's Webb, you . . ."

Strolling from the shadow of the firehouse garage, the shortest fireman Jenny had ever seen came beaming out. "Dr. Jenny, how are you? What are you doing here? You look great. Let me show you how well my scar has healed!" Landis pulled his trousers down to show his right buttock.

"Very nice, Webb. You're a good healer." She gestured for the man to pull up his pants.

"Healin', thanks to you! Who'd have thought that a broken staircase could cause such bleedin'?"

"I'm sorry to impose on you, Webb. This is unusual for me.

Remember you said that you'd help me someday if I ever needed it?"

"Yes, of course."

"I need it now. My brother is here with me." She waved over her shoulder to Jake. "He has a friend who got hurt in a house over on Bond Street at an illegal poker game. Jake wants me to get over there to take care of his friend instead of sending him to the hospital. You see, the friend doesn't want to go on disability. Or get in trouble with his boss. You know what I mean. I was wondering if you'd help me get in without being hassled by the locals?"

"I owe you." Landis answered. "What can I do?"

"Would you be willing to take out one of these big trucks on a test drive? Maybe let us ride until you stop on the corner of Bond Street? We jump out. You just keep driving after that. No one will even know we were there."

Landis nervously combed his hand through his wet hair. "I suppose a quick pass through would work. How about some of the boys and me take the tiller ladder now that it's cleaned? We should test it to be sure everything still works, what with the fresh wash and all . . . okay. Hop in." Landis reached up for the front cab door.

Jenny jumped into the middle cab and pulled on a coat and a helmet, passing a second uniform to Jake. "And Webb, would you mind running the siren for us as well?"

"Sure, why not! Hold on. It's going to be loud and fast until we get to Bond."

Jake leaned over her shoulder. "You're one manipulative surgeon,"

"It's Hartford. I've learned from the ER patients over the years. It's not what you know but what they owe you that gets things done." Jenny chuckled softly. She winked at Jake who half-smiled back.

Jenny adjusted her pony tail sticking out the back of the helmet. "When we get to Digger's house I'll get Webb to block the angles of the mailman and the gas station." He said. "He'll have to stop and redirect those agents to get out of the middle of the street so he can pass by. That should give us thirty seconds to get onto Digger's porch and break through the front door."

When the blaring siren announced their advance on the big

intersection, Jenny rocked back and forth with the truck's movement against Jake. She leaned over and asked, "Is *this* the charge in your belly you get when you're racing building to building getting shot at?"

Jake stared at Jenny in awe. "It's not the same. Let's stay focused. When we get into that triple-decker, we won't know exactly where Digger is. My bet is the third floor. He's not going to be happy to see us . . . or at least me."

Chapter 21

Digger's Apartment Building

Webb Landis shifted back and forth in his seat, violently waving at the pedestrians obstructing the large intersection of Barry Square, the "big BS." Jenny heard him swearing over the siren.

The tiller truck raced into the big BS. Across the traffic circle the FBI agents pulled back to the far side near the telephone pole. The other agents, meandering by the manhole, saw the truck coming and moved to the south side of the street, giving Jake and Jenny the seconds they needed.

"Jump. Run to the stairs," Jake yelled to Jenny. Jenny felt the rush of air when he opened the side door. They both scampered from the truck onto the sidewalk and leaped the stairs.

Jake raced through the front door. Jenny barely made it through, the hinges rattling the door back into place. Their noise and movement were covered by the ladder truck racing further down Bond Street.

Jake leaned against the door, threw off his fireman's jacket and helmet, and pulled out his HK pistol. He helped her pull off her coat with his free hand. The first-floor living room was a barren parquet floor. An empty fire place stained with charcoal split the room.

Jenny recognized that the floor plan mirrored the upper levels, and she could see Jake calculating the size and shape of each of the rooms as he darted from wall to wall. Jake ascended the central staircase, his gun in front of his face. He extended his arm behind him, grasping her shoulder. They paused abruptly on the second floor. She heard muffled voices. Her stomach rolled and she felt a surge of acid when Jake glanced back at her.

The voices grew louder. Across the hallway Jenny saw a single closed door on the second floor landing. From behind it she could hear people talking, dishes clanging, footsteps treading on the wooden floor.

Jake cocked his head at the noise, his gaze squinting back at Jenny. Something was wrong. "The words are running over and over." Jake said. "He set up a recording! We must have triggered it when we came in. I'm sure Digger has cameras on us now. He'll be on the third floor."

Jenny cringed and looked up, feeling the invisible cameras zooming in on her. She watched Jake study the ceiling lights and the hallway rugs; he looked down the staircase, scanning for anyone who might be following them. He waved at Jenny and the two took the stairs toward the third-floor corridor. When they reached the top landing, they could see only a single door.

He turned his large hand over the doorknob, gesturing to Jenny that it was unlocked. He turned it slowly, and leaned forward, looking for trip wires. Once inside, he slid Jenny behind him and headed toward the corner of the living room to give him full view.

Suddenly, a dark object crashed over Jake's head. He fell to his knees and crashed over a floor lamp. A tall man in green fatigues grabbed Jake by the back of his shirt. Jake groaned, then wrapped his arms around the attacker and drove his head into the man's gut, sending the two of them tumbling over the top of the couch.

Jenny spun around and grappled for any free object she could use as a weapon. She saw Jake's gun loose on the floor. Blood was dripping from Jake's forehead. She had a sudden sense that she might lose a second friend in seconds. The attacker flipped the glass table over and jumped back on top of Jake. They bounced off each other. Then hit the floor. The men sat facing each other, like two bumper cars suddenly coming to a stop, gasping for air.

"How come you came here, Jake? I told you never to come. I told you I'd look after Riley. Why did you come back?"

"She called for me. She wanted to see me. Something was happening and she needed me."

The man rested on his knees, partially visible through the worn green camouflage fatigues, panting heavily. "Caught you off guard, one of the few times that's ever happened." Slowly rising, he pointed at Jake's forehead. "You deserved that."

Jake pointed at the black object. "You hit me over the head with a Virgin Mary statue?"

"It's appropriate." Digger sneered.

The two men glared at each other. "Digger, who had her killed?" Jake asked.

Digger sighed and dropped down on his mangled sofa. He looked at the broken coffee table and reached down to pick up a horse-shaped chess piece. "I would have beaten you, Jake, if you didn't just destroy the game."

"Did I get her killed?" Jake replied.

"No. No, you didn't. Riley found a painting she shouldn't have. Some Car-vag-e-o guy. She thought there was some sort of clue in the painting. She had a meeting set up with someone important before going to Ireland."

"Wait one minute," Jenny yelled, finally moving out of the corner.

Digger turned to the young woman awkwardly gripping Jake's pistol.

"Jenny, put the gun down," Jake warned, putting his hand out.

Digger was always armed. He started to move his hand. Jake bumped the older man's elbow, deflecting his thrusting Bowie knife into the plaster wall.

"Wait one second," Jenny screamed at Jake, not noticing the knife passing by her thigh. Before either man could say anything, she ripped her palm across Jake's face.

Digger laughed. "Who's she?"

"That was a cheap hit, Jenny. Put the gun down before you get hurt."

"How's it that virtually every federal agency, some lunatic assassin, and now this pretty lady are trying to kill you Jake?" Digger asked. "How'd you piss off so many people in such a short time?" He laughed.

"Jenny, just put the gun down and I'll explain." Jake pleaded.

Jenny lowered the gun.

"How'd you get her killed?" Jenny snapped.

Digger shot a gape-mouthed glance back and forth from Jenny to Jake. "Jake, you didn't tell her about the thug who's after you?"

Jenny threw up her arms at Jake. "Why and what didn't you tell me?"

"To protect you."

"To protect me?" The words echoed through her while her mind wandered. *Why try to protect me? I want you to trust me. I'm trying to get to know you better than a patient.* She thought.

"Yes. And, you can help me."

"Help? You mean like an 'asset' as you say in your business?"

"No Jenny. That's not how I feel. The emptiness from Riley's death hasn't left me and . . ." Jenny saw that Jake struggled briefly to speak. ". . . and you're different. I don't have a lot of time to explain but this is personal. I need your help. I think she gave you clues. Clues to help me find something so important that she risked her life for it."

"Protect me. Respect me. But . . . don't lie to me." She put her hand up on his chest. He stared down at her. She felt him tremor briefly beneath her hand like he felt her warmth.

"I hear you. And, I know what you're asking."

"Then trust me." She said.

"I will. If we grieve for Riley now we'll lose the chance to redeem her death. And if we grasp the chain of regret be prepared to fill the dungeon."

Jenny's thoughts flashed back to her motivation to enter surgery as a career. *As unsatisfying as it feels I can't tell if I'm seeking revenge or redemption,* she thought. *I need her death to bring clarity.*

"I promise I'll trust you with everything. What were you murmuring a moment ago?" He asked.

Jenny shook her head and exhaled deeply. "Riley always did things with great precision. If she told me something, it was with purpose and motivation, and a few pieces of the puzzle fit together at that moment."

"Jenny?" Jake shrugged.

"When Riley gave me the impression she was meeting the man who was going to marry her. . . for awhile I thought that was you, Jake. I thought the two of you were . . . at least a couple. Now I realize that she meant . . ." she paused to finish the calculation. "She was meeting someone else . . . and that could only be Father John Landry, a Jesuit priest at the College of the Holy Cross. She always said he would preside over her wedding one day and be the man who was going to marry her. That's who she meant as someone important to see before going to Ireland."

Chapter 22

The Globe Theatre
London, England

Bouncing onto the theater stage, Professor Geoffrey Willis waved and beamed. The *Henry IV, Part I* matinee crowd of college students stood and applauded the latest recipient of the 2012 Sam Wanamaker Award.

In recognizing his years of work increasing the understanding and enjoyment of Shakespeare, the Wanamaker Committee encouraged Willis to revel for a few moments in the limelight of the stage, delaying the start of his latest college production.

Off to one side of the proscenium, in the prompt corner, a solitary man in plainclothes—tweed jacket and rumpled shirt—clapped soullessly. But he stared intently at his target. Clean shaven with a black mustache and thinning dark hair, he was more determined than ever to confront Willis, who casually disappeared into his work behind the masking curtains.

The elderly Willis stepped back into the guest dressing room to gather his belongings. The man with the thick black mustache knocked on the door but didn't wait for a response. He opened the door like he owned it and slid inside the small room.

"Professor Willis, could I take a moment of your time to ask you a few questions?" Black Mustache asked, turning to lock the door.

Willis felt a twinge of discomfort and pulled his tweed jacket toward his chest. "I . . . I'm meeting guests."

The man raised his hands. Willis' eyes flinched and he turned away.

"Just a few, Professor?"

Willis nodded in return. But Willis noted that the man was disguising an accent: His pronunciation of the word "professor" made clear that he wasn't British. *Not of any class.* But he couldn't place the country. *Spain? Portugal?*

"Well, yes. But the play is starting soon and my guests will be waiting for me." Willis replied, noting that the stranger's eyes were plain; the lower eyelids thicker than the uppers—making him look more like a tortoise than the cowboy. Willis moved back slowly.

"It'll take just a moment, and I don't think they'll disturb us right now," Tortoise answered. "Professor, can you help me understand a Shakespeare passage that my employer is struggling with?"

"Your employer? I don't understand."

"Nothing is as it seems—" Tortoise responded, but was cut off by Willis before he could finish the thought.

"You're not one of those crazy helicopter parents?"

"No. Just an interested fan struggling with a passage. Let me show it to you," Tortoise said. The man's hand disappeared into his coat.

Willis raised his hands. The man pulled a pen and an index card with a typed excerpt from his shirt:

> 'Tis time; descend; be stone no more; approach;
> Strike all that look upon with marvel. Come;
> I'll fill your grave up: nay, come away;
> Bequeath to death your numbness, for from him
> Dear life redeems you. You perceive she stirs. . . .

Willis glanced down at the card much as one would look into a reptile cage, expecting a strike. He remembered that he hadn't taken his morning thyroid hormone, and sensed his body temperature and stress levels rising.

Willis fumbled for his bifocals in his tweed pocket. Tortoise put the palm of his hand on Willis's coat, "Easy, Professor, go slow."

"My glasses," he said, pulling the glasses from his coat as if he were pulling up the tail of a rat, dangling them in front of the man. He looked again at the card, but this time took in the verses. "This is from Shakespeare's *The Winter's Tale*."

"Yes. We know that. I mean, my boss and I know that. But I need to understand what it means." Tortoise flashed a creepy grin.

"Your boss. Your employer? I recognize your accent. You're Spanish. Basque. Yes?" Willis asked.

"It's not important now. But Bilbao to be exact. I'm not here to discuss that."

"But you came to the Globe Theater on this day of my award to ask me for an interpretation of a Shakespeare quote? You could have looked this up in a book."\Tortoise shuffled his feet and sighed. "Well, Professor, we recognize that you are an authority on Shakespeare and my employer believes the phrase means a lot more."

"Like what?"

"Like a secret to curing illness, extending life." He pulled out a pen, preparing to write notes on the card like a newspaper reporter.

"That's ridiculous," Willis retorted.

"I...We need your help." The Tortoise tilted his eyebrows to one side.

There was a long pause as Willis looked at the card and back. "The Winter's Tale is a both a tragedy and a comedy that highlights a jealous and paranoid King Leontes and his misperception of the world around him. In his madness he loses his queen, or so we believe, until his repentance leads to redemption and rebirth in a happy ending. The importance of this play is learning about the destructive power of jealousy and, ultimately, the renaissance strength of forgiveness."

"But can you explain this phrase and how it relates to the Knights Hospitallers?"

"The Hospitallers? Those Knights from the Jerusalem hospital? No."

The old scholar felt the space closing in on him, as if the room was fading to black. *Surely someone would miss me soon?* Willis looked at the card again and spoke slowly. "This is from act five, when Leontes encounters Hermione's statue and his long-dead wife comes back to life." His hands shook and his words raced, "He's completely shocked. A dead wife. Suddenly alive! It's a sign of redemption, a sign of forgiveness, of love, a love that is redeeming their relationship. But the audience is left unsure whether the statue's coming to life is a miracle or a trick."

The man looked at him as if he'd never heard of love.

"Have I lost you completely?" Willis gulped and palmed his watch. Hoping more information would protect him. "I'll provide context. Queen Hermione of Sicilia was accused of infidelity by her husband Leontes . . ."

"Excuse me, Professor, is that Sicily?"

There was a sudden rumble by the door. Willis snapped toward the noise when the man slid the card quickly into his jacket. "One last question, Professor. Is there any reason why these verses would be written on the gravestone of a Knight who died in Ireland in 1603?"

Willis almost fell over. "That's impossible! 1603?" The play wasn't written until seven years later and wasn't published for another fifteen!"

Chapter 23

CIA Headquarters
Langley, Virginia

Picking up her Jackie Robinson thirty-two-ounce barrel of ash, Karen Smith took a swing with the bat across the top of her desk, a phantom miss over the heaping pile of ancient papers, folios, books, drawings, and photographs.

Her dad had loved baseball, had even spent two years toiling through his bachelorhood in the minors until he dreamed of a family and a hope that his sons would make it to the "Bigs." Instead, he ended up with four girls, who grew into tough-minded young women. They could play the game all right, but their use of time and space differed from the boys'.

Through the years, Smith never lost her love for baseball. She saw the game in everything she did. The flow of play, the interaction of the players, the tools of the trade were prototypical models for her current job. She was a stats "money ball" junkie for the CIA. A veritable Billy Beane when it came to calculated risk.

The bat was Smith's big stick and, though she used it as a distraction from the stresses of the office, hardly any of the men in her life missed it standing in her umbrella rack. Only she knew it wasn't for hitting them in the shorts. Swinging a baseball bat . . . helped her think.

Immediacy. That was all she could think of right now.

Smith couldn't get the word out of her mind. She sensed the immediacy in the play unfolding before her: a terrorist meeting in a Damascus hotel room exploding into a firefight, some old Bedouin man disappearing with a fortune in Arab money, an obscure five-hundred-year-old Caravaggio painting missing for forty years bursting onto the grid and then, nine thousand kilometers away in some godforsaken American city, one of the best special operative men she had ever known somehow linked to the events. Usually she hated instant replays, but this time she wanted one. She was also certain she had to shift from her relatively new role as umpire and head back into the field.

Her CIA operation at the hotel was standard. Maybe that was what the old man expected, or even planned for. He was deliberate and efficient. Discretely in and out in minutes. He seemed to know everyone's positions. No one at the hotel could identify him. He hid himself from all the cameras. But he dismantled the meeting like he was moving through a room full of practice targets on a shooting range.

Then there was this missing Caravaggio painting that was supposed to be at the exchange. *The wild painter was a CIA operative's dream,* she thought.

Poring through books, photographs, and drawings all day long, she was captivated by the file describing a painter she'd never heard of: Caravaggio. As a lifer at the CIA, she saw this guy as the fugitive of all fugitives. His paintings were dark, graphic images of desperate, downtrodden vagrants that acted out the allegories of early Christianity. Each story and painting sucked her in deeper to the depraved world of 1600's Italy. Despite his superior artistic talent, Caravaggio's real life was one street fight after another. He angered virtually everyone he encountered and was on the run from every known military and religious organization of early seventeenth-century Europe. *How,* she wondered, *did such a massive manhunt take place in a time when there were no cell phones, no Internet, no television or radio? This guy must have really pissed off a lot of his fans.*

She opened another book, looking for answers to why this particular painting was suddenly reappearing after forty years and why so much cash was involved in the exchange. Michelangelo da Merisi, commonly referred to as Caravaggio, survived some of the worst years of the Black Plague in the late 1500's. Like many painters of his time, he moved to Rome looking for valuable commissions. By 1592, he was living on the streets, observing the basest of human depravities, including public beheadings, street brawls, and the flesh trade. In 1596, he was hired and housed by a conniving art aficionado and Catholic priest named Cardinal del Monte. Caravaggio's talent as an artist was soon sought out by the Jesuits, recently founded by the Basque priest Ignatius of Loyola. The new religious order was chosen by the Pope to lead the Counter-Reformation and beat back the growing threat of Protestantism. The order would use art and education as primary tools. The Jesuits would aggressively embrace art *as* education.

Smith now knew why Caravaggio resonated with her. He was not the fugitive after all. He was the operative. He was a covert agent spidering his way through the Dark Ages with his secrets tucked into his black coat. When she studied the images of his paintings she felt the cold intimacy of a dark theater—like she was watching a late night horror film. Before long, the shadows flickered and she sensed mysterious movements around her like her soul was running in terror. He could easily have been CIA. *He thrived on immediacy.*

Each and every image of his paintings was savage. The colors were both dark yet lit up by shards of bright beacons; faces were marked by passion. She could feel human sin coming to life. There were gaping wounds and dying saints. Always there was movement, energy, a story being told. No "still life" here. Caravaggio would, she realized, have happily painted the murderous events she'd just experienced in Damascus.

Even though she'd little experience with art, everything described Caravaggio as a man who rejected the traditional rules of painting and lighting, as well as the convention of idealizing saints. Instead, he used as models the men and women of Rome's streets and saloons, her shops and bordellos. He used dramatic contrasting rays of light and dark to illuminate the focal point of each painting. Other painters struggled mightily to copy his magical gift.

Although Caravaggio lived comfortably and painted in Rome until 1605, he was constantly in trouble with the law. Biographers spoke of his time with prostitutes, his sometimes deadly bar fights, his gambling. He was as well-known for swordsmanship as art. His raucous behavior soon became a liability for the Roman Catholic Church that was protecting him. Papal guards were sent to arrest him. They chased him throughout Europe while he painted feverishly from town to town, making a living while trying to stay ahead of his pursuers. Because of Caravaggio's unusual life as an artist, his paintings assumed, long after his death, an aura of mystery and intrigue. There were more of his scattered paintings that had been lost, found, and stolen than those of any other painter in history.

Finally Smith came to entries on *The Nativity*. The painting was, by Caravaggio's standards, a fairly quiet depiction of Christ's birth, done in sepia tones rather than the blood reds and bright yellows of his other works. It was now one of the most sought after and most valuable of the world's "art gone missing." Stolen in 1969 from a church in Sicily, *The Nativity* became part of Mafia lore allegedly traded from don to don. Over the next few decades, various informants would claim to have been the thief or to know which Godfather was currently hiding the painting.

Smith stood and took another swing of the bat, nearly reaching the outside window. She recalled what her dad repeatedly told her and her sisters: *Life is a series of opportunities taken or lost. Think of everything that comes at you in life as a pitch you are about to hit. Sure, think about where it will go, but sometimes you won't know. Just always be ready to hit the ball.* Smith had no idea where this pitch was headed, but she was damned if she would whiff on it.

The door to her office rattled. In burst one of the women from the FBI. "We lost Father Landry. He's disappeared."

Chapter 24

CIA Headquarters
Langley, Virginia

"Father Landry? Who's he?" Karen Smith asked the female FBI agent.

"Father John Landry is a Jesuit priest at a small college in Worcester, Massachusetts, who is considered a world authority on Caravaggio." She said. "Just another ordinary academic—or so we thought until we tracked a call placed from Dr. Riley McKee's cell phone to him last Monday."

Smith's mind flashed, trying to connect the events. Her pulse quickened and she dropped the bat. "How . . ."

"When McKee was mentioned with Caravaggio's *Nativity* in the communiqué out of Syria, we felt we had a breakthrough clue in this unsolved case. The painting has been missing for 40 plus years!"

"What about Landry?"

"Landry had been seen periodically around Europe, but up until now we never paid attention to him, because he traveled in the usual academic circles, occasionally researched in the Vatican archives, and minded his own business in museums. He wasn't someone who came up on the grid."

Karen Smith hesitated, deep in thought, *Riley McKee, a young doctor, is mentioned across the world in a Damascus message about a missing masterpiece and shortly thereafter contacts an art professor in Massachusetts?* "Do they have some preexisting connection?" she asked.

"She was his student at the College of the Holy Cross more than ten years ago," the female agent answered. "We still haven't got her transcripts, but she was an Art History major and they likely knew each other or had friends in common."

"This is one more thing that you didn't tell me. When are you guys going to start sharing information? You lose a Catholic priest and a young doctor and you come running to me because my stud special operative was with her. What else are you not telling me?" Smith's eyes went wide.

A cold silence descended between them.

Smith slowly squeezed her eyes shut and put her hand to her forehead steeling herself. She heard her words echo as she waited. *I hope they didn't screw this up.*

The agent stepped back as Smith opened her eyes. "Dr. McKee was Jake Bolton's sister."

"Sister?! He had a sister? McKee . . . his sister?" she asked, a faint shiver in her voice. "He never mentioned it, never listed her in his records, rarely went home, no family. Are you sure?"

"Yes."

"His sister was killed right in front of him?" Smith picked up her baseball bat, banging the barrel into her hand. She knew her colleagues called it her Al Capone imitation and she didn't care. Right now, bashing in a few heads seemed tempting.

"We only found it because it was deep in *her* medical records." The agent added.

Smith moved around her desk, pushing the green files. After several moments, she spoke again, "Well, someone just woke up Bolton. His chess board is a real one."

"I regret not passing this information earlier."

Smith smirked and turned away. "They're going to regret this. He's back in the game. He comes right down your throat. He's just like a late inning reliever in baseball. The fifty thousand screaming fans in Yankee Stadium, the umpire, the batter, the coaches, they all know the big burly hulk on the pitcher's mound is coming in and throwing fastballs. He's protecting a lead and he's coming after the batter. This is no secret. We need to follow Jake. Don't interfere. Just follow him."

Smith eyed the FBI agent for a brief moment then pushed aside the stacks of folders and pulled Jake Bolton's thick file.

Jake's father was a forty-two year old captain in Beirut in 1983 when the bomb attack hit the marine barracks and the U.S. embassy. Jake's father and hundreds of his American soldiers died. Riley McKee must have been a baby at the time. Jake was only eight years old. Ten years later he joined the Marines.

For years, the Beirut bombing went unsolved. Only Smith knew that Jake was convinced the bombing was the work of Imad Mughniyah, a member of Hezbollah, the Islamic terrorist group in

Lebanon. Mughniyah was known as "The One Who Never Sleeps." He was a ruthless and enigmatic man who planned bombings and murders all over the world, but particularly against Israel and her allies. He was constantly on the run, changing his appearance as he moved between Iran, Lebanon, and Syria. He directed devastating battlefield tactics in the 2006 war against Israel in southern Lebanon; he provided antitank weapons to al-Sadr's henchman in Iraq to use against the Americans; he supervised car bomb attacks against Jews in France and Argentina in the 1990s and was considered the father of Middle Eastern asymmetric warfare. This man was a virtual ghost, totally anonymous, and a forerunner of Osama bin Laden, who armed Hezbollah.

On the night of February 12, 2008, Mughniyah was in Damascus, engaging in his standard maneuvers to maintain anonymity—driving his own SUV, traveling alone, changing his hideouts, never sleeping in the same place twice, and carrying a pistol at his side. He had a meeting at a safe house with the chief spook in Syria and was getting ready for a meeting with President Bashar al-Assad. Seconds after starting his SUV, the car blew up. After twenty-five years of dodging assassination attempts, Mughniyah disappeared in a puff of desert sand in the middle of Kfar Sousa, the Langley of Damascus, Syria's spy central, probably the safest area in the world for him to travel. His death was a mystery that baffled the Syrians, Iranians, and Israelis. They later discovered that Jake Bolton was in Damascus at that time. Now Jake was a target.

"I've been concerned about Jake. Hezbollah wants him dead. If they found out about a sister—they'd kill her too. That's why he knew to keep her secret." Smith added. "They didn't know her identity either. She wasn't killed because of Jake. From the communiqué, I think the bagman from Syria was trading *The Nativity* for cash but, somehow, she and Father Landry found a different Caravaggio painting. The terrorists didn't want Riley's discovery to spoil their sale."

"But the communiqué said: *Have SAM and N by C. Doctor Riley McKee Nativity version forgery. Meeting on track. 25 cold.*" The agent said.

"SAM is. . .?" Smith asked.

"*The Seven Acts of Mercy*, also by Caravaggio."

Smith spun the bat and pointed the butt end at the agent. "Doctor Riley McKee had a painting, a '*Nativity* forgery.'" Smith exclaimed.

"Where did she keep that? Where did her forgery come from?"

"That's probably what she discussed in the phone call with Father Landry. We may need to find him—and fast." She shook the bat as the agent recoiled toward the door. "I might be able to find an expert on this *Nativity* painting and why it's so important."

The door to her office opened forcefully. In burst the male suit from the FBI, rapidly shaking his head. "We lost Jake Bolton. He's disappeared."

Chapter 25

Georgetown University
Washington, D.C.

Karen Smith quickly tapped the clutch of her BMW roadster racing into the left lane of the Key Bridge facing Georgetown University.

She loved the corresponding reverberating growl of the engine, the shift of cross wind in the swampy air over the Potomac River, and the sensory stimulations of the convertible.

On M Street she spotted the black shadow of the Cadillac SUV that had been following her since Langley. She spun the Beemer toward oncoming traffic on Canal Street, split the two lanes of cars, and accelerated, cutting across another car that blocked her way then suddenly stopped. The SUV darted in front of the minivan and disappeared.

In one swift motion her Glock 19 was ready in her right hand and she was standing on top of the driver's seat pointing over the windshield at a family in a minivan. They were bystanders, she realized, and jumped back into her seat. She looked around and slammed the steering wheel. Boxed in by traffic, she jumped from the BMW, and approached the shocked mother in the van.

"Are you okay?" she said, her gun disappearing under her suit.

The woman driver kept her arms up and appeared afraid to lower the window.

Smith rapped on the window, "Are you okay?"

The woman nodded and Smith turned back toward her car. She stopped again and turned. *I thought I saw the red-white-and-blue embassy plates on that van,* she thought. *Those guys are so reckless. Their immunity is ridiculous.*

She jumped back into her roadster. She exited up the Canal Street hill to a little-known back entrance to Georgetown University, past the Jesuit residence, then diverted down the long route toward the chapel next to the baseball field; it was the only college field in the country where there was a cemetery in the outfield. *It gave new meaning to a "dead ball."* She chuckled to herself.

The doors of the church were within reach of a right-handed

cleanup batter with a big swing. The booming of the church organ grew louder as she passed the field.

Smith recalled that John F. Kennedy had attended his last religious service there before his trip to Dallas and his assassination. She hurried up the steps of the Greco-Roman church and headed toward the St. Ignatius Chapel to meet Father Mulready.

"Father, thank you for seeing me on short notice," she said.

The statuesque man with Reagan-like hair steepled his hands in from of the cross hanging across his black shirt.

"I hope it means that I'll see you here more often, Karen."

"I'll do my best, Father."

"You said this was urgent. What can I do for you . . . er, should I say my country?"

Smith smiled at the priest with fondness for his insightfulness. She knew from her Hoya days she could trust him like a doctor. She pulled out a photograph from her briefcase and held it out. "This."

The priest took a deep breath. *The Nativity.* Ah, yes, Caravaggio. What a genius. Tell me you found it. It would make my art history career."

"No. We don't think so just yet. I really don't know. Let's say for a moment, Father, that this painting is mentioned in a communiqué out of the Middle East." She spoke breathlessly. "In the message they mention this painting and the sister of a special agent of the CIA—a trauma surgeon from Connecticut. Two days later the surgeon is killed and the CIA agent is missing. We aren't sure, but we think the painting was getting traded in Damascus, to the Italian Mafia for a boatload of cash. Someone burst in and shot up everyone. The money and the painting are gone," Smith explained.

"I'd say that's all in a day for a Caravaggio. The painting hasn't been seen since 1969, and back then no one really cared about him. I have to ask, where did you get this photograph? This is the sharpest resolution of this painting I've ever seen."

"After Hitler stole paintings, relics, and artifacts during World War Two we created a high-resolution catalog of these priceless objects all over the world."

"The CIA has these files?"

"You know, just in case."

"This is amazing resolution." The art historian shook his head.

"Father Mulready, the usual confidence applies here." Smith leaned over and gazed into his eyes.

"There's something here that no one's ever reported. Your resolution shows it. Look at the banner that the angel Gabriel is bringing down toward the nativity scene." He pointed diagonally across the photo. "That's the greater doxology across the banner."

"Meaning?"

"It's *Gloria in Excelsis Deo*, Latin for 'Glory to God in the highest.' It's from Luke two-fourteen, from when Christ's birth is announced. But it's more than that. Look." He held the photo out in reverence. "The *Gloria* is written on sheet music across the banner."

"I see the little lines. But isn't sheet music five lines?"

A voice from the shadow of a church column yelled out, "Not back then."

Smith grabbed the photo and slid it into her briefcase, then stood up in the aisle.

"It's okay, Karen," Father Mulready said, raising his hand. "This is Father Williams, the organist."

Smith realized that the music had stopped.

"Those are neumes." Father Williams offered. "That's the precursor to our five-line musical staff. It's a Gregorian chant, sung at an exact time and location of the mass."

"Yes. Right after we get to the altar and say the Kyrie." Father Mulready said.

"Yes. That's today. But not during Caravaggio's time," Father Williams said.

"What do you mean?" Smith asked.

"Karen? You need to go to mass more often."

"The Latin mass. The Council of Trent." Father Williams explained. "The Gloria is a chant at an exact position, marking a location in the church." Father Williams moved to the center aisle and stiffened upright, his hands by his sides. "As the priest comes down the aisle he stops, facing the altar, the deacon immediately behind him. He would raise his hands at the word 'Gloria,' join them at 'Excelsis,' then bow at 'Deo.' Right here at the bottom step directly in front of the altar."

"Caravaggio is known for hiding clues in his paintings. The angel with the banner is not just announcing the birth. He's announcing a church location. Maybe it's a secret pathway." Father Mulready said.

"Leave it to Caravaggio to hide it in a chant. He was considered a priestly warrior. A Knight for the Church. And, as a religious Knight he would have chanted during afternoon prayers." Father Williams replied.

"Karen," Father Mulready said, "this painting is the allegory of Christ's birth in Bethlehem, but there's a lot of it that's never been explained, like these two people on either side of Joseph. Notice that the angel is pointing both up and down. Caravaggio's characters never pointed in both directions. Notice also that the angel is trailing, rather than leading, the banderole containing the Gloria chant. There's something profound here—not just the allegory of Christ's birth."

"Like what?" She asked.

"The mystery has baffled art historians for years. It's something about Caravaggio himself. He painted this on the run through Sicily after he nearly killed another Knight."

Smith looked back and forth at both priests. "You're sure that no one has ever seen this?"

"Yes."

Smith patted her briefcase. "There may be another reason why this disappeared 40 years ago."

Chapter 26

Digger's Apartment Building
Hartford, Connecticut

Jenny took in the eerie silence.

It was much like the trauma room after the body had been covered with a sheet. An uneasy chill ran through her and she shivered briefly while she collected herself.

Jake shot back a puzzled stare. For the second time in as many moments Jenny knew she'd knocked him off his guard.

"I...I didn't realize..." Jake hesitated. "That I'd instinctively denied you the information."

"Because if I'm going with you...you need to tell me the truth."

"I was acting on my gut impulse."

"Jake, you need to let this young lady go." Digger warned. "She's at risk of getting shot too. That thug in Syria is still after you. You're breaking all the rules."

Jenny glared at the man, noting that he sweated profusely. This made his skin shine.

Jake sighed. "By the old rules, you're right. But the game has changed. There's something Riley wants us to follow. Riley was sharing clues with Jenny as well as me."

"Like what?"

"Like this tattoo." He grabbed his deltoid. "It's a map. And she gave us different clues. I need to know what Jenny knows."

"Jake's right," Jenny said. Jake's words of support were unexpected. "Riley would want me to solve her puzzle—as difficult and as dangerous as it might be." She felt a stab of anguish. "Listen, Mr. Digger, I loved Riley. We were friends since the first year of college. Right now I want to find out why she died. Will you help us, Mr. Digger?"

Digger shrugged and headed toward the adjoining room. "Just Digger, young lady. You sound like you're not scared right now, but you will be. You will be. Whoever they are, these people don't fool around."

"Don't mess with her, you crotchety old spook," Jake interjected. "No one shoots an innocent female doctor on the walkway of a hospital from five hundred meters out with a 308-caliber sniper rifle."

"That doesn't mean Riley didn't stumble into something and this Jenny won't be a target." Digger said.

"Digger, you owe me. You remember that night in Baghdad; I drove all night long to get you?"

"I don't owe you anything. We were made even in Syria. You never would've gotten out of there alive," Digger replied.

"I didn't want to get out of there alive," Jake said. "At least you owe Riley. What did she want me to know before the sniper stopped her from telling me?"

"I kept an eye on her in this god-forsaken city for you but I couldn't stop some assassin. Riley was the target. You were collateral damage. At least now I'm done in this city." Digger moved toward the outer bedroom. "You need to check out GHARC. Riley worked there sometimes."

"In all those years in the Company… neither you nor I ever took such a shot at anyone so innocent," Jake yelled toward the other room.

"My nightmares come from the faces I see through my scope . . . and live. I don't fear or remember the dead ones." Digger said.

Jenny felt the alarm rising between them and wondered if she'd gone too far. She shifted uneasily, lowering her head and feeling like she was suffocating under a blanket. *Maybe I shouldn't have pushed this guy?* She thought.

Digger turned back into the door and pointed a finger. "How the hell do you know? Throughout your career, if you were five hundred meters away, you probably never knew what they were asking us to do other than hitting a mark. And YOU hit the mark. How do you know you never took out an innocent?"

"Oh, come on. We're lucky if we get orders to shoot with all those fruitcake tree huggers out there in D.C."

The sound of dishes clanging and people talking rattled over a speaker in the corner of the room. Digger ran back into the living room. He turned to a desk near the window and started turning the dials on three television monitors. "Oh, great. They always love those blue and yellow jackets announcing themselves. *Here comes the FBI! Here comes the FBI!"*

Jenny looked over his shoulder. The grainy picture of several men searching the first floor could be seen.

"Nice neighbors you got there, Digger." Jake said with a smile.

"Hey, they always let me know when I have visitors."

"I need your contact in Ireland. How do I find him?"

Digger started to rustle in a backpack on the table. "You can't go through the airport. You need to go to South Boston. Old IRA boat. Find Cleary's Pub. When you get to the bar, wait for the redheaded bartender named Yoke. You'll recognize him by the red handlebar mustache. Ask him to make you a Drisheen. He'll tell you that they don't serve Drisheen there and offer you a Negus. Tell him no, you'll settle for a Mike Collins. Then just listen to what he has to say."

Digger popped the cap off a long red tube and sparked the exposed flare. A bright yellow flame blazed from the top. He opened a small door in the living room wall and tossed the flare down the chute.

"Your usual propane cocktail? How long do we have?" Jake asked.

Digger shrugged. "My guess, five minutes until we burn up or blow up. Or . . . maybe five minutes before those FBI guys get here."

Jake turned to Jenny. "Good old Digger, always burning down the house party."

"Unlike you, they're going to go into the second floor and sweep, and that'll slow them down a few minutes." Digger started packing papers and belongings into a backpack and threw it over his shoulder. Maybe the FBI will hang around the big B.S. and dig into its corruption."

"It's too late." She said.

"I can't protect you from here. I can get you some time, but that's about it." Without hesitation, the older man scrambled to an alcove between the living room and the bedroom and he started pulling out blankets from a wooden chest, tossing them to the floor. "Jake, get over here and help me. I was saving this for me and a friend, but you guys need it." He lifted a large metal handle.

Frosty steam suddenly burst from the chest.

Jenny moved closer, "You have a floor freezer disguised as an old-fashioned hope chest?"

Digger reached into the icy cloud and dragged a large plastic bag into the middle of the living room. Jake grabbed a second bag and tossed it beside the first. Bolton pulled out his bowie knife and sliced the plastic top to bottom. There were two bodies: a man and a woman.

Jenny felt the hair on her neck stand up like static was in the air. A wave of decaying tissue burned her eyes and she felt her skin tighten. She felt her rising anger as she blinked. Looking up she shouted to Digger, "You keep dead bodies in your living room? Are you insane?"

He tossed her a sinner's grin. "Honey, you've got dead bodies in your office. The only difference is I brought these here instead of sending them to you. Besides, the reason they're here is so you won't have to be." He pulled out a pile of clothes from a closet and tossed them onto the couch.

"I need you to change clothes." Jake said sternly. "Give me your wallet, your rings and all your ID's. You're going to need to put these on." Jenny looked at Jake, wondering if she'd just entered a world of no return. "The more we change, the harder for someone to find us," he said.

Jenny nodded slowly, mindlessly, as if the fear had overwhelmed her and now she was moving without controlling her body. Somehow she found herself in the next room.

Jake grabbed his clothes and ran back into the living room. Jenny returned and tossed her clothes down. She watched as Jake pulled their clothes onto the icy bodies. He doused them with gasoline from a container Digger brought from the closet. Digger lit another flare and set the bodies on fire.

He saluted to a startled Jake, and then ran to the east window. By the time Jake reached the window, Digger was attached to a harness on a clothesline. "Jake, there once was a good man, a reliable guy named Shane Walsh, living in Cork. If you get desperate in Ireland, find him. Use my name. We were in Laos together. Flew Air America."

Jake pulled at the harness around Digger. "How are we going to get out of here?"

"Use the other bedroom." He looked at Jenny. "I'm sorry about Riley. She brought hope to this city and had grown like family to me. Jake, remember all the places we've been, we swore we'd bring peace back again? Good luck, friend." With that, Digger Walsh pulled the ring latch and slid down a reinforced clothesline, disappearing onto the back porch of the neighboring house.

Chapter 27

Digger's Apartment Building
Hartford, Connecticut

The burning couch and melting plastic crackled like popcorn in the third floor living room.

Bolton grabbed Jenny's hand. "Follow me if you want to live." Her stomach plummeted.

Jenny hesitated then released his hand. Looking up and down the living room, the fire was spreading from the bodies across the floor onto the bookcases. "Jake? What . . ." Her eyes watered. She could taste the smoke. She heard her mind screaming. *The room is getting darker. A few minutes ago I entered a carnival house. Now they're burning it down! We're trapped.* She turned and ran into the other room.

In the corner window Jake tugged on the thick orange construction pipeline. Shaking the pipe, Jake turned to Jenny, "It's heavy-duty plastic and can hold at least one of us." He leaned into and inspected the chute. "Good. No nails. It leads to a Dumpster in the neighbor's yard."

Jenny peered down the long PVC tube. The drop was at least fifty feet at a forty-five-degree angle. She felt her heart thump in her chest, skipping a beat. She heard the fire engine sirens across the city. *Ugh, Webb will be looking for me.*

She turned to Jake but couldn't speak. The smoke was creeping into the room over Jake's shoulder.

"I need you to slide down the chute and wait for me at the bottom." He said.

She continued to stare at him. She heard him speaking but it was only echoes. Finally, she saw him nodding. The sounds started to make sense. "Jenny. You'll be okay. I'll be right behind you."

He folded his hands into a stirrup and dropped to his knee. She gripped the tube, boosting herself. Her wet hands skimmed off the top. She slid her feet into the pipe.

She crossed her hands over her chest. Then Jake pushed her shoulders as hard as possible to give her momentum. She disappeared into the orange tube. Her body lunged and rocked down the cylinder.

Leaning back she saw the house disappearing amidst the smoke and consuming flames. The top of the tube was no longer visible. Her stomach plummeted into her pelvis. Seconds later she bounced onto a folded mattress curled inside the corner of the green Dumpster. She stood, then turned back and waved.

#

Jake moved back from the window. The hot floorboards rattled beneath his feet. He coughed to clear the smoke from his lungs. Then he ran for the tube, diving headfirst down the chute.

An explosion rattled the house. The window frame shattered from the crippled building. The outer wall of the triple-decker house buckled inward toward the flames.

Jake saw the Dumpster start to disappear below him. Something was wrong. He was slowing down. He looked back. The house end of the construction chute had sheared away. It was going down and he was being cantilevered upward. But he was still moving forward.

Jake felt his body invert as the Dumpster end of the tube shot into the air, seesawing him when the window frame collapsed against the third floor. The centrifugal force blasted him out and up into the free air. He braced himself, but his flank hit the side of the Dumpster.

Jenny extended her hand to help. Instead, Jake pulled her over the side of the Dumpster. They raced through the yard until he spotted a car by the side of the road. Jake jumped into the driver's seat and ripped the wires from under the steering wheel. Revving up the car, he turned north away. . . from the big B.S.

Chapter 28

GHARC
Asylum Street
Hartford, Connecticut

The main office of the Greater Hartford Association of Retarded Citizens on Asylum Street was stark and small, only a few feet larger than a phone booth. Yellow, plastic-covered fluorescent ceiling lights radiated a buzzing sound throughout the room.

Jenny and Jake stepped into the main foyer. The hallway emptied into a linoleum-floored children's room, where tables were lined up for card and board games, with intervening space for blocks and rocking horses, painting easels and toys.

The startled children in the room immediately stopped playing. There was a silence like a hunter had stepped into their forest.

Catherine Gracey took Jake's and Jenny's hands and held them strangely close to her body, as if greeting long-lost friends. She said the gesture made the clients feel more comfortable, and the "hug shake" had become natural to her.

Then, just as quickly, the children returned to their games.

"Thank you for calling ahead. I know you're Riley's friends and that's good enough for me." She looked back at the boys and girls. A few of the children looked up when they heard Riley's name. "They knew her very well. She visits . . . she visited here nearly every Saturday for the last year."

"When she wasn't on call?" Jenny asked, and then she glanced over at Jake. She wondered how he could be in such a very different career from his sister Riley. *But there's something intriguing about his career. Real puzzles maybe?* She thought.

"Yes. Riley always seemed at ease with the kids. She helped them make mazes out of the furniture and was a natural at setting them on little scavenger hunts. I cried when I heard she'd been killed. I don't know what I'll tell the children."

Jake surveyed across the room. "Did Riley spend extra time with anyone in particular?"

"Uh. Possibly . . . little Martin, a shy and difficult boy. Cerebral palsy and Down syndrome, yet smart. A difficult combination."

"Tell us about Martin?" Jenny asked.

"Before Riley came in last week he was terribly upset, running around the room yelling about 'Baby Jesus.' Yelling over and over, 'Baby Jesus is in there.' No one knew what he was talking about, and only Riley was able to calm him down." She looked over the crowd of children again. "Martin would have been extremely upset not to see Riley this week."

"Would have?" Jake asked.

"Yes. He was killed last week when he was walking home from GHARC. He was very capable on his own. He always followed the signs, but the Hartford police said he was crossing the road at a red light and a car hit him. Some of the citizens here went to his funeral. It was very sad."

Jenny felt a knot in her stomach. *He was murdered because he knew something or, his connection to Riley,* she thought. She watched Jake who put a fist up to his mouth. She knew he knew.

"You said that Martin was upset about the 'baby Jesus?' Did you ever learn anything more about that? Do you have a picture of Martin?" Jenny asked.

She pointed to a photograph on the wall of Riley and a young boy smiling. Within the photograph there was a large picture propped in the open doorway behind them. Suddenly Jenny thought she recognized the boy, Martin. She paused for a moment. *Those distinctive features.* "Jake . . . the cam . . ."

Jake clutched Jenny's forearm. He shot Jenny a quizzical look. She felt the reaction between them.

Pulling out Riley's camera, Jake lit up the screen and asked, "Is this Martin?"

"Yes! That was taken here last week." Gracey answered.

"Why did Riley take the picture?" Jake asked.

"Martin was sensitive to the camera, to pictures, to any images. Visuals calmed and soothed him."

"Can you tell me where this is?" Jake asked.

"I'll show you." They followed Gracey into the adjacent room. Boxes and easels filled the storage room. A metal door was off to one corner. Gracey opened the door and they saw a short metal staircase leading down to a cement floor and a large garage. Jake jumped down from the dock and looked around. The space was empty.

"Do you use this dock often?"

"Not really. We share this space with the offices next door. They're very helpful. The Knights of Columbus."

"Let me try something," Jenny said. "They do this stereoscopic-type imaging in radiology all the time." Jenny held up the camera. Jake propped the door open so she could match Riley's photo with the dock space. She held her thumb over part of the screen, focusing her eyes on the remaining picture. "This is a way of creating a 3D image with a 2D picture. She took Martin mentally out of the picture, looking for the remaining details. Looking back and forth from the camera to the garage, she zoomed in on an object in the picture. A framed painting was now apparent that she'd overlooked in the picture. It was leaning on the corner of the loading dock and she magnified the image. The painting displayed a group of people standing over someone stretched out on the floor.

"Do you recognize the image in the corner of the garage," she asked, holding the camera out to Jake.

He took the camera from her. "Let me look at that again . . . that's not a picture; that's a painting of a nativity scene."

Jenny threw both her hands around Jake's. "Jake, you're right! That's THE *Nativity*." She felt a chill run up her spine.

Jake turned back to Gracey. "One last question. Is there any connection between Martin and the country of Ireland?"They moved slowly back into the main room.

"No. But he did have Down syndrome. And Down children have been considered very special in Ireland. Catholics there call them '*daoine le dia*,' Gaelic for 'children of God.' The Irish believe that these children should be treated with great respect, since they are pure and innocent in the eyes of God."

"I know the Nazis made it a point to kill these children." Jenny said, watching Jake gape quietly at the young boys and girls in the classroom. His mind was elsewhere. She looked back and forth. *What was he thinking? Does he have the same interest in helping these children as Riley did?* She thought.

"This all has something to do with Riley's death?" Gracey

said.

"I don't know."

"But you suspect?"

"If it does, I'll get even." He said, his eyes dark.

"If it does, go seek justice. Not revenge."

"Yes, ma'am."

You should say 'Sister.'"

"My sister? She was very smart."

"Sister. As in I'm Sister Catherine."

"Thank you for your help, Sister Catherine."

Jenny and Jake left by the main entrance. Jake suddenly stopped on the sidewalk. Jake turned and shifted closer to Jenny, "that Martin friend of Riley's was hunted down and killed."

She felt the conflict in his voice. She searched his eyes, sensing the anger and her pulse quickened. "Is there any chance it was a coincidence?" She asked. Deep in her gut she suffered with the answer.

"No. Not a chance. Riley is connected to this. My concern is that it all could be tied to me."

"How so?"

"There's been someone after me for awhile."

A sharp panic gripped Jenny. She sensed the urge to run again. *I might be next, if he can't protect Riley.* She put her hand up to her head.

A police siren echoed through the streets. Jake stared at her. She swallowed hard and her lips quivered. *This is new but I can do this.*

"Jenny, it's not going to happen to you. This guy is a different sinner. I think I saw the guy who was after me once . . . in a bar in Libya. He was living it up with some stoned out prostitutes in the corner of this ant hill of a bar in the middle of a dust hole. It was filled with characters you'd never want to meet alone; the whole place stunk of grime and crime. I didn't stand a chance of getting out alive if I took him."

"What did you do?"

"I thought about it. He thought about it too. He's glaring over at me like he'd seen my Dad's ghost, laughing, flirting. I waited, but he just wouldn't leave. My gut tells me this isn't his handiwork. He's not after us. But we still need to get out of here."

Jake walked up to the door marked "Knights of Columbus" and knocked. No answer.

They circled the building. Stacked up against the Dumpster were a few wooden packing crates. Jake grabbed the crates and turned them over.

"Jake, what are you looking for?" Jenny asked.

"Riley worked here to help those children. But she was into something deeper. And the Knights of Columbus are a clue to what she was doing."

"Do you think that the Knights are hiding something?"

"No. But those crates were." Jake pulled one open. Then he slapped his hands together and shook his head at Jenny. "Nothing."

Chapter 29

Alcaiceria Market
Granada, Spain

A jagged splinter of light cut across the small archway leading from Bib-Rambla Square. Nasser shuddered when he saw the transfixing anger on Ashaz Mukhtar's face.

Nearby, local vendors calmly smoked hookah pipes while counting out their tills. Still others hung silver teapots, leather bags, belly dancer costumes and intricate wicker baskets over the alleyway of the ancient market near Granada. They didn't know just how close to death they were.

Though the comforting scent of apple tobacco and mint leaves filled the air, Nasser's heart raced. The fiasco in Damascus had left the team he'd hired dead, the money stolen, the painting vanished, and the CIA on the hunt. He knew Ashaz Mukhtar would want him dead.

Nasser jumped up when Ashaz caught sight of him. He half-smiled. Nasser bit his lip and turned his gaze upward into space, as if he were looking into a different reality, a place or time long ago.

Continuing on toward his boss, Nasser peered hastily down the narrow alleys created by the buildings. The traders surrounding the square played loud music while they cleaned their stalls.

"I'm sorry, Ashaz. Very sorry." He said to his boss.

Ashaz pulled on the hanging scarves. He nodded but did not look at Nasser. Nasser sensed Ashaz restlessness. The scarves jumped back up. The movement seemed to startle Ashaz. *Was Ashaz himself also afraid?* Nasser pushed the blasphemous thought away.

"What happened in Damascus?" Ashaz asked. "How do I know that you didn't double-cross me?"

"I did exactly as you instructed." Nasser chimed. "Something went very wrong. The men were all killed. That Caravaggio painting was not in the room. There were only pictures of paintings. The assassin killed everyone, even a duty agent we hired from the Idarat al-Amn al-Siyasi."

"Why shouldn't I kill you right here?"

"Because it's a much too public place." Nasser said.

Ashaz shook his head.

While the handmade leather sandals, baskets and silk scarves were a stark contrast to the flourishing Islamic economy that had once made Granada the pride of the caliphate, the crowded stalls provided Nasser cover. Nowadays, the locals had been reduced to mere street vendors for Christian tourists. The thought only infuriated most Islamists, especially Ashaz.

Nasser spied Ashaz reaching for the khanjar dagger in his belt, aware that he preferred it over gun. It was a far more effective way to kill a man, less violent and more dignified if done right. The assassin could look a man in the eye as he quietly slid the knife through his chest.

Nasser quickly turned back to look over his left shoulder at the juggling silver teapots. He saw the obscure reflection of a man.

Ashaz Mukhtar started slowly, "Nasser . . ." Then his voice trailed off.

The awareness of the eavesdropper changed Ashaz' mind. Nasser thought.

Nasser answered quickly, "And, the CIA was there. The assassin also killed CIA operatives."

"Nasser . . . I'm going to let you go. Wait by your phone. Say nothing more to anyone."

Nasser had been let off—not forgiven for his failure, only given more time. Minutes? Hours? Days? He didn't know. Ashaz Mukhtar did not grant second chances. Someone else had granted him a momentary reprieve. Nasser turned and ran down the alleyway.

#

The man Nasser had seen in the reflection of a silver teapot emerged from the shadows and sat down on a large handmade basket. He leaned in toward Ashaz. "I gave you a fortune and years of research work. I practically gave you a frickin' map with an X on it. What do you do? Lose the money. Lose the paintings. Lose the trail." Charles Pratt looked with disgust at the proud Arab man. "Are you towel heads good for anything other than blowing up weddings?"

Ashaz looked down at the dagger in his belt.

"Stabbing me would only drain the water pooling in my belly. I'm dying already."

Pratt looked down at his white cotton shirt. The almost silky material contrasted sharply with his darkening skin. He was sure he could see the ugly blue varicose veins bulging from his abdomen through the six-hundred-thread-count cotton. He felt betrayed in many ways.

His doctor had called them *medusa*. An educated man, Pratt assumed the term must be related to the Medusa's head—which had slithering snakes for hair. The marks he bore were also like those serpents, so ghastly to look at that they made onlookers freeze. The doctor had explained sheepishly that there was no mystery involved. The marks were related to Pratt's years of alcohol consumption. The 'Lennox' disease was really cirrhosis of the liver. What he saw were veins growing where they shouldn't. Soon they would strangle his body's blood flow. Not even a transplant could save him. He'd waited too long. Been in denial too long. Charles Pratt knew his only hope was to find the Last Prophet. Quickly.

"Ashaz, I told you to kill him. Why did you let him go?"

"Because when he saw your image on the teapot he gained value. Now he's my insurance. You won't kill me till you find him, and you'll never find him without me. Not in time. I can still find that Caravaggio painting."

"I just lost twenty million Euros looking for a four-hundred-year-old painting called the Last Prophet. Do you think for one second that I wouldn't kill you? And not give a crap about your little drifter? You're only alive because I think you can still help me. The moment you cross me is the moment you'll be hanging from that red tower you worship over there."

Pratt pulled on a long silk scarf draping down from the ropes in the alley market. The sudden movement made Ashaz step back. Pratt rubbed the silk between his fingers. Then his wrists began to flap like a bird's wing. He dropped them down onto the black Stetson on his head to control both his rapid movements and his fear. "Expect asterixis," the doctors had told him. *That rapid hand flapping is scary.* He thought. Pratt's thoughts raced through the list of symptoms, calculating the time he had left. The twenty million was not the issue. Pratt shook his head. He had the money, but not the time. The Last Prophet might lead to the medical secret that could help him.

"Sir, I will do what needs to be done," Ashaz offered.

Charles Pratt looked at the imposing red brick tower in the distance and rhetorically asked, "Do you know why your last stand for your caliphate was up there? It was the marriage of Ferdinand and Isabella that brought together the powers of the Roman Catholic Church. Together they destroyed this final Islamic stronghold in Europe. And, by 1492, they no longer needed to redirect money to fighting the Muslims throughout Europe. The Spanish empire was born."

"I understand that, sir."

"Yes. But Columbus, an Italian, came here because Spain was the world's first superpower. Discovering America then changed the world forever and prevented the caliphate from returning."

Pratt looked down again at his protruding abdomen. "You don't understand the implications of Damascus. You live here in the shadow of Alhambra and your lost empire. The NEW Alhambra has no boundaries."

Chapter 30

Lorca Airport
Granada, Spain

Charles Pratt cursed his bad luck and stupid people while he waited for his private jet to arrive at Frederico García Lorca Airport.

The hangar was hot, sticky and uncomfortable. His expensive cotton shirt stuck to his back and to his distended belly. Sweat dripped from his Stetson.

The small airport south of Granada had a single runway, making it easy for him to see planes landing or departing. Flying had always fascinated him, ever since his science teacher showed him that air moving faster over the top of the wing provided lift to the bottom. He and his twin brother James had tried all kinds of experiments reproducing the Wright Brothers' work. They never succeeded. *Stupid James.*

Later, as his business successes increased, Pratt made a point of learning about Bill Lear, inventor of the first car radio and the eight-track tape. He also invented the private jet and autopilot. The only smile Pratt could muster these days was when he recalled how Lear couldn't afford the booth entry fees to the automobile trade show to demonstrate his "Motorola radio." So he parked his car in the convention center lot and blasted the radio. Attendees raced outside, gawked, and then formed lines to place their orders. Bill Lear was the embodiment of guts, innovation, and persistence.

Pratt blew his nose, thinking with irritation of life's injustice. The inventor never lived to see how the private jet transformed the business world and became its own industry.

He could not avoid comparing himself to Lear. Oh, he knew he was no inventor. But there was creative and then there was ingenious, Pratt thought.

Three years after earning his MBA, Pratt used the money from his earliest investments and a modest inheritance to hire geologists from around the world, looking for oil. He found foreign experts from distressed countries, and then took his time filling out immigration papers. He hired young scientists rejected by universities because they were too arrogant to work collaboratively. He set them in competition with one another. He bribed politicians to change restrictions that might have blocked him from following leads in Alaska, Oklahoma, and Texas. He sent geologists seeking new fields where there shouldn't be any. Finally, the North Sea became what Texas had been. Quickly, before Norway had time to see what the future would be, he sold off his American holdings and invested in Norwegian companies, avoiding the tightening wires of regulations. He made his first fortune.

Pratt grew his millions into billions. He bought his first Learjet 45 so he could take more meetings, negotiate more contracts, and visit more sites. He hired more experts. He expanded his original work in Alaska. He married, he divorced, and he went through that cycle twice more. He had kids. They did not interest him. He always knew that family drained him of energy. Booze, on the other hand, intoxicated him. Not once did it knock him out. He bought better and better scotch and drank it by the bottle. He never, he was sure of it, became an alcoholic. The diagnosis was a total shock. He tried buying a liver. He was told his blood vessels would not sustain a transplant. So now he needed to be ingenious again. He'd nab the right team. He'd pay the right bribes. He didn't care who said he was crazy. They always said that about risk takers.

In his search for a cure, Pratt had tried venoms, folk potions, and magic. He argued with his disapproving doctors that anything that worked would no longer be called poison or magic. "That's where miracles come from," he'd say. A miracle was what he was after now. He had studied the Knights Hospitallers and was convinced they'd become so powerful because they possessed a secret that cured their patients. Then he studied all possible locations where they lived and practiced: Jerusalem, Cyprus, Rhodes, Malta, and Rome. Caravaggio was rumored to have mapped out the miraculous power in his lost paintings; Pratt was sure of it. He had three of those key paintings. Or at least two and pictures of one. He'd "eliminated" that obstructionist Dr. Riley McKee because she'd been swapping carefully-modified forgeries for the originals. If he could find Caravaggio's lost paintings, he could find the most important; the one Caravaggio called *The Last*

Prophet. That was the painting that would tell him how to extend life. *Where was the damn jet?*

He wanted a drink. His doctors had told him to stop, but he knew they were treating him like a typical patient. He fingered his fancy Swiss watch and groaned. He'd been waiting two hours . . . and he didn't have two hours to wait. Once he was home, he would fire these pilots and hire new ones. He had the money.

James Pratt entered and stood behind his fraternal twin, Charles. A breeze was blowing through the screen door. Charles spotted James's reflection in the dirty windowpane.

"Charlie. The jet is late because your Alhambra man drugged the professor and had to sneak him out to the airport in London in a magician box from the stage." James said.

"I really don't like excuses." Charles replied.

"The men we hired in Damascus didn't find the paintings, Charlie. Someone tipped off the CIA. They were there. Someone killed everyone in the hotel room." There was no answer. "I have more bad news."

Still no answer.

"Don't call me 'Charlie.'" He finally answered.

"The girl the assassin killed in Connecticut was meeting a CIA agent."

"Who? Who was the CIA agent?"

"That's more bad news. Jake Bolton. Remember, he was the guy in Kazakhstan that screwed up our pipeline deal to China."

"Oh, good. That's just grand. What was Bolton doing there?"

"The girl was his sister. Dr. Riley McKee. And you had us kill her."

"His sister? He doesn't have a sister."

"He does. Well . . . he did. He's now traveling with another woman."

"But Riley McKee is dead? For sure dead?"

"Yes. But you know Bolton. He's going to go after the assassin, and when he finds him, he will come after you and me and kill both of us." James Pratt sat beside his brother.

Charles Pratt swallowed hard and dropped his chin to his chest. He murmured, "I need to catch a break. I have the desire to live."

"What did you say?" James was likely surprised by what he heard.

"I said, 'I want to live.' I may be desperate but I'm still human." Charles said in a rare moment of self-pity.

"I . . . I don't . . ." James struggled to reply.

Charles seemed to reach a conclusion. "The sister was just an amateur. She'd never have found the paintings, but she was getting in my way by calling in experts that might leak the clues. Bolton has resources. Maybe even better than mine. He'll be looking for the paintings in order to find us. If he leads us to the paintings, we'll be right behind him. Then I get what I need to save my life. If he finds us first, then a quick bullet to my head might be more pleasant than this miserable slow death. Tell half the team to stick with Bolton. Keep the other half tracing McKee's work. Let's see who solves this puzzle first."

Chapter 31

College of the Holy Cross
Worcester, Massachusetts

A flash of sunlight radiated off the window pane in the ivy covered building. Jake Bolton dug out a pair of desert-camouflage binoculars from his backpack.

Jenny pointed to a red brick clock tower. "That's part of the original campus from the 1800's. The Yankees who ruled Boston weren't letting Catholic immigrants into their colleges . . . so the Jesuits built one for them.

"Sounds like the Jesuits." Jake smiled beneath the binoculars.

"This was all farm land. Supposedly, there's an enormous spring here feeding a river-- now covered by the local highway."

"I see two routes in." Jake put his binoculars down. "The shorter one past the church there, but the safer one is through those hedges."

"Through the hedges is the cemetery."

"Cemetery?"

"Yup. Pretty full, too."

"Students?"

"Hey, it's a tough school, but not that tough. No, teaching Jesuits have the honor of being buried on campus." She said.

"Is that instead of health care?" He smiled.

Jenny felt the warm teasing was making Jake more appealing.

Jake scrunched his forehead, "What?"

Jenny awoke from her trance. "I . . ."

"What are you thinking?" Jake asked.

"I want to know what it was like growing up in your family?"

"What it was like for my Mom? She did everything she could to live normal. Waiting day after day for some sort of news. My Dad was in Beirut. And she's standing there staring blankly one minute, then the next slobbering over a sink. Imagine her pain. I didn't want that for Riley. And, I wouldn't want it for you."

Jenny swallowed deeply as a chill raced down her spine. She didn't know how to respond. She waited. His eyes scanned her up and down. Then she realized there was no response.

"There are only two people on this earth that I'm afraid of. And, after that, all the government agencies." Jake said.

"Who are they?"

"It doesn't' matter. There's no satisfaction in killing someone. When you're at work you probably spend hours in political correctness meetings when someone looks at you the wrong way. In the Middle East, they just shoot you. Either way, it's closure. That is, if you ever get closure with death."

Jenny scratched her head and glanced back down the cemetery rows. *His view of death is worldly different than the streets of Hartford that empty into the emergency room every weekend. His normal is not my normal.* She thought. "I'm not politically correct. You have a rank, right?"

"Captain. But that only means something to the men around you."

"Same here. Surgeon. I need to earn my rank every day too. We have a thing called Morbidity and Mortality rounds. This is an open forum of doctors discussing what you did wrong during the care of your patient. If you're not 100% accurate you discuss it. The process can be grueling."

"Isn't that what liberal arts is all about? Doesn't that bring dimension to your character? Bring rank to your soul? The Socratic method?"

"Yes and yes. The first time you go through Morbidity and Mortality Rounds, you throw up. You adjust." She added.

"Just like the battlefield for me."

"Then, you excel."

"Except every patient is probably a little different for you. Just like my opponents on the battlefield reacting to every movement I make."

"Neither you or I can make a mistake and get away with it." *Our worlds are really not that much different.* She thought.

"Just imagine if all those pieces on a chess board were alive."

"That's the Middle Ages." She smiled.

Jake grabbed his binoculars. He appeared to scan the spired rooftops, pausing in front of a large ivy-covered brick facade on the east side of campus. He put the large glasses down and stared at the sky.

Jenny watched the sun passing between the clouds and sensed what he was thinking.

"Our run toward the building will produce shadows, making us more visible to anyone hunting us." He said.

"Hunting us?"

Jake placed the glasses back to his eyes and continued their options. "I think that cemetery hedge will give us the best cover. It looks like it runs directly down to that back door."

"Once we get into the building we've got to move quickly. When the sun goes behind those clouds, we go. Right now I'm going to give you a crash course in tradecraft.

"At some point in the next day or two, we may get separated. If you think that you're being followed, duck into a store and buy something. That can put doubt into your tracker. If I'm nearby and I see you buy something that begins with a 't' like a tie, I know that means trouble, and I'll walk away from you, looking for the person tailing you. Remember, when given the choice, I've got to find Riley's killer. You may need to protect yourself."

"All this spy stuff is unreal. I guess I should've expected anything after Riley was shot. Yet, I can't get that image out of my mind—the two of you on that bridge." Jenny shuddered. *Move Riley. Move! Show me you're alive.* She thought. *A lifeless doll. Her big blue eyes staring through me. Like someone had thrown their toy on the floor.* Riley dead in her arms wasn't part of a puzzle game. The most was a pie in the face. These risks were real. And now, a crash course in spy craft.

"Shake it off." Jake blurted, staring straight ahead. He paused, then turned to Jenny. "I'm sorry. That's instinct talking." He put his hand out and tapped Jenny's shoulder. "You just need to react like you do in the hospital."

Jenny felt an electrical shock race down her arm. Her fingers felt like they were waking from sleep. She glared at her hand waiting for the spark. "When things got real tense in the hospital, Riley would tell me the same joke: A tourist's car breaks down while he's on holiday in the Irish countryside. He gets out, looks around, and opens the hood. While he's staring at the engine, a black horse trots up next to the stone wall. The horse sticks its head over the engine. The man then hears, 'Spark plug.' The tourist steps back, looks around again, and doesn't see anyone. He says to the horse, 'What? Did you say something?' The horse shakes its head and the man again hears, 'Spark plug.' The horse trots off. The motorist follows the horse's instructions, and drives on to the next village, where he stops for new spark plugs and a pint of Guinness. He tells the bartender about his experience with the horse. 'Was it a black horse or a white one?' asks the bartender. 'A black horse,' says the tourist. 'Ah, you're lucky,' says the bartender. 'The white horse doesn't know crap about cars.'"

Jake put down his binoculars. "That's a family joke. My grandfather told it."

Chapter 32

College of the Holy Cross
Worcester, Massachusetts

Jake broke the silence. "I was thinking about that picture we found in Riley's camera. What can you tell me about Father Landry? His work, his travels, that art stuff?"

When she thought about Landry she was reminded of the miracle healing stories from the Gospel. Christ healing the man with leprosy. Healing the paralyzed man.

"I remember one Sunday service in college with particular fondness. While the inside church structure was undergoing restoration, extensive scaffolding, covered with ropes and pulleys and drop cloths, had gradually blended into the sanctuary rafters. The accoutrements of repair had grown as familiar as to go unnoticed. Then, one spring Sunday in the middle of a Father Landry sermon, a young man on a pallet lowered himself down from the ceiling and hung suspended a few feet above the pulpit. At least nine hundred young men and women gaped with horror, unsure whether their classmate's antics would cause Landry finally to lose his legendary goodwill or God to strike the young hooligan with lightning.

"Landry, however, could not resist the opportunity to turn a prank into religious allegory. He switched the topic of his sermon to Saint Mark and the paralyzed man, speaking about the healing as a concept of forgiveness. Jesus' teaching that a mere man, working with the grace of God, could deliver forgiveness for impiety was blasphemous to the Jewish elders. Throughout the sermon, the student on the lowered pallet cowered before the pulpit, unsure what he should do now that his joke had backfired. Landry stretched out his hands, "Get up, son; your sins are forgiven!" The assembled students were astonished and thrilled. They gave Father Landry an ovation while the young man ran from the chapel."

"You're kidding me?"

"Nope." She said.

"He has religious allegory paintings scattered all over his office walls. The Baroque period. That was pretty much the 1600s, especially in Italy. Very dramatic, very eye-grabbing. Lots of great sculpture. The major painter was Caravaggio, the baroque bad boy."

"How do you know so much about art?"

"Liberal arts. You can be an Art History major, an English major and still be Pre-med."

"You and Riley were both Art History majors?"

"Yup. Father Landry taught us. He loved Caravaggio's work. During our Junior year in London Father Landry took Riley for a side trip to Dublin to see a famous Caravaggio." She sensed that maybe he was warming up to her . . . or playing her for the fool.

"What made Caravaggio so great? And why 'bad boy'?"

"Riley would say that he slaps you in the face, kicks you in the guts, squeezes your adrenal glands, and then calls the cardiologist for you. Landry said he was the by-product of his culture. He grew up in plague-infested Milan and watched people die all around him. By the time he made it to Rome, he was looking for life as well as a living. According to Landry, he found them both.

"The Jesuits loved his paintings and put them in most of their new churches. When you see a Caravaggio, it makes you stop, like when you enter a courtyard expecting to find a brick plaza but instead you see this incredible garden and you just go, 'Wow!'"

"For me it's when a gorgeous woman walks across the room. It feels like forgiveness has arrived, like touching her might just be heaven."

Jenny smiled at the newly poetic Jake. *Does he have a heart like his sister?*

"Do you experience this rush where your heart beats fast, your head goes dizzy, your fingers tremble, your feet go numb, and you have to catch your breath?" she asked.

Jake nodded eagerly. "Yes. That's what beauty does to me."

Jenny felt her heart thump. *He seems real enough. But I think he's trying to get me to relax.* She felt like she'd opened his personal diary and her lips quivered. She leaned in toward him like he was pulling her in. Closing her eyes she felt the urge to kiss him. Suddenly, the space around them disappeared.

There was a crack in the distance and Jake's head snapped

forward toward the building. Jenny's head hit his shoulder. "What are you doing?" He asked.

"I was . . . nothing." Jenny pulled back unexpectedly.

"The beauty is another way for life to speak. Far too many people collapse under the weight they bear. That beauty changes the laws of physics. You've got that gift, Jenny. In the way you're able to hold up under pressure and still carry yourself."

Jenny felt another thump. "Riley would talk about breaking the laws of physics with love. That the speed of light slows and charged particles merge."

"You can do that Genevieve Neugold."

"Have you and Digger killed a lot of people?" Jenny rolled to face him. She was looking for emotion inside the shell.

"Yes. But only when necessary. It's not like you see on TV. Each situation is different. You never feel comfortable killing or, saving someone. Either way, it's intense but not emotional."

"Riley could balance that intensity and emotion." Jenny added.

"I agree. Now tell me about the Jesuits."

"The order was founded about the same time Caravaggio was beginning to paint. A Basque soldier named Ignatius of Loyola was wounded badly. Doctors kept operating on his leg. They broke it, set it, and rebroke it. No anesthesia."

"I've had that done to me. Syria. Not by a doctor, though." Jake winked at Jenny.

"Stop interrupting." Jenny grinned at him. "When Ignatius got well enough, he didn't go back to war. He made a pilgrimage up a Spanish mountain and had a conversion experience. Founded a religious order—Jesuits. The order was like a military command.

"Landry told us that the Jesuits became the most powerful weapon ever against the rise of Protestantism. Like the Protestants, Ignatius wanted to reform the Christian Church. But he wanted to do that from within. They established the first formal colleges. The Jesuits sent missionaries throughout the New World. They built churches everywhere, the fanciest in Europe. They believed that art could teach. This is why they connected with Caravaggio."

Jenny ran her eyes up and down his face.

"They've endured the plague, leprosy, starvation and torture. Jesuits go where they're sent. I suppose you could relate."

"I've seen those priests tending the ghettos of Turkey, walking refugees through the mine fields of Lebanon and bathing the incurable in the Egyptian rivers."

"That's them."

Jake looked like he was formulating a careful question. "They still believe in miracles. Do you?"

"Maybe one. Human babies." Jenny winked back. "You?"

"I'm not really interested right now."

"Jake, science is a cold and disaffected universe that sucks life into a black hole. Human birth is the unexplained miracle at the fragile edge of life. Birth restores the energy to life."

"What? You don't believe in science? A doctor?"

"I believe in medical science. Miracles are simply the medical cures I can't explain."

Chapter 33

College of the Holy Cross
Worcester, Massachusetts

Jake pulled Jenny toward the dense bushes near the cemetery entrance.

Jenny leaned against him and could feel his deep breathing. After a while, he relaxed.

"Is it safe?" Jenny asked.

"Jenny, it's time to go. Follow me. Stay low." He drew his pistol and ran through the cemetery, Jenny close at his heels.

When they reached a large white stone crucifix, he paused again. He was scanning the final walkway. Then they ran to the door leading into the office building. The door was unlocked but old, making a disturbingly loud noise.

The main entrance gave way to a wide staircase to the upper floors. The space between each stair was narrow. Each landing had swinging glass fire doors dividing the corridors.

"I particularly hate glass doors," Jake whispered. "They mean we can't hide." They climbed the first set of stairs. Jenny watched him study every window and doorway along the passageway, glancing back every two floors to gauge his position.

Jake continued to lead until they reached a landing a few steps below the fourth-floor corridor. They were now eye level with the fourth-floor hallway and needed only to turn at the landing and rise three more steps to be near Father Landry's office door.

The silence was broken by the sounds of shattering glass and pounding footsteps.

"Jake," Jenny yelled. She dug her hand into his side.

Jake reached around with one arm, pulling Jenny behind him while his other hand brought up his handgun. Behind the frosted glass doors there was the blur of a man running. By the time Jake had covered the last few steps and pushed open the doors the man had disappeared down the end of the corridor.

A cry of, "Help," came from the other end of the hall.

An elderly man dressed in black was struggling to get up. "Help!" he yelled again. Jake ran for the intruder like he was hoping for a confrontation, but once he reached the next set of doors, the man was gone.

Jake turned back toward the fallen man. "Father Landry? Are you okay?"

"I'm not Father Landry. I'm Father Doherty. I came to find him. He hasn't been back to his room. He never made his flight out of Boston and his passport is still on his bureau."

"Where is he?" She asked.

"I came looking for him and knocked on his office door. Then I put my passkey in the lock." He pointed down the hallway. "That man slammed the door open and ran me over."

"Did you get a look at his face?" Jake asked.

He rolled himself into a sitting position, "Who are you two?"

"Jen—"

"Her name is Ellie Svenson. I'm Stephan Contino. We had an appointment with Father Landry. He's going to marry us."

Chapter 34

College of the Holy Cross
Worcester, Massachusetts

Jake and Jenny helped the priest to his feet and walked him to a bench.

"Father, my fiancé is a nurse. Let her look you over while I check Father Landry's office."

Jenny glared at Jake over the priest's head. *What was he thinking, lying to a priest?*

Jake ran into Landry's office and started sifting through the papers on the desk. Jenny watched him browse through the stacks of art books, student portfolios, DVD boxes, conference announcements, and blue exam books. He studied the paintings, drawings, and newspaper clippings on the wall.

She appeared in the doorway.

"Do you see any painting that seems out of place?"

She moved into the room and studied the walls. The paintings were all in neatly ordered rows across the room. There was no change in the wall color to suggest a missing frame.

"I don't see any." She shook her head. She looked under the desk and saw nothing but dust. There were books and a few dying plants on the windowsill.

Jake slid past her and stepped back into the hallway.

Jenny always felt a chill when there was a clue in a room. Usually she found it. This time she was not so sure. She felt the contents of the room closing in on her. Her own life was systematic. This office seemed scattered to the point of meaninglessness. *The intruder didn't find what he was looking for.* She felt.

Her breathing grew louder. Like something was suffocating her. Something that Landry left behind for Riley . . . or them. She reached for the door and pulled herself into the corridor next to Jake.

Jake approached Doherty. "Father, did Father Landry leave any address where he was going in Europe?"

"No. Nothing. We found his passport and plane tickets to London in his room."

"London?" Jenny asked.

"We don't want to disturb anything in his office. Can you find a phone and call the police to ask them to come over?" Jake asked.

"Yes, I'll go to my office and call campus security."

Jake extended his hand to help Father Doherty to his feet.

Something caught Jenny's eye. "Father, if you don't mind my asking, what's that lapel pin you're wearing?"

Doherty patted the pin. "A Knights of Columbus pin."

"Was Father Landry in the K of C also?" Jake asked.

"Yes."

"Any relationship between art and the Knights of Columbus?" Jake looked at Jenny like he was following a hunch.

Doherty folded his hands before speaking. "The Alhambra. The Order of the Alhambra is a secret splinter organization of Catholic men, begun in Brooklyn around 1900. I guess you could say that Alhambra is to the Knights of Columbus what the Shriners are to the Freemasons. Pope Paul the Sixth, Pope John Paul the Second, and President Kennedy were all members of the Order of the Alhambra. The order's first mission is to protect Catholic Church relics and antiquities. The second is to care for the mentally and physically handicapped."

"Where'd the name come from?"

"It originates from the Christian reconquest of Spain, marked by the surrender of the Moors in 1492."

"Church relics? Like art?"

"Yes."

"I suppose that would include Caravaggio art?"

"Of course. So many of his paintings have been lost, stolen, misplaced. He never signed his paintings so who knows where they are. Those that are in churches, the Order of Alhambra seeks to protect. Those that are lost they seek to find."

"Thanks, Father. Could you please go make that call? Also, give them my number as well." Jake handed the man a card.

Doherty walked toward his office.

Jenny and Jake stared at each other. Jenny felt a wave of warmth like his gaze was covering her. *This guy puts together puzzles like his sister!*

"Imagine this," Jake paused and his eyes scattered down the long hallway like he'd been distracted. "The Catholic Church is closing schools, convents, churches all over the world. Sometimes selling buildings in bulk. What if . . ."

"What if," Jenny interrupted. "This secret splinter group, The Order of the Alhambra suddenly comes alive again to go on the offensive to save the treasures of the Church—like the paintings, statues, relics?"

"Priceless antiquities, gold and religious icons." Jake answered.

"And some of these Alhambrans zealously pursued the antiquities in the name of God?" Jenny raised her eyebrows. "To kill to get what they wanted?"

Jake turned around, visibly calculating. "Go into Landry's office again," Jake said. "See if anything looks out of order."

Jenny entered the high-ceilinged room, mentally breaking the office down into quadrants. Everything seemed stacked, as if the room had been tidied into messy piles that represented order to the eclectic thinker Landry.

Jenny studied the office walls. Every inch was filled by a painting or a poster; there were no blanks. The wall opposite Landry's desk was a mosaic made up of Renaissance paintings based on the Bible. For some reason, Landry had copies of both versions of da Vinci's *Virgin of the Rocks*. She remembered how Riley had exploded when the writer, Dan Brown, confused the figures of John the Baptist and Christ in *The da Vinci Code*. You had to know your iconography to get it right. At least, that was what Landry taught them. She said Landry was obsessed that da Vinci was painting a secret about John the Baptist—not Christ—in that pair of paintings. That the two of them together meant something mysterious. A secret about John's importance to the Catholic Church hidden in the pointing motion of the characters.

"Wait . . . I saw something in the paintings. The dusty shadows around the pictures suggested that the frames had been moved. Not just one. It's the coalescence of all the contrasts. It's like a table of puzzle pieces!"

She moved farther back to the wall opposite the paintings. Jenny knew that a person could step back, squint, and curve the eye's lens, altering the rods and cones the same way a painter did when he stepped back and put his thumb in front of his eye. She called to Jake, "I think I see something."

Jake ran from his post at the door. "What? Hurry."

Jenny pulled out a small rectangular box with a gold latch from her backpack. She opened the box to expose a pair of strange-looking glasses.

"What are those?" Jake asked.

"Some people call them loupes, like jewelers wear. They're magnifiers. I use them for surgery. I can magnify forty times and see the smallest blood vessels. But in this situation I can reverse them and make like I'm looking from a mile away."

She slowly moved her head back and forth.

"What do you see?"

"Voilà, there it is. Father Landry, you're a genius. The arrangement of paintings makes for a literal mosaic. The dark shading of the mosaic spells out a message that can be seen only by creating distance between the wall and the viewer."

"For God's sake, Jenny, what does it say?"

"It says 'OK seven.'"

"What's okay?"

"O'Kane Hall is the OK. A building probably named after an alumnus. We called it 'the OK'. That's the red brick building next to us—attached to Fenwick. Seven must mean the seventh floor . . . but, Jake . . . that floor is off limits . . . there's only the exorcism room there."

A door slammed at the end of the hall. Their heads snapped toward the door. Loud footsteps echoed down the corridor. Jake started running toward the noise. Jenny felt the urge to run after him, not wanting to be alone. He stopped. Then looked back at Landry's office where Jenny was waiting. "Jenny, let's get to O'Kane Hall now."

Chapter 35

Lorca Airport
Granada, Spain

Charles Pratt snapped his head from the hanger window when the Learjet pulled up near the outside gate. "Is the woman with Bolton another CIA agent?"

James Pratt opened a notebook. "No. Her name is Doctor Genevieve Neugold. Not only was she McKee's roommate in college, she also spent her junior year in England with McKee. They were both at Cambridge—St. John's College. She's also a trauma surgeon."

"Kill her anyway. Jake Bolton is all we need to get this puzzle solved. He has all the pieces in front of him, just like I do. He doesn't know it yet, but he's going to put them together for me."

"Where are we going now?"

"James, don't ever say 'we.' This is about me and solving a four-hundred-year-old riddle. I am going to London now that my plane is finally here. My two men in Ireland have found other gravestones. More clues from the Knights. Every one of them has those two characteristic symbols from the Knights Templar and Knights Hospitaller: On the left is the cross running through the crown and on the right are the crisscrossed shepherd's staff, lance, and sword through the pivoting two-piece slotted medieval helmet. Each one of them has a different Shakespeare quotation on their gravestone that doesn't make sense. The information I bought said that the secret password was there in Ireland with those Knights."

"Charles, I truly hope that the secret is out there to help you. But a mystery like this is not easy to hide for all these years. Are you sure you aren't just, well, acting out of desperation?"

Charles stood up and looked at his brother, his eyes wild. With the discipline of years spent in boardrooms, he counted down to neutral, walked a few feet away, placed his hat on a bench, then combed his hand through his hair. He returned to face his brother.

"Did you ever hear of the Knights Templar, Jimmy?"

"I went to Harvard too, *Charlie*."

James ignored or simply did not hear his brother's sarcasm.

"When the Knights Templar were arrested by the French King Philip IV in 1307, he didn't just give us the superstition of Friday the thirteenth," Charles said. "He also sent the Templars underground. Many disappeared into the Sovereign Military Hospitaller Order of Saint John of Jerusalem of Rhodes and of Malta. In those days, prisoners were tortured by holding their feet over a fire until their skin melted off the bone, or pulling out teeth, or suspending them by their limbs until they confessed. At times, I feel the same way with this disease. Then the Vatican released Lumen Fidei. It more than protected the Hospitallers. That papal encyclical states that the Hospitallers had some kind of direct line to God. The Hospitallers cured even the victims of the torture. For centuries they've been known to cure the most hopeless patients."

"It's like that Holy Spirit the Catholics talk about. You know, 'We believe in the Holy Spirit, the Lord, the giver of life, who proceeds from the Father and the Son. With the Father and the Son he is worshiped and glorified. He has spoken through the prophets.'"

"How did you know that? You didn't learn that at Harvard."

"Charles, I'm praying for you."

"I don't need your prayers. I need your results. Keep following Jake Bolton. I have a man in Syria trying to find the stolen Caravaggio. I want all the lost paintings we can find. That's why you're going to Sicily. I want the Lazarus painting. It's important. I can sense it."

"Why?" James stepped back and lowered his gaze.

"When the bishop rejected the first version, Caravaggio carved up the canvas with a razor blade. He didn't paint over it. He repainted the whole damn thing. The changes he made are part of his code, part of his map to salvation."

"I, I, I," James Pratt again started to object, then thought better of it. "I'll do my best."

Charles picked up his Stetson and moved to the gangway. He unwrapped a large elastic band from his black-and-white composition book, stuffed with sketches, old news clippings, wire photos, and a time line. "Look at this," he said, unfolding a crusted yellowed parchment. "Charles the Fifth, the Holy Roman Emperor, also known as Charles the First, King of Spain . . ."

James raised a quizzical eyebrow.

"Charles the Fifth was the father of Philip, the Spanish prince who married the English Queen Mary and helped her return England to Roman Catholicism. Mary died, Elizabeth became the Queen, and the country turned Protestant again. The devoutly Catholic Philip was so pissed off he went to the Pope, and tried to invade England. When Philip's Spanish Armada was defeated, out of spite he sent his troops to support the Irish rebellion against Elizabeth."

James let out a long breath. "And?"

Charles flipped to a different page of his notebook. "Listen to this: 'Philip was determined to carry out his father's legacy. He used the Knights Hospitaller to repeatedly thwart England during the Nine Years' War fought in Ireland from 1594 to 1603.' Look at the dates, James! It was a religious war and the Knights died there. The secret the Knights Hospitaller kept must be in Ireland. It's all linked. See the genius of it!"

"Stop. Let me understand this slowly." James said.

"The Holy Roman emperor Charles and his son Philip conspired and converted England back to Catholicism. Then Queen Elizabeth converted England back to Protestant. So, Philip sent the devout Catholic Knights Hospitaller back in to fight the English. Finally, they die fighting in Ireland."

"And, as more and more of them die, they realize they need to protect the Knights Hospitaller secret."

"Sure. But where could the Knights hide their secret and be assured that it wouldn't get lost in time? A place where it couldn't easily be stolen or destroyed? And lastly, where it wouldn't be so obvious to someone unless they went looking for it?"

James squeezed his upper lip between his forefingers while he nodded his head slowly. "The cemeteries in Ireland. With the Knights' gravestones."

"Yes. Exactly. When you get back from Sicily, you're going to Ireland."

Chapter 36

Airborne
Thirty Miles East of Grenada, Spain

Charles Pratt coiled back into the deep blue leather chair of his LJ45 jet. He slowly fingered the decaying pages of a book called *I Modi*. The erotic photos did not stimulate him as they were intended.

Although Giulio Romano had created the erotic drawings, he was, surprisingly, never prosecuted for something that was so blasphemous in 16th century Europe. *Romano must have had something on someone. I know how to do that.* Pratt thought. But Romano was a virtual unknown artist. Yet Shakespeare's reference in a play to Romano is what excited Pratt. He knew it was a clue to unlocking what Shakespeare knew about The Last Prophet.

Pratt's understanding of Shakespeare was not profound. The few plays he studied as an undergraduate he'd read with the help of Cliff's Notes. But his most recent wife, in the waning days of their marriage, had forced him to attend her regional theater's god-awful production of *The Winter's Tale.* It seemed to go on forever. Something, however, caught his attention as the play moved to its happy ending: A statue on stage came to life.

The scene captured his attention because Shakespeare implied that the sculptor Giulio Romano brought a dead person to life. *Romano. The only artist Shakespeare ever mentioned in a play. He gets a profound endorsement from the greatest playwright of his time? Shakespeare says he can bring someone back to life?* He thought. *Romano was nothing as an artist. A zero.*

In Pratt's most recent research on the Knights Hospitaller and his search for Caravaggio, he found the reference to Charles the Fifth commissioning work from a Giulio Romano. He knew Charles V was important because he was a fierce supporter of the Knights Hospitaller and Roman Catholicism in England. But why did he remember Romano?

He went back to the Shakespeare. Pratt remembered how his body actually vibrated when he read the footnote in his ex-wife's edition: "Giulio Romano was a mannerist painter and sometime architect in Italy (1449–1546). As a Knight, he enjoyed numerous commissions from important patrons." Pratt had ripped the page from the thin-papered book.

Now he pulled that sheet out of his composition book and stared at it again. There in the margin was his note, written in a stronger hand than he remembered. "Compared to Michelangelo or da Vinci, Romano was a nobody in the art world. With all the great artists of the Renaissance why would Shakespeare only mention Romano is all of his plays? What was Shakespeare up to?"

Pratt was taunted by the information the Alhambra men had collected on Romano, the Knights Hospitaller, Caravaggio, and Shakespeare. He felt trapped between two worlds: The lost or hidden world of the Knights that might "put breath" into him. And the other world was his, the one in which his liver disease ate away at his body.

The lights in the jet flickered and the wings rattled, the plane broke through the last array of clouds. Now was the time to seek help from the reluctant guest strapped into the seat opposite him. The man was waking up from his stupor.

"Is there any reason that you should kidnap me in the middle of my celebration? Are you going to explain yourself?" The renowned Shakespeare scholar Geoffrey Willis blurted out.

"Professor, tell me about The *Winter's Tale.* Why is Romano so important?"

The professor looked down at his steel handcuffs, pulling on his wrists. He shook his head in disbelief. He tried to stand and think, as was so often his habit, but realized with a start that the leather chair was his prison. "You brought me here to answer questions about Shakespeare? Are you nuts?"

"I assure you, old man, I'm not crazy." Pratt tossed several large photographs into the professor's lap. Willis waved his cuffed hands in defense.

"Where the hell am I?" Willis tossed the images back across the table. "And who are you?"

"You're on my jet. Somewhere over Spain. I need your help with a Shakespeare story. Since you wouldn't help my man from Alhambra he brought you to me."

"That's a bit drastic."

"Not really. I need quick answers. I'm running out of time. Just look at the photos."

Willis studied the images. Simple rectangular headstones with weathered inscriptions stared back at him. Shrugging, he placed the black-and-white images back on the foldout table.

"Professor, look more closely."

"You, sir, are beyond barmy. I've got to get back to my family. You kidnap and drug me to look at your pictures?"

"Look again." Pratt leaned forward, unlocking the professor's handcuffs, and then tossing them on the cabin floor. "Okay, you're free."

"I have no idea what you want of me."

"That barmy I'm not. I need your help solving a very old riddle."

Willis adjusted his shoulders and looked again at the photos. "Will you let me go if I figure this out?"

"Do you see these corners?" Pratt poked at the photo. "There are emblems on each side, coats of arms: the Knights Templar and Knights Hospitaller. On the left is the cross running through the crown, and on the right are the crisscrossed shepherd's staff, lance, and sword through the pivoting two-piece slotted medieval helmet. Each one of them has a quotation from *The Winter's Tale*."

Willis adjusted his glasses and pulled the photo closer to study the enlarged engraving. Though the lines were worn by years of wind and rain, he could make out: *Julio Romano, who, had he himself eternity and could put breath into his work, would beguile Nature of her custom, so perfectly he is her ape: he so near to Hermione hath done Hermione that they say one would speak to her and stand in hope of answer.*

"Good God! That line is from act three of Shakespeare's *The Winter's Tale*."

"There are others, tons of them, all over the country. Like, 'You pay a great deal too dear for what's given freely,' and, 'To unpathed waters, undreamed shores,' and, 'If this be Magic, let it be an Art.'" All those lines are from *The Winter's Tale*, and all are engraved into these Knights' headstones. Nowhere else in the world do you see gravestones that have these coats of arms with these Shakespeare quotes and all from *The Winter's Tale*."

"Eh, that's extremely odd," Willis acknowledged. "But I don't know what it means."

Pratt stared back at him, still hoping for illumination.

Minutes passed. The professor seemed desperate for an answer that would earn his release. "Truly. I have no idea what this all means."

"See if this helps. King Philip the Second of Spain sent his men to Ireland with the Knights Hospitaller, in 1594 to support the Irish rebels in Tyrone's Rebellion. The English did not like that. The Knights' were ferocious fighters and the subsequent Nine Years War nearly bankrupted England. The Irish demanded a free Ireland, the return of papal authority, and a Catholic university. Queen Elizabeth responded with a counter attack. Ever wonder why Ireland is so green but has no trees? The Brits cut down everything but the rock walls. They sent the lumber home."

"Queen Elizabeth did have a temper," Willis conceded.

"The Irish might have ended their troubles there, except for the Knights' decision at the Siege of Kinsale to attack the British. That mistake ended in their own rout. The Knights lost badly and were scattered all over the south of Ireland. By 1603, James became King of England and worried about the cost of punishing the Knights. He offered them leniency. The now "Irish" Knights stayed, bred warhorses, built churches and monasteries, eventually died, and were buried in Ireland. Right there in Kinsale…the southern tip of Ireland."

"You're being a plonker. Just like my students, you aren't paying attention to details. These Knights? The same Knights Hospitaller as you call them—look closely at the graves—one died in 1603, another here in 1601. Those quotes couldn't get to Ireland until the old Bard wrote the damn play! Shakespeare didn't write *The Winter's Tale* before 1611. Maybe, just maybe 1605. And it wasn't published until 1623. The gravestones must be fakes. Someone is playing you for a chump."

Chapter 37

CIA Headquarters
Langley, Virginia

Karen Smith bit her passport between her teeth, checked her Jackie Robinson bat over her left shoulder, and pulled her travel bag with the right. As she spun around, she nearly sliced the FBI man's head off with the baseball bat.

"Hey, watch it!" He said.

Smith glanced back at Felice's visitor the way a batter gawked at a pitcher after a brush back. The agent turned red with anger.

"Listen, Ms. Smith, I only want to say this once. This is our turf, not yours."

Smith leaned in. "I can safely say that there's enough 'turf' on this field for both of us."

"Ma'am, there's no reason for you to go into the field."

"Young man, have you ever heard of the ginkgo tree?"

"Huh?"

"My neighbor got it into his head that the garbage cans in my backyard were stinking up his personal space. He built a fence; then he built a wall; he hung girly candles, started the hang-up phone calls, called the Alexandria police, and even sued me. I dragged him, the judge, and the police around the house, the yard, and the cans, and there was no freakin' smell. Finally, several stinking months later this land surveyor shows up and points out that our other neighbor has a cluster of ginkgo trees. It turns out these trees have seedpods that drop down in his yard, open up, and give off a sticky, slimy substance that smells like a combination of vomit, diaper poo, and unwashed feet. Every time he mowed his lawn he shared this sweaty perfume with the neighborhood!"

"I don't understand. My wife uses that ginkgo biloba vitamin mix and . . . Say, wait a minute. Are you saying we—"

The agent was stopped by a voice from the staircase well.

"Enough!" CIA Deputy Director Felice yelled. "I heard the whole thing. You should feel lucky. Her body turn was more like a bunt than a swing. Karen Smith rarely sacrifices an out with a bunt."

Smith turned toward the deputy director with relief. "Thanks for coming, Kevin. We've got another Jamie Gorelick here trying to frick up an operation."

"Hey, that mistress of disaster wasn't ours." The FBI man added.

"She was your lawyer, another liberal, tree-hugging, myopic lawyer." Smith hissed.

"Whatever." The FBI man threw up his arms in disgust.

"Kevin. Jake Bolton is in for a big fight here. This has a lot more to do with the Catholic Church and some secret medical cure than it does with Caravaggio."

"How so?" Felice asked.

"I think it has to do with the plague."

"Tell me about the plague."

"The true plague is this bug." Smith dropped her bat and balanced her papers on her knee. "Yersina pestis. Named for a Frenchman who discovered how a flea that bit a rat could infect a human. Sometimes called the Black Plague, the Black Death, or the bubonic plague."

Smith waved one hand like a magician with a wand. She knew Felice's interest in biological warfare. "The plague had a fifty percent mortality rate. Just in Asia, where the plague began, the population shrank from a hundred and twenty million people down to sixty million in a few decades. One-third of Europe died from plague in the sixteenth century alone."

"How did this 'pestis' spread so fast if it needed a living delivery system?" FBI man asked.

"There were wars far from home. Soldiers returned with fleas. Trade routes opened, especially between China and Europe. Rats with fleas could hop easy rides along the Silk Road. Fleas living on the rats ran through the garbage on the streets of Italy, Spain, and Germany. I read here that Shakespeare's theater had to close from time to time because of the plague."

"But you're talking about the Renaissance. Da Vinci, Galileo, really smart scientists. They couldn't figure out fleas and rats?"Felice said. "What about the Church?"

"Unfortunately, the Church handled the plague about as well as they did the solar system. The early Church portrayed plague symptoms as warnings from God, and proposed cures from God. They taught that certain streams and pools of water worked miracles. Then people turned to relics, hoping the bones of saints would cure them. Desperate people will spend all their money for desperate cures. Look at the celebrities we read about in the tabloids. Ground avocado won't cure cancer."

Smith realized she was getting wound up. It felt good.

"None of these churchmen helped at all?" FBI man said.

Smith shrugged. She sensed he was baiting her a bit. "It's no different today. You get inconsolable patients making deals with the devil when they've found they have cancer or some incurable genetic disease. On one hand we have women who desperately seek to have a child gulping down all kinds of folklore medicines or vitamins and, on the other, women carrying six fetuses who want gestational reduction surgery." Smith felt a wave of nausea while she envisioned the outcomes. "You know that these situations mess with God's plan . . . and they don't end well."

"When emotion is involved sometimes morality disappears." Felice said. I guess you can't put a price on a long healthy life.

"But here's the kicker. Amidst all this Caravaggio art? There are reports that some religious order in the Mediterranean actually had success curing the Black Plague. Reports. Rumors. No one knows for sure, but they were a pretty powerful, respected, and feared bunch of Knights. They were called Hospitallers because they built hospitals. They were smarter than pushing the sick into streams." Smith felt the urge to slow down before her blood pressure blew up.

There was long pause between them.

"Smith, take a look at this Worcester police report. It just came in."

Smith leaned against the wall, pulled the barrel of the bat from the floor, and opened the file. "They're in deep crap and need our help. 'Ellie Svenson' and 'Stephan Contino' were our operative names when we were together in Rome two years ago. Mine and Jake's. I made Svenson look like she killed Contino. To hide Jake from the Syrians." She said.

The FBI agent nodded as he digested the news. Then he paused. "Now I understand that ginkgo tree. Were you trying to tell me that I've been making a false assumption about Jake

Bolton?"

Felice smiled. "Nah, you were right the first time. She's just saying . . . you stink."

Chapter 38

College of the Holy Cross
Worcester, Massachusetts

Jenny felt her heart pounding against her sternum. They'd raced up the sixth-floor landing of the O'Kane Building.

Jake grasped her hand. Her arm was no longer part of her body. Her heart abruptly stopped and the space was hushed.

An explosion of gunfire broke the silence. The floor rattled like thunder. Slugs zinged and cracked the plaster ceiling overhead. Bolton grabbed Jenny and dove onto the carpeted floor. He rolled her toward the near wall, protecting her from the attack. Automatic gunfire riddled the walls and ceiling; splinters flew across the mezzanine above them. He covered her with his chest.

"Stay down!" Jake pulled his gun forward and saucered away from her. "I can't see them. We're trapped. They're below on the stairs."

"There's only one exit out." Jenny said. "That one behind us connecting to the Fenwick Building." She pointed forward. "And that one down the hall into the O'Kane Building."

Jake rolled on to his back, still screening Jenny. "There's another way. A potential exit." He said.

Jake slapped his hand on the wall. "The building has an arch built into the façade. The dirty brick here was once the outside of the building." Jake added and pointed upward. An array of free-floating wooden stairs suspended only by metal cables, much like an attic ladder, stretched out from the middle of the archway. It went directly toward a wooden door cut from the tower. Jake tilted his head toward the wall. "That's 'OK 7.'"

Shards of brick and plaster rained down on them.

"But we'll be out in the open." Jenny yelled.

"They're trying to drive us into a trap. Chess 101!" Jake yelled as he pointed, "we're going up there . . . no stopping . . . I'll cover us."

"Jake, look out!" Jenny screeched. A large cornice bounced off the railing, missing both of them.

Jake yanked her up with one hand and spidered her along

the wall. He reached up with his other hand and pulled the metal cable down, pinning the stair case with his foot. Firing downward over the railing toward the fifth-floor stairs, he dashed with Jenny up the suspended staircase. Bullets carved the stairs into splinters, the wooden steps disintegrating behind them. Jake hit the door with his shoulder, sending it flying open then bouncing back off its hinges and closing. They landed on the floor in darkness.

Jake used his flashlight to search for something to use as cover. Bullets punched holes in the wooden door and clattered off the brick walls inside the room. Small cylinders of light entered through the bullet holes. Jake pushed an old refrigerator across the door. When the gunfire stopped, he risked peeking through one of the newest and largest holes. "He's gone."

Jenny stepped behind Jake. "The hanging staircase is gone too." The remaining appendages of the staircase swung back and forth in space.

"We're not safe here. We need to keep moving." He said.

Jenny moved across the dark room slowly. "Jake, this room is humid and the floor feels loose."

Jake found an old kerosene lamp and several stick matches along the wall. She lit the lamps. The room began to glow. "I hear water dripping." The area beneath the floor slats reflected the light from the lantern.

Jenny watched him move around the room. *There was no obvious way out*. When she looked up, she could make out the ceiling triangulating toward a spiral peak. On one side she could see the back of the clock glass on the watchtower. "This is a separate building. There are no floors below us." They were in the spire of the O'Kane Building. OK 7 was not a floor at all. The makeshift staircase must have been raised for repair work. *But why the lamp? Why a refrigerator?*

Jake slid in front of a long row of wooden easels. A card table nearby was covered with paintbrushes, water bowls, photographs, and tubes of paint spreading out in a kaleidoscope of stains. Four large rain barrels balanced on the edge of the floorboards. He rapped his knuckles against the side of each.

Jenny listened. She tried to hear from where the water was dripping.

Jake kept staring at the paintings on the easels. Jenny

leaned into Jake's shadow.

"We found Father Landry's studio." Jenny said. "These are his paintings. Look! OMG. Here's that painting in the camera. The card on the bottom of the easel says, *"The Nativity."* This is a Caravaggio copy." She tried to catch her breath.

"Do you remember what Sister Catherine said about the savant Martin? The day that Riley had to calm him down?" Jake asked.

"Yes. He was yelling 'Baby Jesus.' He and Riley must have seen this painting. And it was sitting in the Knights of Columbus garage."

"From what I'm learning about Father Landry, these paintings are trying to tell us something. Something he and Riley figured out." Jake said.

Jenny looked up at Jake's eyes glowing against the flickering lantern light. She sensed a moment of partnership.

"We know that Riley and Martin were killed because of this painting." Jake added. "Is this why Landry has gone missing as well? And why we're being chased by that goon?"

"This place is creepy."Jenny shivered. "Do you think they killed Father Landry?"

Jake said nothing, seemingly distracted by the dramatic and garish paintings.

Jenny scanned the easels of paintings. She felt like a trapdoor had opened and dropped her into a wax museum of lifelike figures of street urchins, beheaded saints, and religious allegories. She took a deep breath and studied the mangled bodies strewn across the Caravaggio canvasses. *These must be copies?*

"Jake, you don't think . . . No . . . Father Landry couldn't be an art forger?" She felt the thought like a sharp needle on her arm.

Jake focused intently on the other paintings like they were about to attack. "We've got to find a way out of here. Quickly."

Chapter 39

College of the Holy Cross
Worcester, Massachusetts

The assassin unfolded his Barrett rifle from the black case and pulled the separate Night Ranger rifle scope up to his right eye. He squinted below his bushy red eyebrow. He had an unobstructed view of the O'Kane tower.

Moments earlier he'd slipped on his stolen Holy Cross College maintenance overalls and zigzagged unseen across the campus to a knoll beside the library.

He needed to get his subjects moving again. He propped open his briefcase against a nearby statue, picked out a small electronic device, and he clicked on several switches to light a map-like screen. A small antenna appeared in the corner of the display and two arrows moved back and forth until a flashing red dot appeared. He tuned the machine to the proper area and key-coded the distinct RF waves of Doctor Jenny Neugold's pager. He confirmed that the strong signal provided by a nearby cell tower had pinged a location on the background map. Neugold was still in the tower. His Stingray device could follow her as long as she travelled with her pager.

#

"I don't like these large rain barrels along the walls, these loose floor boards." Jake Bolton lit another kerosene lantern, moved several dusty chairs aside, and handed the light over to Jenny. He stared at the row of easels holding up the paintings. "Is this really a studio? Do these paintings mean anything to you?"

"Yes. These are great forgeries."

"Forgeries? Landry's an art forger?"

"Yes . . . well, no." Jenny felt awkward believing what she was seeing. This was her beloved priest forging famous art. "These are all religious stories that were typically painted during the Baroque period. They're allegories meant to teach the viewer about Roman Catholicism."

"Do you recognize the stories?" Jake asked.

"I found handwritten index cards stuck on the easels on some of them. The cards are numbered. There's an order to these paintings. Some are easy to match up."

"Do you think he's in trouble because he's a con man?" Jake asked.

"I don't know." Jenny continued to struggle. She didn't want to believe it. She felt a wave of tightness in her stomach moving into her chest. Her mentor was cheating? She tried to focus on the images. "This first one must be the *Supper at Emmaus*. You can palpate the emotion. Look at the apostles' surprise. Intense physical reactions painted into their facial and body expressions."

Jake waved his hand. "How about the rest of these?"

"This one is *Incredulity of Saint Thomas*, you know, sticking his hand into the side of Christ. The graphic physical detail of Christ's skin folds with Thomas passing his finger into the abdominal wound." It was so real Jenny sensed tingling in her own index finger. "And this is the *Adoration of the Shepherds*; you can see the barn animals, the baby, and the men bearing gifts. I wasn't sure of this one, but I found a card on the floor nearby, so this must be *The Nativity with Saint Francis and Saint Lawrence*. Jenny saw the rawness of the newborn and could feel the exhaustion of the post partum mother. I can tell that's the one in the camera that Riley and Martin saw. It's in the Baroque Caravaggio style. The others are all in the same style, so I'd guess they're Caravaggio's also. Only . . . they're not the real thing. None of them. These are watercolors. Caravaggio worked in oil." Jenny worked her way uneasily down the row of floorboards.

"You remember all that from college?" Jake asked.

"Yes. It's easy to spot the Caravaggio style."

"Pretty raw. Emotional." He said.

Jenny pointed upward. "I've got it." She thought she might have a logical explanation. "Father Landry is a Caravaggista. Caravaggista were painters that copied his graphically detailed style."

"Why would Landry paint exact Caravaggio copies?"

"Who knows why? None of these were in his office. He had Renaissance-style paintings there." Jenny said.

"Why would Landry put them here? Jenny, I don't believe he's a forger for money. This has something to do with why Riley was killed and Landry may be in trouble."

"I have an idea. There was a famous 1940's art forger named Van Meegeren who painted fake Vermeer paintings, eventually selling *Christ with the Adulteress* to Nazi henchman Herman Goering; he also did a 'newly discovered Vermeer' *Supper at Emmaus* that made a fool out of a famous Dutch art expert who called it an authentic masterpiece. Van Meegeren did it for revenge in a perversely fun way. No. There's no way Landry could be an art forger." She spoke like she was trying to convince herself.

"These are water colors. No one would want these."

"There must be a reason . . ."

"But you said there are oil supplies here. Don't artists make a preliminary painting?"

"Yes. Usually a drawing. But then again, Caravaggio is the only painter in history to paint freehand without drawing—he was just that great. I still don't believe Landry would cheat anyone."

"I've seen all kinds of con men. Crooks disguised as charismatic leaders. Guys like Yasser Arafat, who put a diplomatic face on the PLO, yet stole billions of dollars for himself."

"We've got politicians in D.C. doing the same." She said.

"Could Landry be one of these crooks?"

"Not like you think. The typical art forger is a narcissist with a big ego, a con man that frequently can't keep his mouth shut. Landry is quiet and unassuming. He was up to something else here."

"What if Landry and Riley were trying to create forgeries to trick the smugglers and art thieves?"

"To protect the original art! That would be justice!"

"What if Landry and Riley were trying to deceive someone with a painting?"

"Exactly!" Jenny's heart raced. She felt like her hero, Landry, could be vindicated.

"There are thousands of fakes that are hanging in museums and art collector's homes."

"Landry and Riley were intent on deceiving. Much the way Caravaggio would deceive the viewer. Caravaggio spent his life hiding secrets in his paintings, deceiving the viewer with light and dark. Deception. There's no better way to do it than with a

Caravaggio! But they were doing it to help the art world. Not to fool the art experts . . . but to fool the criminals who were trading art for cash."

"Either he or someone very good is making them. These oil supplies have been used here, too." Jake said.

"If we can find the oil versions, we can find Riley's killer." Jenny grimaced with the words. She blinked as she stared at the vivid images of tortured saints. The ominous saintly figures seemed to stare back at her calling for forgiveness, something that she wasn't ready to give.

"The paintings are all one style, right?"

"Look here, this is *The Crucifixion of Saint Peter.* This is partly in oil. You can see how the men have nailed him to the cross and are straining to turn him upside down."

"Upside down?"

"Yes. Peter was crucified upside down. And this last one is *The Raising of Lazarus.* I really think these are all copies of Caravaggio paintings. But the reds? The red colors are all in oil." She carefully touched the painting.

"Pull out Riley's camera again; snap pictures of each one of these. There may be something that they have in common besides Caravaggio." Jake waved his hands as if painting the scene before them. "Maybe a theme? Also, get a wide shot of all of them just in case Landry did that thing again where you stand back like you're taking in the whole forest."

Jenny bit her lip, entranced with the images. Jake turned and ran a hand along the walls, seemingly looking for an exit. *Okay*, she thought, *to each his specialty.*

She started taking pictures.

#

The assassin spied a small van driving up to the main college gate and froze. The van drove past the grassy embankment, followed a curve in the road, and then disappeared. He crouched slowly like a spider and brought his bushy red eyebrows up to the scope. The building had wide steps and classic columns. He homed in on Jenny Neugold's signal location one more time and read off the Stingray quadrants: *Range . . . a hundred meters, elevation . . . forty-one degrees, wind five west.*

He readied his final firing position, noting the moisture on the knoll while aiming toward the clock tower. He could not see his target but knew where she would be. Pratt had ordered him to take out the woman—assuring him Bolton would stay on the trail for the paintings. The sharpshooter would follow the orders with precision. Pratt would get his information. But, most importantly, his other boss, his religion, his Order of the Alhambra held a higher calling for the shooter. He wanted the paintings.

The sharpshooter calibrated his shot across the quadrangle.

#

"I wish I had a CAD," Jenny muttered.

"A what?" Jake answered.

"A CAD. But for painting. We have computer-aided diagnosis technology in medicine to help with patient examinations. It's this complex computer program that takes thousands of laboratory tests and images or sounds, and then looks for a pathologic pattern. It can be helpful for early detection of a disease the human eye might overlook. For example, even the best radiologists can pass by a cluster of calcification on a mammogram that might be an early warning of cancer, or a cardiologist may miss a specific sound examining someone's heartbeat with a stethoscope that might tell us that there's a birth defect. If we had the CAD for painted images, I think we could figure this one out."

"Maybe if we find Father Landry we won't need one."

"Why don't you give this display a look?"

Jake glanced up and down the row of canvases. "I don't see anything. Religion. The Bible stories. Saints. I don't get it." He knelt down and rocked on the unsteady floorboards.

"Keep looking. Try again."

"Yeah. There's *some* kind pattern here. Simple but . . ."

"What? What do you see?" Jenny asked. She could feel that he had Riley's gift that could decipher the clues.

"Reaching out to us. There's someone pointing in every one of the paintings. This one, the first one in the row, this figure points toward us." Jake gestured at *The Supper at Emmaus.* He moved to the second canvas, *The Burial of Saint Lucy.* "This dead person has her hand out, calling us in."

"Yes. Yes." Jenny stumbled with her excitement. She stopped and caught herself, exhaling quickly. She walked to the third easel. "Here's Christ pointing to Saint Matthew—"

An explosion sounded overhead and an avalanche of white glass from the clock face came raining down on them. Jake raised one hand to protect his face and extended the other toward Jenny, pushing her head down to safety across the room. The easels tumbled down onto the floorboards. Bullets blew apart the clock tower.

"We've got to get out of here." Jake yelled.

"There's only one way."

"No. They're trying to force us out that door again."

"The police should be here soon."

"They're tracking us somehow. Did you make any calls with your cell phone?"

"No."

"Tell me exactly what's in your backpack."

"There's nothing in my bag but some medical instruments and a few personal things."

"Like what?" Shards of glass fell around them.

Jenny unzipped her backpack. "My gun . . ."

"A gun? You're carrying a gun?"

"Yes. Riley and I each got one. Working in Hartford is dangerous. She took me to the range a few times."

He looked at the black Ruger 9 mm. He murmured, "this will stop the guys."

She continued digging in his bag. "My night kit, stethoscope, loupes, drug book, dressing materials, emergency aid kit, pager. Two pairs of socks and a change of underwear. A toothbrush and a comb. I'd brought my guitar but couldn't fit it. Riley's camera."

"A pager? Let me see that." Jake reached. She handed it to him. He flipped it around in his hand. "This is a radiofrequency device. The hospital has this number. The shooter has it. He's got a Stingray."

"I assume a Stingray is a tracking device?" She asked.

"This is how they've been following us." Jake saw the large hole in the roof where the clock once was. He wound up and threw the pager out.

The bullets hit the upper corner of the room. The sniper had to be shooting from a lower angle. Jenny could feel the floorboards shaking under her feet. Suddenly one of the rain barrels rocked and fell, spilling the water. She heard a second splash. *Water hitting water? Is that water below us?*

"Jenny, the floor is breaking! Grab this board and hold on to the wall!" Jake put her hand on a piece of wood extending from the brick face.

Jake lost his footing and disappeared into the darkness below the vanishing floor.

He hit a pool of water and submerged. Darkness. No sound.

"Jake! Jake? Where are you?"

"Below you. In the water. The floor's on top of a pool of water." She pulled a lantern and saw the rain barrels emptying their contents into the pool. The paintings were floating around him, their colors dissolving in the vat of water. "Get in," he said. "This must be the way out. There's air coming up."

"What about the paintings?"

"Forget the paintings. There's no time. They're gone. Hurry. I feel the water level dropping. The barrels must have triggered the drain. Jump toward my voice. We're going for a ride."

Jenny blew out the air in her lungs. *I can do this. This is it, I'm going with him.* She turned back and plunged through the open boards and landed next to Jake. He put her hands on his shoulders. "Hold on to me."

The water level dropped, then started to swirl, sucking them rapidly down an enormous pipe. Into darkness.

Chapter 40

Airborne
Sixty Miles East of Grenada, Spain

Charles Pratt jumped from his chair, propelling his fold down desk into the air. His notes fluttered about the jet cabin. "The graves are real."

Professor Geoffrey Willis wind milled his hands and grabbed some of the papers. His voice clamored. "I said you're being mugged. The headstones on these Knights' graves record them dying twenty years before *The Winter's Tale* was printed or performed. Twenty years!"

Pratt threw his hands out, pressing downward on an invisible flat surface, calming himself. He closed his eyes and sat back in his chair. "I missed that. *This* is why I need your help."

Pratt reached down and clutched a fistful of his scattered notes from the floor. "As you can see, Professor, I have all kinds of pieces of the puzzle. I have information on Shakespeare, the Knights Hospitaller, Romano, King Charles the Fifth, and Caravaggio. I need someone like you to help me pull it together." He got up and walked hand over hand between the leather seats of the Learjet.

"Caravaggio?"

"Yes."

"That mad painter?"

"Maybe, maybe." Pratt's voice trailed off, as if the secret were a balloon that had just deflated. "He might be the most significant clue to the secret of the Knights Hospitaller."

"What secret?"

"That's where I need your help."

"I'm afraid I can't help you. I don't know much about Caravaggio."

"I don't expect you to. I found a priest who's a Caravaggio expert but he got away."

"Got away? What do you mean he 'got away?'"

"Like I said, I had him . . . and he escaped."

"You're a crackpot. Most people just look up information

in a book or on the Internet. You, you . . . . kidnap the experts and shake them down?"

Pratt threw the papers back onto the floor of the plane. "The Internet is more public than you realize. I don't think it'll be a secret if I'm searching for paintings the FBI has on its most wanted list, paintings that some high-powered Knights have hidden for hundreds of years." He interlocked his fingers behind his head, and then looked down at Willis.

There was a long moment of silence. Like they'd ended their arguing. "You'd have to explain the dates on the headstones." Willis said.

"Let's assume they died right there during the war in Ireland around 1600. Then suppose these headstones were put up well after the Knights were buried."

"Are you sure there're Knights actually buried there?"

"Yes, we dug a few of them up."

"You dug up dead bodies?" Willis screeched. "You dug up some dead Knights? And you're worried that the FBI will come after you for searching paintings on the Internet? Now that's balancing the scales of justice, lad."

"Cut the crap." Pratt hissed back.

"I'm satisfied. There's no battle of conflicting morals going on inside you. You're just solid in your depravity."

"We reburied them when we were done."

"Very thoughtful. I don't want to know what other unspeakable wrongs you've done." Willis paused. "Just tell me how you know they're Knights?"

"We didn't know for sure that the Knights were buried in Ireland until they were discovered at St. Michan's Church in Dublin during a renovation." Pratt stood. "A catacomb was discovered that contained innumerable burial chambers and rows of caskets. The caskets were suspended in limestone and engulfed by methane gas. That combination preserved the cadavers. In one of the chambers, our archeologists found a man buried with a long sword and his legs crossed. That doesn't just happen because a corpse is too tall for a casket."

"It sounds familiar." Professor Willis agreed.

"Beginning around 1550, English writers started referring to tombstone effigies with crossed legs. They make clear that this was an honor bestowed only on kings, queens, royalty, and . . . crusading Knights. The Knights Templar elsewhere are all buried with their legs crossed."

"And you know the men with Shakespearean verses on their gravestones were Knights Hospitaller because . . . ?"

"The graves we found also contained men whose legs were crossed. Just like in St. Michan's."

"But that just makes them Knights." Willis said

"Yes. But the tombstones all had a mysterious marker. A cross running through the crown. The King's crown. A crisscrossed shepherd's staff and lance. A medical lance. They were doctors . . . of sorts. Only the Knights Hospitaller used the medical lance in their symbols."

The Shakespeare scholar scuttled across the cabin. He bit his thumb like he was calculating. "Yes. I can recall effigies on the coffins in the Temple Church and Westminster Abbey in London—they're all cross-legged."

"Yes. A few royals. And many men known to be Knights Templar, fighters who were buried with their swords."

"I still don't understand what all this has to do with Shakespeare and Romano in *The Winter's Tale*."

"Caravaggio and Romano were religious men of the Knights Hospitaller. I believe that Shakespeare knew the clues that first Romano, then Caravaggio concealed in their own art. They knew the secrets of their own religious order. I think Shakespeare immortalized Romano in *The Winter's Tale* by calling him a sculptor, making it his own contribution to the secret treasure of the Knights Hospitaller."

"There are enough professors in London who'll claim that's a conspiracy. Romano was a complete unknown when it came to art."

"Shakespeare calls Romano a sculptor. One who brings someone alive in the play. But Romano was never a sculptor, right Professor?"

"True."

"Why doesn't Shakespeare mention the great Michelangelo or da Vinci as artists of that generation?" Pratt asked.

"Agreed. They were much more influential artists." Willis said.

"Romano knew something."

"But Romano wasn't a sculptor. It's a dead end."

"Aha!!! But devout Roman Catholic King Charles V was his biggest patron. And Romano was part of the Knights Hospitaller—King Charles' men!"

"Is Romano's name a reference to the Knights Hospitaller?" Willis murmured.

"The Knights Templar disappeared when the Crusades ended, about 1300 A.D. But the men who were Knights did not just go away. They were absorbed into the less controversial and more clandestine Knights Hospitaller. The Templars' money, their power, their influence, their land all slowly dissolved into the hands of the Knights Hospitaller. The Templars used the Knights Hospitaller to disappear in plain sight? To enter society even more rich and powerful?

"Throughout the Mediterranean, the Middle East and Asia the Knights Hospitaller were the most feared and respected Knights. They were smart and sublime. And uber wealthy. They saved hundreds of thousands of lives, including the enemies they defeated, in their hospitals with 'magic.' A magic that no doctor could replicate."

"Then what is the connection to Romano and Shakespeare?"

"Wait." Pratt raised his index finger. "Those Knights were constantly on the move from Jerusalem, Cyprus, Rhodes, Malta, and Rome. Fighting to the last man alive. As if they knew they wouldn't be that last man. Never the last man." Pratt emphasized the last two words. "The new Templars, had only one mission: preserving their society's greatest treasure, the secret to eternal life on earth. With time and modernity, their numbers dwindled. They couldn't allow the secret itself to be lost. So they concealed the mystery." Pratt felt the heat of excitement rise around him like a curtain. He wiped his forehead fully expecting to be drenched in sweat. He felt that the secret was right there pulsating near him. In a space hidden by time or history . . . lurking behind some shade that needed to be pulled back. He'd grasp the secret and hold it up as his own. Everyone around him would then say, "That was so obvious, why didn't we see that?"

"Where?"

"I think the Knights buried it in Ireland in such a way to guard the secret."

Charles Pratt ran his hands through his thinning hair. Professor Willis looked out the plane's window as if considering whether he should jump.

Chapter 41

Bottom of St. James Hill
Worcester, Massachusetts

The sound of rushing water filled Jenny's ears. The darkness grew deeper as she swung from side-to-side inside the high-speed water slide. Jake wrapped his arms around Jenny holding her steady.

Jenny looked down at her feet, hoping to slow her frenzied descent. The ride was unstoppable. Her gut tightened with each turn and she shivered in the waves. Foam battered her face. She gasped for breath and shook her head. Her stomach clenched. She turned back to survival mode. *There was a raging river beneath the college. The runoff pipe from the tower must connect with groundwater.*

Jenny could see a light exploding into the view in front of her. She burst into the open air and rolled to an abrupt stop. A drenched Jake was behind her, sitting in the shallow water.

She coughed precipitously, forcing the water from her mouth and nose. The stark feeling of choking came over her. Her chest hurt so much she felt like her lungs were falling out. She swallowed and spit, then felt the relief of breathing easier. She puckered and faintly whistled out the air in relief.

"Whew!" Jenny sat in the small pool, recovering from the wild ride. "Now that was a baptism I don't want to do again!"

Sitting in a concrete viaduct, Jenny fisted her hair dry. She took in the surroundings. A second large pipe at ground level sank into the earth, clearly designed to pick up any storm water and carry it under the nearby highway overpass. Jenny snapped back and recognized that they'd reached the bottom of the hilly campus, well outside its main gates. Light bounced off a billboard on the nearby highway. They were alone. It was safe for them to rest.

She grasped the concrete curves of the viaduct and pulled herself up. Kaleidoscopic graffiti covered the concrete walls of the highway overpass. Exaggerated cursive script blurred into stylized print. Intricate, interlocking calligraphy and round popcorn lettering bubbled into murals, some with surprisingly good 3-D effects.

"Is this how Alice would feel lost in a twenty-first century wonderland?" Jenny observed.

Jake extended his hand to her. *He wants my hand. We made it this far, we're in this together now for sure.*

"We need to keep moving." Jake pulled Jenny out of the stream of water and began walking toward the highway overpass.

Jenny collected her wet medical bag and started following him. Something bothered her. She felt a sense of familiarity to the dark street. A coldness ran down her back like fingertips on her spine. She turned back and studied the scene. *Like someone was watching.* There was a street sign dangling from the fence post. She could just make out the block letters: NO OUTLET.

"It can't be." Jenny blurted out. "Riley used to joke about bringing one of those signs to work during one Urology rotation." *Riley knew how to take the simplest things in the world, turn them on their side, and find humor.* She went over and touched the sign in affectionate memory; it fell to the asphalt, echoing under the bridge.

"Quiet!" Jake hissed.

"Not my fault. It just fell."

The sign landed on its face. Jenny put the edge of her foot on the metal square. One word, written in bold, red cursive, cut the sign's diagonal: "Riles." Jenny lifted the sign and silently waved it to Jake.

Jake forced out a whisper. "What?"

"Riley wrote on the back of the sign. She was here."

Jake grabbed the sign from Jenny. He stared at the letters. "Give me a minute to think." He looked back up the hill toward the college. "How did she know," he murmured.

Jenny walked into the viaduct, looking more closely at the graffiti diffusely decorating the walls. The first part of the façade looked different from other parts of the mural. She pondered the scenes on the mural. *The ship "in the distance" seemed right. As if floating away from the water in the viaduct. But there was something . . . yes, below the ship. There it was.* A stack of bold letters, distinct and blocked out from the remainder of the wild drawings.

U R O L O G Y

Q S T A B R F

D C V Z W H E

G K K X D I R

A O L T V X Y

A S R F I L G

T T B D V K D

Q R Y X H Y O

Jenny quietly took the sign from Jake's hands, and then led him to the ship image.

He looked up and down the wall. "It's a cipher." He said. "Riley was here. This was 'just in case.' Riley knew she was in trouble. And she staggered the clues on the path. This is why she contacted me."

"Notice the first line says 'urology'? She's shouting 'Jenny, remember our urology rotation.' She knew I'd make it here with you Jake."

Jake smiled. She felt the warm response. *It's something.*

"She always called me her backup and this is why she had me do so many of her puzzles." Jenny placed both her hands on Jake's wrist. She felt the powerful muscles in his hand. Jake didn't change his gaze from the wall.

"Yes. It's a cipher." Jake said. "The first row is your clue. 'Riles' on the sign was meant for me. My pet name for her. My wonderful, annoying sister had plans for us, Jenny. I'm sure of it. This was a Hail Mary. Regardless of what the prize at the end of this road is, Riles got in way over her head."

Jenny studied the letters. She felt a sudden rush of recognition. "The J, U, and W are missing. Those are absent from the Latin alphabet. The rest of these eye-chart lines make for a Latin cipher." She said.

"How do you know?"

"I've studied Latin. My Mom always told me Latin would help me in medicine." *I didn't think I'd need it to track my best friend's killer.* She thought. "We need to get this."

There was a sudden cracking noise.

Jenny pulled out the camera. Jake turned to say, "No," but before he could, the flash shattered the darkness beneath the bridge.

"Quick. Give me the damn camera." Jake shouted.

#

Jake placed the camera into his backpack. Then he felt the cold steel barrel of a gun against the back of his neck. He slowly raised his hands.

#

"Don't move," instructed the man standing behind him.

Jake assessed the threat. The barrel felt like a generic street gun; it was pointing up, so the man was shorter by at least six inches, right-handed. His accent was vaguely Hispanic. The man sounded nervous, and his voice came from the side, as if he were looking around. The odds were extremely high that this was a local gang member. Jenny was in front of him, momentarily screened from danger.

"I'm not armed. I won't move," Jake said, sounding like they were instructions to her. He dropped his backpack.

Jenny turned and waved her hands at the man holding the gun. "Hey, get the frick out of here!"

"What?" The startled young man moved his gun, shifting to this new target. That split second was all Jake needed. He swung his elbow downward, sending the gun to the asphalt, and then kicked backward into the man's groin. He grabbed the gun and, in one swift motion, emptied the rounds onto the ground. He quickly found his backpack and retrieved his own loaded gun.

He covered the few feet to Jenny and glided her to the ground with his left hand. There, near the corner of the underpass, another assailant started running. Jake fired over the bushes. As the man disappeared, Jake grabbed the man on the ground. He emptied the man's pockets and threw his car keys into the pool of water.

#

The young man studied Jake and Jenny. Seventeen at the

oldest. "Who the frick are you guys?" He asked.

"I can't believe I just did that." Jenny shuddered.

Jake pulled out the man's belt and rolled the man onto his stomach before tying him up.

"He's not part of the hunt. Just a coincidence. But nothing brings cops like gunfire. Put a fire under those feet, Jenny. We need to get to Boston."

Chapter 42

CIA Headquarters
Langley, Virginia

"It looked like I killed Jake. Craziest frickin' move." Karen Smith jerked the knob of her baseball bat up to her chin and glanced away from CIA Deputy Director Felice.

"How so?" the FBI man asked.

"You should read his file." Smith stopped, pondering whether she should ask, *can you guys at the FBI read?*

"Give me the Spark Notes."

"Jake Bolton is a master in Raumschach chess. Do you know what that is?"

"No."

"It's three-dimensional chess. Three-D. It's played on eight checkerboards suspended on each other. Looks like a Hungarian Dobos tarte. It requires the player to control spatial resolution, anticipation, actuarial analysis and mathematical modeling into a game of war."

"Like majoring in ORFE at Princeton?"

"OAR . . . FEE?" Smith knew the man was bragging about his degree. *But that arrogance isn't going to save your butt out in the field.*

"Operation Research and Financial Engineering." FBI man replied.

"You could say for Jake, he's an ORFE major on steroids. The rook moves through the six *faces* of a cube in any rank, file, or column. A bishop, for example, moves through the twelve *edges* of the cube. The knight makes leaps up and down, enabling it to control 24 different cells from the board's center. Of course, the queen can combine the moves of all three. Playing this game gives Jake the vision to see action and reaction in the world around him. He's like a real knight."

"What move did he pull in Rome?"

"In counter-sniper tactics it's called a Rush."

"I've heard of it. At the FBI Hostage Rescue Unit."

Yeah, they always hear about it in their classrooms. Then there are those that live and breathe it like Jake. She thought.

"Like a sniper attack, we were pinned down. They were going to pick us off one by one. Let's just say he pulled a knight move on one of those eight layer chess boards."

"What happened?"

"Jake and I were in Rome working with the Swiss Guard to foil an assassination attempt on Pope Benedict when we got a promising midnight tip about a tattoo artist sitting on a potential lead.

"Soon we're trudging down this godforsaken backstreet of Dumpsters, parked Vespas, and feral cats when shooting erupts. We're pinned down when four guys in ski masks close down the alley on us. No way out.

"They were real pros, automatic weapons, closing tactics, suppression fire, brick fragments raining down on us, the whole blazing mess . . . Jake and I were crouched down in the corner behind a Dumpster. I figure we're toast." Smith paused to visualize the memory. "Jake Bolton was cool and cunning. He sets out a plan. He runs out into the open, firing his two guns wildly so the gunmen will dive for cover. He turns to have me shoot him dead center in his vest. As he spins and drops to the ground, three of their guys are so stunned that they show themselves. Just enough time and space. Jake rolls and nails the two of them in succession and I get the third. The other one bugs out. A couple of deep breaths and he's back in form. We'd been set up, of course."

Smith turned to look at Felice and the FBI agent. There was no response.

The agent spoke first. "Holy crap. What if you missed?"

Felice shook his head.

"Who set you up?" the FBI agent continued.

Felice turned to the agent. "It was the Syrians. They've been after Jake Bolton ever since they suspected he knocked off Mughniyah right in their front yard."

"You're talking about a guy who's cameled the Sahara Desert, tackled a charging lion and, for fun, swims with Great White Sharks off the coast of South Africa. To do all that Jake does, you need cunning, vigilance and a belief in immortality."

The FBI agent looked uneasy scanning the hallways for an exit.

Smith nodded. "Kevin, he's not warning me. This isn't a telephone number in the police report. These are coordinates. He's sending me a message," Smith continued. "He wants me to meet him in Rome!"

"How about Jake is trying to tell you this is a trap? He's warning you to stay away." The FBI suit asked.

"Not Jake's style. Not mine. He knows me."

Felice seemed worried. "Anytime Jake comes out into the open he's a target of one of these nut-job assassins. We've been very careful with information on Jake. You sure you want to jeopardize his cover?"

"His cover is blown already. Do you remember 1995, Kevin? When we found out how much KGB counterintelligence we'd swallowed? All because we thought the Soviets were so inept and we were so superior? It was premature closure and arrogance. And all those years we didn't even suspect our own moles, like Ames and Hansen and Pitts, were feeding them Intel. We make incorrect assumptions that we find a way to confirm. Then we base our next decisions on that Intel. Don't underestimate the world from your enemy's perspective. Jake doesn't."

"It was an embarrassing mistake." Felice nodded.

She turned to the FBI agent. "Do you know what game theory is?"

"Of course." The agent said.

"It's a science now. Jake understood it long before people studied it for the sake of strategic thinking.

"We all study strategy at the academy."

"Game theory is much deeper than strategy. That's what makes him a great chess player. And, a great operative. He gets into the head of his opponent. It's not about what HE would do in the opponent's position. Uses their own quirks, fears, and strengths against them. Out in the field . . . he doesn't work like he's inside another man's shoes. He thinks the way the opponent thinks in *their* shoes. He'll do this with the young doctor he's traveling with."

"All the more reason we should go in." The agent said.

"No." Felice added.

"You think you're playing chess on a single flat board and Jake is several levels above you, looking down. Right now? He's already in deep hunting the *Nativity* painting because it leads to his sister's killer." Smith said.

"Okay. I'm letting you back in the field. But not alone," Felice added.

They both looked at the FBI agent leaning against the wall. "No. Not you. I dread the paperwork of an interagency personnel loss," the director said as he walked away.

Smith threw her bat over her shoulder and sauntered down the hallway.

Chapter 43

Airborne
Ninety Miles East of Grenada, Spain

"Yes, Professor. Shakespeare and Giulio Romano. I assume you recognize the connection from your own doctoral thesis?" Charles Pratt wagged his finger in his guest's face.

Professor Geoffrey Willis nodded.

Either the turbulence across the jet wings or the weight of the Romano connection stole Professor Willis's legs from under him. He thumped back into his chair.

"There's no proof that Shakespeare ever got out of England, let alone to Italy. Let alone saw Romano's paintings."

"What if this detour within Shakespeare's play is intentional? The Bard was notorious for double meanings, for hiding truths so the viewer could ferret them out. Was he concealing a truth about Romano?"

"Go on." Willis replied.

"Let me read those key lines from *The Winter's Tale* again: 'newly performed by that rare Italian master, Julio Romano, who, had he himself eternity and could put breath into his work, would beguile Nature of her custom, so perfectly he is her ape.'" Pratt put extra emphasis on the word "breath."

"So?"

"You said it yourself, Professor."

"I never said that."

"Your thesis did. Shakespeare doesn't describe the appearance of the statue of Hermione, but rather how Romano *could make* her appear. Even after Shakespeare describes the queen, you still have no idea what she looks like. It's about how he *could make* her. You understood this once. Hermione is described only in the terms of Romano's greatness and skill as a sculptor, as an artist, as a purveyor of *reincarnation*."

"Shakespeare is using Romano to praise himself. He's saying that an artist can confer eternity." Willis sculpted several curves in the air with his hands.

"No. Shakespeare is talking about something else altogether. He's talking about something Romano really could do. He wasn't describing a beautiful queen. He was describing Romano as a Knights Hospitaller." Pratt said.

Willis flushed red. "Hogwash. I think I'd rather be locked up with a cage full of Oxfordians nattering that Shakespeare isn't Shakespeare!" Willis retorted.

"Romano is indeed a nobody to academics. Even if Shakespeare ignored da Vinci and Michelangelo. But to the world Romano lived in, he was a Knight with knowledge that could bring breath into God's work. A doctor Knight. Like all of them. With knowledge of a secret that could cure man from his illnesses." Pratt insisted.

"It's hard to know exactly who was important during that time."

"Really? Why Shakespeare's emphasis on "sculpture" when Romano was only a painter? Think about it. You claimed in your thesis the importance of Romano's one famous sculpture. One and only one. Describe it."

Willis swallowed hard. "Christ points out at the visitor to the grave."

"What does that pointing mean professor?" Pratt emphasized the word "pointing."

"During that era, pointing to the viewer had profound religious implications. It meant the power to reincarnate. To heal. To cure."

"And this same sculpted pose of Hermione is the inspiration for Caravaggio's renowned Lazarus painting in Sicily. Caravaggio specifically said it was." Pratt then spoke in staccato fashion, emphasizing each and every word. "Christ extends his hand out toward Lazarus. It's not so much the identity of the characters that's important but rather that the pointing is the power to reincarnate."

"A desperate desire to see a pattern. So you make one up. Don't you have anything better to do with your time?" He took off his glasses and squinted at his captor.

"As a matter of fact, I don't have time."

"You're mad. Starkers. Is this some midlife crisis?"

"Worse. Much worse." Pratt ran his tongue across his lower

lip. "I'm dying."

The professor stiffened. He puffed his cheeks with air and blew outward. "Then indeed you're the 'man clothed in purple and fine linen'?"

Pratt sighed. "If you say so."

"And you think there's a cure out there for you? A way to save yourself from the inevitable? Death is going to skip over you? Maybe you should be looking at *Hamlet* instead of *Winter*. You might find real consolation there."

"Don't underestimate my commitment to finding this answer. A great medical cure. I have the resources."

"And you think you can change destiny by finding this secret? You're digging up dead Knights to find it? You're kidnapping people to get your hands on it?

"I've found the Caravaggio paintings."

Pratt cocked his head upward. "You mean your hired guns are stealing paintings too?"

"Within a year of Caravaggio leaving Rome, he'd painted his greatest masterpiece, had been forgiven by the Pope for a brutal murder, had been ordained a religious Knight of the Hospitallers, had been imprisoned on Malta, escaped, excommunicated and was then on the run with virtually every military and religious organization in Europe trying to find or kill him. A manhunt of epic proportions . . . for a painter?! Come on! I think his easy escape suggests a greater mystery. I think *some* Knight set him free so he could paint the secrets the Knights Hospitaller held over the Roman Catholic Church. A secret cure in the wrong hands that would make the Church obsolete. But the Pope lured Caravaggio back to Italy with a rumor of a pardon so that the Spanish guards could kill him and spare the Catholic Church the embarrassment of an ugly trial."

"Then you're willing to do anything. You *are* the 'man clothed in purple.' Who are those other men helping you?"

"Men from the Order of the Alhambra. They share the goal of recovering lost religious art. They're devout. They'll do anything to help find the art. I told them they can keep the paintings when I find my secret."

"The Knights' secret." Willis insisted.

"I only need to borrow it." Pratt replied.

"What else have you done?"

The wealthy man ignored the question. "Romano was hiding something. The Roman Catholic Church knew it. Charles the Fifth respected and feared it. Shakespeare embraced it. Then he saw what it was. He saw what Romano had done. By 1610, Shakespeare knew he was dying of syphilis. He knew he couldn't get to Italy and be cured, so he left a clue for his great patron, Lord Wriothesley. While the Knights Hospitaller were dying in Ireland so late in their years they preserved the secret. In their last act of chivalry they engraved lines from Shakespeare's great play of resurrection on their own headstones. Those lines are preserved in history and geography where no one would move them. I'm dying and I need that secret now."

Chapter 44

Cleary's Pub
South Boston

Jake stepped out of his third stolen car of the day into a dimly lit parking lot. He circled around to the passenger side. Jenny awoke and got out. He lifted her up in one swoop when she stepped into a puddle.

Across the street rose a long row of buildings, each seeming to have split like an amoeba from the building beside it. Fading yellow light bathed the cornices but barely penetrated the alleys. The parent building was a dilapidated triple-decker. Its top porch was screened in and anchored by a spring-loaded fire escape. Old-style antennas mixed with modern satellite dishes rising like antlers from the roof. The bar on the first floor had been lengthened out from the house. Metal gratings covered its small windows. A banner hanging above the door announced a local sports show hosted by Dennis & Callahan.

He felt a rush of adrenaline race through his chest. An alley was visible at one end of the old pub building. At the other, he saw a cinder-block wall sprouting weeds. The wall was meant to hide a large Dumpster now overflowing with white plastic bags. The dark street facing Cleary's Pub melted into a highway.

Jake studied the orange light from the street mixing with a flickering neon Budweiser sign. The shadows cast by even his slightest movements made him uneasy. The haphazard alignment of the cars reminded him of how difficult urban warfare was in Afghanistan. Normally he identified enemies by noting signs of disorder, incongruity, and unexpected movement. The orientation of the lights and cars was thwarting his surveillance routine.

There was sudden chatter behind them.

Jake wrapped his arm around Jenny's shoulder so they could look more like two lovers. Or two drunks. "You and I are now in the business of saving lives." Jenny's eyes twinkled. She moved in closer to him as they walked.

"Jake . . . I just. Never mind."

"Really? I just saved your pretty little butt back there." Jake declared.

"Oh, you did, did you? You want a gold star? I was the one who got the guy to drop the gun. Those guys are chickens. They back down."

"You move like a queen on a chess board. No boundaries."

"You have a problem with that?"

"Nope. As long as you're on my side."

"I am."

"Where'd you learn that?"

"Catholic school." Jenny replied. Jake shot her a smile and lowered his arm to her waist.

Jake thought she looked seductive. She squeezed her arm on his waist.

"Once you enter this bar Jenny, some nasty people will have seen you. They will come after you. You can turn back now and I can go on from here. This is your last chance."

"Like I said, I'm staying in. With you. I want to find Riley's killer."

#

Jake smiled. She knew he liked her spunk. *He senses what Riley had seen in me.*

At the back of the building, the door opened suddenly. A man with two hands on his belt rocked back and forth as he ran into the metal garbage cans, grunted, then started urinating against the Dumpster wall. Jake kept her moving past him before the door closed.

The darkness of the hallway concealed years of spilled beer, and a sweet stickiness pulled at their feet. Jenny thought of the man at the Dumpster and grimaced back at Jake. The smell of vomit was much more sour than at the hygienic ER. The sounds of a televised baseball game blended with the shouts of disgruntled patrons. Fluorescent ceiling lights blinked like slot machines.

Jenny and Jake exited the hallway and entered the bar area where the shadows melted into three-dimensional people shrouded in smoke. A few waitresses weaved between small wooden tables. Some patrons threw darts at a grubby target, while others rested their bellies beneath the edge of a horseshoe-shaped bar.

Jake's eyes darted back and forth, seemingly deciphering the haze. He moved his arm off her waist and placed his hand in hers, displaying a new warmth. He elevated his head and appeared to survey the room cautiously. Then he turned to Jenny. "I see Yoke. Wait here by the bar. Here are the keys. If there's trouble, just run to the car. I won't be far behind."

Jenny jumped onto a lone open bar stool, trying to ignore the dirt and sweat she was sure would make a Petri dish come alive. She was thinking of a long soak in a bathtub of hand sanitizer when an aproned bartender broke her reverie. "What can I get you?"

"Guinness, please."

She studied the grey rag used to clean the bar. Visions of a New Jersey gas station attendant came to mind.

Jenny jumped when she felt a hand passing up the inside of her right thigh. A middle-aged man smiled from the next stool. "Would you like to play with my darts, sweetheart?" In his right fist he clenched a couple of feathered spikes. She half-sneered a smile but lost all sense of courtesy when he exposed his oyster shell teeth.

Jenny browsed down the bar. Jake was talking to a big man with a greying red mustache. The man gave a curt nod to his left, lifted the bar railing, and gestured to Jake to follow. They disappeared into a back room behind the half doors. Jenny looked her neighbor up and down.

"Sir, please remove your hand." She said in a gritty voice.

"Oh, sorry, I was trying to get your attention."

"You did. Move it."

"I was just being friendly."

"Instead, you hit my cremasteric reflex. Do you know what that is?" She shifted on the stool with a pained glare.

"No. Sounds like something I want to know."

Jenny clawed the forefinger and thumb together on her left hand. "There are these tiny primitive sensory and motor fibers that extend from the lower lumbar spine and innervate the thigh. When tickled at the thigh, they cause stimulation all the way up into the pelvis." She lifted one eyebrow toward the man.

"Whoa. I like the primitive and pelvis part."

"I bet you do. Let me teach you a similar trick. Did you know surgeons can stretch your skin so thin you can't feel anything penetrating? I'll just take your left hand off my thigh and put it up here on the bar."

"Okay."

Jenny lifted the man's hand onto the bar, then gently separated his thumb and forefinger and held his hand splayed on the oak board. "You see the forefinger here and the thumb here? Now let me extend them a bit. See? There is a web of skin between these fingers that can be thinned out. Let me stretch your fingers just a bit more to demonstrate."

The man nodded in recognition.

Very gently, Jenny used her own fingers as calipers. "When skin is stretched, like this, there is decreased sensitivity." Then, with one swift motion, she grabbed the darts from his right hand and slammed one through his left, nailing the offending hand to the wooden bar. The man screamed in pain.

She took the second dart, spun, and fired it across the room, hitting the dartboard from twenty feet away. Patrons applauded.

Jake appeared from around the corner and pulled up to her side. He looked at the third dart still in Jenny's hand. "I didn't know you played darts." Jake took the dart and hit the board, right next to Jenny's shot.

The man next to Jenny was still trying to pull the dart from his hand. Jake looked at the man whose hand was bleeding profusely onto the bar. "Wow, you'd better be careful. Those things are sharp. Maybe my friend can help you. She's a doctor."

The man pulled out the dart, and headed to the washroom.

Jake took Jenny by the elbow. "Sorry to take you away from your new friend, but we have an appointment. Gloucester Harbor. We leave for Ireland at oh four hundred."

Chapter 45

Leonardo da Vinci Airport
Rome, Italy

Karen Smith took a deep breath as the plane hit the runway. Her first instinct was to secure her briefcase.

By its military role and conspicuous size, the Lockheed C-130 was perfect cover for her CIA persona. The plane turned toward the U.S. military hangar. The pilot parked the Hercules perpendicular to the hangar, blocking any peripheral view of her arrival.

Greeting her in the hangar were Mary Palazzo, longtime Rome station chief, and Giancarlo "Slo Fiz" Carbone, two smart colleagues but unfortunate scapegoats of the Niger yellowcake uranium forgeries. Like many good people in the intelligence community they were bright, hardworking, and dedicated. They were not, however, infallible.

Carbone and Palazzo were both working in Rome in 2002 when the Italian military intelligence service, SISME, passed vetted documents to the CIA suggesting an active contact between Saddam Hussein and the purchase of uranium from Niger. Their synthesis misled the Bush administration and Congress that Hussein possessed weapons of mass destruction. Eventually, the documents were revealed as forgeries. When Iraq was liberated and no WMD was found, Carbone and Palazzo were quietly demoted in the intelligence community.

Although Smith had faith in Jake, she was wary that some phantom message hidden in a Caravaggio painting could be her own downfall.

"Mary. Slo Fiz, good to see you."

"Welcome back. It's been too long. We've got your Caravaggio brief." Palazzo said.

"It's been a long time since I was in Rome. I have some idea where to start, but we've a lot of real estate to cover. I appreciate your help."

"Jake is out there. Smith, is this personal?" Palazzo asked.

Smith bristled. "No. Not me. It might be for him. You don't just kill Jake Bolton's sister in front of him and get away with it."

"We've contacted the Vatican and they'll give us immediate access," Carbone said.

"Great. Do you know where we should start?"

"We identified an expert on Caravaggio who's worked in Rome. But you won't like this. He's that Jesuit priest Landry who's gone missing." Palazzo replied.

"What?"

"Yeah. Jake and Genevieve Neugold were looking for Landry to help them." Carbone said.

"Curiouser and curiouser. Have you found Landry?"

"No. We're looking. In the meantime, Slo Fiz asked for a substitute who could help us at the archives. They assigned us another priest." Palazzo pulled down on her suit jacket between her thumb and forefinger, a nervous twitch that reminded Smith that she'd had never been in the field.

"The Vatican liaison will meet us at the secret archives area in forty-five minutes. He knows this Caravaggio stuff."

Chapter 46

Airborne
One Hundred Miles South of Heathrow

"The Knights Templar didn't just die." Pratt insisted. "The King of England mysteriously let them keep the Middle Temple in London, where they moved in with the Knights Hospitaller. Why did the King allow them to keep it?"

Willis looked exhausted. He rubbed his temples. "This is like a game show. I don't know. Ask me something else about Shakespeare."

"Oh, I will. Play nice and I may even let you go."

Willis lifted his head. "All right. Why did the Templars merge with the Knights Hospitaller?"

"Because they were more powerful than the Templars. They controlled more land, more money, the hospitals, the Mediterranean Sea. They were smart spooks. Most importantly, the hospitals. There was no way the King could unwind that. And they couldn't be identified or rounded up like the Templars. They were already ghosts, blending into society at every level of nobility, every profession, and every business."

"And Shakespeare was involved?"

"Shakespeare knew a lot more than he ever let on, right? Always misdirecting people?"

"Yes . . . and?"

"He staged *Twelfth Night* at the Middle Temple in London on Candlemas in 1602. Candlemas is one of the Twelve Great Feasts of Christendom."

"So what?"

"Queen Elizabeth was there for opening night."

"Perhaps. So?"

Pratt ignored Willis.

"It was also common for a young playwright like Shakespeare to take on a nobleman like the Earl of Southampton, Lord Wriothesley, to be his patron, his sponsor. But this Earl was a Catholic sympathizer and his father had aided the famous Jesuit freedom fighter priest Edmond Campion? And the Earl also had a tempestuous relationship with the English Crown!" Pratt added.

"Yes. And?"

"So maybe Shakespeare also had some Catholic guilt in his blood?" Pratt asked.

"Probably after he contracted syphilis," Willis thundered back.

"This play was staged in the Knights' Middle Temple on an important religious holiday. Shakespeare is staging a play about the Epiphany in front of the anti-Catholic Queen Elizabeth? Don't you see the irony . . . or the message?"

"Yes, but . . ."

"To this day, the Middle Temple is exempt from the jurisdiction of the mayor and city of London. The Knights Hospitaller's Middle Temple is their own independent country granted to these knights in the middle of London! It still has a status commensurate with the Vatican in Rome."

"I see the barristers walking around there all the time. It's where they cut their teeth."

"Exactly. The lawyers."

"Okay, Mr. Pratt. Now you've put all your actors out onstage. Shakespeare, Romano, the Knights Hospitaller. How does Lord Wriothesley fit in with the mystery of the Knights Hospitaller?"

"Lord Wriothesley moved his entire library of Shakespeare's writings to St. John's library in the early seventeenth century. Across from your office."

"Yes, agreed."

"Lord Wriothesley, powerful English nobleman. Catholic sympathizer. Financial backer of Shakespeare. He was Knights Hospitaller just like Romano and Caravaggio. He shared the secret with Shakespeare."

"Okay . . ." Willis said.

"Shakespeare ignores da Vinci and Michelangelo. Instead, he immortalizes Romano because of his power in the Knights Hospitaller."

"Possibly . . ."

"There was a college student from the United States, Riley McKee, digging in Lord Wriothesley's archive of papers years ago."

"You Americans are always digging in our laundry." Willis said bitterly.

"I think the Knights hid their secret with Lord Wriothesley in the Middle Temple. Shakespeare concealed that secret. When the Lord was dying, he moved it to St. John's—and Riley McKee found enough information to start to unravel it. I think it was there she figured out the Romano link to Caravaggio and the secret of the Knights Hospitaller."

Chapter 47

Cripple Cove Landing
Gloucester, Massachusetts

Jake pulled his binoculars up to his eyes. A faded white seafood warehouse traced the edge of Gloucester Harbor down to a long plank platform rippled by an early morning tide.

Low wooden jetties extended from the main dock of Cripple Cove into the harbor. These were vaguely bathed in the glow of a lone Coca-Cola machine stationed at the top of the platform. Jake Bolton liked this ambiguous time between night and day. It suited his preference for shadows.

Jake made out the shape of a man at the end of the dock, a suspendered Humpty Dumpty seated on a bench. His grubby beard of black and grey hung like an inverted beehive from his neck, his eyebrows were thick patches of white, and his legs looked like they were screwed on backward. For a moment, Jake wondered whether the man was actually a piece of tourist art, one of those permanent sculptures craving a pose. But the man turned his head toward Jake and lifted one of his eyebrows. Jake elbowed Jenny, cueing her to ask the question he had taught her.

"Are you the captain of the *Dorenkamp*?" Jenny asked.

"No. I'm a chemistry professor."

"Huh?"

"Of course, I'm captain. Captain Frank Hardy."

"Jenny Neugold and Jake Bolton here."

"You're late." The captain rolled to a standing position and passed them on the dock.

Jake signaled Jenny to let him speak. "Yoke told me to be here at oh four hundred."

"We *leave* at oh four hundred. You should've been here earlier." The captain stood and waddled toward the largest ship in the slips. Jake and Jenny followed.

The *Dorenkamp* rolled slowly side to side at the end of the dock, its booms extending from the stern of the fishing boat and rising high over the dock like high-tension wires. The three of them descended the stairs next to the ship, guided by an orange glow emanating from a large room in the center of the boat. A thick black anchor dangled out over the bow. Jake assumed the wide, hidden berth once carried shipments of IRA guns but would now hold a week's catch of fish.

As they boarded the boat, the captain turned toward the lighted room. A small crew sat along a table, drinking the day's first coffee. A few of the men looked up as the captain introduced Jake and Jenny simply as "the passengers."

Jake took inventory, attending to facial features, ear shapes, scars, tattoo marks on the hands. He didn't recognize anyone. He and Jenny moved past the benches and descended with the captain below deck.

Hardy walked down the narrow hallway and opened a door. "Mr. Bolton, I'm a little tight on short notice. Best I can do for you and the lady is this room here." A bunk leaned against the wall. A small wooden chair filled the corner. An oval mirror hung above a stand with a basin filling the rest of the floor space.

"I'm sure this is fine, Captain Hardy. We just want to get across the pond unnoticed."

"That's the whole trick, isn't it, son? Since the Irish won the war, I haven't had as much business, but I know what I'm doing. I'm going to the wheelhouse to get us under way."

Jake tilted the chair against the wall. "You get the bed, Jenny."

Before she could protest his gallantry, Jake was asleep.

Jenny fell face-forward onto the bed. The boat made its way noisily into the Atlantic.

#

Three days later
The *Dorenkamp*
Atlantic Ocean
One Hundred Miles West of Kinsale

Jake dreamed of bright blue water and turquoise sand. He

was a teenager; Riley was a child. Riley began to struggle against the tide. He dove under the water, trying to catch her body. But someone else was pulling her away. He could see his sister thrashing her arms and legs; he saw bubbles billowing around her. He could not make out the man stealing her from him. The water seemed to explode like glass. He saw a face. A dark face with an unusual slash across the forehead.

Jake sat straight up in the darkness. "Riley!" he screamed.

Awake but confused, half still in the dream and half in the dark space, Jake reached instinctively for his gun.

Out of the corner darkness he heard a voice call, "What's the matter?"

He dove across the bed and threw his body over Jenny. She grunted in response.

"What the hell are you doing?"

"Riley?"

"It's Jenny. What's the matter?" She pushed Jake off her and held his shoulders firmly. "You're having a nightmare!"

"Where's my bag? We've got to get out of here."

"We're on a boat in the middle of nowhere."

"We're in danger. I recognized him. At the table. Sitting third from the left."

"Who? You mean on the boat? Who's *he*?"

"He recognized me. Grab your bag. We're in danger."

Chapter 48

The *Dorenkamp*
Atlantic Ocean
One Hundred Miles West of Kinsale

Jake pushed Jenny ahead of him as they raced down the hallway. He knocked with a thud on the first mate's door. No answer.

Jenny bent down and touched a dark liquid oozing from the light beneath the door. She raised her fingers to her face and inhaled. She felt a cold tremor in her chest.

"It's blood."

Jake covered his hand with his sleeve and tried the door latch. He pushed the door open. The lamp was on but overturned, casting a freakish shadow across the floor. Jenny peered past him. The lifeless first mate was sprawled half out of his bunk, facedown. Blood seeped down from his chest and pooled on the floor. Jake felt for a pulse. He shook his head.

Jenny leaned over to see his face touching the floor. The handle of a knife stuck out of the seaman's chest. The hilt was so broad it held the body off the floor.

"This just happened. The noise woke me." Jake said.

Jenny thought of Riley dying in her lap on the skywalk. *Another murder around us . . . and we're trapped on this boat.*

"We have to get to the captain."

Jenny's mind raced, calculating like a surgeon. "Blood like this is fresh. It's coagulating. We're only seconds away from the killer."

Jake grabbed Jenny's hand. He extended his head out the door. He looked up and down the narrow hallway. She felt him pull. He raced them toward the bow of the ship.

"Speed is now more important than caution," Jake said. She ignored the sound of her feet pounding on the metal stairs. Once topside, he pulled Jenny with him onto the navigation bridge. The captain was bent over nautical maps. His pilot seemed busy at a distant instrument panel.

"Captain, we've got a problem," Jake yelled.

"Not now, Jake. Whatever it is, I got a bigger problem."

"Frank?"

"Jake, *not* now."

"Someone killed your first mate. I think you've got a traitor on board. We may have endangered your trip."

Captain Hardy let out a deep breath of frustration. "Crap. Cripe."

"I found him facedown with a knife in his chest. Minutes . . ."

"We're being followed," Hardy said. "For the last fifty miles."

Jenny stepped toward the glowing electronic screens. "How do you know?"

Frank rolled his eyes. "I turned off my navigation detection device twenty miles ago. I was performing my best 'angles and dangles,' even though this isn't a submarine. You know, like a water skeeter. We've been watching him with binoculars following all our moves." Frank scratched his beard. "He's gaining on me. Bolton, you know what we've got to do."

"We can't outrun him?"

"I'm a souped-up fishing trawler, but not that souped-up. He's gaining quickly. He'll be on top of us in thirty minutes. If I had a torpedo . . ."

"Thanks. You did what you could." Jake pulled his bag further up on his shoulder. "Let's go now. What kind of raft can you spare?"

Hardy yelled to the pilot. "Turn east twenty, and when I signal, slow to ten."

Hardy led Jenny and Jake out the bow door. Hanging crosswise was a black rubber raft with "*Nellie*" painted in white lettering across the side. "She's never failed me. This thing is a valiant, seaworthy boat. She's reinforced TPE covered with double rubber tubing. She's got a great engine for these seas."

Jenny felt strong winds blowing along the port side of the boat. She shivered and looked down at the dark water. *Here we go again,* she thought. *I bet there isn't an aqueduct at the end of this ride.*

Hardy cranked the handle, releasing the rescue boat into the water on the port side, where it skipped alongside the boat, a tether holding it in place. Hardy turned to the bridge and waved to the pilot. The *Dorenkamp* slowed.

Jake passed a rope to Jenny and told her to shimmy down. He grabbed her bag and waited for her to reach the boat. Tossing her the bag, he turned to Frank Hardy. He threw his right leg over the railing. "Can you slow them down?"

"I'm going to do more than that for you, son. I'm going to stop them."

Jake tumbled into the boat and started the engine. He sat with one hand on the rope line and one on the handle of a small but powerful Mercury engine.

The captain tossed a compass down to Jake. "If you head north by northeast you should pass Fastnet Rock. Shane can find you there. I'll radio him now. If I can't stop this thug, you won't be able to outrun his boat. You've got to meet up with Shane if you're going to have any chance to reach Cork. . . ." Hardy's words suddenly trailed off. His body froze. His back arched backward and his head shot upward. He dropped and turned, folding like a blanket over the port railing of the ship. Jenny spotted the hilt of another knife sticking from Hardy's back.

The man with the scar threw his hands over the railing and looked down at Jake and Jenny, reaching behind for another knife.

Jake revved the Mercury motor and the boat leaped into motion.

Jenny then saw Hardy lurch upward, swinging wildly at the attacker.

Chapter 49

Atlantic Ocean
Forty Miles West of Ireland

Jenny fought down nausea.

The frigid water splashing over the sidewalls of the reinforced rubber TPE soaked her clothes. But the swells made her stomach uneasy.

Jenny righted herself and checked Jake to see how he handled the swells. Blood dripped from his right side. Jenny crawled over to him and struggled to lift up his shirt. Jake pushed her hand away. "What happened? Did he get you with a knife?"

"I sort of sliced my side when we jumped out of Digger's house. I bandaged it up pretty good, but I guess I opened it up again."

"Sort of sliced? It looks more like a shark got you."

"Fix it. Hurry. I'll give you two minutes."

"This wound needs stitches." She spun around in the narrow boat. After collecting what she needed from her back pack, Jenny placed a blue towel next to Jake on the bench. She dropped a needle driver, suture, alcohol, and scissors onto the towel, trying to steady her hand.

"Can you cut the motor for two minutes? I'd rather not stitch your arm to your navel."

"No. We have to veer away from Fastnet Rock. They'll be looking for us there. It's an old IRA dead drop for Libyan guns. We have to head north instead."

"Can we at least slow down?"

"Wait until we reach land."

"You can't wait until we reach land. You're losing too much blood." Jenny looked down at her sterile field, soaked with blood and seawater. *It's like the spray of a waterpick.*

Jake put his hand over the wound. "I've got pretty good insurance."

"Yeah. It's me right now." She smiled.

Jake looked over his shoulder. "The *Dorenkamp* is gone."

"Gone as is in sunk?"

"No." Jake pointed as Jenny looked past him. "Hardy's still alive. He's heading the ship east to get those tracking thugs off our tail. Impressive. Hardy's gruff, but he's sure smart and dedicated to helping Digger."

Jenny looked again at his wound and assessed how much blood he'd already lost. Jake throttled down, slowing the raft to a roll in the waves. "Okay, sew me up quickly." Jenny lifted his shirt and began cleaning the wound with alcohol. Jagged scars were scattered haphazardly all over his abdomen. "Human cells aren't immortal. This laceration is right over your liver. Skin can replace itself only so many times."

Jake looked back at her. "How many times?"

"Huh?" she replied.

"How many times can a human cell replace itself?"

"It's called the Hayflick phenomenon." Jenny paused. "Are you sure you want to hear this?"

"Yes. I like hearing you speak." Jenny suddenly felt warmer.

"Until about forty years ago, we thought cells were immortal." Jenny probed the depth of his wound with her gloved finger. Jake didn't move. "Scientists then discovered that cells can replicate only about fifty times before they shut down. Life lasts only so long."

"Then the cell dies?"

"Sort of. The better way to think of it is that a cell just stops being able to replace itself. The end of the DNA strand gets too short and it shuts down. Cancer cells work just the opposite. The cancer cell has the ability to say, 'Keep replicating and don't shut down,' until the abnormal cell multiplies and ultimately outlasts the good cells. The cancer then kills its own host."

"Meaning the person dies?"

"Yup."

Jenny's hands moved swiftly across the wound with a running stitch. She was in awe that he didn't move as each needle stick pulled his skin together. She quickly covered it with a dressing. "It's not pretty but it should hold."

"Thanks."

"Your body is a mess. You know, with your shirt off, you don't look at all like a spy. You've had the crap beat out of you. Come to think of it, you don't look like a spy with your shirt on either."

"That's the best compliment you can give a spy. What does a spy look like to you?"

"Shouldn't you be wearing a tuxedo?"

Jake laughed. "Would you like to see me wearing a tuxedo?"

"Maybe, someday." She winked.

"Are you flirting with me Doctor Neugold?" Jake revved the Mercury engine and the Viking rescue raft jumped up onto the waves and sped north.

The words warmed her back.

Chapter 50

Atlantic Ocean
Forty Miles West of Ireland

"How fast do you think we're going?" Jenny asked.

"Not fast enough. We're going to run out of time. Short of the coast." Jake glanced at his watch and rapped his knuckles on the top of the engine. "At this speed they'll catch us in twenty minutes or less. If they can find us."

"Can't we use the signal flare Captain Hardy gave us to alert Shane?"

"No. It'll direct the bad guys to where we are. We have to ditch them first."

"Can we make it to shore?"

"Not enough gas at these speeds." He stared out toward the horizon.

"Any more good news?"

Jake patted his bandage. "Nice job on the stitching. You're useful out in the field."

"Useful. Gee, thanks." She felt the sting.

The two fell into silence.

"Are you scared?" he yelled over the growl of the engine.

"Of course I'm scared. My hands are shaking, I'm sitting on a carnival ride in the middle of the Atlantic and my body is tensing up in the cold. I don't want to die out here in the dark. I'd be stupid not to be scared. You're saying you're not?"

Jakes shrugged. "Sure. But I'm doing something about it. Focus on the mission."

"You just don't care about living?"

"That's different. I said I was scared. What's the point of focusing on it? I'm just using it against itself. You have to think that you're immortal out here. Turning the fear into a good thing."

"C'mon. Fear is a natural response to danger."

"I bet the first time you did surgery you were scared? Your hands shook? After watching you today, I doubt that happens anymore. You're a cool cucumber."

"Yes. It comes with practice."

"And it's hard to be compassionate while being a tactician?"

"Yes. So, what makes you scared?" She asked.

He paused. "Walking across the gymnasium floor to ask a girl to dance."

"Seriously? You're kidding me!"

He smirked. "It's the moment before you enter her confessional . . . but she sees you coming across the room. She wants to dance. I want to get to know her. At that moment you're completely defenseless and she knows what's coming. I'm putting my life in her hands."

Jake's words startled her as they penetrated. *He displays a shocking sense of emotion,* she thought. *Or, was he just distracting me? It's working. He's got me thinking. When are we the most vulnerable?*

"I feel the fear in my own way."

"You can control it." Jake declared.

"How?"

In the distance, a light was flickering. It got brighter, then turned red and exploded across the horizon. "Crap." Jake hissed.

"What was that?"

"They just blew up the *Dorenkamp.*"

Jake turned the boat northward with one hand.

"They're getting closer. I can see their spotlight. We may have to get into the water, Jenny."

"Do I get to be afraid of freezing to death or should I just shoot myself with the flare gun?"

Jake stared, distracted in deep thought. "You gave me an idea. We'll be okay. Keep your life vest inflated. We'll drift toward shore."

"I'm sorry. What? Drift?"

Jake unscrewed the gas cap on the Mercury engine. "A half tank."

He stood up. He slid past her and untied the bow line. He lifted the metal casing that covered the floor of the boat, balancing it at the bow. Beneath the casing of the raft he pulled up a larger polyethylene board responsible for the oval shape of the Viking raft. He signaled Jenny to lean back on the engine and keep them moving while he pried it up. Once it was free, he motioned for her to kill the engine. He tied the line to the handle of the Mercury motor, then tied the other end to the metal tubing at the bow. Back at the engine, he picked up a screwdriver and slammed it into the lower end of the gas tank. The gas started to leak out into the ocean.

"What are you doing?"

"Here, help me." Jake lifted the long polyethylene board and floated it into the water next to the boat. "Hold this in place for now."

"We can't survive in this water. It's too cold. Maybe fifteen minutes max till hypothermia sets in." She said.

Jake spidered across the boat, quickly shifting any loose weight to the front. "We won't survive in this boat either." He bellowed. "We have to take chances to save lives. Hold this!" Jake tossed her a mirror.

"Take chances? We're going to freeze to death!"

"Get out on that board. I'll hold it in place." She felt a long shiver. She turned and slid her body prone onto the long surfboard.

She took up most of the space on the board, waves washing over the edges. Jenny shivered again. Jake grabbed his bag then Jenny's, pushing them into her arms.

Jake jumped into the freezing water and held one hand on Jenny's board and the other on the boat line. When he pulled back on the line, the engine roared. He released the line, and the empty rescue craft leaped west at full speed. Gasoline trailed off into the waves. Jenny threw her hand at the water, imagining she could grab the line on the boat. She looked back at Jake dangling from the board.

"Jake. You're going to freeze. Fifteen minutes, tops. Too cold." Jenny's voice rattled.

"I know."

Jake raised the flare gun and pointed toward the *Nellie.* "One . . . two . . . three . . ." He fired at the rainbow of oil in the water. Yellow flames raced over the ocean. The *Nellie*'s engine exploded, igniting the trail of gasoline in the water. The burning boat continued to race away from them, chased by the flames.

"We're sitting ducks in this water." She pleaded.

"Just remember this: As Riley lay there on the bridge dying, she told me to 'find the barrister.' If I don't make it, remember that clue. 'Find the barrister.' And, my arm tattoo. They mean something important."

Jenny swallowed hard, sensing that this too was going to end badly.

Jake held the board again and started kicking the water. "Here's the compass. There's the mirror. Just keep us moving east."

"You just sent our boat blazing off into the distance and now you're swimming a floorboard toward the Irish coast?" Jenny felt breathless.

"Yup."

"Can't we negotiate with these guys?" Jenny asked.

"They just blew up Hardy's boat. Don't think so."

"One of us needs to survive. I'm trying to create time and space between you and them."

Jake's teeth chattered.

"Wait a minute. You . . . you used the boat as a flare?" Jenny's tone changed. She recognized Jake's move. She could see the assailants' boat turning west and toward the flaming boat racing away from them. His plan was working.

"It was our only chance. It's a game of chess, you know. Maybe I lost. You may have a chance to float directly toward the coast. You'll start to see the lights of Cork City in 15 minutes. Just let the waves carry you. The water should warm from the Gulf Stream and carry you right into shore."

She was awed. "It was a gutsy move. A smart risk."

"Like that exploding Vacutainer bottle? We tried, didn't we?"

Jenny grabbed his frigid hands. "Smart move." She rubbed both her hands on his, trying to warm him.

"Use your mirror on the moon." Jake mumbled. Then he passed out.

She squeezed his hands tightly, holding him on the edge of the board.

Chapter 51

Airborne, Grumman Albatross
Forty Miles West of Ireland

Shane O'Toole banked his Grumman Albatross so tightly that his copilot's face flattened against the glass.

He scanned the horizon from the Albatross as he approached the lighthouse on Fastnet Rock. He saw a signal flash. Circling the small quartz island jutting out of the Atlantic Ocean, he didn't see any rescue boat. But when he raised his binoculars, he spotted a long flickering yellow line on the western horizon. *It was not like a flare but more like something . . . something burning in the ocean.* Looking out the side window of the old seaplane at Fastnet Rock, he realized he had to make a decision. *It must be him*, he thought. Shane turned the plane west and raised the nose. He cranked the throttle.

Looking down from the cockpit of the hulking amphibious seaplane, Shane spotted the flash and he slowed the engines to descend. In the distance he could see a larger boat racing toward the other end of the flaming line in the ocean. He circled around and took his plane down toward the signal mirror.

Shane and the copilot both looked down and studied the source of the signal.

Another strange flash.

The copilot pulled out his binoculars. "Yikes"

A woman was down in the ocean floating on what looked like a board. She seemed to be rotating a mirror to send up the flash. Sprawling halfway off the panel was a second person, most likely a man. *Is that Jake Bolton?* He thought.

The copilot signaled to O'Toole to turn the yoke back. O'Toole traced the blazing waterline over the plane's nose and saw the collapsing boat in the distance. O'Toole turned again to head toward the struggling boat. "Is that Frank Hardy?"

The copilot didn't answer. O'Toole didn't want an answer. He would just say, "Shiite," over and over again as he headed toward the doomed ship anyway.

Descending to fifteen hundred feet, O'Toole flew over the

Dorenkamp's flames. The boat's nose was inverted and hopeless. O'Toole screamed, "Holy shiite!" and banked sharply to the north toward the torch in the water, nearly ripping the wings off the behemoth Albatross. He knew there was nothing he could do for Hardy now. *Might as well save the passengers Hardy contracted for*, he murmured.

O'Toole continued north, mentally calculating the distance and speed he would need to safely reach the two people on the life raft. The copilot pointed west and O'Toole drifted closer to a converted naval patrol boat that was clearly not engaged in a rescue mission. Men on the patrol boat seemed to be positioning themselves to engage the plane. O'Toole quickly banked away. And then they fired. Round after round of tracer fire lit up the sky.

"Oh crap, another hot LZ!" O'Toole knew all too well that landing a seaplane in the Atlantic Ocean called for less than four-foot seas with an approach of at least two miles, that is, if no one was shooting at him. He also made a quick calculation: *that blaze in the water was a diversion that gave me the only chance to save Bolton. Bolton is not at the end of the blaze. He's on that board clinging to life.*

Even on the best of days, landing the Albatross was like skimming a Winnebago RV into a backyard swimming pool. The six-ton banana body of the plane created enormous drag as it approached the shifting air currents running over the water. That drag could make the plane stall, drop, or even land explosively. He knew he didn't have the time for the three-one rule of three miles for every thousand feet of altitude. He would have to get out as far as he could. "Here's hoping I'm far enough out before I descend to pick up Jake . . . and before the gunmen are on top of them."

O'Toole had made up his mind. He rattled off the kneeboard checklist while the copilot lowered the flaps and trimmed out the wings. Once he'd brought the plane perpendicular to the six-foot swells and in line with the raft, he trimmed the wings further. The altimeter dropped below five hundred feet.

During his decades of contract work picking up American guns and money from the Boston Irish, meeting Gaddafi's henchmen for Libyan dead drops, being chased by the Brits, and the CIA, O'Toole had landed in just about every possible abyss. Usually he had some sort of backup. He always seemed to escape.

But this was supposed to be a limo ride, not a firefight. *Need to fight the urge to descend too fast,* he thought.

It was time against distance. He couldn't buy time now.

Passing east of Jake and Jenny, O'Toole managed a punishing landing. He quickly turned the amphibious plane back toward the raft. The copilot took the helm while O'Toole ran to the cargo door and opened it. The young woman reached out her hand but kept pointing to the man half in the water. "Jake's in hypothermic shock. I need blankets. I need to get him flat now."

O'Toole pulled the board next to the door. The six-foot swells continued to rock the plane as he braced himself against the door and pulled Jake's two-hundred-pound deadweight up into the bay. He extended his hand to Jenny and grabbed her arm, pulling her aboard. The two of them rolled Jake on to a car mechanic's creeper before O'Toole raced back into the cockpit.

Once he'd throttled up the rotary Pratt & Whitney horses, O'Toole quietly thanked himself for loading the tank with jet fuel for a JATO takeoff. Out his port-side window he could see the patrol boat within two hundred meters. Given the plane's new weight, he needed at least a mile to take off. "Shiite!" he yelled again without interrupting his instinctive movements across the instrument panel. The copilot bit a rough cuticle on his left thumb and wondered aloud, "this is going to be one close call. Too short and my wife a widow."

#

Jenny rolled Jake's body off the creeper onto a low-lying burlap bunk hanging from the wall of the fuselage. She kicked off her wet shoes and composed herself. Everything seemed to slow down in the ER when there was a trauma. *Amygdala,* she murmured to herself recalling the peanut-size gland in the brain. Fear made humans experience nightmare events slowly. Now she was living one.

Jenny quickly moved toward the cockpit, vaguely aware of the ocean racing toward her from the window as O'Toole began takeoff. "I need your help. Jake's hypothermic. We need to save him. He only has minutes."

"Minutes? Look out the port side window! We only have seconds before those thugs kill us."

Turning to look past the pilot's shoulder, she spotted gun

tracer flashes arcing toward the plane. Looking aft she saw bullets blasting holes in the steel skin of the cargo bay around Jake.

"Jake!" she yelled. She ran back into the cargo bay.

Chapter 52

Airborne, Grumman Albatross
Forty Miles West of Ireland

Jenny dove across the cargo bay, throwing her body on top of Jake.

"Jake!" Jenny yelled, grateful that she'd safely placed him flat on the bottom bunk. A small car in the cargo area would protect him from the initial slugs, but not from ricochets. "A car?" She bellowed. "What's a car . . .?"

Suddenly the gunfire stopped as the plane put distance between the attackers. She stood briefly but then crouched to look around the cargo bay. Her heart thundered as she moved ropes and wrenches off the bench, and then pushed tarps aside.

The hull of the seaplane bounced off the water as the Albatross fought the ocean's drag; then she felt the sea release its hold on the plane. *We're airborne.*

\#

O'Toole let out a triumphant howl, high-fived his copilot, and then turned his head back toward the cargo bay. Jenny couldn't hear him. Again he turned the plane over to the copilot and made his way back to the cargo bay.

\#

"We reach the coast in thirty minutes. What can I do to help Jake?" O'Toole yelled over the groan of the engines.

Jenny looked closely at O'Toole for the first time. She knew what she had to do. *I have to run my own code.*

"We need another flat surface, stat!" She screamed at O'Toole.

"Lady, this ain't a hospital. This is a tin can with wings."

Jenny looked around the modified cargo area for a flat surface.

"Clear this crap out of here." She pointed to the stack of tarps and ropes very much in her way.

"Lady, stop tearing apart my plane. I'm trying to find you a bleedin' stretcher."

"Stop calling me 'lady.' And what the heck is this car doing here?"

"That's my Fiat! Hardy didn't give me time to clear it out. Shiite! Hardy's dead, you know. He must be. I hope to God you two are worth that man's life."

Jenny felt the pilot's growing anger. It was the same anger directed at her by relatives of her ER patients when their loved ones didn't make it. She couldn't afford to lose O'Toole's focus now. She knew what she had to do. She stood and stared nose-to-nose with the older man, steadying him with her eyes. "Let's make sure Frank Hardy's last mission was a success. I need your help. Just do exactly what I say, exactly as I say it." O'Toole swallowed deeply and tugged on his drooping grey mustache.

"Okay, lady. You got it."

Jenny stripped down to her boxers and sports bra as O'Toole stood back and stopped moving. She grabbed a scalpel from her bag, pulled off Jake's belt, and then cut his pants north to south, yanking several times, finally ripping them off. She used the belt to secure his legs to the bunk. That would have to do. "Let's get on with this. Get that area clear."

Jenny directed O'Toole to collect three folding chairs, and then had him arrange them as her second gurney. She dug deep in her trauma bag and found intravenous tubing, two large-bore needles, and a steel Kelly clamp. She stuck several strips of silk tape on the side of the bunk. Grabbing an alcohol wipe from her bag, she cleaned off Jake's right groin area, rolled off the pulsation of his femoral artery under her fingertips, grabbed the cap off the needle with her teeth, and then stabbed the adjacent femoral vein. The tubing started to ooze dark red deoxygenated blood. Taping the needle into place, Jenny slid onto the three chairs parallel to Jake. O'Toole put his hand to his forehead, gasped then froze.

"Stay cool, Doctor Copilot." She said.

She cleaned off her left groin area. "Take that clamp." She nodded to the Kelly.

O'Toole clamped the tube where Jenny pointed. With the needle she then jammed her own femoral vein. She calculated in her head how much time she needed. *The human body contains about six liters of blood and the femoral vein probably flowed at about point-five liters per minute. I can transfuse for four minutes and both of us will be safe.* "Open the Kelly clamp." O'Toole did as he was told.

Jenny put her legs up on the back of the chair. She saw that her blood was reversing and going into Jake. O'Toole looked catatonic.

"We induce hypothermia to save patients in the ER all the time." She yelled casually to the stunned pilot. "The body has a primitive response called the dolphin reflex. Time is of the essence. The hypothermia also slows down the body—a natural way to protect itself. It prevents brain and heart damage. The cooling reduces the metabolic rate. Jake's at risk for anoxia if it goes on for too long and his heart stops."

O'Toole's expression shifted as he moved the surface of his index finger over his mouth.

"It's like slowing the engine on your car to an idle so the cells in the body need less oxygen and the cell membranes become more stable. It reduces the blood pressure in the brain and that shifts the blood circulation into the brain. But we usually do this by pumping cold saline through the body, not throwing the patient into the Atlantic Ocean."

O'Toole nodded his comprehension. "And you probably charge for it, too."

"Yeah, but we also don't get paid." Jenny laughed.

"I need to get back to the cockpit."

"I need your help. Here's the problem: Raising the temperature back is more dangerous than dropping it. That part usually needs to be done slowly. Fast can work but it's also extremely painful. Think of it like when your leg goes to sleep and then you feel this tremendous tingling as it wakes up; if you move fast, you howl. That's just your leg; this is going to be Jake's whole body. But right now we don't have time for slow."

"What do you need me to do?"

"I'm transfusing my blood into Jake, which should warm him. But I can only do that for so long without . . . well, without dying. In no more than four minutes, I need you to clamp this line, raise his bunk, and lower me to the floor. That will shift blood back to me and help keep my blood volume and keep me conscious."

"What if he has a reaction to your blood?"

"He won't. I'm O negative, which means I'm a universal donor. Either way, we don't have time to cross-match blood."

A crescendo propeller noise cracked through the cargo area.

"Holy shiite! They really want you dead. We have a plane chasing us."

#

O'Toole made his way quickly back to the cockpit. He grabbed the railings and jumped into the pilot seat.

The copilot yanked the yoke to the starboard as the blur of a tail rotor flew past. He yelled, "He's shooting at us!"

"Not a plane. A chopper. Shiite again and again!" O'Toole set the alarm on his wristwatch for three minutes, thirty seconds, hoping his guesstimate was right.

Chapter 53

Airborne, Grumman Albatross
Five Miles West of Ireland

"Head east. *Now!*" O'Toole yelled.

The copilot quickly rolled the yoke and the hulking seaplane lumbered into a turn.

"The Cliffs?" The copilot asked.

"Yes. Let's see how fast he is." O'Toole said, jumping into his pilot's seat and pushing the overhead throttle forward.

"Speed two hundred kph, ceiling a thousand feet. We can't outrun him, but we can maneuver pretty shifty in this big lug." The copilot added as he checked his watch. Leaning back from the cockpit, he looked into the cargo area but could only make out only Jenny's extended feet.

#

Jenny lifted her head and looked at Jake. She reached over and felt his radial pulse. *Still thready. Skin's cool.* She passed her hand under his nose. Breathing is still agonal. Jenny squeezed her legs together to increase the pressure in the transfusion line. He needed more blood. Forty seconds had gone by. *If I go any faster he'll stroke out.* She released the pressure on her legs.

#

The Albatross was still trudging up to speed. Suddenly the small dual blade rotored helicopter buzzed across the top of O'Toole's wings. The large glass front to the Helo looked like the face on a fly. A *rat-a-tat* of bullets strafed the nose of the plane.

O'Toole studied the chopper's design. "It's a Dragonfly." The prototype had been developed especially for archeological exploration. "I've never seen one with mounted guns."

O'Toole leaned forward and the Dragonfly passed to the port side. "We need to go faster." He looked back down into the cargo compartment, then back at the helicopter racing away. "I need to reduce the plane's weight. We're too heavy." Then he unlatched his belt and turned toward the rear of the plane. "Oh crap!"

O'Toole stopped at the edge of the cargo bay and sighed. He knew what he needed to do. Just a little larger than a phone booth, "Rosy," his Fiat 500, was small enough to fit into the bay of his Albatross. He'd picked it up for sale from an Italian car thief a few days ago, but found he couldn't part with it. Until today.

O'Toole grabbed the handle on the industrial door opener and pressed the green button. He stared at Jenny lying next to Jake, and then checked his watch. Twenty-eight seconds. The metal chains began to ride over the teeth on the door's locking wheel as O'Toole released the winch on the rear of the car and untied the lines. The wind gushed through the rear of the plane. He rushed to the front of the car and pushed up and down on the hood to get the car moving. He then jumped out of the way as Rosy disappeared into the darkness. The plane quickly lurched up and forward. He closed the door.

O'Toole moved to Jenny's side.

"Clamp the line in forty-five seconds." Jenny said.

"My count says twenty-five."

"You've got forty-five. Go do whatever you need to do up front."

#

Thirty-five seconds to stop the transfusion. O'Toole thought.

O'Toole jumped back into the cockpit and yelled, "Where is he?"

"Our six. Two clicks and closing."

"Let's go for it." He pointed toward the jagged Irish coastline.

A few miles ahead, the Rocky Needle rose out of the crashing ocean waves just below O'Brien's Tower, the marker for the highest point on the Cliffs of Moher. Stunningly beautiful and utterly dangerous, the Cliffs were a treacherous home to rapidly changing wind currents. And O'Toole knew it was his best chance to defeat the faster Helo.

"Five hundred feet and turn!" O'Toole barked at his copilot.

Grabbing the pilot's yoke, he strapped on his seat belt and

harness.

#

Jenny checked her pulse against her watch. She was starting to feel a wave of nausea. Her eyes blinked and she could feel sweat on her forehead. She took a deep breath—in through her nose and out through her mouth fighting the wave of sleep—realizing it would maximize her oxygen intake. *I'm going to dose off for just a second. . . .*
Jenny Neugold was unconscious.

#

The plane's gyroscope momentarily spun on its side. The copilot released the yoke as O'Toole took control. The magnificent rock of the 'Needle' extended out of the frothing Atlantic waves, and then split like a needle's eye before closing again. O'Toole grinned at his copilot, and then turned his plane on its side as he passed through the needle.

His alarm watch buzzed. He set it for another twenty seconds, then looked back and saw the Dragonfly increase its altitude just in time to miss the collision with the Rocky Needle. At two hundred–plus meters of shale and limestone rock, the Cliffs were an imposing wall of defense. But O'Toole knew the chase was not over. The Cliffs could also be used on the offensive.

O'Toole pointed to the Sea Stack Rocks. Like bowling pins sticking out of the water, the rocks near the vertical face of Hag's Head funneled winds so strong tourists had been forced to surrender their spectacular photo op. According to folklore, the winds generated such a downdraft that the dolphins dried off as they leaped out of the ocean below.

O'Toole turned inland toward the Cliffs, taunting the helicopter to follow him upward . . . he started to slow the plane.

The copilot yelled. "O'Toole? Speed?"

"I know. I'm drawing him in."

"You're what? He's shooting up our frickin' tail!"

O'Toole quickly turned the plane upward toward the top of the Cliffs while the down drafting winds further slowed their flight.

The copilot rattled off the dropping airspeed: "One eighty . . . one sixty . . . one forty . . . Shane frickin' O'Toole?"

"I know. I know. Keep pushing." They were rapidly approaching a hammerhead stall. And they did not have the room to release, because the rock face was directly in front of them. O'Toole's alarm buzzed. But there was no leaving the pilot's seat now.

#

Jenny was tossed off her chairs by the plane's new direction. She rolled to the opposite side of the cargo area with such force that the tube connecting her to Jake was jerked free, blood still running through it. Jake grunted as the intravenous needle ripped out of his groin.

#

O'Toole watched the sudden shudder of the helicopter. The nose tipped, the blade stalled, and the Dragonfly spun wildly and dropped out of sight toward the ocean. "Shiite, yes! I'm still the best." The Albatross blasted over the top of the Cliffs and leveled off.

His watch buzzed, and he released his belts and turned toward the cargo bay, patting the copilot on the back. "She's all yours." He sincerely hoped the lady had been right about her timing.

Chapter 54

Airborne, Grumman Albatross
Lahinch, Ireland

"Jenny!" Jake yelled.

Unbuckling his legs from the bunk, he rolled onto all fours, disoriented to his position and space. Was he in Ireland? No. He was on a plane. Where was Jenny? He saw the crimson stain on the floor and found the tubing, tracing it back to a crumpled Jenny. *What was going on? The flowing blood couldn't be good.* He pulled the needle out of her groin and put pressure on the wound. She winced but didn't wake up. Jack leaned over her body to protect her from an approaching figure.

"Who are you?" Jake yelled.

"I'm Shane O'Toole. Great to finally meet you, Jake. Frank Hardy called."

"What's going on here? What happened?"

"This lass just saved your life. You came out of the Atlantic frosty as a Popsicle. She transfused her blood into you."

"How long has she been out?"

"Just minutes. Maybe just one. I had to go to the cockpit when this helicopter started shooting at us, then take us into the downdraft at Hag's—"

"What? A Helo shooting at us?" Jake grabbed his head feeling the pulsating headache.

"That wasn't all. We picked you up on your raft. I suppose you created the torch trap? We thought those guys were with Frank. Darn nearly shot us up when we flew over them!"

"Raft? Torch trap?"

"Why's she with you? Frank said you always travel alone." O'Toole asked.

"Slow down! I have such a headache."

"Is she pregnant? Is that why you're supposed to go see old Doc McGrath?"

"What are you talking about?"

"Jake, we've almost been shot down twice in the last thirty

minutes. I don't know where Frank Hardy is. I'm fair into thinking Frank Hardy *isn't* anymore. You show up floating on a board with this lady flashing a mirror at us. Dead as a Dosser. She strips down to her Gee Gee box. She brings you back to life. Now she's flat-out cold cocked on the floor. I'm supposed to get you to Cork City and then you need to go see Doc McGrath."

Jake looked at Jenny and then back at O'Toole. He shook his head to wake up. "How far?"

"Maybe thirty minutes until we land. Then a quick slant over to his thatch."

Jake took several deep breaths in and out. "Where are your blankets?"

"Is she pregnant?"

"No. She's not pregnant. As far as I know, anyway. Shut up and help me now."

"Then why does Frank want you to get over to Doc McGrath?"

"It must be something about . . ." Jake's voice trailed off. The events were becoming clearer. This doctor must have some information for him.

Jake looked over at Jenny. "We need to do something to help her now."

"Like what?"

"Show me what she did. What did she tell you?"

Jake went to lift Jenny and almost keeled over. O'Toole picked her up and brought her to the bunk as he explained about the transfusion method. Jake studied the tubing and rolled his hands over Jenny's groin, gently probing the needle into the original wound. He waited until the blood oozed out of the tubing; then he lay flat on the chairs and punctured his own groin with the needle at the other end.

"Jake, this blood is a lot redder. It seems to be flowing faster than before."

"Give it a minute. Get some blankets over there and put them on her."

Jenny started to cough and groan. Jake yelled, "Jenny, Jenny."

She turned her head toward him and shivered, then took several deep breaths. "Whoa, what's happening?"

"Easy, Jenny. We gotcha."

"No, Jake. Too fast. Stop." Reaching out onto the floor, she grasped the Kelly clamp and squeezed the tubing. She then pulled the needle from her groin and compressed the area with her free hand. "You hit your artery. It's okay. That was sort of lucky. For me."

Sitting up, she pulled out the needle from his groin and put his hand into position to compress the area. "I sure hope you're O negative, or else I'll be puking all over this plane."

Suddenly the copilot yelled from the cockpit, "Twenty miles, O'Toole!"

O'Toole stared at Jenny and Jake sitting on the floor and shook his head in disbelief. "I lost my Fiat over this. I hope you guys are through saving each other. Now do you suppose you'd be wanting to put on your seat belts? Or at least your pants?"

#

O'Toole jumped into the pilot seat and looked over at the copilot. Staring back, the copilot started to recite the kneeboard checklist. O'Toole flicked on the wing lights and strobes and picked up the microphone. "N-seven-eight-three-eight delta. North eighteen."

The microphone crackled back. "Cork City. N-seven-eight-three-eight-D. North eighteen. Barometric thirty-two. Wind four. Easy."

O'Toole took the Grumman Albatross through the darkness, descending onto the north runway. The plane turned quickly toward the eastern hangar and disappeared into the shadows.

Chapter 55

Seven Heads Bay
Kinsale, Ireland

"I'm gonna be sick." Jenny said.

Jenny rubbed her forehead and leaned against the window of the black MINI Cooper. "Ugh. My head hurts."

Jake downshifted the small car borrowed from O'Toole's used car lot. Jenny closed her eyes on the narrow Irish road, tightly bordered by hedgerows.

Jake pulled into a side road, stopped the car, and rifled through Jenny's bag. He found a sodium hydroxide ice pack, popped it, and placed it on her head. He took a water bottle from beneath his feet and handed it to her. "You're dehydrated."

"Thank you, Dr. Bolton, but I'm worse than that. I think I gave you too much blood." Jenny caught herself yawning. She knew she was compensating for her low blood pressure. "That wasn't a textbook resuscitation." Jenny felt herself becoming sweaty. She opened the car door and crawled out onto the grass next to a stone wall. She lie down and put her legs up on the wall, taking several deep breaths, gulping the cold water as quickly as possible.

"We're two miles to Dr. McGrath's house. Do you think you can make it?" Jake asked.

"Yeah. Just give me a minute to finish this water and get my stomach settled."

"How much blood did you give me?" Jake asked.

"Too much!" she growled, hoping the anger might help her feel better. "I don't know for sure. I blacked out."

"Great. With all that girly blood I probably won't be able to read maps anymore."

Jenny laughed. It helped her blood pressure rise. She thought about her own five brothers. While she felt the urge to keep up with them in contact sports, the experience gave her the "locker room" philosophy that she loved about trauma medicine. Girls playing on a boys' hockey team wasn't always comfortable but it was a great life lesson. The idea of working together at high speeds. Unexpected changes in direction. The wins and losses brought them together. She felt the warmth of the uniform.

She shot an eye over at Jake again. "You handled yourself pretty well out there."

"It was one cold water baptism."

"I'll make you think twice about committing any sins!"

"You're not so bad at patching me up."

"Is it really that terrifying to walk across a dance floor and ask a girl to dance? Or, were you just trying to distract me?"

"You should try it sometime."

Jenny felt a warm tingle up her spine. *This guy knows how to dish it back.* "In the ER a lot of times we're teaching each other not to quit. If you like one another like a teammate, you work harder." *It was the intensity of the "like" for one another that allowed them to take jabs at each other. On the outside someone might call it sexist but in the heat of a trauma code the bonding and trust worked.* "Hand me another bottle of water!"

"Feisty, aren't we?" Jake tossed her another bottle. "You okay buddy? Last one."

"Do you think the guy who shot Riley is still out there after us?"

"Don't know. But he's not the problem."

"How so?"

"It's like those cancers you treat. The shooter is just one cancer cell. You've got to take out the source before you treat the whole cancer. Whoever that source is, that's where you direct your cure."

She hunched forward and rubbed her eyes. Jenny had a vision of the cancers she'd seen in young patients and the sadness it brought on. Her focus slowly changed to the green valley in front of her. "Beautiful country, huh?"

"I've been in and out of so many countries I make it a habit not to look."

"See the beautiful patchwork plots of land extending as far as the eye can see, the different shades of green, the stone walls carving up the properties?"

"Yeah. Reminds me of a green chessboard."

Jenny laughed.

"That comes from the 1802 British Land Act. The Brits ran Ireland then. They realized that the Catholics were multiplying like rabbits and might become a political problem. So Parliament passed a law requiring each family to split up their land based on the number of kids they had. They realized that with each successive generation the Catholics would have less land to farm and eventually would starve . . . or move." She stopped to drain the water bottle. She was still thirsty. "The Irish were one adaptive and stubborn bunch, though."

"I've got one for you . . . The Brits were like those guys who may still be hunting us. They were trying to create a Zugswang, as we call it in chess."

"What's that?"

"It's when your opponent tries to put you into a position where any move on the board is a bad move. It's not check mate. But, you're trapped."

He spread his palms apart.

"What do we do?"

"That's when you Zwischenzug."

Jenny shot him a puzzled look. "I had to ask!"

"It's a tactic where you do something completely unexpected. Totally confuse them. Sometimes you need to think rogue to beat your opponent."

"Like blowing up your own boat?"

"Yeah."

"I thought we were going to die out there." She said.

"Like all the Irish, we need to be stubborn to stay alive. We don't quit so easy. Don't die so easy either. Let's roll."

Chapter 56

The Vatican
Rome, Italy

The black Mercedes slowly crossed the Largo del Colonnato in front of St. Peter's Basilica, turning with equal caution onto the Via del Fondamento.

The driver stopped to present papers to an ornately dressed Swiss Guard blocking his way, pulling into a parking space near the Stradone dei Giardini.

Mary Palazzo turned from the front passenger seat to face Karen Smith. Before she could speak, Smith pointed toward the door of the Cortile del Belvedere. A tall man stood there with his hands crossed over flowing red vestments. "Mary, that's not a priest. That's a Cardinal."

"Yes. He'll personally guide us to the secret archives. I'm glad to see he's also early. One cannot always be sure with Cardinals."

Slo Fiz Carbone sprang from the car's backseat, circled around its front, and opened Mary's door with an accustomed courtesy. Smith was collecting her bags in the back.

"You only need to bring your briefcase and computer; the driver will stay with the rest," he told her.

Smith hesitated. Since the advent of USBs, micro disk drives, and micro data cards, she'd become aware of personnel losing secret information in places that compromised or embarrassed the agency. She conducted a mental inventory: Her bags were clean. She grabbed her personal briefcase. She let Slo Fiz assist her from the car and joined Mary.

Approaching the doorway, Smith's instincts kicked in. She found herself looking to her left and right, beyond the Cardinal into the shadows. She studied the man himself, noting his olive skin and dark hair, his comfortable stance. The Cardinal had raised his hand to shield his eyes from the sun as his guests approached, making the fabric of his red galero shimmer. A snippet of parochial school training clicked into place: Cardinals' red was meant to represent their canonical place as the lifeblood of the Church.

"Your Eminence." Smith knelt to kiss the ring on his left hand recalling what she'd been taught. But the Cardinal laughed and caught her, raising her back to a standing position.

"No need, no need. I'm Cardinal Sergio Manuel. It's a pleasure to be your guide today."

"Your Eminence. Was your staff able to find the documents that we requested?" Palazzo asked.

"I'm sorry. Did you send a list?"

Carbone rolled his eyes toward Palazzo. "We sent a list two days ago. Caravaggio documents? The archives? Did you—"

"No, my office didn't receive any list."

"I have another copy here."

Mary Palazzo glanced over at Smith. She looked embarrassed in front of her CIA boss. She balanced her briefcase on her knee and clicked it open. She pulled out a file listing documents, letters, death certificates, ceremonies, catalogs, and papal decrees. Smith took the manila folder, reviewed it quickly, and then handed it to the Cardinal.

Cardinal Manuel barely glanced at the file's contents. "Okay, okay. Let's see what we can do. Please follow me. We haven't much time."

"We don't have much time?" Carbone asked.

"No. I didn't mean it that way. *You* will have plenty of time. I need to get you over to the archives and then run to another meeting."

The Cardinal waved them toward the ornate stone arch off the Stradone. They moved through the large shadow of the arch. They quickly found themselves back outdoors on the walkway of an enormous courtyard.

Cardinal Manuel sped them along and waved them ninety degrees back toward a large building transecting the courtyard. Smith noticed that he looked down at his feet as he walked, the way that three-year-olds do when they're surprised by what their feet are doing. She wondered if it was the robes or the speed. Was he *uncomfortable*? She hurried to walk side by side with him, though she realized Palazzo and Carbone were on her six and losing pace.

She twisted sideways, taking in the tourists, gardens and statues that populated the quadrangle. The quadrangle was a part of the Vatican grounds that Smith had read much about. She wondered if the Vatican had any CIA files in their library. She touched the Cardinal's sleeve.

"The Belvedere Courtyard, yes? Too bad Bramante never got to see his masterpiece finished."

"Yes. Yes. Bramante."

The courtyard was surrounded on all sides by the papal library, the neoclassical columns of the Vatican museum, and the papal apartments. The inner walls were fifty feet high with a repeating pattern of cornices and recessed walls. The center, divided by an asphalt cross that surrounded four separate manicured lawns, was marked by a fifteen-foot bronze-plated rotating sphere. Groups of tourists posed for pictures in front of the sphere, replacing one another with startling efficiency.

At the end of the walkway, Smith's group approached the center of a building that had a recessed semicircular exedra crowned by a half-dome. Two large, concentrically rising staircases joined to form a terrace beneath the semicircular plinth of the triumphal arch. Smith immediately recognized the symbolic pine cone capping off the terrace. She'd seen the same design atop the Pope's sacred staff.

Smith knew that the Roman Catholic Church built the Vatican over the ruins of the Temple of Isis, aware that Isis had represented eternal life for her worshipers, gleefully installing the fountain as a centerpiece of their courtyard. The pine cone represented the pineal gland, the human organ controlling the body's melatonin and circadian rhythms. The gland was called by some the "third eye," because it contained cells much like the retina. *It was probably the secret to a woman's astute intuition.* She thought. Although the literal translation of "pineal" was "face of God," Smith felt that her CIA was the third eye of the U.S.A.

They covered the length of walkway to the exedra, turned into a bustling corridor of tourists, and then turned back again before entering a long hallway. At the desk, a guard took their cell phones and locked them in a drawer.

At the far end of the hall, Smith spied a frescoed, barrel-vault ceiling that looked like an inverted staircase, giving the effect of waves coming at her as she walked. Each step was divided by a series of short gold-framed illustrations of the lives of the saints, accentuated by recessed lights hidden above the walls. *He's sure in a hurry.* She noted. The speed at which the Cardinal walked risked orthopedic injury and neck strain.

The chamber appeared to close in on them until they reached a white marble staircase spiraling around a caged elevator that led to a study sparsely furnished with a metal bookcase, a few computers, and a long metal desk lit by banker's lights. Smith paused briefly, assuming they'd stop. But they didn't. The Cardinal rushed them through another wooden door and entered a windowless room with thirty-foot ceilings. Though the walls were covered with colorful frescoes depicting Saint Paul's shipwreck in Malta, there was no furniture or lighting.

The Cardinal finally spoke again. "I will ask you to make yourselves comfortable for the moment. I will be back with your papers."

"Thank you, Your Eminence," Smith said.

The Cardinal left them.

Chapter 57

Seven Heads Bay
Kinsale, Ireland

Jake gunned the accelerator until the engine squealed.

In the distance Jenny could see the thatched roof of a small house, perched like a Monopoly hotel in the middle of a green grid. The country home of Dr. McGrath was not marked, but its location was obvious from Frank Hardy's description.

Jake pulled to the side of the road. There was less than a foot of grass between the road and a stone wall. Jenny stared at the rocks that had been culled and stacked by years of farming.

He pressed on the brakes. "Hey, thanks for what you did back there. It was a gutsy move on your part."

"You're kidding me, right?"

"No. You shouldn't have done that. You're not deep into this business like I am."

"You still don't get this. She was my best friend. She got me through college and medical school. I can't just close some book and walk away. You're part of her. And you're more than a patient."

Jake stared blankly, seeming to absorb Jenny's thoughts. "I can still see Riley smiling as a teenager when I took her fishing. She'd be happy to see us together. "It's not just a mission anymore."

"I think I had your consent to act." She said.

"Is that why you transfused *me*? When you could have left me as a field casualty?" Jake said.

"Riley would have wanted me to save you. But I also wanted to save you."

"I see. It's not just you acting for Riley anymore? Good. I feel the same way."

A boxy green fiat came racing around the corner. Jake looked up from the dashboard. He appeared to instinctively scan the car, the driver, and the plates as they went by. *He was mechanically storing the information.* She thought.

"For years I've separated these parts of my life. Riley understood why that was so important." He said.

"I know. As an Art History major she didn't look at paintings like they were splotches of color. She saw more than the story or the allegory. She looked for the artist's emotion or the deeper message. She saw something far more complex in Caravaggio and I think she's right. I'm not sure what we're chasing in this Last Prophet. But Riley found something, as only she could. And someone or some people don't want us to find it."

"We can do this."

"I know we can. But it's still scary."

Jake smiled. "It could get worse as we get closer to the truth."

"Like walking across the dance floor? I'm ready."

"Okay. Hardy said Doc McGrath was a retired obstetrician. Apparently he's blind now, over a hundred years old. You may be able to pass yourself off as Riley. Just follow what I say at first, you then take the lead. He might have information on the cipher that Riley left us. He might also know who was after her."

Chapter 58

The Vatican
Rome, Italy

Smith took a deep breath and exhaled impatiently. "I get the feeling I've been here before." The CIA director scanned the walls like she was analyzing her escape.

"Really?" Palazzo asked.

"Just a sense. You know, like its all familiar?"

"It's probably those hills surrounding Rome." Slo Fiz Carbone pointed off the balcony, where he'd opened the porch doors to let in some light and air.

Smith joined him at the marble railing, and then looked out at the hills.

Carbone gazed at his watch. "Why is it taking the Cardinal so long to pull those documents?"

Smith muttered, "The hills. Those hills."

"Is there something wrong, Smith?"

"'One of the few places you can still see Rome's seven hills across the Tiber River,'" she whispered, quickly turning back into the room and scanning the floor. She circled the room again, this time with her back to the walls.

"Oh my god!" Smith yelled.

"What?" Palazzo asked.

There it was. This is what I sensed. Something she hadn't quite processed when they entered: an eight-pointed rosette inscribed in marble in the center of the floor.

#

Heathrow Airport
London, England

"Lord Wriothesley was Shakespeare's best friend and financial backer. Wriothesley's entire collection of Shakespeare papers was there in that round church-like building. Right there at St. John's College." Pratt jabbed his finger toward the library while clutching the professor's arm with his other hand.

"And you believe that the clue is somewhere in those papers?" Professor Willis asked.

"Yes. Imagine for a moment that the Knights Hospitaller had some secret that could extend life. A cure that was so powerful that it would change the world? It would bring down the Catholic Church. Faith in all gods would change. Imagine how people would fight to get their hands on it? Dictators and politicians would be overthrown, wars would be fought, all kinds of bribery, bargaining, depravity and extortion. Health care would be transformed. Its a mystery carefully hidden from mankind."

"In those papers that hundreds of years and thousands of scholars have not uncovered?"

"Yes."

"I've spent my entire career teaching, lecturing, and researching Shakespeare. I don't believe there's anything there."

"I do. And I think some wet-behind-the-ears college student stumbled on it a few years ago. You know, a fresh look at something that has been staring us in the face for years? She realized that she came close to putting two and two together . . . but, I was in line ahead of her."

"Why don't you just ask her to help you?"

"Can't. She's dead."

"She's dead? Did you kill her?"

Pratt pursed his lips.

"You're really an effin' bastard, aren't you! I suppose you plan the same for me?"

"Do you know what Caravaggio's epitaph says?"

"No. Tell me."

"'Michelangelo Merisi, son of Fermo di Caravaggio—in painting not equal to a painter, but to Nature itself.'"

Geoffrey Willis blanched. He leaned back like he'd seen Shakespeare standing before him.

"Yes, Professor. It's too familiar. A Shakespeare quote on Caravaggio's grave. He died in 1610. That quote would be from *The Winter's Tale*. The play you say wasn't printed until years later." Pratt exclaimed.

"Crikey!"

#

The Vatican
Rome, Italy

Smith moved to the south wall and stared at the elaborate fresco. Looking up and down the wall, she swung her arm like she was waving a runner around third base while she analyzed the religious allegory. *That was it. That was the reason for this déjà vu. Or, one of the reasons.* She felt a wave of nausea.

"I can't believe that I didn't recognize it before. We've been betrayed." Smith said.

Palazzo and Carbone exchanged glances.

"How do you know?" Palazzo asked.

"See the hole?" Smith pointed to the fresco. About five meters up on the wall a genie was blowing wind over the ocean. The genie's mouth was open and light from outside the building blazed through. "This is the famous Meridian Room." She palmed both hands downward. "The balcony outside is one of the few places you can still see Rome's seven hills across the Tiber River. This fresco is 'The Calming of the Storm on the Sea of Galilee' by Pomarancio. I saw this in my briefing notes. The Pope's calendar was calculated right here in this room . . . by the Jesuits."

Palazzo and Carbone stared at the fresco while Smith raced for the door.

"That was no Cardinal. He took us here to hide us. To delay us while he stole the documents."

The agents followed Smith back across the room and into the study. Palazzo held out her hand. "How do you know this?"

"I missed it at first. He introduced himself as Cardinal Sergio Manuel. Right?"

"Yes. So?" Palazzo stared blankly as he spoke.

"He should introduce himself as Sergio Cardinal Manuel. The first name goes first. There was no ring on his left hand. The fisherman's ring belongs there! I sensed the details were wrong. Damn it, I knew. The jet lag, caffeine deprivation, I missed the subtle truth staring me in the face. Then his audacity? Stashing us in this room. Nobody has been in the Meridian Room for years. Except a few art historians. Yet he knew how to get here. Count on it—those doors are locked." She pointed to the exit.

Carbone rattled the door handles, and then pounded on the

thick door with his fist. "You're right."

"He's stealing the Caravaggio documents." Smith added.

Pallazzo picked up the phone but there was no signal. Carbone checked The Meridian Room computers but they were disconnected.

How long before we'll be found?

Chapter 59

The Vatican
Rome, Italy

Fifteen minutes later, the white double doors rattled open. A tall man in white gloves stood alone, short of breath.

His red boot covers, high white ruff collar, black beret, and distinctive blue-red-orange-and-yellow Renaissance uniform marked him as a Swiss Guard. He wore a long sword on his left hip and a SIG Sauer P220 handgun on his right. He placed his hand on the grip of the gun.

"Are you with the American embassy?" He asked.

"Yes, I'm Karen Smith. This is Giancarlo Carbone and Mary Palazzo. What's going on here? A man dressed as a Cardinal and calling himself Sergio Manuel brought us here. He told us to wait while he went to get documents we've requested from the archives."

"I'm sorry. You've been deceived."

"What's happened?" Palazzo asked.

"Cardinal Manuel is on his way here now. The real Cardinal. He waited for you at the Cortile del Belvedere and you didn't appear. He returned to his office and called the American embassy. They called me. I'm sorry it took so long, but I traced you here. This isn't a place you should be."

The guard's walkie-talkie crackled. He moved closer to the outside balcony.

As messages sputtered between the guard and the box, another man in red flowing canonical vestments appeared in the room. He paused, folded his hands, and surveyed his guests. Smith looked to see that he was wearing the ring of a fisherman. She bent to her left knee and reached out to kiss his ring. "Your Eminence."

"I'm deeply sorry for what's happened." He said.

Smith looked up at the Cardinal as she rose. "Can we still get into the archives and get to our research?"

"I'm sorry . . . when the guards called and told me that you'd been abducted, I also sent a guard to the archives. I had set aside the documents you requested this week. They've been taken."

"All of them?" Carbone shouted.

"Yes. Including the letter the Bishop of Caserta wrote to Scipione Cardinal Borghese. I'm afraid this impostor was playing with you as well. This is the Tower of the Winds."

"The Tower of the Winds? But Ms. Smith just told us this was the Meridian Room." Carbone said.

The Cardinal fired a curious face at Carbone. "Yes, it's that too. The Meridian Room is the center of the Tower. This room is a bigger secret than the famous Vatican Archives. It's off-limits to the public and is rarely seen by dignitaries. How do you come to know of it, Ms. Smith?"

Smith hesitated, unsure how much she should divulge from her CIA analysts. "Some friends from Georgetown showed me some . . . sketches . . . of the room."

"Ah, the Jesuits. You're trying to make the connection between Caravaggio and Bruno, right?" The Cardinal directed his words to Carbone.

Carbone nodded, his mouth still agape.

"This is the original Vatican observatory. Science and the Church. Yes, Copernicus, Galileo, Bruno. After the Council at Trent, the Church sought to correct its misdeeds. One area we needed to improve was our understanding of science. Unlike our enemies, we do like to seek penance. This building was finished in 1580 to study the cosmos. The Jesuits started here on this very spot to study the science of earth."

"I'm told that the line on the floor is the marble meridian used to identify the spring equinox. At noon the light enters from that hole in the wall, marking the exact time of the spring equinox." Smith pointed.

"Ms. Smith, your Jesuit friends taught you well. The Council of Trent reaffirmed that Easter should be celebrated on the correct day, the first Sunday after the first full moon after the first equinox. The Church discovered, through science, that the calendar established by Julius Caesar was wrong each year by two hours and, after fifteen hundred and eighty-two years, was off by ten days! So for the only time in history, Catholics moved faster than everyone else and the Church made time speed up. The Council of Trent declared that October fourth, 1582, was followed by October fifteenth. Years of incorrect assumptions were corrected, and the

Gregorian calendar was born."

Carbone whispered toward Smith. "And embarrassing us?"

"What better place to embarrass us?" Smith asked. "The very location of the Pope's astronomy lab? A place that wasn't known for five hundred years? Where the very seat of God sought to use science to calculate the exact day of Christ's resurrection? I think the Cardinal is going to tell us again that it has something to do with Caravaggio and Bruno."

"You are again correct, Ms. Smith. Giordano Bruno proposed heretical views of the cosmos years before Galileo. Years! Bruno was the one who predicted that the stars were suns and that the earth was not the center of the universe. He wrote that nature could be understood through scientific investigation and systematic experimentation. This was a threat to the Church. A big threat! It challenged the Church's infallibility."

"Bruno?' Palazzo asked.

"Yes." The Cardinal responded.

"The Church doesn't like that." Smith added.

"The Church doesn't always know how to live in the real world."

"The Church *is you and me*, Cardinal Manuel." Smith replied.

"The Church wanted to go slow . . . study the issues. Bruno was moving too fast. We burned Giordano Bruno at the stake in 1600 for cosmic misdeeds. We now know that Caravaggio was there in the town square. Likely horrified at the sight. Anyone paying attention must have gotten the message: Ideas can be deadly. The Church is made up of men and women who made and continue to make mistakes." He closed his eyes as he spoke. "All human churches have their sins."

Smith thought about the CIA's mistakes.

"Looking back, someone might find that easy to understand, but in 1600 we were correcting the transgressions of thoughtless religious leaders while trying to care for the masses dying from the Plague. People like Caravaggio, Galileo, and Bruno were ahead of their time while we were lost in time."

"And that symbol on the floor?"

"That eight-pointed rose is a symbol from the Knights Hospitaller."

Chapter 60

Heathrow Airport
London, England

Charles Pratt slammed his fist into the table.

The Lear jet rattled his tea cup in unison on the fold out table. The landing gear bounced. Professor Geoffrey Willis wished he could toss Pratt's tea in his face. He was growing tired of his captor.

Pratt tore open three packets of sugar and stirred them into his cup. His hands shook like a rattlesnake tail.

"And don't forget, Shakespeare introduced a novel and dangerous notion of romantic love into his plays." Pratt said

"So?"

"Controversial for the era in which he lived?"

"Probably."

"Shakespeare wrote a play called *Love's Labor's Lost* while he was trotting around London with Bruno, the most influential philosopher of his time. It was Giordano Bruno's notion of an intense intellectual love that inspired Shakespeare. He embraced Bruno's theories of freethinking, science, and the cosmos, then used the arts to advance those ideas."

"And the Catholic Church was not happy about it." Willis threw the sugar packet on the floor.

"Not funny. If you're no use to me I might as well find someone else. Did you know that Caravaggio was there in Rome when Bruno was burned at the stake?"

"I didn't. I'm happy I missed that one."

"Don't tempt me, Mr. Academic. What if that *love* was code for the secret that the Knights Hospitaller possessed? A secret love? A power that could 'beguile nature' and bring back life?"

"So what's your point?"

"Forget about the early plays. I think *The Winter's Tale* holds the key that unlocks the secret of the Knights Hospitaller. The reference in the play to Romano as a great artist is irony. He's a Knights Hospitaller. Shakespeare knew secrets were dangerous. Bruno was killed, and Shakespeare made plans to retire. But first he baked a very big plum into *The Winter's Tale*. A clue meant to last for all eternity—or until someone put the pieces of the puzzle together."

"And that someone would be you?"

"He cites Romano in *The Winter's Tale* just by accident? And then after Shakespeare dies, someone adds epitaphs from that play to all those Knights' headstones in Ireland because why? They knew. The Knights Hospitaller knew that Shakespeare knew what Bruno knew. What Caravaggio knew from the same source? What that annoying Doctor Riley McKee may have figured out. Bruno had discovered the Knights medical secret to extending life. Uncovering that secret will keep me alive."

"Good God. Do you mean the fountain of youth?"

"Better than that. The fountain of life. Did you know that those Knights all lived into their hundreds? During an era when the Black Plague usually knocked you off by age forty? It's not a coincidence."

The professor threw his arms up. "What am I supposed to do about any of this?"

"You're going to help me interpret the Shakespeare papers I need."

"Since you have all this figured out, why do you need me?"

"Your own thesis reported that Romano's only sculpting was the epitaphs on gravestones, like Baldessare Castiglione's gravestone in Milan. There's a thread within your thesis that pulls everything together: Romano, Shakespeare, Bruno, Caravaggio, and the Knights Hospitaller. They were all hiding a secret. A secret so powerful that Napoleon destroyed the island of Malta looking for it, Hitler chased it all over North Africa, and the Roman Catholic Church has fought to protect it for hundreds of years. I believe that it's something that can save me from this liver disease eating away at my body." He pointed his two index fingers at his bulging abdomen.

Pratt looked up over Willis's shoulder, his attention caught by a blinking red light on the wall. Pratt picked up the phone and answered.

"It seems we've located Father Landry."

Chapter 61

Vatican Archives

Cardinal Manuel rubbed his hand across his forehead as if he were shining an apple. "There's something I found that might interest you."

"Related to Caravaggio?" Slo Fiz Carbone asked.

"Yes. Those letters you asked for? I looked at them closely yesterday for the first time."

"What did you find?" Smith asked.

"Something very curious. I've studied art history for years but what I read baffled me. The Spanish authorities were pursuing Caravaggio because of a murder he committed in 1606. Yet he was accepted into the most prestigious religious military order of the time, The Knights Hospitaller." The Cardinal pulled a handkerchief from his alb and rubbed his hands. "He's made a Knight after committing a murder? And he wasn't the required eighth-generation nobility."

"As required by the Knights?" Smith's voice trailed off, her CIA senses triggered.

"Yes. There's something strange about his acceptance into the Knights Hospitaller. Shortly thereafter, he's thrown into jail on Malta by members of that same religious order. He escapes from a so-called inescapable prison carved out of solid rock. He's now running from the Knights Hospitaller, the Spanish guards, and the Pope. But yet, he returns to Italy?" Cardinal Manuel's voice cracked.

Smith considered Caravaggio's dossier. "Spanish guards protected the area." She turned away. *Why Italy? That's where the Knights, the Spaniards and the Pope would be looking for him.* She paused.

"He was hiding something. Or he learned something that he shouldn't have known. Meanwhile he was sending his last paintings to the Pope. While on the road. He was looking for forgiveness and . . . protection." Smith said.

"Exactly. Then Caravaggio dies. His belongings seem to disappear. A letter suddenly appears from the Bishop of Caserta in

Naples to Scipione Cardinal Borghese in Rome, dated July twenty-ninth, 1610. It states that the Marchesa of Caravaggio is holding two John the Baptists and a Magdalene that were intended for Borghese."

"The Marchesa?" Smith asked.

"Yes. Merisi was nicknamed Caravaggio after his hometown. The Marchesa was the wife of a prominent political family from the town of Caravaggio."

"Why was he carrying the paintings to Borghese?" Carbone asked.

"These paintings were presumably the price of Caravaggio's pardon set by none other than Borghese's uncle, Pope Paul the Fifth. He set the price of forgiveness! But note there are only three paintings listed."

Smith studied the Cardinal's eyes and his facial expression as her pulse quickened. She saw a twinkle in his eye and a nervous shift in his smile. *He knows more. This Cardinal would make a good operative. He doesn't telegraph all his knowledge.* "But you don't believe that, Cardinal Manuel, do you?"

"No. There's another letter." The Cardinal replied.

"Another letter?"

"From the hospital nun that says Caravaggio died there with six paintings, not three. And this same letter—announcing that Michelangelo Merisi da Caravaggio died in the hospital Santa Maria Ausiliatrice in Porte Ercole--is dated July eighteenth, 1609."

"So it must be a fake letter? Right? He died in 1610."

"Yes. You'd think so. Or else someone made an ignorant mistake when they were trying to create the one *that is* the fake." The Cardinal answered.

Smith reflected a moment. *I wish I had my baseball bat right now.* She gyrated and looked around the walls, taking in the Meridian Room. She spun the point of her Jimmy Choo around the eight pointed rose. *This is why the imposter Cardinal brought us to this room! The very place where the Church recalculated the true date and time for the calendar.* "The calendar was mathematically estimated here in The Tower of the Winds!"

"Exactly, Ms. Smith. You see the irony of this fraudulent Cardinal."

"I don't understand," Carbone said. "Please explain, Your

Eminence."

"The diocese of Siena hadn't adopted the Gregorian calendar at the time that Caravaggio died." The Cardinal said.

Smith started to see the puzzle pieces on the table. "Siena, where he died, still used the Julian calendar at the time of Caravaggio's death! Of course!"

"Yes. Precisely." The Cardinal said.

"So 1609 was indeed 1610 when Caravaggio died?" Carbone asked.

"Yes. At least in Siena."

"Both letters might, just might, be real. But only one of them was written in the area where Caravaggio died. That letter used the Julian calendar which means there were six paintings, not three, when Caravaggio died. The other letter used the Gregorian calendar."

Smith pulled one of the desk chairs beneath her, looking up at the Cardinal. "That's not what's really bothering you." *I know he knows more. He's speaking like a Jesuit, daring us to ask more questions.* "What's the real problem?"

"Three paintings, six paintings, 1609 or 1610?" Carbone asked.

"Naples was controlled by Spain when Caravaggio died. There's a notation from the Spanish viceroy that a Knight of St. John of Cyprus, Rhodes, and Malta appeared in the Naples area and seized three paintings from the Marchesa. The Knight claimed that Caravaggio was also a Hospitaller and that all his possessions rightfully belonged to the Knights, even though it was well known that Caravaggio had been expelled in 1608. After the Knight took the three paintings the viceroy probably took the remaining three paintings. Those three were the Magdalene and two Saint Johns."

"Have the six been identified? Or just three?"

"We only know of three. The Magdalene and two Saint John's. And there were rumors that Caravaggio died with something called the Last Prophet."

"The Last Prophet? Like Elijah?" Smith asked. She paused, realizing that the three missing paintings were likely the most important paintings. "The three Caravaggio paintings given to the Pope were for forgiveness?"

"Yes! And . . ." The Cardinal waited.

"The other three paintings were . . . The Last Prophet!" She exclaimed. "Lost, stolen, traded?"

"Yes to all!"

"What better place to hide a secret than in a series of paintings? It was a painted riddle!" *This guy was a CIA operative's dream.* "It's not one clue in one painting. It's three clues in a series of paintings that make up The Last Prophet!"

"There's been many references to it in Jesuit history." The Cardinal answered.

"Is there any real evidence or is it folklore?" Smith asked.

"The Jesuits were meticulous historians. The teachers, the smartest and the missionaries. I believe you will find validation of these paintings in the documents the fraudulent Cardinal stole."

Smith walked out toward the open veranda. Her heart was racing. She could taste the sweet gratification of history unraveling. "Tell me how they viewed the prophets at that time in history."

"The prophets were the gadflies of religious irritation. There were some that did miracles, others that preached against inequality, some that felt that they were speaking God's message."

"Like Jim Jones or Charles Manson?"

"No. When we talk about 'prophets' in their day we're talking about agitators and predictors of the future, interpreters of God's will. When John the Baptist and Christ came along there were seen as different prophets."

"How so?"

"Christ spoke to sick people who equated sin with their disease. He healed their illness by forgiving their sins. This was something that had never been seen before. And, it confused a lot of people. But his followers like Luke, who was a doctor, marveled at healing disease by forgiving sin. John the Baptist cured people in the Jordan's waters. His ministry was growing in size and power. The Jews might have made him King . . . if Salome didn't demand his head."

How does Caravaggio create three missing paintings and call one or all of them The Last Prophet? "Do you know what the three paintings are about?"

"I don't know what those three are. I don't know if one of them is a painting of a Prophet or if two of them contain pictorial clues. I wouldn't even know how to identify them because he never signed his paintings."

Smith's section chief mind kicked in. "Let's go back to the three paintings you know about. The one's that supposedly weren't seized by the Knight.

"A very smart Caravaggio biographer located one, *John the Baptist Reclining*, in Argentina."

"How?"

"The Spanish guards patrolled the area of Italy where Caravaggio died. The viceroy likely took it back to Spain. At the time, Spain was claiming much of the land in the Americas thanks to the Treaty of Tordesillas. That arrangement made Spain very wealthy. The Spanish conquered the South American Incas and brought home Inca gold. Argentina was created as an extension of Spain. The painting was probably traded or given to an Argentinean dignitary. It's now in Germany, in a private collection."

Cardinal Manuel moved into the fading shaft of light passing through the balcony window. He turned toward Smith and her Italian colleagues.

"A Caravaggio painting called *Youth with Ram* made it to Borghese. It's likely that painting is the Baptist painting we have here in a gallery in Rome. The Magdalene disappeared, along with the other three."

Smith smoothed the wrinkles from her skirt. "How many Caravaggio's are here in Rome?"

"Twenty-seven."

"Too many. We don't have time to study them all."

The lone Swiss Guard, who'd remained so still that all had forgotten him, had moved with them to the door. There he again assumed his statue-like pose. But without changing position or expression, he cleared his throat.

They all turned.

The Cardinal signaled to the guard to speak. "Yes?"

"Actually twenty-eight, Your Eminence. I believe the historians fail to report the one here in the Vatican."

The Cardinal looked the guard up and down. "Interesting. *The Entombment of Christ*. Everyone overlooks it, even though it may be Caravaggio's most important and profound spiritual work."

Palazzo surprised them with a quick outburst. "Why?"

"Location, location, location. They miss it because it's at the entrance to the Sistine Chapel. They pass right by. Yet the *Entombment* is the only painting that Napoleon took during his invasion of Rome. It's the only one protected by the Vatican."

Smith and the Cardinal moved to the center of the eight-pointed star.

"What makes the painting more important than his others?"

"It's not the painting, but who's in it."

Simultaneously, Smith and Mary spoke: "Who?"

"Nicodemus. He's in no other Christian painting." Caravaggio is the only artist who's ever painted him.

Chapter 62

Dr. McGrath's House
Kinsale, Ireland

In the small living room, Jenny eyed the elderly man in a wooden wheelchair sitting near an open fireplace, peat simmering on the black metal grille.

Years of burning the earthy lumps had smeared the hearth but the characteristic smell of burnt dirt warmed her. Two small wooden chairs, covered only with a colorful flowered cloth, faced the man.

"Good day, sir," Jenny said. "Do you remember me? Riley?"

"Riley, my beautiful lassie. You got my message!"

"Yes, Dr. McGrath, we came to find the clues." Jenny studied the obstetrician. Hands like lion's paws rested on the arms of his wheelchair. His feet were firmly planted on a thinning rug. A colorful red, gray and white knit blanket of reversible stitched cables covered his lap. He displayed good muscle tone when one hand reached for a wooden trunk table and lifted the metal latch. A dense crest of white hair sloped back from ruddy cheeks. Though his blue eyes moved aimlessly, they were not clouded. His smile was broad and welcoming. Jenny would have tagged him as a healthy septuagenarian rather than a centenarian.

"*We came?* Who's with you? A boyfriend? Let me hold your hands, Riley." McGrath lifted his hand off the table, leaned forward and stretched. She noticed that his eyes wandered briefly before focusing downward. He ran his hands up and down her fingers, and then dropped them to his lap. She felt a release of the earth's gravity when he slowly tightened his muscles on hers then relaxed.

"Evelyn, can you put some more peat on the fire?" He interrupted. The old man took rolling papers from his vest with his right hand, poured some tobacco with his left, and attempted to roll a cigarette in his lap. His hands shook. "I'm not as nimble as I once was." He laughed.

Evelyn split the swinging doors from the kitchen, entering the living room kneading a towel to dry her hands. The double action bronze hinges rattled back and centered the doors. His caretaker was tall and slight, with two tints of dark coloring in her hair. The skin in her neck gave away her age at around sixty.

Evelyn grabbed the cigarette. "Now, you know better, Doctor. This isn't good for you!" She swept the extra tobacco into the fireplace, and then made an efficient exit from the room back through the swinging kitchen doors. When the thwacking doors stopped, he pulled a single Winston from his breast pocket. "She doesn't know about these." He chuckled, stroked a Bic lighter into flame, and then deftly guided it into place.

"You'd think she wants me to live until I'm a hundred and fifty. I'll have no idea who I am for the last forty. It's like lathering a beached whale with sunscreen." The larger than life McGrath swung his head back and forth with a laugh. "Who's the young man with you, my young lass?"

"This is Jake Bolton, Dr. McGrath."

"Let me see your hands, young man." Jake glanced over at Jenny. She nodded an approval.

Evelyn yelled back from the kitchen, "Now, Red, you know you can't see his hands."

"Red?" Bolton asked.

"I used to be a redhead, young man. Still got the thick plumage. Just not red anymore, so they tell me."

Jenny thought about what her anesthesiology colleagues frequently discussed. They always told her that redheads required twenty percent more anesthetic compared to dark-haired patients. Because of their bad experiences, redheads were twice as likely not to go to the dentist. She looked at McGrath's smile. Sure enough, his teeth were etched with black. *Then again, at least he* has *teeth at his age.*

McGrath's big hands matched Jake's in length but not girth. McGrath murmured something indecipherable then moved like he was dissecting a liver transplant. Encircling Jake's wrist, the old man felt his pulse, then his palm, and then ran through his fingers. He nodded slowly and closed his eyes, like he was counting.

"Sir, I'm Riley's brother."

"Riley, you never told me she'd a brother." He turned to Jenny.

"He's been in the service. I called for him because I knew that we'd need help."

"It's great to meet you, Jake Bolton. If you're Riley's brother, I know I can trust you."

"We wanted to talk to you about the things you've taught me." Jenny said.

"Oh, don't worry about that. It's not important."

"The key seemed important. What does it open?"

"Nothing. Let me tell you a new joke I heard."

Jake shot a perplexed look at Jenny while Evelyn reentered and placed a tray with teacups, sugar, and spoons in front of them.

"An American tourist was passing by a farm and saw a beautiful horse," McGrath went on. "Hoping to buy the animal, he said to the farmer, 'I think your horse looks pretty good, so I'll give you five hundred Euros for him.' 'He doesn't look so good, and he's not for sale,' the farmer said. The tourist insisted, 'I think he looks just fine and I'll up the price to a thousand Euros.' 'He doesn't look so good,' the farmer said, 'but if you want him that much, he's yours.' The next day the American came back in a rage. He went up to the farmer and screamed, 'You sold me a blind horse. You cheated me!' The farmer calmly replied, 'Now how could that be? I told you he didn't look so good, didn't I?'"

McGrath's voice broke into a profound belly laugh. Soon his laughter brought on a fit of coughing. Jake and Jenny both laughed politely. Jenny put her hand out on to Jake's thigh. Jake looked down, covered her hand and nodded approval to Jenny.

But Evelyn wasn't laughing. Not even a smile. Jenny looked over at her, carefully hiding her hands behind the chair.

"Riley, now you tell me a joke," the doctor demanded.

A sharp panic gripped Jenny.

There was an uneasy silence in the room. Then the peat shifted on the hearth. Jake looked over at Jenny and back at Evelyn. Jenny glared at Evelyn and her mind wandered. Evelyn's distant eyes gazed cryptically and didn't move even when the kettle in the kitchen started to whistle.

"A joke, Riley? Remember, I told you some of my favorite jokes." The old man demanded.

Jenny felt the heat building in the room and shifted in the small chair. She heard a click, like the safety on a gun, from Evelyn's direction. She stared at her but she didn't respond.

Jenny leaned back in her chair, bringing her hand up to her

face. *Riley save me.* Suddenly she remembered, and told the joke about the horse and spark plug.

The old man burst out laughing. Evelyn's demeanor changed and she gave a broad smile and a nod to Jake and Jenny.

Jenny exhaled. Jake started to nod and laugh. She knew Riley had given her the clues she needed to help Jake.

Dr. McGrath's face suddenly grew serious. "Evelyn, let Riley see the palimpsest." Dr. McGrath's voice changed to a serious tone.

Evelyn nodded. She reached into the cloth backing of Jake's chair, pulling out a long brown wrinkled cloth and placing it on the table. "Palimpsest animal hide?" Jenny said, "I've heard of ancient stories being written on parchment—that the monks often used stripped animal hide for writing. They reused it by cleaning off the old story."

"They found this up in the cemetery." McGrath said. "Do you have your special glasses Riley?"

Jenny looked at the old fabric, browned and wrinkled with age, its edges ragged and irregular. She gently touched a corner. The only glasses she had were the loupes. Relying again on instinct, she took them out, unfolded them, and looked down at the table. She closed her eyes, brought her thumbs together in focus then turned to the small column of letters on the parchment.

QSTABRF

DCVZWHE

GKKXDIR

AOLTVXY

ASRFILG

TTBDVKD

QRYXHYO

The cipher that Riley had painted on the underpass, minus the UROLOGY code. She released Jake's hand. She felt a sharp pang in her stomach and peered over the loupes at Jake. She took several deep breaths and stood up, admiring the parchment and hoping that it would get her closer to understanding what Riley was working on.

"You need to take it with you." The doctor said.

Evelyn spoke. "You need to get going. You're still in danger. You've been followed."

"Where are we going?" Jenny asked. "I'm confused." She looked at Jake who stood and put his arm around her. She felt a pulse of warmth down her shoulder as he blinked affirmation.

"Old Head. To the golf course." Dr. McGrath pulled a heavy, shawl-like sweater from the back of the chair and Evelyn helped him squirm into it.

Jake helped the doctor out of his chair and held his arm outward as a brace. The three of them walked to the door. Jake said, "We'll take your car, Evelyn."

"I'll be okay, Evelyn. Thank you." McGrath replied.

Evelyn folded her hands. "We did what the Knights asked us to do. It's time to move on. I'll be right behind you."

When she said "Knights," Jenny's heart jumped.

Chapter 63

Old Head Peninsula
Kinsale, Ireland

Jenny gazed in wonder while Dr. McGrath slept during the car ride to Old Head.

She couldn't decide if it was the calmness of his pose while the car thumped over the undulating roads or the years of experience and knowledge he possessed that captivated her imagination. The brown plaid of his wool jacket dressed him in a stately pose. His folded hands were like catcher's mitts. *He smiled in his sleep.* She smiled back when she calculated that he'd delivered more than six thousand babies during his career. Jenny had laughed when he'd said, "the Mom's did all the work, and I just celebrated."

Jenny read the directions to Jake from the envelope Evelyn had given them. Otherwise, there were long moments of silence.

They reached a small gravel parking lot and pulled in. The car crackled over the rocks. McGrath woke immediately. "Now, don't you be worrying about the climb. You each take an arm and I'll be fine. More than fine. Spectacular!" McGrath said.

They walked up the slope of a cliff at the doctor's slow pace. Like a tour guide his speech was clearly one he had given before.

"The air of Old Head of Kinsale tastes like warm Murphy's Stout but knocks you back like a cool ocean breeze. This emerald peninsula thumbs its nose out into the Old Irish Sea, smells like burning peat, and sounds like cracking palm branches thumping at its two-hundred-foot cliffs. With one black snake of a road, this quaint village hangs like the last teardrop off the southern coast of Ireland, its lighthouse winking from the edge of the cliff and flirting good-bye to Europe." They reached a stone bench at the top of the cliff and Jenny and Jake carefully settled the doctor onto it. "I love it here."

Jenny sat beside the obstetrician. "It's very beautiful." *It's a real blue. Completely surrounding us,* she thought. *Unlike the ER—where we use the painted blue to hide the horror.* Jake looked over at Jenny and smiled. She sensed a glow of warmth from him.

She winked back.

Jake turned around to look East then North. The blue sky completely surrounded the stack of land that jutted its jaw out into the Irish Sea. "It's an impressive elevation of rock. Tremendous views." Jake added. He looked down at the raging sea waves crashing against the rock face. "But I'm concerned that we might be trapped here."

"We, who grow old watching you young, constantly blink. Babies become boys. Girls become women. Time stands still while speeding up. Looking back makes us want to look down. Numbers lose their meaning. Here, at the edge of my world, it all changes."

"I still look at the world strategically." Jake said.

"I can relax here. Ponder the years."

"We don't have the time."

"I'm a hundred and five years old, young man. I practiced delivering babies all over this corner of heaven for sixty years. I just hope some of them come to my wake." He let his right arm drop to where Jenny was sitting. She squeezed his hand.

The doctor pointed over Jake's shoulder to his left. A stunning green and black chessboard of land radiated toward the East. "We lived a few miles over there near Cobh. In 1912 we were so poor, we reboiled cabbage for the flavor. But we had faith. I had five older brothers. One day an enormous boat made a stop before heading to America. My ma saw hope and put all five of them on the ship. A note to the relatives in New York. A few punts in their pockets . . ." The doctor shook his head roughly.

Jake was looking back up the cliff, only half listening. Jenny sensed something terribly wrong with the doctor and leaned her head in toward his chest. "What is it, Red?"

"Imagine losing five sons when the ship went down in the frozen Atlantic? My ma never recovered."

"My God. They were . . . on the *Titanic*?" Jenny asked McGrath, looking anxiously over at Jake.

"Oh, and yes, but wasn't the mother wrecked. She couldn't care for me. In a tizzy. Lost in her soul. Blaming herself. She sent me to Killone Abbey in County Clare. The nuns washed me in Saint John's well. Prayed for me. Fed and clothed me. I showed an affinity for the sciences. Math. Anatomy. They cared for me. They prayed some more. Then they sent me into medicine. Now it's over."

Jenny stroked McGrath's hand. The frail skin moved like a ripple on the ocean. He nodded. She felt a spiritual bond with the aged doctor. *Like the lives he touched were passing on to me. The medicine he knew before the books were ever written. The knowledge and experience of his practice must be amazing,* she thought.

Jake turned quickly to McGrath. "Doctor, I'm concerned that you brought us here. We're trapped on this peninsula. If those thugs come here, there's no way out."

"You Americans. Always looking out over the horizon for your escape. You're fragile, scared and clueless souls trying to figure out how the world works. Stop and ask yourselves 'why' I say. Then you'll understand."

"I find safety a natural concern."

"I'll tell you what's natural. You Americans build a wall and it falls down even when you use cement. We Irish put up walls without cement and they last for centuries. You Americans come here with your bags of money. You see this huge rocks sticking out into the sea . . . you see it as a golf course. So you start digging. Before long you find a graveyard. Some druid graves, Stones of Accord, unmarked graves, even some Dolmen Stones. Great curiosities for you."

"Not all Americans." Jenny replied.

"These Americans kept digging over there behind us and hit what we call BFRs."

"Okay, I'll bite. What are 'BFRs?'" Jake asked.

"Big frickin' rocks. Except these weren't rocks. They were more gravestones. Lots of them. Right back there to your right on the golf course. At least they built the fairway around the cemetery—out of respect you know, like a dog leg. While they dug around the graves the golf course architect found writing on them. Quotes from Shakespeare. These were the graves of my forefathers. The Knights Hospitaller."

There was a long moment of silence between them. The wind hissed over the long isthmus in front of them. "Are you saying you're a Knight of the Hospitallers?"

"Yes. One in a long line of physicians, nurses, aides, midwives who've cared for patients all over the world. The scalpel is our sword. When I left the abbey I was knighted and swore my oath: 'I, Michael Gregory McGrath, now in the presence of Almighty God, the blessed Virgin Mary, the blessed Saint John the Baptist, the Holy Apostles, Saint Peter and Saint Paul, and all the saints, sacred host of heaven, and to you, my ghostly Father, the superior general of the Society of Jesus founded by Saint Ignatius Loyola . . ..'"

Jenny felt McGrath's hand tightening.

"Young lady, you're not Riley. Don't try to lie to me. Who are you?"

Jenny suddenly felt lightheaded and her heart thumped in her chest. She started to stand but McGrath pressed his hand downward.

Jake quietly moved away from where he'd been standing near the bench and reached into his backpack.

Chapter 64

Old Head Peninsula
Kinsale, Ireland

"Young man, I suggest you don't move from this rock. This bench isn't built into the cliff rock. There's a small attachment in the wall. Once I sat down—I removed it. Our weight keeps us here. Unless the young lady and I get up simultaneously, the free boulders on the wall of this cliff will explode and avalanche into the ocean." McGrath's face grew red with anger. "Now tell me who you are, missy, or you're going to eat those thundering waves."

Jenny winced. *I shouldn't have lied to him. He's a surgeon. He knew me by the touch.*

\#

Jake surveyed behind the rock bench. He could see that the bench had been cut from the cliff but the back wall was unattached to the rock face. What looked like primer cord extended into the cliff. He looked up and could see the ridge of the golf course. He might be able to jump back and get free. But the boulders on the wall would still take McGrath and Jenny tumbling into the raging ocean.

\#

Jenny felt a draft wind disrupting her balance. She moved her hand on to the bench to steady herself. She felt a knot in her stomach like a wave of guilt. *He knew all along about the lie,* she thought. She leaned forward and looked up at Jake. He nodded his preference that she tell him the truth. "Where's Riley?" McGrath asked.

"Riley is dead, sir," Jenny said, pushing her hair aside and fighting the wind.

The man looked down at her feet. He was waiting.

She could see the emotions rippling through McGrath's body. Anger. Fear. Sorrow. Jenny noticed tears welling in his eyes. She took his hand again and squeezed tightly.

"I sensed something. But you have hands like hers, like a surgeon. And you, young man, calluses and dirt. Are you a caretaker, Mr. Bolton?"

"No. I work for the US government. But Riley really was my sister."

"Unlucky."

"No. Very lucky. She was a great woman."

"Vengeance seek you?"

"No. Justice."

"Be careful. Vengeance is like an unfulfilled appetite. Justice should be your meal. Don't ever confuse them, young man."

"Never." Jake said.

"She didn't tell me she'd a brother. There must be a reason. She was one smart young woman."

"To protect both of us. My job is hazardous. Our relationship couldn't be known."

"What's it you do?"

"I work in special operations for American intelligence. There are some nasty people I've pissed off in the past who'd love to get a piece of me. If any of them found out that she was my sister, she'd be in danger. Was there any other reason that she might've been killed?"

"Yes, of course."

"What, Dr. McGrath? Why?" Jenny asked. "We're looking for the secret she may have uncovered."

"The Order of the Alhambra set you on this path to find me. They used you. To find the secret of the Knights Hospitaller. Young lady, who are you?"

"I'm Genevieve Neugold. I am . . . I was Riley's best friend. Yes, I'm a surgeon. An emergency surgeon, like Riley."

"Damn. I'd wished Riley would take up my sword. Dame of Hospitallers, she'd be. I was teaching her the gifts of a Knight of eighty years. She was the one. She'd the gift." There was a long moment of silence then a tiny squall blew dust in front of them. "Jenny, my lass, I'm afraid you'll need to take Riley's place a bit longer."

"I think she wanted it that way, Dr. McGrath. The two of them were surgeons. She'd discreetly taught Jenny the clues she'd need. She played puzzle games with her to teach her." Jake said.

Jenny felt a wave of tenderness from Jake's approval. She inhaled deeply and shook McGrath's hand up and down.

"We may still be in danger." Jenny said.

"They're coming for you. I know. And, they won't stop." McGrath said. "It's possible Evelyn might fight those hooligans off first."

Jake looked startled. "I should go back."

"Don't. She can handle a shotgun. And she can handle herself. She's also a Dame of the Hospitallers. She's devoted to the cause and will give those men a battle they've never seen before. She's willing to die before she lets them catch us."

"Who are they?" Jenny asked.

"They're members of the Order of Alhambra. A few who've gone rogue. They were hired by a cheating man named Charles Pratt, an American with lots of Black Sea oil money. He's taken their zeal and confused them. With self-righteousness in one hand and a knife in the other, he's been carving everything in his way."

"Alhambra?" Jenny asked.

"Yes."

"We heard about them while we were in Father Landry's office. They're an offshoot of the Knights of Columbus. They care for the physically disabled, mentally challenged, handicapped." Jenny added. *My gosh! Riley was sending paintings through that dock at the Knights of Columbus office at GHARC. Martin saw the painting and was killed. Riley was using that office to deceive the Knights who were also in the Alhambra!*

"Yes. But they're also devoted to preserving the antiquities of the Catholic Church. Their zeal is to protect ancient artifacts, art, statues. But these men are being paid handsomely by Pratt."

"And they're especially interested in Caravaggio paintings owned by the Church?" Jake asked.

"Exactly. That's what they're really after. They could care less about Pratt or his illness."

"What if Evelyn can't stop them?" Jake added.

"Then they'll come here next." McGrath said.

"There's no escape off this peninsula that I can see." Jake warned.

"I don't want them to escape. Sometimes you need to do the unexpected."

"Like what?" Jake asked.

"About a hundred years ago the German U-20 U-boat spotted

the *Lusitania* right over there." The physician pointed south. "Captain Sweiger ruthlessly fired his last remaining torpedo and killed a thousand innocent civilians. Then he raced off to hide. Sweiger then did something that was considered unorthodox, perilous: He came to this side of Old Head, took his boat into the shallow water, and slid into one of the big caves that run under this peninsula. He was cornered if they'd searched for him there. But sometimes something so unexpected can work in your favor. The Brits sailed by three times and, thinking that the captain would never do something so stupid, just moved on. At least five other boats went by, never suspecting that the U-20 was hiding right there." He pointed down the cliff.

"I agree that such a maneuver can work. But we can't get you down into those caves."

"You don't have to. I'll take care of them."

"What can we do?"

"First, you can prove to me that you are who you say you are. You want to help Riley? Do you want to escape and carry on her quest?"

"Of course we do." Jenny said.

"Did she tell you the name on the key gravestone? I gave it to her."

Jenny paused and then looked at Jake. She smiled and nodded. Then she mouthed the word 'barrister.'

"Then find the clue in the cemetery." McGrath threw a thumb over his shoulder toward the golf course above them on the ridge. "Quickly!"

Jake looked back at the bench, realizing that Jenny couldn't get up.

"It's safe now Dr. Neugold. I just replaced the pulley. The bench is secure. The lassie can join you Jake."

Jake reached out and over the man and pulled Jenny up onto the ridge. Then he leaped two feet up onto the grassy area, grabbed her hand, and started to gallop toward the graveyard in the middle of the golf course.

A short stone wall encircled the broken graves. The green fairway of the golf course had indeed been doglegged around the gravestones. Jake and Jenny looked up and down the rows. There was writing on the stones that was remarkably preserved, because they'd been buried underground for many years. He started looking at the names, dates, and epitaphs, reading them out loud: "'Patritius Moran, 1632,' followed by some poetry. 'James Kelly, 1625,' and some more verses."

Suddenly Jenny yelled out, "Jake, oh, my God! Look here. I found it."

"What?"

"Barrister! Johannes Barrister, S.J., 1633. A Jesuit priest . . . or Knight! The Barrister! Remember what Riley said—'Find the Barrister'?"

"Yes. She did it again."

"Look at the ornate engravings on the top corners of the headstone. A cross running through the crown. A crisscrossed shepherd's staff, lance, and sword piercing a medieval helmet. That must identify something." Jenny knelt before the headstone and ran her fingertips over the letters. She couldn't contain her excitement. "There are some verses below the name. It says, 'Could put Breath into his Worke.' Jake, what does that mean? 'Breath into his Worke?'"

"I don't know. Let's get back to the doctor." He quickly grabbed her arm and they raced back to the edge of the cliff, down on to the ledge. Jake moved his hand down her arm into his hand. Jenny beamed back at him. When they reached McGrath, he was smiling, his face turned up facing the sun.

"You found it?"

"Yes," Jake affirmed. "Riley's last words to me were, 'Find the Barrister.' We found him alright. All this time I thought we were looking for a lawyer in London. Johannes Barrister, S.J. A Jesuit priest. A Knights Hospitaller."

"Those markings on the top of the stone are from the Knights." Jake added.

"But the verse?" Jenny said. "I don't understand. 'Could put Breath into his Worke' doesn't make sense to me."

"Young lady, you need to read more Shakespeare." Dr. McGrath said. "Those are all Shakespeare quotations on the Knights' graves. Dozens of them, to confuse and mislead. But that one leads to something greater. The ability to cure mankind's illnesses, to extend life. The gift described in the gospel of Luke." Suddenly they heard a loud chugging noise getting louder. A car grinding its way up toward the top of the cliff. Dr. McGrath gave them a stern look and yelled at them. "They're coming. That's not Evelyn. There's no more time. You must leave now."

Jenny bent toward the doctor to take his arm. "We can't leave you here. Those men are evil."

McGrath pushed her hand away firmly. "It's time. I can stop them here. They won't follow you anymore."

"No. We'll get out of here together." Jake demanded.

"Enough. This is where the Knights last stood to fight the Brits. This is my battleground."

"But . . ." Jenny said.

"I said ENOUGH." McGrath yelled. "You see a dirt path down to the left?"

Jenny stared down the rock ledge and noticed a narrow dirt path between the low scrub bushes. She traced it until it faded down the cliff side. "It looks like it disappears into the bushes?" she said.

"Follow it." He instructed. "With each switchback you'll descend lower and become invisible to the previous path. It'll take you down to a short ridge behind the lighthouse. There's a rope ladder down to a rock ledge. At the ledge you must jump thirty feet into the water. You will see many boats. Take the red Donzi, bobbing about a hundred yards offshore. The key is in the life preserver. There's enough fuel on board. Head due east into the Bristol Channel, then over land straight into London. You'll find Father Landry waiting for you in the National Gallery. Room number fifty seven. He comes there from the Jesuit house each day at noon hoping for Riley."

"We can't leave you here." She said.

"I refuse to leave. Jean Parisot de la Valette refused. I refuse."

"Who?" Jake said.

The Knight froze. He was not an easy man to startle. Maybe he'd softened in his old age. "Who refused?" She asked.

"Valette was the Grand Master of the Knights Hospitaller when the Turk Suleiman attacked the Knights' island stronghold. He refused to leave, even when his attackers beheaded his men, tied them to wooden crosses, and floated them into the harbor." He spoke quickly.

He swiftly ran his finger across his neck. "In response, Valette had all the Muslim prisoners dragged to the walls and beheaded. According to legend, the Knights then loaded the heads into the cannons and fired them at the advancing ships. The horrific cannon shot brought down the Ottoman sails and shocked the sailors. Within days, the enemy size had been reduced by half. Defeated, they returned to Turkey."

"I'll keep going." Jake replied.

"You must. And you must never give up."

"Let's go. There's no time." Jake said.

Jenny put her hand onto her head and pulled on her pony tail. She looked at Jake. He nodded slowly. Jenny leaned over toward Dr. McGrath, grasping his head in her hands and kissed him on the forehead.

"You're warm Dr. Neugold. Now go." McGrath said.

Jake turned away toward the path. Then he hesitated. He leaned back toward McGrath, "What does the phrase on Barrister's stone mean?"

"Hurry. It means *the* breath. *The* Holy Spirit. You're looking for the Holy Spirit. When you find it . . . make sure that Pratt doesn't get his hands on it."

"What about you, doctor?" Jake asked.

"Sir Jake. She's your Dame now. Take care of her. Protect the secret. It will make her a better surgeon. The breath of God on earth! Now hurry! Go!"

Chapter 65

Old Head Peninsula
Kinsale, Ireland

Jake circled around to the side of the bench that led toward the path. He felt a large palm grip his arm, slide down to his wrist and squeeze. He snapped back, looking at the obstetrician.

"Protect that young Dame." McGrath said.

Jake tensed. The deep sigh he let out couldn't be heard over the blowing wind. The sightless doctor couldn't see Jake purse his lips. But he might have felt the electric charge racing through Jake's body. "I will. I am. She's something special and Riley would have wanted her for me."

"Take this." McGrath held out a small brown leather packet the size of his palm. "I'm trusting you, Riley's brother."

Jake bit his lip, aware of the determined change in McGrath's demeanor. His voice was deep and serious. He was a now a man that had completed his mission. Jake looked down the path and saw Jenny waving to him. He studied her tall frame and her long bright red pony tail flutter in the wind. She looked inviting but regal. He felt an urge like he wanted to ask her to dance. A deep sense of urgency. He signaled to Jenny to keep moving. He then turned back to the old Knight. "What's this?"

"It's the palimpsest and the cipher disk you need. Vigenere. You know it?" Jake felt the flush of responsibility. A fellow warrior passing a map. He'd been in these positions in his career. He recalled bonding with a wounded Northern Alliance mujahedeen in the early days of the Afghanistan war. The dying man stayed behind to cover Jake's advance into the mountains. He knew that McGrath trusted him like an allied soldier.

"Yes. I know Vigenere's cipher. But I need the code word."

"I don't know it. That part is still hidden. Keep the palimpsest from the Pratt's of this world."

"I know what I need to do."

Jake looked down the path again, then back at the physician. Jenny disappeared. He could hear the footsteps of the pursuers on the gravel lot getting closer. Then he snapped his head back and quickly raced down the dirt path after Jenny. Jake veered along the snake-like path through a set of scrub bushes, cut between two small pine trees leading down the cliff, and descended onto a dirt path. He shortened but quickened his steps on the steepening path, picked up speed, disappearing into the descent carrying him forward to catch Jenny.

#

Two men in rumpled suits raced panther-like across the open golf course, scanning side to side, and handguns in front of their face.

The taller man in a dark tattered jacket carried a Llama Mini Max pistol. He headed toward the cemetery and he lightly stroked the checkered neoprene grip and its ten-shot magazine. The other man held a Glock 26 pointed out in front of his face. The taller one nodded to his partner and hissed the words, "Remember, the Caravaggio paintings—we get those first. Show Pratt how the pros do it."

The white plumage of Dr. McGrath stood out against the rock wall. The llama crept slowly forward toward the ledge, his gun pointing at the top of the obstetrician's head. Glock converged from the opposite side of the ledge in a classic flanking maneuver.

Llama yelled toward Dr. McGrath, "Don't move!"

McGrath put his hands up. "I'm not going anywhere!"

Glock stepped out onto the ledge. He pointed his gun at the doctor's temple. "Put your hands on your knees . . . slowly."

"I'm just an old man. What's this about?"

"You know what this is about." Llama climbed down onto the ledge from the doctor's right flank.

"Where are the American agent and the girl?"

#

Jake caught up to Jenny. He grabbed her hand and slid past her. Then he stopped suddenly and turned toward her. He stared at her.

Jenny looked up at him, "What?" She saw the quizzical look in his eyes, like he'd also solved a complex puzzle. *Or . . . was he looking for redemption?*

"It's nothing. We're going to do this." His mouth was open. Like he wanted to say more. He shook his head and turned.

Together they reached the lighthouse. He drew his H and K pistol with his free hand. Turning the corner, they found the lower ridge and rope ladder. He pulled on the ladder and detected that it was attached from below.

"I'll go first," he said. "Can you swim?"

"Can I swim? Absolutely. Let's go."

Chapter 66

Old Head Peninsula
Kinsale, Ireland

The two assassins moved closer to the doctor, leaned out over the cliff, and looked down. The sound of the crashing waves muffled the noise from Jake and Jenny racing along the path.

McGrath shuffled his feet below the bench while resting comfortably on the teetering ledge. He felt the click of the lever. Then he sat back quietly on the stone bench against the wall of the cliff, turning his face up to the sun and enjoyed the last warmth of its afternoon rays.

"I'm not going to waste a lot of time before I shoot you." Llama said.

"You'd better hurry. I might just die here with a smile on my face without you."

The Glock approached the bench and rapped his gun on the doctor's knee. "Stop being smug, doctor. Where are they?"

"Smug? Whom are you referring to?"

"The two Americans."

"You can see that I'm all alone." The doctor smiled, aware that most of what he was saying was lost on his captors.

Sitting down next to McGrath, Llama pointed his gun and growled into his face, "I may just want to shoot you. That old maid of yours put up quite a fight. Shotgun and all."

McGrath turned toward the angry voice. He ground his teeth and let out a deep breath.

#

Reaching up from the frigid water, Jake grabbed the aft platform of the Donzi 38 ZRC and pulled himself onto the water ski platform. He slid next to the Kawasaki Jet Ski secured on the platform. He reached down and grabbed Jenny's arm and wrist in the classic Navy SEAL motion.

He raced quickly around the boat.

He found the key in the life preserver. He placed the key in the ignition then froze. He looked back up at the cliff and realized that they were strategically blocked from the view of the bench. Jake took a breath in quickly through his teeth. He turned the key and the twin Mercury outboard 700 horsepower engines growled to life.

#

The noise of the Donzi engines barely echoed across the cliffs and into the cemetery when the assassins stood from the bench. Dr. McGrath blessed himself. He knelt forward at the same time, releasing the weight of the rock wall. He felt a sweet sense of victory. *Ah, the air does taste like Murphy's stout.* The blast rattled down the cliff and shook the lighthouse. Smoke mixed with stone and bodies ascending out over the ocean. The bench, the wall, and their bodies tumbled forward then bounced down the cliff.

#

Jenny looked back at the sudden explosion of rock. It reverberated through her chest and assaulted her ear drums.

"No!"

She felt the urge to lunge back toward the sea cliffs. She turned and ran to the aft of the boat. Reaching out she saw the dust and stone bounding down the side of the rock face. Tears welled up when she saw Riley's friend falling helplessly into the ocean.

Chapter 67
Vatican Art Gallery

"This is the greatest art gallery in all of Rome. Yet you'd think it was a secret. The Vatican Pinacoteca," Cardinal Manuel pointed to the perpendicular hallway. "Most tourists overlook it because they rush to the Sistine Chapel over there." He pointed in the opposite direction.

It was unusual to see the art historian Cardinal moving through the throngs of tourists, delivering what seemed to be a private lecture to a group. The Cardinal's role was primarily one of curator and researcher. Occasionally a special ambassador would request a private showing, but that was rare. The unusual activity was attracting attention from passing sightseers, and the Swiss Guard periodically turned to speak anxiously into his walkie-talkie.

Slo Fiz Carbone eagerly turned to Smith. "Da Vinci, Raphael, Lippi, Michelangelo—they're all here."

The Cardinal folded his hands and smiled his approval. "The Caravaggio *Entombment of Christ* down the corridor is the most important work in the Vatican. Probably his most important allegory. At the time he created it, his contemporaries and all of Rome recognized him and this painting as the greatest of a generation."

Karen Smith fidgeted with the small brass lock on her briefcase. She could no longer be silent. "What makes the painting so important?"

"Caravaggio told the story of Christianity like no one before him, evaporating the space between the viewer and the gospel message. He wanted you to experience their suffering. To feel the emotion of the developing scene. But he also hid deeper unexplained allegories in many of his paintings."

The Cardinal slowed as he approached the painting.

Karen Smith looked up at the enormous canvas towering over her. She swallowed hard, feeling a sudden electric shock down her back. Reverberations ran through her body. She stopped in the middle of a deep breath and felt the rising pain in her chest. Dark visions of her father's burial came to mind: the lifeless body in the coffin, her own inner darkness at his death, the wailing of her mother. She remembered the men lowering the straps on his coffin into the hollow grave. The memory tensed her body, but she could not pull her eyes away from the image in the painting. The ten-by-seven-foot canvas loomed overhead like it was coming down on top of her. She mouthed the words, *My God*, but nothing came out.

Slo Fiz and Mary stood motionless.

Smith felt herself engulfed by the story of Christ's burial.

While the Cardinal described the scene she was hypnotized. "Look at this painting and the chaotic heads and hands moving across the canvas. The strain of this man lowering Christ into the tomb. Look at the graphically dirty toenails on the dead Christ. How can you avoid being shocked and captivated by the scene? It's just so real. You cannot escape it. Because *you* are part of it.

"Michelangelo rejected what the eye can see, while Caravaggio painted what the heart was feeling. The sorrow, the depravation, the fear. Caravaggio's genius was in rebuffing the classical idealism of the Renaissance and replacing it with the realism of human life and death. He defied the rules of art with astonishing originality, clarity, and realism. The storytelling astounded the viewer, while his paintings shocked the world around him. The commoners of Rome saw their own neighbors' faces on the saints, and the clergy only saw profanity. All recognized the street urchins, prostitutes, and gamblers that he used as models to portray Mary here, Joseph here, and Magdalene here. Life and death hit too close to home for the many who gazed for hours."

Smith finally exhaled the breath she'd been holding. The agent inside her perceived that there was more to the story. "I'll say it does. But that's not enough to explain the Church's reaction. Why has this been hidden in plain sight all these years?"

"The painting was meant for the Oratory church called Santa Maria in Vallicella. It depicts the gospel story of Christ's 'deposition,' or burial. This is not a utopian moment in the Church. It could have all ended here in 33 A.D. It captures the darkest hours of Christianity. The religion dies here. And, in 1600, Caravaggio felt we were at that point in time . . . again. He used this moment to make it all too clear that the Church needed to change. Radically change. *The Entombment of Christ* was a commentary on the Church, on you and me."

"It's scary," Smith muttered. "There s no glory, no landscape, just darkness."

"The early Christian Church was lost. Dead. The message of this painting in the 1500's was that the Roman Catholic Church was lost." The Cardinal said. "Caravaggio knew something about the death of the Catholic Church."

"I'm worried that our Church is dying today." Smith thought of the lapses in her own Christian life. *My days at Georgetown led me away from the deeper faith of my youth. My agency career never reconciled those doubts about life, death and the depravity of mankind.* She shook herself back to the gallery. "Your Excellence, you said that Caravaggio put all kinds of clues in his paintings, secret messages. Anything here?"

"Yes. We recently discovered a self-portrait of Caravaggio in another painting. He's in the reflection of a wine glass in front of Bacchus. Elsewhere he painted a bowl of fruit that cast a shadow the shape of a fish, intended for Christian symbolism. We suspect there are clues here in the characters Caravaggio chose."

"The characters?"

"Yes. This is someone unique. Nicodemus—the large distorted man holding Christ."

"Why?" Smith asked.

"Because he was likely one of the most powerful Jews on the Sanhedrin, the council that governed Jerusalem during Christ's time."

"I've heard him mentioned in the Bible." *I think I've heard him in the church masses of my youth.* She thought.

"Yes. But you'll never see him painted again in a Christian Church allegory."

"What does his presence mean?"

"I think he represents the emotional suffering of another lost 'prophet' or 'savior.'"

"There were all kinds of 'saviors' that appeared during that time. And the Romans executed *all* of them." She said.

"Yes. But Christ was a healing prophet." He said.

"Is this where John the Baptist also ran afoul of the Romans?" Smith inquired.

"His message was very powerful. He spoke out against the Roman leader. If he had more missionary time before he was beheaded who knows what would have happened?" He asked rhetorically.

"People were flocking to him. A healing prophet was unique. He was healing and cleansing with water." She answered.

"I believe that before Christ's death, Nicodemus learned something in his private, midnight meeting—something about healing, eternal life." The Cardinal said. "Something transformative. Remember, Christ was a different type of prophet. He was also a healer."

"And Caravaggio learned about it also?"

"Yes. Personally, I think Caravaggio believed that this secret was reaching out to heal him in his troubled life. To redeem him for his failures. He was emotionally rattled and searching for redemption." Then he returned to Italy.

"Your Excellence, you said that Napoleon sent this painting to France?"

"No. I never said he sent it to France."

"Napoleon left all the other Caravaggio's here in Rome. He thought this painting was so important that he carried it with him into battle."

Chapter 68

Bristol Channel
England

"Jake, Father Landry must be in terrible danger." Jenny said.

Jake gazed at Jenny and then slowly turned back at the azure water of the Bristol Channel. The Donzi 38 engines were churning out boluses of foam. The boat bounced over the waves toward Burnham and Berrow Golf Club. The golf course on the eastern side of the channel would help him navigate north toward the mouth of the Severn and then Portishead. He admired the large green cliff walls covered with white floating seagulls. He studied the small dot-like rocks that jutted out from the coastline like stubble on an old man's chin. He knew he could slip discreetly into the large docks across from the Portishead oil basin. There he could find a car that he would "borrow" for the trip to London.

#

When the boat slowed within the channel, Jake pulled the cipher disk out of the leather case and held it in front of Jenny. "The obstetrician gave me this."

She opened the case and looked at the crude bronze cipher wheel. In the center was an emblem of a knight. She slowly turned the dial and studied the letters. She had never seen such an instrument. She handed it back.

"What is it?" she asked, while Jake touched the small, flat wheel with near reverence.

"It's used to translate alphabetic coding text. These two concentric disks rotate around each other and can be used to encrypt messages."

"Like that same message under the bridge and on the palimpsest?"

"Exactly. McGrath told me it was a Vigenere cipher. The Confederacy used these ciphers during the Civil War. It's derived from an Italian model, the Alberti cipher disk. It would have been in use during Caravaggio's lifetime. The beauty of the design is that the decoder can't be used without the key code. The Vigenere cipher requires the user to shift at each position in the text, and the value of the shift is determined by the code key word or phrase. The cipher is considered unbreakable."

"What's the key word?"

"The doctor didn't know. Although we have the code words and the disk, we need that code key."

"That's it, Jake. Riley figured out the code word, I'll bet you anything. She could piece together a differential diagnosis on a patient faster and better than most senior doctors. Her mind worked by coalescing fragmentary signs and symptoms into a conclusion that often surprised her colleagues. It was a gift."

"You can do this Jenny. When you enter a patient's room, you study their signs and symptoms for a diagnosis." She felt a rush of warmth. She knew that he wanted her with him.

"Yes. She's given me some signs but I'm not sure which ones are important."

"Exactly. That's why she wanted us to be together. When I enter a room I examine everything. Let me test you."

"Okay. Go ahead."

"Let's take Dr. McGrath's house. When he reached into his jacket. Was he right or left handed?"

"Left."

"Yes. What was the design on his blanket?"

"It was a colorful stitched wool. It had a lumpy pattern of red, white and gray. In the center was a design . . . like the Red Cross. An eight . . . pointed . . . cross."

"Exactly. And what was on the wall above the fireplace?"

"It was a picture. A gold framed picture." She paused for a moment to envision the room. "A childbirth. In a barn with animals. Family all around. Like a nativity scene. Like that Nativity."

"And, I'm willing to wager that's a copy of a Caravaggio painting. Maybe sent from Father Landry? That's why they killed her. Those rogue Alhambrans don't care so much for the secret. They want to recapture and preserve the Caravaggio paintings." He said.

Jenny felt the exciting wave of discovery crash into despair. Her stomach panged and she felt the heat of anxiety around her temples. She resisted the hatred toward Riley's unknown killer. "Now she's gone. Over a stupid code."

"Yes. But we need to find it before they do. She felt this was important." Jake added.

"She was going to meet with McGrath to decipher the palimpsest. She left us signs to the ultimate clue. I'd bet my life on it."

Jake folded his index finger across his lips like he was weighing Jenny's words carefully. He quickly dropped his hand and nodded, signaling that he'd made a decision.

"Take off your jacket."

"What?"

"Trust me. Let me borrow your jacket."

Jenny shrugged off her blue linen jacket and handed it to Jake. He signaled for her to take the helm. Then he took his knife and sliced down the jacket's seam. He inspected the thin layers of fabric. Carefully, he inserted the wheel so that it lay flat. He then took the palimpsest and threw it into the channel. The heavy cloth bobbed for a while, then sank. Opening Riley's camera he pulled out the data card and slid it into her jacket next to the wheel. "We have what we need in that card."

"You need to hide the key too." Jenny added.

Jake reached out with his hand and pointed toward her hair. "May I?"

"I trust you. Go ahead."

He pulled out the small key they'd found in Riley's apartment. He grabbed a lock of her hair and rolled it in his fingers then slid the hair down through the eyelet of the key. He then smoothly rolled several more locks of hair and braided them to lock the key into place. She felt a tingle in her nerves when he maneuvered his hands through her hair.

"I know you can sew. Close this jacket up and keep it with you at all times." He took over the steering. He revved the engines. Jenny smiled when she opened her medical kit and began suturing her jacket. She looked up at Jake and studied his deep blue eyes.

"Her wounds still haunt me." She said.

"Tell me, what's it like being a female surgeon in a House of God?"

Jenny laughed. "I'm surrounded by a room full of boys."

"Oh God, you're not a whiny liberal looking for sympathy?"

"No, just the opposite. I just need to be better than all of them."

"Do you get nervous before operating?"

"Only before my first surgery."

"What did you do?"

"I went into the john and threw up. Only to find my colleague in the next stall doing the same. Both made me feel better."

"Not Riley?" he said.

"Never. The only thing she didn't like was flying. It feels different when it's someone you know." She said.

Jake paused and slowed the engines on the Donzi. "She'll be with me every day. You'll never believe how much I can love someone. It's scary. You realize that you'd throw yourself in front of anything to save them."

"I often wonder myself. Those lifeless patients in the ER with their sightless eyes staring through you like they've already moved on somewhere else like heaven. Have they figured out the world? Are they still trying on impulses? Feeling pain? Is there anger or just love?" Jenny's eyes blinked repeatedly.

"Riley was dynamic. Hypnotic. She could touch a life with what she understood in their heart. Like game theory in a chess game. She could change life but not just in the flesh we see but in the air we . . . breathe . . . Jenny!!" He replied.

"Yes. That's it. She had learned the gift of the Knights Hospitaller from Dr. McGrath. She could also put 'breath into her work!'"

They heard the waves lapping louder against the hull and they both looked up to see a large cargo ship heading down the channel. Jake revved the engines again and spun the wheel closer to the Eastern shore.

"Ever heard of the Chamberlen secret?" she asked.

"No. What's that?"

"There are some secrets that can live on for a long time. We overlook them. We forget them. Or our own visual bias makes us pass over them."

"I've seen it throughout the Middle East."

"Childbirth was a pretty risky adventure for mother and infant until modern times. Mothers died regularly during childbirth. I'm sure you've heard of midwives?"

"I think I dated an English one once."

Jenny groaned her opinion. She stitched the jacket and taught. "Midwives were in great demand straight through the late 1500s. Their learning was experiential—it was not a coincidence that midwives were women. Men knew nothing about birthing babies. But the midwives brought a lot of superstition along with skill. That's why many were accused of being witches. Their knowledge seemed secret, and they added practices that seemed magical."

"What, they used spells?"

"No, they applied a kind of coincidental knowledge. Take Ireland. A midwife actually performed the first modern C-section there. They were the obstetricians. But scientific discovery was not their forte. Midwives might respond to a difficult labor by unlocking all the doors, lifting the bars from the windows, or letting the cattle loose. They might even toss the mother in a blanket, or flip her upside down on a ladder."

Jake grimaced. He looked down at the wounds on his legs. "Just repositioning the mother might actually have helped."

"Around 1600, along came a barber-physician named Peter Chamberlen. He had his own secret, but it wasn't magic. He would enter the pregnant woman's room carrying a gilded box. He'd place the box at the side of the bed, blindfold the expectant mother, and then cover her naked legs with a sheet so attendants couldn't see him either. He would slide underneath the sheet and do something to deliver the baby alive, even breech babies. Peter Chamberlen was so successful he became the obstetrician to the wives of King James and his son, King Charles.

"He became famous. Revered. Worshiped. Expectant mothers traveled long distances to have him deliver their babies. In the beginning he was known as a barber-surgeon, but the British monarchs awarded him the title of "doctor," a word usually reserved for scholars of divinity. He became the first person called a medical doctor.

"Unfortunately, Chamberlen died without passing his secret on to fellow physicians. It was hidden and then lost for hundreds of years. It took a great deal of time for the medical community to recover his device . . . and his knowledge."

"What did he have in the box?" Jake asked.

"The instrument he created was derived from separating the two branches of a sugar clamp. It formed two spoons facing each other and articulated in the center. Each spoon was placed on either side of the baby's head and then Chamberlen would pull. It was this forceps that enabled safe delivery. Obstetrics was born. What amazes me is how long it took the world to understand. Chamberlen's own family hid the secret."

"How could they do that?"

"Easy. The family buried the forceps under the floorboards of their house after he died. The instrument that explained the secret of delivering children headfirst was lost when the instrument of delivery was lost. Medical ethicists now refer to a 'Chamberlen secret' when they debate the morality of keeping a lifesaving instrument a secret, especially for reasons of profit. . . ." Jenny's voice trailed off and she looked back toward the last waves of the Irish Sea.

"How does this help with our decoder problem?"

"What if there was some sort of secret that Caravaggio possessed that made him the most wanted man in the Holy Roman Empire? What if he knew his life depended on keeping the secret? So he hid his secret in a secret. A kind of decoder. He thought he was in control. But then he died and, instead, the decoder was buried beneath the floorboards of time."

"If the decoder is in Caravaggio's work then we're looking for the same paintings that the Alhambrans are seeking BUT for very different reasons." Jake replied.

"That phrase on the Knight's gravestone, 'could put breath into his worke' might be the thread we need. It probably works with the code that Riley found."

"If this involves a cipher I can be helpful."

"What if this secret is not a painting at all, but the message in those paintings?"

Chapter 69

National Gallery
London, England

The sudden blast of an AirZound bike horn knocked Father John Landry out of his trance. *Probably racing between the cabbies*, he thought. The daily gridlock circling the Trafalgar Square roundabout was taking shape.

Landry sat on a cushioned bench in room fifty seven of the National Gallery. He twiddled his fingers over the open letter on his lap, looking with a mixture of hope and irritation at his watch. This was the longest hour of his day and had been every day of the last week. If prayer could bring about a miracle, Riley McKee would be alive and would walk around the corner and join him. The Toad-like man with the flat face and suit would be proved a liar. Then his treasure hunt with his former student would continue.

Landry enjoyed all the seventeenth-century Italian artists. But he had to admit he'd become a bit obsessed with Caravaggio. He feared the obsession might be affecting his judgment. As a scholar, his thinking was guided by a set of rules that he believed were more than valid; they were crucial to good judgment. Those rules, derived from an analysis of concrete evidence and historical context, provided coherent explanations for various interpretive conclusions. They brought him into community with generations of scholars who shared the principles of objective verification.

Riley, whom he himself had trained in this method, may have fallen down a rabbit hole and lured him in behind her. Then again, her innocent view point had shown him some enlightening findings in Caravaggio's paintings. It seemed that when she had him paint oil copies of Caravaggio's paintings—that is when he started getting worried. What was she doing with the one's he'd already sent her?

The strange note he'd received a week earlier from Riley held only a phrase. *Just like a doctor to use Latin*, he thought. He looked at the letter again hoping for inspiration even though he'd memorized the phrase: *Pellentesque semper ante oculos tuos: eo quod in January lubricum iter est.* Always put your pants on. . . ." He knew what the Latin words meant but not what she was trying to say.

He kept coming back to the Caravaggio hanging in front of him—hoping for inspiration. No matter how many times he studied *The Supper at Emmaus* painting, he just couldn't figure out what Riley had seen in the series of Caravaggio paintings she'd asked him to paint. Sometimes she acted too much like a physician focusing on what wasn't there instead of the painting in front of her. She kept asking him to paint images that he just didn't see. He hoped he wasn't making forgeries for her to sell. He felt they were exact copies she was using in her treasure hunt. Clues he didn't understand. *Perhaps she was randomly searching or probing like a physician inside the body of a patient? What was it that she perceived that no one else grasped?*

He let out a deep breath. Then he folded the letter and put it in his breast pocket. She wouldn't come today. Again . . . she wouldn't come.

For a week he'd taken this seat every day at noon. He and Riley had made a promise: If there ever was a sense of danger, they would head to London immediately. He would leave his U.S. passport and travel using his EU Gaelic passport. He was Eoin Rouge. Irish citizen. The system allowed him to travel with his Gaelic translation of John Landry. No one would find him. Each day at noon, the first to arrive would sit and wait for one hour. He was now becoming despondent that this former student, a friend and muse, was indeed dead. The strange post-wedding visitor had scared him. He left everything behind. He was sure that his fellow Jesuits would be looking for him.

Landry's mood was broken by a new arrival to the gallery room. A very large man and a tall woman seemed to be looking at him. She looked familiar. The couple kept walking.

#

Jake asked Jenny, "is that him?"

"Yes. He's aged. But that's Father John Landry." She studied his plaid wool coat and neatly pressed trousers. His feet were locked together like a statue.

#

Landry watched the couple turn and walk back toward him. He stood to meet them.

"Father, my name is Jake Bolton. This is Jenny Neugold. I'm

Riley's brother. It hurts me to say the words, and I know they'll hurt you. Riley was killed several days ago. You're in danger."

Landry bowed his head and closed his eyes. His lips moved, his shoulders dropped but he couldn't make a sound. He looked up and blessed himself with the sign of the cross. He stared into Jake's eyes looking for an explanation. "So it's true. I was visited by a strange man who was looking for Riley. He said he was from the FBI Art Crimes Team. He was an impostor."

#

Jenny stepped forward and mouthed the word toward Jake, *Alhambra*.

"He also mentioned Caravaggio's painting, *The Nativity*." Landry said.

"*The Nativity?*" Jake blurted out. "There's a picture of that painting we saw in the GHARC garage."

"GHARC?" Landry asked.

"The Greater Hartford Association of Retarded Citizens. Right next to the Knights of Columbus." Jenny added.

Landry kept looking over at Jenny Neugold. "I know you. You were in class with Riley. You were always together."

Jenny smiled. "Yes, Father, she was my best friend. I'm also a doctor now."

"I sent my painting to the 'K of C,' care of Riley. My copy. The hoodlum who visited me asked about *The Nativity* painting. The original, of course. I thought it a strange coincidence that I painted a beautiful copy of it and sent it to her at the Knights of Columbus." Landry added.

"Tell me about this imposter who visited you." Jake asked.

"He claimed Riley was mentioned in a cable out of Damascus, along with the painting. *The Nativity* is a Caravaggio masterpiece that has been missing for forty years. Riley and I have been conducting some . . . research on related paintings."

"What were the two of you doing most recently?"

"Riley asked me to paint a series of Caravaggio masterpieces and put them in a specific sequence. She told me to hide them until she was ready and she'd come find them. She didn't want to use the internet because the allegories had unusual subjects and she was concerned that she might attract attention from the wrong people. If either of us ever ran into trouble our plan was to meet here. I've been waiting days."

"Is there anything else you can think of, Father?" Jake interjected. "The others? Other work on Caravaggio?"

"Of course. She had me paint several. Very real copies. Beautiful oils. I matched his reds perfectly. I sent a few of them to her weeks ago."

"Why?" Jenny asked.

"She said she wanted to see them up close and . . . in sequence. I thought this was a tad risky to be hauling around copies that looked so original. Maybe so, but I had fun. She seemed to be enjoying herself." Landry said.

"Where did you send it?"

"I said, I sent it to her."

"Where exactly?"Jake asked.

"Oh. To her office at the Knights of Columbus in Hartford." Fr. Landry answered.

"Oh my God!" Jenny said.

Fr. Landry turned to Jenny. He tilted his head wondering what she knew. "I don't understand."

"How did she have you paint them?" She asked.

"I started with the water colors in my studio and I positioned them so that they would be destroyed in the event they were discovered—just what Riley instructed. Then I made the oil copies. Almost exact copies of the original masterpieces. But a little different."

"How so?" Jenny asked.

"Though I did them in oil, I signed them." Landry answered.

"You signed your name?" Jake asked.

"No. I signed 'Fra M' for Caravaggio. He never signed his paintings so I don't know why she wanted them signed." Landry added. "But they looked great."

"Which ones?"

"This *Supper* here on the wall. All the rest were saints: Lazarus, Januarius and Lucy. And, and there was an unusual one— Saint Panteleon. Sent them all to her. What does that have to do with her death?"

"Father, I'm not sure. I have a hunch that she was . . . well, she was sending you a message in those paintings." Jake said.

"Like what?"

"I'm not sure yet. I don't have enough information."

"Is there anything else you can think of? Anything related to Riley?"

"Yes. This is the first time these two da Vinci versions have ever been together. There is something unique about *The Virgin of the Rocks*. Riley wanted to talk to me about these."

"We saw both of the versions in your office." Jenny said.

"I put those prints together for a reason. Artists like Leonardo da Vinci embedded clues into their paintings. But never in multiple paintings that might be commissions in different churches." Landry said.

"I can see some differences." Jake offered.

"I've had my theories over the years. The background might be a real place. The rocks. The crashing waves. And the hand positions of the characters mean something. But she thought there was more."

"Like . . .?" Jenny asked.

"Riley suspected something Caravaggio and da Vinci knew. Mind you, even though they painted 100 years apart. She understood that Dan Brown wrote that thriller novel and got it wrong about John the Baptist and Christ in this painting."

Landry pointed to the painting and Jenny turned to look.

"Like what?" Jake asked.

"The Christ is not correct. He was swapped with John. It was intentional by da Vinci. John the Baptist is the key to this painting. Not Christ. She said da Vinci wanted to draw attention away from the background scene. The crashing waves against the rocks. She didn't say what it was. And she said we would discuss it soon."

Jake scanned back and forth from the painting and nodded to Jenny. He moved closer to the painting and scrutinized the landscape.

Jenny sensed that Jake recognized the scene. Like he'd been there. A real place.

Jake pulled out his cell phone and attempted to make a call. "Jenny, Father. I need to call my boss and get you to safety. I think Riley did figure out what Caravaggio knew."

Chapter 70

National Gallery
London, England

"I need to get you out of here quickly." Jake ran his hand across his crew cut and turned around within the gallery.

He pulled up his cell phone and dialed Karen Smith. The number wouldn't go through. He closed the phone and shook it. Then he looked up at the walls.

"Jake, a lot of galleries like this are marble. It reduces the risk of a fire spreading. But it also blocks out cell phone signals." Father Landry said.

"I need to step out near a window to get a signal. Jenny, stay with Fr. Landry." Jake pointed toward the front of the Gallery building. "I'm going out there on to the portico."

"That's the Getty entrance, Jake." Landry replied.

"I'll be right back. Stay here in the public space." Jake turned and dashed toward the front of the Gallery building and found himself exiting beneath the Getty archway out onto the open portico. He squinted and adjusted to the sunlight. He waited momentarily. Then he quickly dialed up Smith.

"Jake. What have you been doing? Burning down a building with the FBI in it?" Smith asked.

"Smith, I can explain."

"I thought you wanted to meet in Rome?"

"Yes. I thought it was there." He spoke in a staccato voice. "It's the secret the Knights Hospitaller has been protecting for hundreds of years. Something that this Pratt guy is looking for. Something about the breath of life on earth? I thought all the clues pointed to Rome. I know where it is now. I need your help. I'm in London at the National Gallery."

"Let me guess. Caravaggio?"

#

Jenny was captivated by one of Fr. Landry's lengthy descriptions of Caravaggio's Supper *at Emmaus* painting. They hadn't noticed that three strange men had slipped quietly into the room through the three entrances. They weren't looking at the art collection but rather circling and flanking them.

Jenny glanced up and noticed the men. She reached for her jacket with one hand and stood quickly. One of the men grabbed her bag. She reached out with the other hand toward Landry. "Father, we need to move," she said quietly, looking around.

It was too late. They were surrounded.

A man dressed in a Black Jack Stetson and black alligator cowboy boots, a white cotton shirt and a baggy pink cotton suit jacket brushed past the three men. He side mouthed some instructions to one of his men. "Sit down, Ms. Neugold."

"Who are you?" Jenny asked the man, then looked over at Father Landry and whispered, "Don't move until I do."

"I guess I should say Dr. Neugold? It's much more important that I know who you are." Jenny looked around for Jake Bolton and contemplated yelling. She stopped when she saw that one of them men had pulled a knife and now had it on Fr. Landry's neck. The other two men were blocking her move in either direction. She rubbed her hands together and felt the sweat. She could feel her breathing quicken.

"I wouldn't make a noise right now."

Fr. Landry looked over at Jenny, his pupils expanding. He shook his head, telling her to keep quiet. She turned. "Who are you?"

The man moved closer to Jenny. She slid back onto the bench and swallowed deeply.

"I'm Charles Pratt. Jake Bolton can't help you right now. Nor his sister—Riley Catherine McKee. I need you and Fr. Landry to come with me. Quietly."

Jenny stood defiantly, ready to strike back. But she had nothing to fight with. She looked back and forth from the men.

Pratt laughed out loud. "No, no, Dr. Neugold. You really want to cooperate. Right now my men in Rome have Jake Bolton's incredibly efficient and entirely predictable case officer, Karen Smith, under surveillance. She's not in immediate danger. But you should cooperate."

Jenny felt out of her realm. She continued to look around for an escape. "Dear, dear Karen Smith. When she alerted her staff at Langley to wire her info on the Damascus robbery, she inadvertently helped me on my quest." Pratt said.

Pratt turned his head toward Father Landry. "That man who visited you in Worcester was mine." He then snapped toward Jenny. "I believe you watched my men also fall to pieces in Ireland, Dr. Neugold. Or make that 'blow to pieces,' eh?" Pratt laughed. "I won't miss those two clowns. I have other friends from Alhambra who are much more valuable. They would've had you back at that college if it weren't for the tower. You do seem to like blowing things up."

"Sir, I'm happy they weren't that good at their jobs." Jenny replied.

"Don't get cute with me." Pratt spit the words out.

"Cute. Not me, sir." Jenny said, placing a knee back on the bench.

Pratt slowly moved a long finger up to Jenny's face. She snapped back and turned her head away. His three thugs looked around the doorways, making sure that no one was coming. Jenny looked over at his men. Surely there was a more honest organization behind their zealotry. She decided to try something. "Your men don't know how sick you are. Killing innocent people like Riley."

"Of course they do. They want the paintings. They'll have them when I have the secret. If my men in Rome don't hear from me in thirty minutes they'll kill Karen Smith."

Pratt moved his yellow, spoon-like fingernail closer to Jenny's face and then traced it down to her neck. She felt the sharp fingernail against her skin. She didn't move. She gazed from side to side around the room, scanning for an escape. There were no viable options. His men had them surrounded.

Pratt stared into Jenny's eyes, grinned, then pushed the fingernail into her neck and drew it down like a penknife. A small amount of blood oozed from the linear cut. She didn't flinch. She felt her blood pressure rising. She gritted her teeth back and forth and the sound clattered in her ears.

Jenny Neugold stood her ground. "You're nuts."

"Ah, Dr. Neugold. Very resourceful. You're just not used to seeing this side of the trauma."

Pratt stuck his long, bloody digit into his mouth and sucked the blood off. She noticed his finger start to twitch. He grabbed it with his other hand and pulled it away.

The last stages of liver disease. She thought.

She instinctively turned back to her bag. Pratt's man held the gun out from the open bag. "Now, now, Dr. Neugold."

She pulled back and ripped it from his hands. "I'm getting something to stop the bleeding."

"Leave her alone. It's me you want." Father Landry interrupted.

"Why did you kill Riley?" Jenny could feel her anger in her temples.

"Because she tried to stop me or mislead me. But she only succeeded in helping me!"

"How?" She asked.

"She was taking Fr. Landry's forged Caravaggio paintings and swapping them for the real ones. I caught on when a heist in Syria went bad. And, she helped me by leading me to Fr. Landry. He can help me interpret the Caravaggio secret."

Jenny felt the carotid pulse throbbing in her neck.

"I have nothing to fear. What are the police going to do to an old man dying of liver disease? I can bond myself out of jail within two hours. What are you going to do, kill me?" Pratt added.

Again her vision swept the room hoping for Jake to return. *Stall for time. Stand my ground.*

"It's you, Landry, who hold people hostage. If you don't help me, then Jenny will die with me." Pratt raised his hand toward the doorway and one of his henchmen brought a chair over for him to sit facing Father Landry.

#

"Yes, Caravaggio." Jake answered.

"That painter either travels with trouble or creates it." Smith replied. "Five hundred years later and he's still stirring it up."

"I found Father Landry here at the National Gallery in London. Riley McKee was supposed to meet him here." Jake felt a pang of discomfort. Speaking about his sister in the past tense—like she was a stranger. It was no longer necessary to hide her identity. Her loss was sinking him deeper. He felt the urge to explain to Smith but she replied before he could.

"Jake. I'm sorry. I now know about Riley. I had no idea. I wish you'd told me you had a sister. We could have taken precautions."

"I felt that *I* needed to take precautions. I didn't want the information in the CIA files. After our father was killed in Beirut and that Op in Syria it was my responsibility to make those decisions."

#

"Father Landry, you've been difficult to locate. I'm not going to ask how you got here off the grid, but I'm going to ask you some questions about Caravaggio. He put clues into his paintings, yes?"

Landry looked over at Jenny, then at *The Supper at Emmaus*, and then back at Jenny. Jenny nodded that it was okay to respond. *I know the ciphered letters are here somewhere.*

"Listen Landry." Pratt moved closer to his face, his eyes dilating with anger. Extending his hand backward he snapped his fingers toward his thugs. One of them pushed the rubber grip of a large knife into Pratt's hand. Pratt grabbed the back of Jenny's head with one hand and jerked the knife forward and pointed the working end toward her cheek. Jenny pushed back and tensed her neck muscles, trying to scream.

"Stop. A lot of painters put clues or symbols into individual works." Landry started. "For example, Da Vinci painted cryptic letters and numbers into the eyes of the *Mona Lisa*. Michelangelo painted God shaped out like the entire human brain on the Sistine Chapel ceiling."

"What about Caravaggio?"

"Of course. Look right here at his *Supper at Emmaus*. There's the beardless man in the center. Christ is never painted without a beard—except by Caravaggio. He paints the symbol of a fisherman cast by the shadow of the bowl of fruit."

"I think he put a group of clues in a series of paintings. Many artists put one clue in one painting. He was such a genius he required you to put together the clues from several paintings." Pratt said.

"No painter has ever put a series of clues into a series of paintings. The paintings were usually commissions for different churches."

"We've been doing similar research, Landry. We both seek his clues to the mystery of the Knights Hospitaller. Their secret for preserving life."

"That's fantasy. I don't know about that. He was an artist. . . ."

Father Landry's voice trailed off.

Jenny suddenly looked over at Landry. She sensed the priest was hiding something. The gallery Riley had asked him to build in his studio came to mind. She realized with horror that Pratt might be right. That studio held the series of paintings. Except Pratt never saw them. He needed Father Landry to explain the history behind the paintings. And, for some reason, the key ones might be in oil.

"Remember, Landry: He was a member of the The Knights Hospitaller. The Sovereign Military Hospitaller Order of St. John of Jerusalem, of Cyprus, of Rhodes and of Malta. They cured the incurable. No one ever figured out how. Ring any bells?"

Landry swallowed. "There were rumors that they possessed special healing powers or their doctors were gifted with skills known nowhere else in the world. Just fantasy. No proof was ever found." Landry said.

"Until now. Proof. The secret. That's what I need now. The Knights' secret."

A noise in the hallway outside the gallery caused one of Pratt's men to move from the doorway. Jenny looked over at the other two men. She thought about making a move but knew she couldn't protect Landry. She had to wait for Jake.

"I'm taking you to meet a Professor Willis across town. The two of you seem qualified to decipher the little museum I've created."

#

"I need your help getting Father Landry and Dr. Jenny Neugold to safety. Can you send someone from the London office? Take them to a safe house?" Jake asked.

"Of course." Smith replied.

A loud piercing siren jolted Jake away from the railing. He pulled the phone away from his ear and turned back toward the Getty entrance. Then he looked out on the front esplanade of the main Gallery entrance. Instinct told him Jenny and Landry were in danger. He held the phone out and he looked around and over the portico. He could hear Smith yelling into the phone. "Jake, Jake!"

He pulled the phone back up to his ear, turning to run toward the Getty entrance. "Smith, get to London now." Tourists were flooding out of the entrances.

Jake ran back through the Gallery into room fifty-seven. The cushioned benches were empty. He then quickly moved to the hallway that extended to the main entrance. Men and women were rushing toward the front.

He made a decision. He ran back toward the Getty entrance and out on to the portico. Fire horns echoed in the distance. The London police were moving past the fountains in Trafalgar Square. He scanned the crowd emptying down the stairs into the square. Jake jumped up onto the stone railing and pulled his gun.

#

Pratt's men held their guns under their jackets and pushed Jenny and Landry past the fountain and the statue. They moved intentionally, matching the speed with the crowd. Pratt turned back and saw Jake Bolton standing on the railing surrounding the Getty Portico. He saw an opportunity. He waved for his men to continue to the van.

He spotted a policemen moving from the curb onto the concrete promenade toward the National Gallery. "Sir, there's a man up there." Pratt pointed to Jake. "He's waving a gun wildly and started this riot. People are scared."

#

Jake spied Jenny and Father Landry surrounded by several men and scurrying into a car past the Napier statue. Jake looked down for a place to jump. Chaos spilled across the sidewalks. Patrons were screaming while pigeons scattered from the Square.

He looked down again. The height was at least ten feet to the concrete. He skirted side to side and noticed a large umbrella covering a hot dog cart. He jumped on to the umbrella and passed through on to the cart, bounced, then landed in a three point stance. He started running diagonally across the square between the crowds, his gun overhead.

Jake passed the fountain at full speed. A huge wave of blue hit him, knocking him back. The three large policemen tackled him to the ground and his gun rattled onto the cement. Jake rocked back and forth and two more policemen jumped on top of him. He wrestled sideways and saw the white van pull away and disappear into traffic.

Chapter 71

Wood Street Police Station
London

Jake Bolton jumped up and grabbed the cold steel bars of his prison cell.

The dark room looked more like a warehouse than a prison. The light from the outside door cut a trapezoid across the cold stark room. A dripping faucet in a dingy small sink rhythmically broke the silence of the room. A metal key clicking against the outside lock suddenly echoed through the hallways. Karen Smith thanked the police captain and he closed the door behind her.

CIA station chief Karen Smith's stare sliced through Jake and he felt the pain of failure. He looked down in disgust. He'd lost Jenny and Landry. And the man who took Jenny had flipped him off after he pointed out Jake to the local police.

"Another one hundred meters and I would've caught the guy. I would've ended this cleanly." The thought made Jake even angrier. He needed to get back on their trail. He'd grown attached to the young Dr. Jenny Neugold and recognized a lot of Riley's traits in her—the inquisitive nature, the problem-solving, the playfulness.

"Jake. I'll get you out of here . . . in a few minutes. The captain is an old friend of mine and he understands that he shouldn't ask a lot of questions."

"Good. They jumped into a van and headed out of Trafalgar Square. Smith, this guy took . . ." Jake started but Smith abruptly cut him off.

"His name is Charles Pratt. Businessman. An American. We tracked him through some payments to the thugs you knocked off. It's always the money trail, eh?"

"He's the guy who knocked off Riley."

"He hired the shooter." Smith said.

"Because she was about to discover the Knights Hospitaller secret. I'm also willing to bet that she was going to make sure it stayed hidden. *If* it even exists. The idea of a power that can cure diseases would create chaos all over the world. Just imagine how nutty people would get? Dictators. Worshippers. Pilgrims. Every

nut with an army. They'd fight to get a hold of it and stay alive."
Jake said.

"What is it?"

"I don't know. But this group? These Knights have long been known for their medical prowess. Riley was being trained to be a Dame of this organization. She spent a year here in London. Met a physician Knight in Ireland. He tapped her to take over the secret. She died before she could get back to him. The path to the mystery is somehow hidden in a series of Caravaggio paintings. But to solve it, you need the code key for an old Vigenere cipher . . . you know, the one's they used in the Civil War. I sewed the cipher wheel and the code words into a disk in Jenny Neugold's jacket. This guy Pratt doesn't have the code key or the location of the secret. But I think I do."

"Pratt came after Riley because of the Caravaggio painting, *The Nativity*."

"Smith, I think I know what she was doing. She was having Father Landry paint exact Caravaggio copies and she was working through a branch of the Knights of Columbus called the Order of the Alhambra. They are devoted to preserving the Church's relics. I think she discovered that someone was after the Knight's secret and she substituted forged paintings to confuse or misdirect them."

"She ran out of time."

"And space." Jake felt the heavy burden of his own words. He'd not fully dealt with Riley's passing. A knot formed in his gut, much like one he experienced immediately prior to a parachute jump. He grasped the steel bars again and quickly shook himself back to the present.

"You can start with that *Nativity*. I met with some art historians. Showed them some high def images from our CIA archive. You know, post World War II we catalogued everything because of what Hitler did?"

"I didn't know that." Jake replied.

"There was something in the graphic detail of that painting they hadn't seen. From our photograph of the original. There's this banner with music on it. It's the Gloria. It's sung at an exact location in the church at a specific time during the religious service."

"Yes. In front of the altar."

"The *Nativity* images the historians were using don't have the banner detail. It's a forgery. I think the original painting was Caravaggio's stealthy way of hiding the location within a church. The guy would have been a great operative."

Jake paused to take in the information and digest it with his own. He realized that Jenny was in big trouble if Pratt found the photograph of the detailed image, the cipher disk and the code words. She was in greater danger than he first thought. He needed to find Pratt. And quickly. "I need to get to them. She's not going to like it, but she's not capable of doing this alone."

"I know." Smith said.

"Get me out of here."

"I can't. You're done."

"Huh? You can't send the police in. I need to go in alone. I need to find this secret and make sure it stays hidden. That's what Riley wanted."

"That's not what I want. I'll get you out. But you're done. Leave this to the authorities."

"He'll kill her." He shook the cell door.

"You can't let your emotion get in the way."

"We can't just leave her." Jake thought about how he'd come out of the shadows only to have Riley killed. *She kept saying, 'you've got to protect your queen.' She wasn't referring to herself; she was referring to Jenny, in case she didn't make it.* He thought. *But Smith isn't going to let me out of here unless I agree to shut down this op.*

"Jake . . . ?"

Jake closed his eyes and turned around. There was a tense silence between them. He could hear the faucet dripping again. His heart beat matched the cadence for a moment.

"Okay. I understand."

"Karen Smith took the key from her pocket and opened the cell door."

"Smith. I'm sorry . . ."

"Don't you dare. Jake, you can't bring Riley back to life."

"I know that. I'm in control."

"So, don't make a mistake in rage." She said.

"Smith," Jake raised his a bent finger upward. "Do you know why the knight on the chess board makes those funny moves . . .

like up one and over two or, down two over one?"

"No."

"Because the knight is specifically meant to protect the queen. To sacrifice himself if need be."

"Jake, this isn't your fight." She said.

"I can't stop. She's all I have now."

"Karen Smith pursed her lips then bit her tongue."

Jake stood at attention and glared down at her. He tried to cut her with his stare. She dropped her head. Then she turned and shot one eye back over her shoulder at him. She was calculating.

"This is off the books. I can't support this." She said reluctantly. "But, should the authorities somehow hold off for twenty four hours, you might be best to get moving."

Chapter 72

St. John's College
London, England

The tall man with the large gold-bladed knife lingered in the office doorway.

The man then turned away, placed the knife into his belt and started backing into the room. Despite her professional honor and ethics, Jenny felt the urge to grab that knife and plunge it deep into his liver.

Carrying the front end of a very large crated box, he shuffled through the door. Juggling the other end was another big man. A second pair of men brought another large crate. Pratt hurried them toward the far side of the room. They placed the box down and left the room.

"Hurry. We don't have much time." Pratt waved at them.

They brought in another box, crossed the large, rectangular, dark red and grey floral rug, juggling the heavy crates. Professor Willis' office had twelve foot corniced ceilings of darkly-stained oak with recessed stone walls. The large brown leather chairs gathered in a square around a low white granite table. Shelves of books ringed the outer margins of the office, a large white board on the end wall. The beveled brownstone windows opened out onto a courtyard and Jenny could see a familiar arch across the quadrangle.

"The St. John's Gate," she murmured to herself. The gate was modeled after the headquarters of the Knights Hospitaller. The Order was recognized by Henry VIII's Catholic daughter, Queen Mary but subsequently dissolved by her Protestant sister; Queen Elizabeth I. Shakespeare's plays had been licensed there. The Gate was a dramatic stone and brick tower of Jacobean Gothic style that created the entrance to the college. Vaulting crenulations of stone surrounded the imposing pillared porticos, overlooking the arch. Adorned with the arms of the founders, the red rose was flanked by mythical beasts possessing antelope bodies, goat heads and elephant tails. *This is the library where Riley had studied when they were in London.* Jenny thought.

Pratt pulled a key from his pocket, yanked Father Landry up by pulling on his handcuffs, unlocking him. He rattled the steel rings onto the rug. He gestured for Jenny and Landry to sit on Professor Willis' office floor.

Jenny turned to Landry. "What are they doing?"

Landry shook his head and rubbed his wrists.

Pratt pointed to Landry and said, "I understand Riley had you paint and assemble a series of Caravaggio paintings. Smart girl . . . Bad girl for trying to mislead me. She attempted to disrupt my purchase of *The Nativity*."

Jenny's heart dropped into her stomach. *Had he figured out the mystery? Did Pratt understand all the clues? It's not possible. He would have killed us by now.* She calculated to herself.

"Those Alhambrans were tenacious in searching for the painting once I gave them the money. Finding these other obscure paintings would have taken me years without their help." Pratt added.

Two of the men crow barred at the first box, then stared over at Father Landry and Jenny sitting on the floor. The taller man pulled out his gun. Jenny pushed back with her feet, putting her cuffed hands out in front of Father Landry. "No. Wait."

"Not yet, young Doctor Neugold. I still have use for you." Pratt intervened between the men. Pratt moved back when the door to Willis' office opened again and his two other men brought in Professor Willis. A gun was pushed against his back.

Father Landry turned to Jenny. "I recognize that man with the gun. He's the one who came to my church. Said he was from the Art Crimes Team of the FBI. He lied." Jenny felt the pang of disgust. She wasn't sure if it was just the imposter from the FBI or that Landry had created some art forgeries. She thought to herself, *certainly Riley knew what she was asking him to do.*

Pratt paced back and forth while the men started to open the other crates. Finally, he grabbed some small wooden slats and started to stand them in the middle of the room. He unfolded them like they were lawn chairs and they grew into easels.

He reached into the crate and pulled up several unframed paintings, the canvases pulled over their wooden stretcher bars. The men plugged in several large steel studio lights. Jenny felt dizzy from the rapid assembly within the room. Pratt placed each painting on an easel he'd put together.

Jenny looked over at Landry again and saw that he, too, recognized his art studio series of paintings. But Jenny saw that these were different. These were all in oil, some of them with the musty glaze of centuries of wear. *These are the originals.* She swallowed deeply and sighed, realizing that she was looking at millions of dollars worth of Baroque-style paintings with Bible-themed stories. She studied Landry and noted that his eyes were straining while he reached out, trying to touch the paintings. *He's an expert. Maybe he understands what they all mean and we can get out of here?*

"Landry, did you know Caravaggio is the only painter in history who neither sketched nor primed his characters and scenery? And he never signed his paintings. This made it very difficult to identify his work." Pratt said.

Landry leaned to stand. The man with the gun moved forward but Pratt waved his hand that it was okay.

"He took the back of the brush and scarred the canvas before painting quickly, sometimes finishing a master work in hours." Pratt said, his face glowing with excitement. "No one has ever matched his gift for painting."

Jenny glared at the pistol grip in the hand of one of Pratt's men. The working end of the gun pushed Willis toward Landry. "Father Landry, I see you've met one of my Alhambran men." Pratt said.

Father Landry tried to stand again. Pratt's man turned and flashed his knife. Jenny put out her free hand flat and lifted it up and down, signaling to the man to hold his ground. Father Landry froze while Willis moved to sit.

"Easy, easy. All of you," Pratt warned. "Stay down."

Jenny twisted her head toward the Jesuit. "Father Landry, don't say anything."

"Father Landry has already tipped his hand, or should I say his brush?" Pratt asked. "You recognize these paintings, don't you, Father Landry?"

Father Landry looked at Pratt, then over at Jenny. Jenny fidgeted cross-legged on the floor. At that moment Jenny realized the impact of sitting near Riley's real killer, Charles Pratt, and felt a guilty rush of hatred for the man. Jenny nodded to Landry.

Landry turned back to look at the paintings and stumbled to his feet.

"I've never seen this many Caravaggio's. I've also never been in the presence of such an evil man." Landry said.

"You're a confused man Mr. Pratt," Willis added. "But you're still a man nonetheless and you'll go the way of all of us . . . 'life's but a walking shadow' for you."

"Very nice. What's that? Macbeth? Well then, this is my 'hour upon the stage' professor and how I know I'm still feeling alive."

"The feeling is there. But without the soul you'll have no redemption." Father Landry said while he stared intently at Pratt.

"So you still feel the shock in your stomach? Your mouth goes dry? For Caravaggio's paintings or for me?" Pratt asked.

"All those. And more for you. My feelings toward you can only be forgiven by my God. The paintings . . . there's deception there too. But honest deception. I'm not sure if it's the shimmer of the portable studio lights or the artist's play with light and darkness that deceives my eyes. I can now see why so many seventeenth-century parishioners had talked wildly of Caravaggio's magic, why the Cardinals sought after his paintings, and why the Vatican had feared his message." Landry grimaced and answered.

Jenny suspected he saw more than he was saying. He turned to sit back down, winking at Jenny. But Pratt grabbed his arm forcefully. Pratt reached out with his free right hand and swam his fingers in midair toward one of his thugs. The man reached into his belt and passed the handle of his nine-millimeter gun over to Pratt.

Turning to face Father Landry toward Jenny and Willis, Pratt held the gun up to Father Landry's temple. "Listen. I'm only going to say this once. He's going to help me or he's useless to me. He recognizes something here."

Jenny could not contain her hatred toward Pratt. She instinctively lunged forward and slapped the gun down. Pratt turned, his eyes red with anger, and pointed the gun into her face. She leaned back with the barrel leveled at her eyes.

Jenny nodded to Father Landry that it was okay to respond.

Father Landry moved closer to the painting on the nearest easel. He moved around the painting like he was building a relationship with it. Jenny expected him to drop to his knees at any moment. It was the allegory from Mark 16, portraying Christ's appearance during the moment of recognition at the Supper at

Emmaus. Landry spoke and Jenny detected the quiver in his voice.

"This is the *Supper at Emmaus.*" Landry moved closer. "See the man dressed in black with a black goatee and black hair? He's wearing the white Maltese cross on his vestments." Landry looked up, and then back down. "Recalling the pictures I've seen . . . this is Caravaggio in his own painting, a self-portrait. A Knight of the Hospitallers. *Dear Jesus, may this your servant have been redeemed.*"

Jenny turned to speak to Pratt, "Caravaggio!"

"Yes, all of these," Pratt replied. "In the flesh."

"But where? How? Did you steal them all?" Jenny asked.

"I've only borrowed them. I have no long-term need of them."

I hope that I can make your need shorter, Jenny thought to herself. *He's made a deal with the devil.*

"I made a deal with the Order of the Alhambra. They did the work. I paid the bills. They can have these lost paintings once we're done with them."

Jenny felt hollow studying Pratt. She cupped her hand over her mouth instinctively holding back what she wanted to say to him for stealing the masterpieces.

Landry squinted at Jenny.

Pratt's men were assembling a gallery of authentic Caravaggio paintings in Willis' office. Jenny thought. Looking down the row of easels, Jenny saw many familiar topics for Caravaggio paintings: Mary Magdalene, John the Baptist, the Adoration of the Shepherds, many suffering saint stories. "Are they all . . . ?" Jenny asked.

"Genuine? Yes." Landry added.

"Some of these have been lost for years. Hundreds of years. Or never been seen. This is the benefit of having the money to give to these Alhambrans."

"These men are not true Alhambrans. The real Order of the Alhambra is dedicated to the care of the intellectually disabled." Father Landry replied.

Pratt answered. "And they started out with a devotion to preserving church relics like these paintings."

Chapter 73

St. John's College
London, England

Jake Bolton lowered his binoculars and studied the roof above Willis' office. No entry there.

Crouching below the archway he could see that the windows were no joy. They'd been beveled outward and downward, just like a castle, to prevent oncoming attackers. *It must be the college students now*, he thought. He couldn't go in the front door—he knew from Trafalgar Square that Pratt likely had too many men surrounding him.

Jake looked through the binoculars again. The adrenaline racing through his veins raised his awareness of the surrounding castle structures. Then he thought he felt the motion from the second hand of his wristwatch. He looked partially away from the binoculars, like something had caught his peripheral vision. He put the glasses down again.

The central courtyard was surrounded by a curtain wall of stone. A wall walk extended out and around the courtyard with a bordering outer parapet. Stone merlons jutted upward in a saw tooth pattern with intervening crenels that opened to the courtyard. He paused momentarily. Looking around he saw nothing.

He stepped forward. Moving across the wall walk like in a low-ceiling attic, he felt at any moment he could step through the floor, trapping his legs.

#

One hundred yards across the castle walls, the black spider crawled across the wall walk. He wore a thin wool cap and a black Lycra running suit. His face was gaunt yet tanned, accentuating his bushy red eyebrows. He moved across in a practiced crouch, a hunting cat in a field. He knew that his prey, though now invisible, would be coming across the parapet on the south side of the building.

He dropped his bag at the edge of the stone wall, knowing he had a clear sight line. He briefly leaned forward from the shadows of the corner arch. He unfolded his sniper rifle, placed the bipod on the stone wall, and removed the scope to check his target point. He rotated the suppressor on the end of the rifle.

#

The Jesuit moved toward the last painting in the row and struggled to identify the narrative. "But how can these be genuine?"

"You unwittingly helped me . . . when you supplied some beautiful forgeries. I used those to replace the originals."

Father Landry looked back at Jenny. His shoulders dropped. He rubbed one eye with his thumb.

"It's okay. You did what Riley asked you to do." Jenny replied.

He turned back to the painting. It was another beheading . . . one that he didn't immediately recognize. A man stood before a king on a throne. Beside the man were several dying soldiers lying on the stairs with slits in their necks. He looked around the scene for clues to the allegory. He saw an executioner's blade, a large snake, a rope hanging from a tree, an ocean in the background. The man was carrying a gold box and a lancet. *Ah! Those were the identifiers. The man portrayed was a . . . physician.* He thought. "This is Saint Panteleon! He's the saint venerated during the anointing of the sick. He was felt to hold the hand of God that cured the sick."

"Panteleon? I've never heard of him. Keep going. What do you make of all the other paintings? Do you see a series of clues yet?"

Landry seemed so excited it was as if he forgot where he was. "Saint Panteleon was the patron saint of physicians and midwives. The Emperor Maximilian's troops repeatedly tried to kill him. They attempted to drown him in the ocean, burn him, and drop him in a cauldron of molten lead . . . that's why . . ."

"Enough!" Pratt yelled.

"The priest paused, then stepped back again. "The blood! There's blood dripping from the lancet. Drops toward the corner of the painting creating the signature, 'f.michelang.o' in red."

"So what?" Pratt asked.

"I know of only one other painting Caravaggio signed. And this is 'Frater Michelangelo.' The Brother Knight. It must have been painted AFTER he left Malta, AFTER he was made a Knight of the Hospitallers." Landry said.

Pratt quickly pointed to the other paintings. "No signature. No signature."

Landry looked behind the Panteleon. He moved down the line of paintings and suddenly stopped. "I see another painting with 'f.michelang.o' emblazoned by the blood dripping down from a beheading." *The victim must be one of the martyred saints. There is also something peculiar.* He thought. "The background here was from the famous *Virgin of the Rocks*. Da Vinci understood the code, all right. I knew it."

"What does it all mean?" Pratt asked.

There was an uneasy silence. "Landry? What are you thinking? I want to know the stories and where they are hiding the secret to the Knights Hospitaller." Pratt asked.

"Will you let us go now?" Landry asked.

Pratt raised his gun like a cobra preparing to strike.

Chapter 74

St. John's College
London, England

Jake inched forward from the shadows like a predator. He surveyed the quadrangle. Scanning across the parapet surrounding the courtyard, he looked for any signs of movement. He pulled back instinctively and breathed the air in deeply, trying to fill his senses. A subtle flicker distracted him momentarily within his peripheral vision, like something was moving on his flank. He froze. His head flinched.

There was a sudden shimmer to his right, like light passing through a drop of water and he instinctively dove to the stone floor. *I'm not alone.* He braced himself on the stone wall. He raised his head slightly to focus on the office building where Jenny was being held. *Jenny is trapped inside that dungeon.* He thought. *And, I might be trapped here.*

#

"You're lucky that it's summer and there's no staff around." Willis yelled as he twisted his body in the handcuffs. Willis kicked the side of the conference desk that crossed the room.

Pratt instructed his men to uncuff Jenny. They then roughly pushed her into a chair beside the enormous desk.

Willis gaped over at Jenny. She nodded back.

"For the moment—consider all of us kidnapped by this guy Pratt." Jenny pointed indignantly at their captor.

She surveyed the windows across from the desk and determined that the drop was too far for a safe escape. The castle walls looked like an impossible climb. *I'm on my own now with Jake gone.* She thought. The leafy vines on the windows partially obscured the view out into the courtyard. *A single exit. Pratt's smart. No escape. He won't keep us here for long.*

Pratt pointed toward Professor Willis and Father Landry. "The two of you need to talk. Caravaggio and Shakespeare."

"Under normal circumstances, Father, it would be a pleasure to chat about this subject, but I assure you, this is not my idea of an appropriate situation." Professor Willis sat stiffly at his desk. He, too, looked tired.

Father Landry struggled to laugh. "This man seems determined to figure out how to save his life through Caravaggio and, I take it, Shakespeare."

"Indeed. That about sums up our task. Whatever happened to the simple principle that one lived. Then, when time was up, one died?"

"Enough!" Pratt slapped both hands on the large desk. His moist hands briefly stuck to the sheen finish. The noise stopped the exchange.

Father Landry turned and moved his chair across from their reluctant host. "Professor Willis. One of my favorite students, Riley McKee, may have come close to figuring out the Caravaggio secret. She loved clues, symbols, and mysteries. Her skills made her a great doctor. This man Pratt had her killed probably because she would have re-hidden the greatest puzzle in Renaissance history."

Willis looked over at Pratt. "Riley was my student as well. During her Oxford term. Bright girl. Such a bright girl." He looked over at Jenny. "My dear child! Light finally dawns on Marblehead! You were her tall friend!"

Jenny smiled wanly. There was little comfort to be reminded of her lost friend. Riley had started her last days with such optimism for meeting her brother and going on this treasure hunt. Now Jenny felt alone, trapped and struggling for answers to the puzzle Riley solved. There was a heavy weight in her throat as she swallowed.

Landry rubbed his palms together and tried to steady them over the desk. "Riley wanted me to meet her at a specific painting at the National Gallery. Instead, this man showed up."

Willis shot an angry look over at Pratt again. "What was the painting Riley wanted to see?"

"*The Supper at Emmaus.* Some people call it *Supper on the Road to Emmaus* or just *Supper.* Caravaggio painted Christ in that one without a beard, as if to make him unrecognizable to his disciples and the viewer. But then he put a mysterious clue on the table—a shadow of the Jesus fish, the ichthys symbol. You can see the shadow in the center of the table. The fish tells you that Christ is present in disguise."

Pratt pulled out his book of notes that he'd collected on

Shakespeare and Caravaggio. "I don't understand." Willis said.

"It all started there. In that painting. Some imperative Caravaggio felt. Conceal. Hide code meaning into the paintings." Pratt replied.

"It all starts right here. It starts at the end. *The Supper at Emmaus*, when Christ met his disciples, who didn't recognize him. Hidden in plain sight. At the center of the painting he's reaching out and pointing at you, the viewer. He is calling you into the secret." Landry added.

Willis stroked his chin thoughtfully. "What's this painting's original provenance, Father Landry?"

"It was painted for Philippe de Bethune." Landry's professorial voice trailed off.

"The French ambassador to Rome. And Shakespeare's patron, Lord Wriothesley, worked for that ambassador." Willis said.

"They were all one group." Landry said. "The *Supper* was painted soon after Caravaggio's other friend, Giordano Bruno, was burned at the stake in Rome by the Catholic Church."

Willis rapidly tapped his fingers on the desk. Help me understand. "At the same time there was a Catholic rebellion in Ireland being put down by Queen Elizabeth, the King of Spain reached out and sent the Knights Hospitaller to Ireland to fight alongside the Catholics? And, at the same time, she imprisoned Lord Wriothesley for conspiring with the Catholics. That angered Shakespeare?"

"Yes!" Landry and Willis exclaimed simultaneously.

These scholars could not help themselves. Jenny looked over at Pratt with an expression of disdain. Pratt smirked. He knew his dream team was coming together.

Landry practically jumped with excitement. "The same Lord Wriothesley that was the 'fair youth' in Shakespeare's sonnets?"

"The same! And Wriothesley, the Earl of Southampton, was on the French ambassador's staff with none other than Giordano Bruno. Both of them were imprisoned at about the same time." Willis added. "I've always believed that Bruno was burned at the stake because he gave the odd book called *I Modi* to Wriothesley. Bruno spoke of a different type of love, one that was contrary to the Church's teachings."

"One that could destroy the Church?" Father Landry asked.

"What if that forbidden or superior love was, in reality, some sort of power that was really a threat to the Church? Some secret that the Church could not afford to release to the world?" Pratt asked.

Jenny felt a spike of horror down her back at the thought of such a powerful secret. Exposed to the whole world it would destroy the Church she lived and loved.

Willis proceeded to answer the question. "I believe that Lord Wriothesley shared the Romano book with Shakespeare, who couldn't help but be amused by the graphic sexual content. Remember, there was no Playboy TV channel, no *Hustler* magazine, no Internet porn sites. I mean, good lord, there weren't even female actors. Shakespeare couldn't help but be excited by Romano's drawings. The raunchy verses? They probably couldn't contain the thrill. And the ties that bind. He rewards Romano for giving him this pleasure, making him the only Renaissance artist he ever mentioned in a play!"

Landry stood up and leaned even further in toward Willis, grabbing the sides of the desk. Pratt's men moved forward but Pratt raised his hand to hold them back. "It can't be as simple as that, paying the bill for titillation? What is Caravaggio's The Last Prophet—the secret that can extend life?"

"No, of course not. At the same time that Caravaggio used the Romano drawings to do his resurrection paintings on Sicily, Shakespeare wrote The Winter's Tale about the resurrection of Hermione in Sicily." Willis added.

Pratt kept flipping through his heavy book of notes. He mumbled, "Is the secret in Sicily?"

Willis elaborated. "This part of *The Winter's Tale* is not about Hermione's appearance, but rather how Romano could *make* her appear. Even after Shakespeare describes her, you still have no idea what she looks like. It's about how *he could make her*. How that *love* could make her come alive! She is described only in the terms of Romano's greatness and skill as a sculptor, as an artist, as a purveyor of reincarnation. Only the gift of Romano's sculpting could make her appear so real—that she became real."

Jenny looked away from the windows toward Pratt. She thought back to her own Catholic Confirmation. The prayers, the recitations, the communion. She believed it was a gradual transition toward religious conversion as an adult. Her stomach knotted. The thought of this man getting his hands on such an important power. Could this man Pratt even believe in a higher being? What if this gift of life required a belief in God to even see or experience a conversion? "So, Mr. Pratt, is this the gift of life that you are seeking? You need a sculptor like Romano?" Jenny asked.

Chapter 75

St. John's College
London, England

Jake rolled onto his back and, in one swift motion, pulled his HK Mark 23 pistol and released the safety.

Someone was tracking him. From somewhere along the opposite castle wall. A sniper. His breathing initially quickened. He looked back and up to see that there was no one on the roof top above him. Gathering his senses, he took a deep breath, closed his eyes briefly and slowly, pulling himself to his knees behind a stone merlon.

He recalled an operation in Kabul when a Taliban sniper had him dead to rights but hesitated. At that instant a truck drove by and kicked up some sand obscuring his view. That gave Jake the brief moment he needed to escape into a culvert. Eventually he flanked the sniper and knocked him off with a single shot.

He listened intently for movement. *Was he on my right or left?* He thought.

#

Father Landry put his hand over the gun barrel. He stared into Pratt's dark eyes. Pratt lowered the gun.

There was a long, uneasy silence and Jenny noted the hesitation in the man's movements. *Was it his disease?* Jenny stored the information. *I might need to use that against him.*

Pratt finally looked down at Jenny, then over at his men, who also had readied their guns. "Pretty brave of you, Father."

"Not really. I'm an old man. I don't need to put up with your bullying."

"I still don't have my answer, Father."

Pratt raised the gun again and pointed it this time at Jenny. She tilted her head in disdain. She disliked guns but it was more conceptual. She'd only seen the damage they did to patients and the work they created for the trauma rooms at Connecticut General Hospital.

Father Landry turned and Jenny nodded her head in return.

The priest again put his hand over the barrel of Pratt's gun, this time gently pushing it in the direction of the paintings. "That third painting with Caravaggio's signature is Saint Januarius. He's the patron saint of Naples and famous for the Blood Miracle." Landry said.

"Who? The what?" Pratt asked as he stepped back.

Taking a deep breath, Jenny looked at Willis. *Had the Brit figured it out? Did he know what* The Last Prophet *was?* Jenny continued to scan the room realizing that an escape would have to wait. The room layout, the brownstone beveled windows recessed into rere-arches and the height of the jump was too much to overcome. She made an inventory of Pratt's men—the knives and pistols they carried. *Now I know what Jake feels like.* She thought.

Willis laughed. "You really don't know southern Italy, do you? Tell him the story, Father Landry." Willis said.

"Saint Januarius was the Bishop of Naples. He was martyred for protecting Christians and refusing to disavow Christ during the pagan Roman Emperor Diocletian's reign. He was thrown to the wild beasts, but they refused to eat him. He was thrown into a furnace but came out alive. When he was finally beheaded, blood flowed from his decapitated head and was caught in a vial by a woman. To this day, a portion of the dried blood is kept in a sealed vial in the Naples Cathedral and is taken out three times a year. The blood is brought to the altar and mysteriously liquefies as the congregation prays. If the blood does not liquefy then the parishioners believe a great tragedy will hit the city, like the eruption of Mt. Vesuvius or the massive Naples earthquake in 1980."

"So, is the secret in Naples?" Pratt asked.

"No. The liquefaction of the blood is the clue. Naples has become known as 'Urbs Sanguinum.' Meaning, 'The City of Bloods.'"

Jenny cocked her head to the side. "I'm sorry, Father Landry, but it must be a trick. Clotted blood can liquefy, but once it does, it will never return to solid form again."

"I didn't say I believed the miracle, Jenny. I said I knew the legend. And that's the clue." He turned back to Pratt. "Tell me you've been to Little Italy in New York City?"

"Yes, of course." Jenny answered.

"The San Gennaro festival? The highlight of the year? The

locals of Neapolitan descent march through the area with an enormous statue in front of the parade." Father Landry said.

"Never saw that." Jenny replied.

"San Gennaro is Saint Januarius. Professor Willis? Guess who went to Naples and took home the majority of the blood sample early in the sixteenth century?"

Willis smiled. "King Charles of Spain again!"

"Exactly!" Landry said.

"So, Caravaggio was there in Rome when Bruno is burned at the stake by the Catholic Church. Bruno was a pal of Shakespeare and worked with Lord Wriothesley. Lord Wriothesley was Shakespeare's financial backer and preserved all of his works there in a library dedicated to the Knights Hospitaller. Romano has a gift. A gift unknown as his role as a Knights Hospitaller. Finally, Caravaggio, also a Knight, paints masterpieces with secrets like a madman murderer on the run." Willis said.

#

Jake Bolton sensed the sniper was readying his position, waiting for him to move into the open. He noted that the firing spaces on the wall walk were limited. Any good sniper would set up his final firing position with a location for escape. *He must be near the north corner*, he thought.

Jake calculated like he was playing his three dimensional chess game. He loved the game. Unlike standard chess in two dimensions, Raumschach chess more closely resembled modern warfare where the opponent could use unconventional moves, attack from below or above and escape over great distances. But, these players couldn't leave the board. And, this sniper was also trapped on the wall walk, knowing his first shot was his best shot.

Jake sensed he needed to increase his odds. Escape required calculation and misdirection. His H and K .45-caliber pistol was another board piece on his side. It was his game theory analysis and anticipation which moved the weapon around his board.

Chapter 76

St. John's College
London, England

Jenny stared at Pratt. She perceived an element of satisfaction in his face. Like an awareness of his surroundings.

For the first time, she looked at him like a patient. The pasty white shine on his skin, the redness from his unfolding lower eyelid, the brittle appearance of his hair all reminded her of a cancer patient being eaten slowly by his tumor. She sensed fatigue and dehydration. His demeanor was a man in a trance, at times in a fog moving without thought. A man with an inner battle with liver disease and an outer battle to find a cure.

Pratt reached on either side of his chair to pull himself up. "Please explain."

"These Caravaggio paintings are the work of a man fighting to save his soul." Landry started. "They're an attestation of faith, a plea for forgiveness, while Caravaggio imagined a way to tell a story that might gain him redemption. He painted that story not into one, but into several paintings to illustrate a pathway to salvation, to healing. Remember, for him, painting was communication."

"You need both Shakespeare and Caravaggio's clues." Willis suggested, raising his hands in excitement.

"I agree. Shakespeare knew of the secret but probably only Caravaggio experienced it." Father Landry blurted out the message Riley had sent to him: "*Pellentesque semper ante oculos tuos: eo quod in January lubricum iter est.*"

Pratt wiped his brow with a handkerchief. Jenny sensed that he was fighting back much needed rest.

She looked toward the bottom of his untucked white shirt. Hanging over his bulging abdomen she could see the dilated veins of a caput medusa, a sure sign of portal hypertension. The elevated abdominal blood pressure caused fluid to build up in his abdomen and the veins to bulge. Pratt occasionally seemed to doze briefly as he leaned back to sit. *He was suffocating in his own vat of blood and water.* "What's that gibberish?" Pratt asked.

Willis burst out laughing, and then translated the line for Pratt. "Latin. The old mass, Father? 'Always put your pants on first, because January's road is slippery.'"

Jenny smiled and murmured, "Never lower Tillie's pants! Just like Riley and the carpal bones in the hand."

"What?" Pratt asked.

"It's a mnemonic." She replied. "We use them in medicine all the time. To remember code sequences, to treat patients, to recall protocols. Riley created her own for Caravaggio's secret—to this . . . this *Last Prophet*. Panteleon is first, then Januarius, then the Road. The paintings are all the signed ones. The Saint Panteleon is first in the order and the Supper on the Road to Emmaus is last."

Landry nodded.

Professor Willis considered the paintings, and then spoke directly to Jenny and Landry. "All of these stories are about saints or a Christ who would not die."

Pratt suddenly became alert. He rolled from his flimsy chair and sauntered to one of the paintings. "The two saints are painted in a mysterious place. It's exactly the background in the *Virgin of the Rocks*. We need to find this place."

#

Jake pulled his knife from his back pack and scraped the stone merlon. Shards of stone broke free and landed at his feet. He eyed two golf-ball sized rocks and placed them in his hand, much like a split fingered hold on a baseball. Leaning forward he threw the stones out over the wall to the opposite wall walk.

As the stone spread out they hit separately in a clack, clack against the stone wall. At that moment, Jake dove across the crenel and spun into the corner.

The hiss of the gunfire preceded the sparks flying from the stone. The wall near his feet exploded in a fusillade of bullets. Stone splintered off the walls.

Jake buckled backward and leaned into the covered archway. Lunging forward from his knees he leapt up onto the outside parapet, his pistol moving into his right hand. Jake raced across the parapet toward the north side of the castle, his pathway obscured by the angle of the merlons.

#

The sniper looked away from his scope. The sudden move

caught the sniper off guard. He pulled his rifle scope away and looked for any movement. *Nothing. There was no way off that wall walk.* He thought. Instinctively, he pulled the gun apart and quickly placed it back in the case. He drew his pistol and listened for any sound.

#

The unexpected popping sound froze Jenny. She snapped her head toward the courtyard window.

Pratt thumped his hand on the desk again.

"Even when we get there, I'm not sure where to look." Jenny pushed herself up from the chair. "Let them go. I can help."

"Don't worry, Doctor. You will all help."

"You don't understand. I'm Riley's best friend. She was training me to take her place."

"How romantic," Pratt said smugly.

"I'm a first-class decoder. She had Father Landry make those paintings and arrange them in his gallery just in case. They were there for me. That's why she wanted to go back to the College before Ireland. And I do know. I know the background in the Panteleon painting. The secret is there. The second clue is Januarius; he couldn't be beheaded. The blood was miraculous. Last, Emmaus refers to transubstantiation. You know, conversion of matter into spirit? Eternal life." Jenny became uneasy with the mention of transubstantiation. She knew that beneath Pratt's callous surface was a cold atheist. Even if he found the secret he may not be capable of believing that it was a religious conversion that he required.

Pratt's face was flushing red, but now with excitement, not fever. "Where? Tell me where."

"Let them go. I know where the secret is. They don't."

"I can't do that."

"We're prepared to die. I'll take the secret with me if you threaten my friends again." Jenny warned. To her, Pratt's threats were mere fingernails on a blackboard.

Jenny felt a sense of reluctance as she stared at the faded reflection in the table. She thought about asking for a pass for her youth. Then the visions of her Confirmation came back to her. The feeling of conviction warmed her, comforted her. She smiled over at Landry who said, "I'm with you. All the way."

Chapter 77

St. John's College
London, England

Jake shot a glance around the outside wall of the castle. Nothing there.

He looked down through the hole in the wall walk floor. He knew he had to be aggressive. *Game theory*, he thought. He was taking chances. But it was his best one. He was cornered and he didn't have a rook to castle out with. A straight-on unexposed attack was not possible. Decision time. *Make my move. To save the queen,* he thought.

He dropped down through the machicolation, the hole created for dropping stones on medieval invaders. Hanging from the intervening stone battlements momentarily, he then moved hand over hand across the outside castle wall. His movement was slow, strained but steady. The sniper couldn't see him from above unless he charged toward him along the wall.

Finally, he pulled himself upward, leaping up onto the merlon from one corner. He dove for the crenel, facing the arch. With both hands steadying his pistol he squeezed. Two shots hissed from his gun into the darkness of the arch.

A grunt echoed from the shadows.

Jake kept rolling, hitting the stone wall at the corner of the crenel and merlon. He leapt onto one knee, his gun pointing forward.

\#

Another strange cracking sound echoed into the room. Jenny gazed over at the window.

Pratt tossed his gun to one of his guards and moved toward the window. "We're almost done here." He moved back and stood over Jenny in her chair. The confused guards looked back and forth at each other.

He leaned into her and whispered, "Hear those gun shots? It seems your hero Jake is here. We need to hurry."

Jenny tried to stand but her legs felt weak. She pushed herself up from the chair but she felt unsteady. "Jake," she murmured.

"Is the secret at the Knights Hospitaller headquarters in Rome? Naples? Sicily?"

Landry put his hand up to her face and then down on her shoulder. She mouthed the words, *Trust me*. She felt a tingling from the nerves firing down her neckline and into her body.

Jenny rushed her voice. "No. It's still in Malta. Something happened in Malta." She felt the need to help Jake, if there was a chance. She was in charge now.

Pratt shook his head in violent disagreement. "That's not possible. They would have taken it from Malta! Hitler, Napoleon both went there. One of them would have taken it . . . or destroyed it. More bombs have hit Malta than any other place in history."

"Of course. If they'd found it. But they didn't," Landry replied.

"The pieces are coming together," Jenny said. "Caravaggio escaped from a jail on Malta. A lockup no one had ever escaped from. Someone must've lowered him a rope and he got away. Right?"

"Not possible." Pratt exclaimed.

"You see the jagged shoreline, the crashing waves? In da Vinci's *Virgin of the Rocks*. In these other paintings? That's Malta." She said.

Landry waved his hand at the easels. "Look at the particular paintings he produced on the run AWAY from Malta. All of them point to something profound. All pointing backwards. From Syracuse to Messina, from Messina to Palermo. This is a map. A painter's map."

"But where on Malta?" Pratt demanded.

Willis and Landry looked at each other, each arching an eyebrow. Jenny then felt the weight of their stare. They knew she knew.

"What?" Jenny said. "Riley was assembling this . . . for me . . . 'just in case.' This is what I can do. I put clues together. She had nearly all the clues. But not all." Jenny said.

Father Landry gave Jenny a thumbs-up sign. "*The Burial of St. Lucy* in Syracuse. *The Raising of Lazarus* in Messina. Last, *The Nativity* in Palermo. They are part of the sequence. I'm convinced. Riley had asked me to paint those in oil." The priest replied.

Jenny turned, "Doctor McGrath said—'Put breath into his work?'"

"Yes?"

Jenny pointed to the Lazarus painting. "Look at Christ pointing at Lazarus. There is light shooting across the room from behind Christ. Lazarus is in rigor mortis. Crucified shape. The palm of Lazarus's right hand should block the light. But the light is too powerful and goes past it without creating a shadow over onto the right side of the frame. His left hand is reaching downward. Why is that, Father Landry?"

"More allegory. He's pointing into purgatory. Entombment. Where Lazarus' soul descends to wait. This painting teaches us that even the rigor of death cannot stop the power of life." Landry said.

Jenny rubbed her fingers together. *Is Jake alive? Do I stall or do I rush this?* She wished that Jake or Riley were with her.

Father Landry put both hands above his head and leaned back as if to capture all of Caravaggio's hidden secrets. He leaned forward. "There's more. There should be a shadow on Mary and Martha's right side in the *Lazarus* painting. But there isn't. Christ doesn't cast a shadow. This is Caravaggio's intention. Here is the supremacy of life." Father Landry spoke faster and faster. "I know the face above Christ's arm is Caravaggio's. He's showing wide-eyed optimism. In the mirrored position on the right is Mary Magdalene, who has long been portrayed as a sinner—like Caravaggio. Together, they are looking into the scene, like they just arrived on the event, for their own healing and redemption. Caravaggio paints himself and us into a scene like no other painter can. Imagine the sacrilege and outcries this painting caused?"

"Look at how Christ's power to heal distracts all the actors in the painting except one: Martha. Look at Martha stooped over Lazarus, blowing air on his head. Martha, not Christ, is breathing life into Lazarus, helping to heal and raise him from the dead." Father Landry turned to Professor Willis. "Didn't you say it was Romano who could 'breathe life into his work'?"

"Yes, but those are not my words—"

Jenny interrupted the professor, calling on her catechism of her youth. "When Christ died, what happened to the disciples? They were confused, lost, scattered, disorganized, and fearful. Right?"

"Yes. The Church was dead."

"Their lives were a mess. They didn't know what to do. What

happened to Lazarus? He was a refugee. I'm sure you know."

Father Landry smiled and nodded. "I think I know where you're going with this. In the Gospel of John, 'the chief priests consulted that they might put Lazarus also to death. Because that by reason of him many of the Jews went away and believed in Jesus.'"

"This was a time of life and death for the entire religion. Christianity could have all died right there." Willis said. "Evaporated into history. Another dead religion."

"I've lived there in the Middle East. The population has endured repeated exiles after persecutions, entire peoples on the run, and seismic shifts in geopolitical populations. Getting killed just for your religion. You breathe in the history with the sand. Recall that Judeo-Christians scattered all over the Mediterranean after Christ died." Landry answered. "But Lazarus hung around Jerusalem to talk about his own resurrection. Then he got scared. With Christ gone, were the Christians going to try to make Lazarus king? He escaped to Cyprus and lived long into his hundreds. He supposedly healed many illnesses and diseases. And guess what? When the Knights of St. John of Jerusalem left, where did they go?"

"They joined him in Cyprus." Willis answered.

Father Landry stood in front of *The Burial of St. Lucy*. "Do you know the story of Saint Lucy? It's said that Lucy prayed with her mother at the tomb of Saint Agatha. Her mother's long-standing illness was miraculously cured. Lucy was also stabbed in the neck during her torture and persecution."

"Father, there's more." Jenny, who'd been wondering about Jake, jumped into the conversation. "I see the pattern. This is where Riley may have connected the paintings. Look at the very center of the painting. The most important person? Kneeling over the body is a woman with two hands up to her cheeks, blowing air onto the dead body of Lucy."

"Yes, that's the same woman within *The Nativity*. The painting that was stolen by the Mafia in the late 1960s. He reused his images and character positions in separate stories but with the same intended meaning." Father Landry said. This is a series of clues that can only be deciphered with the paintings together, something that he hoped would take place with the right person.

Pratt snapped his fingers in agreement.

"That painting may have turned up in Damascus a few days ago." Landry added. "Riley may have been aware of it. And she had me paint a copy to prevent you from getting it. Then it disappeared."

#

Jake spied the sniper lying motionless on his side. He moved forward, his gun readied. The tall man with the red eyebrows groaned and a pool of blood radiated from beneath his arm. Jake leaned over the man and a wave of recognition hit him. The black Lycra suit covered part of his green fatigues. Jake swallowed deeply as he lowered the gun. Disgusted, he leaned against the archway wall. *Digger.*

#

Jenny suddenly recognized the distinct sound. Another loud gunshot sputtered from outside the building.

Pratt turned to Jenny, "that should be the last we hear of your Jake Bolton."

"No!" Jenny screeched.

"It seems that Jake's Digger Walsh is my Digger." Pratt said.

#

"Why? Digger?" Jake begged as he knelt beside his former colleague. Jake's face was red with anger.

Digger rolled his face upward toward Jake. He groaned. He pulled his free hand, covered in blood, out from under his flank. His own blood.

Jake's face tensed further. He felt a deep mixture of denial and betrayal. *It shouldn't be this way.* Jake turned around and kicked the arch. He turned back and there was a tense stare between them. Then he hit his pistol barrel over and over on the stone wall. Finally, he let out a deep burst of exasperation. "Why?"

Digger was struggling to roll on to his back. He murmured something incoherent. Jake pulled his gun up from his hip and rotated the barrel at Digger's head. Jake then lowered the gun toward Digger's groin and fired. Blood flowed rapidly on to the stone floor. "Riley could have saved you from this Digger."

Jake bent down over the dying friend. He put his hand on Digger's carotid pulse and felt it slowly disappear. He then stood over the man briefly, shaking his head.

"It's just beginning Digger." Jake watched as he gave out his last breath. He reached into his pocket and cradled the 308-caliber bullet. Looking down at his former colleague he flipped the bullet on to his dead body.

#

Jenny collapsed back in her chair. Silence.

Landry made a quick sign of the cross.

Willis glared back and forth at Pratt and his men.

"It seems you've taken Jake's place, Doctor Neugold." Pratt said.

Jenny stared blankly at the table. Her anger bubbled and churned in her gut. She felt her muscles twitching and tensing. They were fighting the adrenaline speeding through her arteries. *Riley. Now Jake.* She thought. She felt like a dream was coming over her, a visible mist of desperation, not knowing where it came from. She needed to act. Now. She recalled Jake telling her the story about the veterinarian. The advice about going into a room determined to show the dog who was the boss.

"Or did *The Nativity* disappear?" Jenny asked with an angry look, her eyes bearing down on her captor. *Now I'm alone.* She thought.

"Huh?" Pratt asked, confused.

It was exactly the response that she wanted. She wanted to take control. To put doubt into her captor. "It was a piece of the puzzle that Riley was looking for." She said, intentionally ignoring Pratt's comments about Digger and Jake. "Let's talk about *The Nativity* painting you've been seeking. Were you deceived because someone in the Order of the Alhambra swapped out the original? Maybe you're missing something within the real one?" Her voice trailed off. The doubt in her voice echoed from her deepest feelings.

Pratt again sat down. He raised a defiant fist and shook it at Jenny. "You know where Caravaggio's *Last Prophet* is? Tell me where or I'll kill you."

"The paintings are all pointing back to where the Knights' secret is. I know the place. If you let these people go, I'll take you there." She quietly breathed in, hoping her bluff would work. She knew it was Malta, knew she still had the key and the cipher disk, but to put it all together would take time. She was trying to buy time.

Pratt looked at Jenny and then back at the two professors.

Jenny recorded his hesitation.

"No. We go together." There was a long uneasy silence, while Pratt's eyes bulged and his face tensed facing off against Jenny. Her practice skill in the ER helped her hold her ground. Finally he exhaled.

"You've convinced me. But how can I trust you without my hostages?"

"Let them go and I'll help you. Besides, you don't need them to solve anymore of this puzzle. All the pieces are here." Jenny said, pointing with one finger to her temple. "I'm more valuable to you now. It's easier to travel with me alone and let them go. Traveling with a big entourage will attract attention."

Charles Pratt stared into Jenny Neugold's clear eyes and made a decision.

"My men will hold Willis and Landry for twenty-four hours. Then they can go free. They will come to no harm as long as you find the secret by then. But I can't have them calling for help. If you don't find the secret by then my men here will kill both of them." He turned to his men. "The pretty doctor will be going with me. Take them to my place on the other side of London and wait for me to call."

Pratt once again raised his gun, but this time just as a gesture. "I mean 'free' as you Catholics say. Free of this earth if you're unsuccessful. Or free to go if you help me find the secret. We're leaving immediately."

Chapter 78

Malta International Airport
Luqa, Malta

Doctor Jenny Neugold stepped from the Learjet and studied the two men guarding Pratt. She did her sums and realized he ran his own little army.

There are too many mercenaries in the world. These guys look well trained. I might be able to escape, but Willis and Landry would be killed. She was running out of time to figure out the remaining clues.

"We need to go to St. John's Co-Cathedral," Jenny said. Her gut told her that it would be there. *I've seen the images on the church floor and the wheel Jake gave me works there.* She tried to convince herself. *They wouldn't hide it in the hills.*

"I knew it," Pratt exclaimed. "That was on my original list. My men searched. Hitler and Napoleon tore the place apart looking, too. Then, they focused more on St. Elmo."

Pratt signaled to his driver. He moved to the front of the lead SUV, keeping Jenny and two guards blocked behind the chauffeur's glass. Jenny watched Pratt grab a cell phone from the glove compartment. He barked something into the phone, turned, and smirked at Jenny.

#

Jake recalled that working alone carried its risks. No one to watch his back "in country." But being alone made him faster and more mobile. Working with a teammate gave him the advantages of flanking an opponent. But his partner would know that, if the chips were down, the mission came first and one of them may need to be sacrificed. But with Jenny he knew he was on a different level. If he had to make a decision on the mission it would be difficult to leave her behind or allow her to be vulnerable.

Back at the National Gallery in London he recognized the background in the Caravaggio and da Vinci paintings, something he'd seen during his trips through the Mediterranean: Malta. Both Virgin of the Rocks paintings were about the location in the background. *Da Vinci knew. He painted the secret.* The secret was on Malta and that is where Pratt would take Jenny. Karen Smith called in her jet and he landed ahead of Pratt, setting up outside the airport.

While Pratt spoke to his pilot, Jake studied the wind blowing across the tarmac and the sun beating down on the waiting black SUV.

The weather around the island was the most stable in the world. In contrast, the waves regularly hitting Malta were the most violent, and he knew that might help him. The undersea stone arches and complex rock formations around the island were the most sophisticated a Navy Seal could enter. There were underground blowholes, rogue waves and iceberg stones that could trap them when they swam ashore.

From the hill beside Luqa Airport, not far from the capital of Valletta, he spied Jenny through the binoculars. He calculated his chances of rescuing her. Each option he considered was difficult. Each was blocked by the number of Pratt's soldiers and Jenny's inexperience. He needed to protect Jenny. Pratt had her at his side.

Jake jumped into his own SUV and turned to race toward Grand Harbor to get ahead of them. He knew where they were going. He needed to alert Jenny that he was there.

After racing down Triql Ghassarra for a few miles, Pratt's driver turned onto Xatt Pinto. Jenny looked out over the sandy seawalls. She tried to think like Jake. *If he were here what would he do? Like that chess game he played. I'm a moving piece on that board.* She saw that two large cruise liners were docked along the seawalls. Given the time of day, many of the tourists would be on the island. The crowd in the Cathedral might help her. She saw many other boats exiting Grand Harbor, their international colors flying from their masts.

Jenny had contemplated misleading Pratt and his men, maybe to Fort St. Elmo, which she knew from Father Landry was the original stronghold of the Knights. But this solution would be fraught with risks. If she could quickly lead them into the ancient maze of underground prison cells, she might be able to get away. But, then again, not alone. *Why couldn't she have kept her mouth shut? No, she had no choice.* She would have to take them very close to the secret itself.

#

Jake slammed on the brakes, pulling up to the dock immediately off Ta Cejlu, 100 meters south of the Ferry to Sicily. He knew that Pratt was an impatient man and would likely take the fastest road to the Cathedral.

Jake jumped off the dock and revved the three Mercury engines on the Donzi 38 ZSF. He pulled the speedy boat out into the harbor and studied the road next to the seawall. The Xatt Pinto was a serpiginous road following the harbor exit toward the Cathedral. His speed was slow as he paralleled the traffic, 30 meters off shore from the Valletta boatyard. He needed to find Pratt's SUV before they descended into the tunnel beneath Fort Lascaris. He studied the cars entering the highway, waiting for the SUV to appear. From there they would turn west and head toward the Cathedral. He would then break for land. He only wanted to get Jenny's attention.

The small white captain's roof held three fishing poles. Attached to one of the poles he'd carefully placed the large distinctive white flag that he'd taken from the shoreline flagpole at Senglea. The lifeguard nearby wasn't happy.

Suddenly, the large black SUV turned the corner on to Xatt Pinto and the Donzi leaped on the water, dashing deep into the Grand Harbor. The flag was nearly straight out in the wind as he approached 45 knots. Turning back, he saw the flashing blue light of the harbor master boat trailing him, well beyond the imposed speed limit. He hoped that the harbor master didn't stop him first.

#

Jenny locked her fingers together and squeezed her hands. She looked out toward the city approaching fast on her left. She glanced out the right side where the harbor flashed between the large cruise ships.

Between several small boats a single boat bounced at a high speed across the water. The trailing white flag of the Red Cross caught her eye. The colors made her recall her days as a lifeguard in Connecticut. But, the flag outsized the pole and the rear of the boat. A single captain held one hand on the wheel and stared in her direction. She rounded up her pupils, squinting to bring the distance into better focus. *No. It couldn't be.* She thought. Her heart beat jumped. She quickly looked back toward the front of the car. She looked down. *Jake! He's alive.* I need to signal him. *He wants me to know he's there.* Looking around there was nothing she could do without alerting her captors.

#

Jake snapped his head forward and studied the Xatt Pinto road disappearing ahead of the SUV. His boat continued to hit the wakes of the smaller boats and bounce. There was less than a kilometer before Jenny and the SUV disappeared into the tunnel or he was stopped by the harbor master. There was nothing he could do to get her attention without alerting Pratt as well. He might kill her if he saw Jake.

Suddenly, the side window shot downward and Jenny's head stuck through. She lowered her head and the hair on her bright red pony tail blew up and over her head. She jerked back like she'd been yanked back into the car. *She knows I'm here.*

#

"Don't do that again, Doctor Neugold." Pratt said.

"I felt car sick from the ride." She replied. She glanced out the window and saw Jake decelerating the boat and turning toward shore. *He saw me.*

#

Pratt raced to a stop in front of St. John's Cathedral.

Jenny looked out the car window at the humble building. Two bell towers flanked a lower central archway that was covered by a Maltese cross. The white and yellow papal flag waved above the cross. The Cathedral looked like the military fortress it once served. The checkerboard of sand-colored limestone blocks marked numerous replacements and repairs to the six-hundred-year-old church.

There were two small cavities carved out of either side of the church facade—exedras waiting for saints to inhabit them. One of the bell towers was adorned with three large white dial faces with black arrows—one each for the month, date and day of the week. A large semicircular staircase spilled out into the road, creating a wide but low terrace.

Once they were parked in front of the large sandy-brown Cathedral, Pratt's men fanned out around the car. Pratt exited first. The men then waved for Jenny to exit the passenger door. Pratt closed on Jenny. "Remember, one false move and I'll kill your friends in London. You know I will. I don't care about the crowds. All your friends will be gone." Jenny glared at Pratt. Then she spun around looking for Jake.

Entering the large Cathedral doors, Jenny absorbed the noise from hundreds of tourists and pilgrims searching the nine chapels and naves. While the overhead lights were dimmed to protect the valuable artwork, the interior erupted with its own glimmer from the gilded walls and the rich rainbow colors of the inlaid marble floor.

Jenny grabbed a tourist map from a wall mount and studied it. Like most Medieval churches it had the standard cruciform shape. She sensed someone watching. She looked toward the altar. Moving through the crowd she saw the tall man in dark glasses, staring at her. *Jake.*

#

Jake recalled an operation in Malta from five years earlier. He'd been assigned to pick up an asset escaping another coup d'etat in Niger and carrying valuable information regarding uranium stores in the south of the country. It was the second time in seven years. He thought about how poorly the French, unlike the British, performed in supporting their former African colonies. The French never left behind an educational system, infrastructure or government. The French liked to colonize and celebrate culture. *Live and love.*

While waiting for the asset to appear five years earlier he'd pored over the elaborate design on the Cathedral floor. The hundreds of inlaid marble tombstones created a chess board kaleidoscope across the floor. Each one was elaborately decorated with religious motifs and covered with epitaphs. Six feet below each colorful rectangle an heroic Knight was at peace. He wondered again if his fate was to die with such glory like the Knights buried beneath the Cathedral floor: many had their heads cut off or their bodies quartered. He wondered whether someday he'd fight some great battle like the siege of Malta.

He felt his gun beneath his shirt and rotated his back pack over to his opposite shoulder. He needed to get Pratt and his men into a trapped position where he could get Jenny out.

Jenny had the Vigenere cipher disk and key. *They must decode something in here,* he thought.

#

Jenny turned her focus back to the inside of the Cathedral. The ceilings, columns, cornices, lamps, and arches were lavishly decorated with gold tiles and leaf, ornamenting elaborate and sculpted swirls. *Gold, gold, and more gold. Solid gold everywhere.*

Jenny glanced over at Pratt, who seemed indifferent to the splendor. Pratt tilted his head and said, "Well?"

"I'm still looking," Jenny answered. The two guards seemed in awe of their surroundings, but Jenny doubted they were distracted enough for her to make a move.

She studied the multicolored floor in front of them. It was covered by a mosaic stack of inlaid marble tombstones, each Knight interned below. Each of the four hundred marble tablets told the symbolic story of a valiant Knight of the Hospitallers. Symbols such as lions and stars represented valor; fleurs-de-lys and bear paws represented royalty; skulls and skeletons spoke of death and eternity. All the tombstones were surrounded by angels, beasts, and inscriptions that described the military deeds and spiritual history of the dead Knight. Built at the height of the Knights' power and prestige, this Cathedral was still considered one of the most important and magnificent churches outside of Rome.

Jenny checked her map. She read aloud, "'*Deo Optimo Maximo,*' 'To God, the best, the greatest.' These men were devoted to fighting for God."

Pratt's two hired hands remained in a trance at the opulence of gold and precious stone. "I'm going to have to fire them. Good help was becoming increasingly tiring to locate even if I promised them the Caravaggio masterpieces." He murmured.

"It will be difficult to identify the location from floor level," Jenny said. She looked deliberately to each side of the cathedral. She pointed to a small door at the side of the nave. She started to lead Pratt's small parade single file to the door. Pratt jumped in front of her and blocked it. He nodded to the first guard. "One of my men goes first." He demanded.

"Okay. You're the host." Jenny said, knowing she was mocking her captor.

Climbing up the stairs behind the black-suited guard, Jenny

paused. *This was a rare right-to-left fortress spiral staircase.* Because most Knights were right-handed, they built their staircases spiraling left to right so that an attacker trying to climb the stairs would have to fight upward with his left hand, while the defending Knight would likely use his dominant hand. Perhaps, she thought, she could use this knowledge to her advantage.

They reached the top floor and faced a small wooden balcony supported by a balustrade in front with side wall plinths. Jenny turned toward Pratt, who gave her a warning glance.

As if reading his mind, Jenny unwound the linen blazer from her waist, where it had been tied by the arms.

#

From across the Cathedral Jake studied Jenny taking off her coat. *Smart woman. She's trying to figure it out.* Jake looked her up and down. Jenny was more than an asset now. In a brief moment he dropped his guard, studying her slender figure, her glimmering red hair. He snapped back to the present.

#

Pratt looked confused and stretched out his hand to intercept the jacket.

Jenny shook her head. "Don't worry. There's no concealed weapon. It's the final clue you need." Jenny dug her nails in and tore open the seam, then pulled out the data card and the cipher disk. She placed them on the balustrade.

Pratt picked up the cipher disk and rotated it on the palm of his hand. "Doctor Neugold, you've been hiding information from me."

Jenny nodded upward toward the front of the church. "They've been hiding it from people like you."

She grabbed her camera back from a guard. She loaded the data card and pulled up the image of Riley's message written under the bridge. Jenny held her palm out to Pratt. Pratt reluctantly passed her the cipher disk. She magnified the image as far as the small screen allowed, then started to decode the letters with the cipher.

Pratt looked over her shoulder. "I thought Doctor McGrath didn't know the code key?"

"He didn't. The Knights were smart enough to separate the pieces of the puzzle. It's called compartmentalization. Riley had figured it out. She's been trying to tell us. And Doctor McGrath was probably preparing to give her the cipher disk."

Pratt was clearly excited. "Which cipher is it? There were so many in the sixteenth century. Even da Vinci wrote backward so that he could hide his ideas."

"Jake taught me. It's a Vigenere cipher. The French call it '*le chiffre indéchiffrable*,' 'the indecipherable cipher.'"

"I know it. But you need a code key to decipher the string of letters. What's the code key?" Pratt asked.

"The code key is 'Romano.'"

Pratt rolled his eyes. Jenny looked at him with obvious amusement. "Yes, Mr. Pratt. That's what Shakespeare's tip to Romano was about. Since he was pissed off by what the Queen did in Ireland. He wasn't about to turn over this secret of the Knights Hospitaller to her."

"Romano is a mere code word?" Pratt shook his head.

"Riley had located the palimpsest and the cipher in Ireland. Before you killed her, Doctor McGrath was grooming Riley as a Dame of the Hospitallers, appointed to protect this legacy." She held out the string of letters on the camera and the brass disk. "And, before your Digger killed Jake, he guessed Romano was the code key."

Pratt sniffed. "Well, obviously, we didn't really need her, now, did we?"

Jenny stopped and glared at Pratt. She couldn't visibly control her anger. She felt her facial muscles tighten. "Before this day is over, you and your men will not make it out of here alive."

"Just decipher the code and shut up!" Pratt said.

Jenny turned the dials on the cipher disk.

#

Jake turned around in the cathedral like he was studying the tourist map and pointed toward the nine chapels each dedicated to one of the nine langues, or tongues, of the Order of St. John: the French, the Spanish, the Portuguese, and all the other nations that sent Knights to the order. He mingled in the crowd of tourists. He looked back at Jenny and Pratt leaning against the balustrade. *Did I teach her what she needed to use the cipher? Would this be another clue leading to an additional clue? Or would the secret be here?*

#

She turned to the disk again and matched the ROMANO code key with the letters from the highway underpass and the palimpsest.

Finishing the decoding, she stared at the letters. *Nine letters. One word?* It still did not make sense: *minutilli.*

"Neugold, don't try to deceive me now," Pratt warned.

"minutilli."

"Latin?"

"No. Not Latin. And if you divide up the letters it doesn't make sense either."

Pratt moved to take the cipher from Jenny, but just as his hand touched hers, the doctor jerked back.

"Wait. Look at this tourist map." She said. "Minutilli. It's the name of one of the Knights. A single Knight. It's easy. The gravestones are all numbered. He's gravestone three sixty-seven."

Pratt opened the tourist map and held it in front of him to overlay the church interior. "There," he said, pointing down and to the right toward the Oratory.

Jenny laughed as she pointed to the tourist map. "Giovanni Minutilli. A Knight's grave. In the Oratory."

#

Jake saw Pratt and Jenny point toward the side entryway to the Oratory. He knew they'd go there next. He noticed a large tourist group moving out of the room. He moved to the side aisle of the church passing slowly past the columns and casually along the walls inconspicuous to Jenny's captors. He needed to find a place to hide but observe. To wait to make his move. As he moved, he read about the history of the Oratory:

It's located where three Caravaggio paintings are located. The part of the cathedral that was added on well after the main church. The grand master built this Oratory as a place of devotion for the young novices. It was built '1602 to 1605.'

Caravaggio was here then. I need to get there before them.

Chapter 79

Oratory
St. John's Co-Cathedral
Valletta, Malta

Jake slid into the crowd of exiting tourists and raced down the Oratory toward the chancel.

There it was racing into view: Caravaggio's masterpiece, *The Beheading of St. John the Baptist.* The painting was placed low on the far wall.

He moved forward and then froze. He murmured. "This is the right spot. I think I know why *The Nativity* was so important to Caravaggio, to the Knights Hospitaller and, especially, to Riley."

Jake stood on the precise location in front of the altar that Karen Smith had described. She'd told him, "I've seen it during mass in the Church of the Holy Sepulchre. A novice in the Knights or a Roman Catholic priest will pause at a fixed position in the Oratory to sing the greater doxology, 'Gloria.' *The Nativity* was important to Riley because only the original painting contains the banner with the four line chant, 'Gloria in excelsis deo.' Riley recognized this, and eliminated it in the version she had Landry paint. She wanted to keep Caravaggio's secret hidden."

He looked down at the ornate gravestone in the floor. He rubbed his hand on his deltoid, recognizing the elaborate design on the Minutilli grave. The red-and-white fleurs-de-lys, the angels, a lion and anchors. *They're all there.* He briefly thought of Riley. *We're getting closer. This is where I need to trap Pratt. The secret is beneath here. Jenny can find this spot.* He turned to see the last tourists exiting the Oratory.

Jake spun over the red security ropes, past the kneelers, around the stone columns and into the shadows of the Oratory altar.

#

Pratt and his men entered the Oratory with Jenny in the lead.

Her head down, Jenny counted the gravestones as she

stepped across the floor. She looked up when she stopped on Minutilli's gravestone. "This is Minutilli's grave, but it means so much more." She spoke loudly and it echoed across the room. She hoped Jake was listening.

"Where's the secret?" Pratt pressed.

She ignored him. "It was here that the novices would have stopped in front of the chancel. There would have been an altar here in front, intentionally obscuring the lower half of that Caravaggio painting." She pointed.

"Why?"

"Just like all of Caravaggio's paintings—Landry said so himself—they were positioned in the church for effect. As the novice Knights approached, they would gradually see the executioner . . . the prisoner in the background staring . . . Salome waiting with a silver platter for the decapitated head. When they advanced further, they'd reach this spot. Only then, would the lower half of the painting appear. They would see the prostrate Saint John the Baptist with his slit throat. They would freeze in horror. It would be here that the young Knights Hospitaller would be reminded of the siege of Malta. Was this their fate? Would they also be willing to be decapitated in the name of Christ?"

"We need to examine this gravestone." Pratt instructed one of his men to stand by the door of the Oratory and look official. He was to allow the last tourists to leave but not permit any new tourists to enter. The cathedral was not a museum but a working place of worship and it didn't have guards or docents.

The other guard fanned out and gave a cursory search to the sparse room.

\#

From his position across the chancel, Jake could see the men holding Jenny captive. Jenny suddenly looked up. He saw her beautiful blue eyes twinkle in the light glow of the chapel. He felt a brief warm comfort—like she knew he was right beside her. But he didn't like the prospect of protecting Jenny and stopping three men. He hoped they would split up further.

\#

Jenny read out loud the writing on Giovanni Minutilli's grave. "Italian Knight, the same as Caravaggio."

Pratt threw his hands to his side. "How do I know that you

aren't just dragging me around this church?"

"Quiet."

Pratt snapped back, seemingly stunned by her response.

"I'm examining the grave."

The six-foot-by-three-foot gravestone of Fra Giovanni Minutilli was embossed in red-and-white fleurs-de-lys surrounding an altar. On top of the sculpted altar, two cherubs carried the Minutilli coat of arms, a lion with anchors bisecting its body in several directions. Resting at the top of the altar stone was the gold-plated head gear of the Knights Hospitaller and a skeleton. On the side, there was another image: a boulder balancing in front of a small cave.

Jenny smiled inwardly as she studied the coat of arms. *Jake's tattoo. From a picture that Riley sent him. This is the right place.*

At the bottom of the tombstone there were Latin phrases.

Jenny translated. "'*Siste, viator*' means 'Stop, traveler.' '*Ora et labora*' means 'Pray and labor.'"

Pratt leaned closer.

"Anything that talks about a secret, about Caravaggio, or a cure for illness?" Pratt asked.

Jenny pointed to another word. "Look—'*Spiro, spero*'! That means: 'Breathe and hope.'"

"Latin, ugh." Pratt murmured.

Jenny knelt and moved her hands across the tomb like it was an Ouija board. "You have to read it in context. It says, '*Cruci dum spiro spero*,' which means 'While I breathe, my hope is in the cross.'" Jenny paused and then added, "It goes on to say, '*Sic itur ad altum*,' meaning 'Such is the way to heaven.'"

"Look at the bottom, right above his date of death." Pratt directed.

"'*Omnia mea mecum spiro in factum.*' That means, 'My wisdom is my breath into my work.' That sounds a lot like Barrister's headstone in Ireland!" Jenny stood and spun around.

Pratt put his thumb and forefinger to his upper lip and rocked back and forth. Jenny could hear his breathing speed up. He then said, "That's Romano in Shakespeare's *The Winter's Tale*!"

Jenny turned back to Minutilli's gravestone and knelt. Reaching down, she ran her palm over the stone and studied the angel like a doctor would probe the abdomen of a patient. "This cherub is blowing wind down on the skeleton. Like the *Saint Lucy* painting. Like the *Lazarus* . . . the breath of life?" She moved closer. She saw loose sand filling its mouth. "This angel has an opening right here." She cleaned the sand away, revealing a small round hole in the cherub's mouth.

Pratt knelt next to Jenny who sat back on her knees. She reached back with both hands into her plaited hair. Twisting her braids she pulled out the key that Jake had hidden there. Pratt shook his head.

Jenny studied the key. She blew the remaining sand from the crevice, and then carefully placed the small, ornate key into the mouth of the angel.

When she rotated the key, Jenny heard a loud click of tumblers beneath the enormous marble stone. A sudden rush of air exited around the stone and raised it a few inches above the floor.

Pratt reached around the gravestone. "I can grip the edges. There's a small space beneath this marker."

"I don't think you want to disturb a dead Knight." Jenny warned.

Pratt snapped at the guards. "Here, help me move this stone."

"There should only be a coffin with Minutilli's skeleton in there," Jenny said.

"Not if Caravaggio is correct. I think this is the place we're looking for." Pratt said.

Chapter 80

Oratory
St. John's Co-Cathedral
Valletta, Malta

Pratt sparked his cigarette lighter and held it over the open tomb. He snapped back when an abrupt gust of air billowed up from below and doused the flame.

He flashed the lighter again and leaned forward toward the chamber. "Stairs. It goes down!"

Jenny took advantage of the moment. She spun around the Oratory, looking deeply into the dark shadows. She stopped when she saw the corner of the chancel. *That is the only place he could be,* she thought. She smiled . . . then winked . . . into the darkness.

#

Jake studied Jenny's lean body in the light. She barely cast a shadow across the room. She turned around the room like one taking in the splendor. She stopped. He saw it. It was an unmistakable smile and wink. Directly at him. She 'had this moment' and would meet him on the next level of the playing board.

Jake knew that Pratt would never let Jenny out alive once he had the secret. Jake also knew he had to act soon. He sensed an opportunity. He pulled his suppressor from his pocket and slowly placed it on the barrel of his H and K pistol.

A dark confined space was an ideal location to take away Pratt's advantage. Pratt couldn't triangulate Jake in the darkness.

But he knew he still needed cover for Jenny. *They will split up when they go down in the undercroft. I can rescue her there.*

#

"One of my men will go first. Doctor, I warn you. I'll follow. We're all armed and we're accurate." He pointed at his man near the door. "You stay here. If I don't come up first, kill Landry and Willis for me." Pointing at the other man he said, "You lead. I'll be directly behind Neugold."

Before they descended into the dark chamber, Jenny glared at Pratt. She felt the anger and depravity of this soulless man. She wished she could throw him down the hole. Once Pratt had his prize, he would kill her. "We're going into the darkness of hell. I'm going to be damned with you."

"You'll be damned when I tell you." Pratt replied.

When they reached the bottom of the stairs, Pratt flicked his lighter. He grasped three torches mounted to a metal wall frame. Pratt lit them, giving one to Jenny and one to the guard. She heard the faint sound of water dripping, noting that the floor was slippery, damp.

Pratt shoved Jenny forward. She pushed Pratt back and held her torch in front of his face. She felt the urge to hit Pratt over the head with the torch but spotted the working end of Pratt's gun appear beneath her nose.

"Get moving Neugold." He said. He snapped his forehead signaling her into the lead.

#

Jake eyed Pratt and his men move the gravestone and descend. Two guns.

Back in the Oratory his one guard attended to the doorway, his gun ready. Jake studied the room. It appeared to have only one entrance or exit for the tourists. But he knew that the Knights would never allow themselves to be trapped. *There must be another exit.*

A three foot red drape cut across the chancel and descended behind the altar. This shielded the spot lights that focused upward onto the Caravaggio painting. On the other side of the chancel a red rectangular curtain hung from the wall. The outer borders were covered with carved stone blocks suggesting a doorway.

Jake crawled across the chancel floor. He stopped, grasped a loose plug and cut the wires with his knife. He looked up, uncertain he wasn't casting shadows on the painting hanging just above the altar level. He reached the curtain and spied the door, likely leading outside to the cemetery. He pulled on the lower end of the curtain and slid up against the door. He exited to the outside cemetery and jammed the plug in the door.

He raced along the outside wall of the Oratory to cover his movements. He found the side door to the main church and entered. Turning left, he located the staircase. From the staircase there was a small door to the side of the Oratory directly behind the guard. He slowly pulled on the door. No noise. He readied his gun. Sliding behind the stone pillar, he eyed the guard.

#

Leading the way, Jenny suddenly felt the floor disappear beneath her. She fell backwards. She felt the rush in her stomach and her body sped downward for a few helpless seconds. She slid into a dark chamber, losing her torch. The torch sparked, rattled off the stone, and then extinguished.

The guard jumped toward her and also disappeared into the darkness.

Jenny felt like she'd landed inside a hard box. There was a sting in her back. She rubbed her back which had taken the brunt of the fall onto the hard surface. She ran her hands along the sides and detected a cold metallic feel. Movement behind her. She put her hands down and felt the struggling legs of Pratt's goon. They appeared to be sitting in a steel coal car.

She spun around, reached over the edge and splashed rushing cold water, realizing they were in a river driving them downward. She could hear Pratt yelling through the sliver of light above. The sudden compression-decompression effect of the moving coal car splashed gushing water past her, over and onto her head, pushing them through the darkness. Her pulse raced and she swallowed deeply. *Here we go again*, she thought.

The car rose upward then swung left as thousands of gallons of water suddenly entered from a chamber on their right flank, rolling off the walls as if a fire hydrant had opened up. Jenny felt abrupt dunks of descent followed by soaring while she and the guard sped through the water bouncing back and forth in the car and on the water.

She let out a short scream. Leaning back she felt the guard's gun leveled between her shoulders, his feet braced against her pelvis.

Pratt's voice was now coming from behind, not above. He'd also fallen down the fissure. He was in another container and, not far behind. Looping, cutting, spinning back and forth and swirling through the geographic maze.

In the distance Jenny spied a light shooting into view. Her odd craft burst into the open air and out onto a stone floor, skidding to a stop. Moments later Pratt shot out of the water onto the stone floor. Jenny braced when his car clanged against hers. Pratt had his gun drawn.

#

All three stepped onto the rocks and shook the water from their clothes. Jenny studied the undercroft chamber of vaulted limestone beneath the cathedral. Although the torches were lost there was natural light entering the barren room.

Pratt stopped abruptly. "Shhhh, do you hear that?"

Jenny cocked her head. "Sounds like more water crashing."

Pratt gestured with his gun. "This way." They followed him toward the roar of crashing waves.

Chapter 81

Undercroft
St. John's Co-Cathedral
Valletta, Malta

Jake needed to make his move on Pratt's men. This was his way out, his way of saving Jenny, himself. And he needed to improve his odds, change the balance of players on the game board. There was an armed guard in the undercroft and one nearby in the Oratory.

He slowly closed in behind and startled the guard. Elevating the grip of his gun he hit him on the back of the head with a "thud." The man groaned and twisted forward.

The larger slid off the wall, giving Jake the time to slide behind. Jake punched him in the temple. The man staggered and dropped his gun. Jake dashed forward at him. The man threw a round house punch. Jake ducked downward. The swing missed. Jake dove into his gut. The man grunted and leaned back. The man shoved back. Jake then lunged at him driving his head into the stone pillar. The man murmured some faint sounds, his eyes rolled to the side and he collapsed on the floor.

Jake ran to the front of the Oratory and grabbed the gold post and ornamental red ropes from the portable barrier system near the altar. He unlocked the ropes and threw the post over his shoulder. He dashed back to the entrance doors and slid the gold post through the handles, locking the room. He then tied the ropes around the feet and legs of Pratt's man.

He pulled out his cell phone and called Karen Smith, realizing this might be his last phone call. He alerted her to the man and that he was going into the undercroft. He asked her not to move on Willis and Landry until he secured Doctor Neugold.

#

Jenny marveled at the gold glow emanating through the hallway extending from the undercroft.

When they turned the corner, the passageway opened into a large cave of jagged rock carved from years of ocean currents. The ceiling was thirty feet high with walls bulging forward from moist, large limestone boulders. At the base of the walls there was a smooth stone walkway encircling a flat, depressed center floor. A few puddles of water intermittently vibrated within the uneven center floor. On the far end of the rocks, the ground sloped steeply downward toward a second small cave where the sound of crashing waves emanated and generated the vibrations.

She nodded briskly and murmured, "The scene in the *Virgin of the Rocks.*"

#

Jake raced down the hole beneath the Minutilli grave. He studied the rushing water before jumping in. He used one hand for a torch and one hand paddling with the current. He grabbed at the slippery side walls, gulping and spitting water. The rushing water deposited him on the stone ledge hidden from view of the main cavern. He pulled his gun again and peered around the stone boulders.

He now had Pratt and his guard trapped in the cavern. Or . . . they had Jenny and him.

Behind the large rocks his position was covered. He listened. Then he took a quick glance at the cavern. He saw the alternating flash of waves smashing against the rocks on the opposite side of the room. Pratt stood with Jenny and his guard studying a stone pedestal. *The queen blocked by a rook and a pawn.* He thought.

The thundering sound of water entering from beneath the dungeon-like room sporadically drowned out Pratt's speech. Jake moved closer and spied the surging water at the far edge of the room. An explosion of seawater burst upward from below and then shot across off the far wall of the cave.

A blowhole, he thought.

The water level was at least ten feet lower than the stone floor. The arching waves rose rhythmically above the floor. This distance kept the pedestal in the center of the room dry. *That rapidly changing natural distraction could be better than a slab of C4 explosive.* He recalled Digger setting up an escape for him in Damascus years earlier. A series of oil drum explosions set in nearby buildings created the chaos and pathway he needed to get around the checkpoints after he knocked off Mughniyah. *Digger,* he thought, *why?* Jake felt the anger deep in his stomach.

There were no candles or torches in the cavern. Yet, the walls appeared to drip with gold, radiating geological phosphorescence throughout the room. There was an occasional flash of light when the blowhole water receded. It shone as if the light came from nowhere, yet it was everywhere. He spied the metal glint of the handguns. Pratt gestured with his gun.

But what was the secret? Though they'd cracked the code, Jake still didn't know what secret this elaborate cavern contained.

#

Jenny grabbed Pratt's arm and pointed at the platform. "Look!" Pratt instead looked down with anger at his arm.

There in the center of the cavern was a rock-like pedestal. The light in the room appeared to coalesce and focus around the football-shaped object on the top of the pedestal. *Was that it? The secret?* Jenny was puzzled. *All this splendor and mystery for a lump of black fibers?*

Jenny circled slowly around the room, balancing her hand against the moist rock face, focusing on the center pedestal of rock.

She moved closer to the center. "There's a red liquid at the base of that lump on the platform." Rotating further in position, she added, "that lump is a face—a face with eyes and a nose. It's a head. Not a skull. But a head! A head with long black hair flowing toward a severed neck. The neck is resting on a silver plate that's collecting drops of the red liquid."

Jenny reached over and dipped her finger in the red ooze. She brought her finger up to her mouth. "Fresh blood. It's noncoagulated blood." She said in a shocky voice. "But the head is old. Ancient. Given the way the hair looks scraggly." She furrowed her forehead.

A tall man appeared out of the shadows on the near side of the rocks and entered the light. He wore flowing canonical black robes marked by the classic white eight-pointed cross of the Knights Hospitaller. He carried a long sword by his side.

Pratt shouted over to the priest while pointing to the central podium, "Is this . . ."

Jenny finished his sentence: "This is a baphomet. Like the Knights would use to lead their army. Given how decayed this looks, it must be at least six months old. But it shouldn't bleed."

The man didn't answer.

Pratt moved toward the Knight. The Knight put his hand on his sword and turned to face Pratt. "Sir, you don't belong here."

"I'm Charles Pratt. I've spent a lot of time and money searching for the secret of the Knights Hospitaller. I'm dying and . . ."

"Sir, you don't belong here. You must leave now." The Knight replied.

"I won't be stopped." Pratt answered. Pratt's guard moved forward behind Jenny with his gun drawn.

"This is the head of John the Baptist." The Knight said. There was a tense silence. "You will not . . ."

A large wave cracked off the walls. Jenny swallowed deeply and shook her head. "The Baptist? After two thousand years there should be nothing left but decaying bone. I've seen decaying corpses in the morgues and autopsy rooms. Even with embalmed bodies, there's significant decay. And that's after only a year."

"No. It's the actual head of John the Baptist."

Jenny understood. *The Knights* believe. *Like Doctor McGrath. Like the religious pilgrims to Lourdes or Jerusalem.*

\#

Jake knew he needed to make his move.

His mind drifted to one of his "Ops" two years earlier in Helmand Province. His team was hunting for a Taliban war lord when they broke into a house during the filming of a beheading of a local American sympathizer. The unaccompanied video camera was recording from its tripod, bright shade-less lamps filled the room and a Taliban operative held a bloodied sword over the headless body. *A cheap horror flick,* he thought. He'd opened fire in anger.

This could be the confusion I need.

\#

"A preserved head?" Jenny asked.

Pratt shouted back over a sudden crashing wave before the Knight could answer. "No way. There's no way to do that."

"It is he. There's no preservation. This is his natural state."

Jenny gazed in awe.

Pratt fell to his knees, but not in worship. "Is this what I'm looking for? Saint John the Baptist?"

Jenny grew impatient. "Tell us the truth. Too many people

have died."

"It is he. *The Last Prophet.* Many have been saved." The Knight answered.

"Recall Elijah in the Old Testament." Jenny said, "Or, Christ and his disciples in the New Testament. The authors of those stories marveled at 'prophets' as those who could cure the sick, drive out demons, bring people back from the dead. They worshipped prophets. We're dealing with First Century legend." *Taken and guarded by the Knights Hospitaller. The Knights who could cure the incurable?* "Prophets were not just men who spoke for God. They were agents of God's breathe on earth. I said Lazarus escaped Jerusalem for fear his resurrection would make him glorified."

Pratt looked up from his kneeling position. There was hope in his face. "The Islamic religion teaches that John was the last prophet before Muhammad."

"Caravaggio saw this but struggled to believe." She said.

"This is what Napoleon was searching for? This is the baphomet that guided the Knights in battle? This gave their healers saving powers? This is what I need."

Jenny stared over at Pratt while he stood up. "We should take this back to the laboratory and study it. If nothing else, there may be some ancient anticoagulant at work. The body should decay much more rapidly than this. The medical secret could save lives."

The Knight gestured toward the head. "It's not the head alone that saves. You need to have faith. It doesn't decay because its John's own breath at work. Prayer has the power to save you. But it won't."

#

Jake leaped forward from behind the boulders. He fired a quick shot at Pratt's guard who hit the stone wall, then rolled, lifeless, into the small pool of water. A puddle of blood formed beneath his arm and moved slowly across the center floor, hitting the water and diluting it.

Jake turned toward Pratt, "Uh uh. Don't move." Pratt wrapped his arm around Jenny and pressed his cold gun against her temple. Jenny's eyes blinked rapidly.

Jenny felt a rush of excitement. "Jake!" She yelled.

"Don't move, Jake. Or I'll blow her head off just like this religious icon." Pratt nodded toward the pedestal.

For the first time, Jake spoke with contempt. "Jenny, you can't take this with you. John the Baptist was a threat to Herodias because he criticized her marriage to Herod, right? Just imagine how big a threat his living head would be to all mankind. Dictators would send their armies to capture it. Men and women would sell their souls to embrace it." Jake circled slowly around the room toward Pratt.

Jenny shook against Pratt's grip. "Jake?" Pratt jammed the gun tighter against her head.

The Knight returned Jake's warning with his own. "Worshippers believe the head of John is in the Umayyad Mosque in Damascus or possibly in the Church of San Silvestro in Rome. Hundreds of thousands of religious pilgrims travel every year to those places hoping to live forever. The sick and dying would be killing each other just to touch his head. To seek a cure. Imagine the chaos?"

Jenny struggled against Pratt, his grip tightening on her neck.

Pratt's face grew red. "No. This is the real deal. This is what Caravaggio found four hundred years ago. He traveled here from Italy to find forgiveness. He then painted his map to help other penitents! Even for murder."

The Knight scoffed. "You hardly strike me as a penitent."

"I'm taking this with me."

Chapter 82

Underground Cavern
St. John's Co-Cathedral
Valletta, Malta

Jake steadied the sight of his gun at the exposed corner of Pratt's head. He was trying to hide behind Jenny.

He knew he needed to secure the head and disarm Pratt as quickly as possible. Once Pratt had the head, then Jenny would be useless to him. The madman would never let them go.

#

Pratt sensed Jake's movements and inched backward. He grasped the Baptist head off the pedestal, pressed it against Jenny's chest and dragged her slowly off the ledge of the center floor.

"Jake. Stop or I'll throw her into the blowhole."

#

Jake was familiar with the natural power of blowholes from his experience in the water off the coast of Turkey and Malta. Their force and speed could reach thirty miles per hour. *That is enough.*

Jake spied the Knight pulling his sword. Jake knew this was the shift in balance that he needed.

Pratt briefly turned his gun away from Jenny. He fired wildly toward the Knight.

The bullet flashed off the stone wall and ricocheted toward the ceiling. The Knight spun back and disappeared into the shadows. Pratt fired again when a wave crashed behind him. The bullet sparked off the stone boulders.

#

Jenny dropped down and drove her elbow into Pratt's groin. Simultaneously, Jake fired a shot at Pratt. He missed.

Jake raced forward and dove onto Pratt. He grabbed Pratt in a head lock and forced the Glock from his hand. A quick pop of the gun was muffled by a blast of water shooting up from the blowhole. He pulled him closer when Pratt pushed backward, the Baptist head pressed between them.

Jenny dove free to the ground.

Smoke hung like a curtain shroud circling the room.

Pratt broke free of Jake's hold and slashed the side of his hand with his knife. Jake's gun flew into the water. Pratt barely held the Baptist head.

Jenny raised her clenched fist in the air to hit Pratt.

Jake yelled out, "No, Jenny!" Pratt was reaching up behind her. He grabbed the top of her shirt, pulling her to the ground. They rolled closer and closer to the blowhole.

Pratt dropped the knife and awkwardly scrabbled for his fallen gun, still holding the head.

Jake dove across the rocks headfirst, breaking Pratt's arm loose from Jenny's shirt. Jake sensed his feet slipping on the wet ledge. Pratt grunted as he rolled off the edge into the water coming from the blowhole.

Jenny stood up shakily.

Jake dove into the blowhole water on top of Pratt.

Pratt paddled desperately toward the rocks, grasping for a hold on the slippery edge with his free hand. Jake emerged briefly. He took a deep breath. Then he dove under an enormous blast of water.

The explosion tossed Pratt against the rocks. Then he tumbled back.

They both disappeared into the foam when the blowhole wave disappeared back out of the cavern.

"Jake!" Jenny screamed as she shimmied sideways along the ledge. Her faced tensed and her heart plunged into her abdomen. *No, Jake! He was gone.*

She felt the searing anger of losing both Riley and Jake. She moved back and forth along the ledge looking for him. She saw the churn of foaming water race back and forth in the blowhole. She thought of her father's death. *Should I jump in? No, Jake would want me to protect the queen for battle. He was gone in the crashing waves.*

Then, she leaned forward . . . but stopped. *Not again!*

Another burst of waves crashed through the blowhole and she jumped back into the cavern. She turned to see three Knights appear, light shining down on the empty pedestal.

Chapter 83
Outside Connecticut General Hospital
Hartford, Connecticut

Karen Smith swung the baseball bat and hit her Lincoln Continental tire with a thud. Her driver jumped in his seat. "They found Pratt's body twenty miles down the coast." She yelled out.

Jake Bolton stood like a shade in the darkness beneath the Skywalk staring at the emergency doors of the Connecticut General Hospital. He looked up and shook his head. Finally, he turned and smiled. "I heard everything turned out okay."

"The Knights are very happy. The head remains with its rightful owners. No one believes the rumors, so the secret is safe. And you've taken one rotten man off the grid."

"He slipped on his own sin." Jake said.

"I don't think there's a prophet that can help him now." Smith said. "What did it feel like staring into his face in the churning waters?"

Jake shot her a solemn stare. Like a fog covered him. "Unlike a bullet—I saw everything. The fear. The rage. He got his baptism into hell."

"Did it take away the pain of Riley's death?"

"No." He shrugged. "For a while there, I thought I'd never see her again." Jake nodded his head toward the hospital ER.

"You're hesitating to go in?"

"I guess I was hoping to see the young surgeon come out."

"She doesn't know you're alive."

Jake's smile faded.

"You should have noticed by now . . . I don't die easy."

"How'd you get out?"

"When I hit the blowhole I knew the best way out of there was to go out with the current. I knew that the tide would carry me out. You look for the sliver of light beneath the rocks. The key was swimming with the flow when the water rushed out of the cavern. Pratt died because he fought against it." Jake said.

"Fr. Landry? Professor Willis? Did you hear?"

"No."

"They've struck up a friendship. Working on exploring John Shakespeare, William's devout Catholic father and his influence on religion in Shakespeare's works." She said.

"I hope they're careful with the religion they dig up."

"I gather you learned a little about the faithful?"

"And I learned a little Latin along the way," Jake said.

"Speaking of Latin. You asked for this information. Before I give it to you I have something important to say to you. Jake, the CIA doesn't take out American citizens."

"Someone leaked the information that got Riley killed. I just need to know who set Riley up."

Smith held up the manila folder in her hand and bounced it against Jake's chest. Jake didn't move. "You're not targeting any Americans. Ever."

"I promise."

"I know you do." She released the file into Jake's strong hands. "So, are you going into the ER?" She asked.

"What do you think?" Jake scratched the toe of his shoe across the sidewalk.

"Can you imagine what Caravaggio felt? Fighting to get back to the Italy he loved? To reach for the God he feared?"

"Don't you think I know the feeling? Like a need to talk to her?" He said.

"You know why you can't. Caravaggio didn't want to hurt anyone. Just like you don't want her to get hurt."

Jake fell silent momentarily, like his mind had wandered to another place. "She knows."

"Ah, alright, I'm sure she does." Smith jumped back into the Lincoln, settled back into her seat, resting a hand on top of her bat.

Jake felt his face warm at the thought of Jenny. He whispered to himself, "to protect the queen."

She didn't seem to hear him. "Jake, I need you back in the field."

Jake leaned into the car. "Okay, Smith. I know you. What's on your mind?"

"You see this Hillerich and Bradsby bat? The game has used this same white ash wood for almost a hundred years. Almost all of it northern white ash harvested from either Pennsylvania or New York. It's hard, durable, strong, good weight, but also has the right feel."

"What does that have to do with this information?" Jake asked, looking down at the file in his hand.

"Because you have a gift. I need you to stay in the game. That's the gift that sets white ash apart from maple, oak—all the other woods."

"I understand that."

"In 2001, Barry Bonds hit an amazing seventy-three home runs using a *maple* bat, and other players started changing their bats. They thought it must be the wood that helped. That is, until they discovered he was juiced on steroids the whole time."

"I know. It'll probably cost him the Hall of Fame."

"That's it, Jake. You need to win the right way. Sure, you need to find justice, but promise me you'll play by the rules. He's on American soil." Smith pointed the butt end of the bat up at Jake's chest and pressed hard.

"I understand. *Justum perficito, nihil timeto.* I told you, I learned some Latin.'"

"Do you need a ride somewhere?"

"Nah. I'm going to hang on here awhile longer."

"Which hurts more? Losing Riley or leaving Jenny alone?"

"Neither?" He looked up and down the dark street. "Convincing myself that she'll forgive me for staying away from her."

"Asking for forgiveness can be very painful."

"Her skill as a surgeon brings forgiveness to these streets."

Smith smiled. "I'll be calling you. China."

"The twin is in China?"

"And, Jake? Next time, warn me when you're on a date." Smith tapped her bat on his arm and pointed off to the side toward the hospital ER exit. "She's a Dame of the Hospitallers now."

Turning, Jake saw Jenny in her long white coat strolling gracefully, her beautiful long red hair blowing in the wind. She walked in the opposite direction toward the parking lot, her smile lighting the way. Jake was distracted by her beauty.

He turned back toward Smith. She was gone. The car. The bat. The boss.

Jake looked up and noticed he was standing alone beneath the Bridge of Sighs. His eyes lost focus. He swallowed deeply and felt the pain searing in his chest. It was changed. Forever changed.

#

A short while later Jenny clicked on the key lock to her red BMW 328i. She jumped into the driver's seat and eyed a change on her front dash. Like someone had moved her belongings.

The three inch piece of plastic balancing just above the GPS system startled her. She picked up the piece and studied it closely. The white chess queen rested sideways in her palm like she was sleeping. A scratch in the plastic at the base made it uneven.

Jenny smiled. She felt her face flush for an instant.

A hollow blackness followed his disappearance into the waves. It was a deep, dark despair. *A heavy wave of grief had crushed me. And, I wondered if I'd ever surface. I could see my pain in the mirror. When I did come up for air . . . I was a different person.*

Now he's alive! She thought of the churn of water closing in on Jake. *This time . . . Jake got out.* Her mind and eyes focused back to the present. The anger was gone. The nightmare was over. Replaced by hope. Refilling the emptiness. Her heart raced.

She quickly opened the door of the car and got out. Turning around, the lot was empty. She waited. Listened. She heard the sounds of cars moving on different levels of the parking lot. She closed her hand and murmured, "Protect your queen."

Epilogue

July 17, 1610
Feniglia Beach, Porto Ercole, Italy

Michelangelo Merisi tilted his head toward the angry
Tyrrhenian Sea and sensed the morning fog billowing in on him
like the sails on a Maltese galley. In his delirium, he perceived an
eight-pointed cross flying above the smoking waves. It was only
clouds.

Yet as sure as the waves were wet, a real Templar ship was
somewhere in that fog, in that shadow brushed over the ocean. Fra
Michelangelo crabbed across the blowing sand, finally reaching
an upper terrace where he hoped the winds might be less fierce.

He fought his way across the winding spit of the Maremma,
aware that the Tuscan cliffs cast a shadow that betrayed his
footing. Across his shoulder he carried a leather bag. It held three
canvases rolled into gray plumes. These three signed paintings
were more important to him than the others that had been taken
from him the night before. Though his senses fluctuated in the heat,
he knew he must make a decision whether to protect or destroy the
canvases and the secret they held.

Dressed in black, a long sword dragging between his legs,
a rapier reaching down toward his knees, he was sure he
resembled nothing so much as a giant spider crawling toward the
small fishing village of Porto Ercole. His breathing was louder to
him than either wind or waves; his chest ached. He guzzled down
the swirling air. His tongue and lips were dry, caked by salt. He
wished he could savor it but he had no sense of taste. His
perception was failing. The heat was winning its battle over his
faculties. Only his hearing remained uncontaminated. He
wondered whether he had finally begun a fight he could not win.

A sudden convulsion of wind tugged his frame toward the
ocean as if he were a seagull fighting the thermal gusts. The earth
was not to be trusted: One misstep and he would sink in the wet
sand and be swallowed like a ship's anchor. Exhausted, he willed
himself forward on the beach as if he were painting the scene

before him.

Merisi squinted at the rising sun and imagined two white birds hovering a few feet over the bluff ahead of him. They barely moved their wings—much like gulls. But, at this hour, surely they must be doves? Then he reconsidered. Maybe they were gulls. Maybe they knew he was dying and were awaiting his decaying carcass. No. He was not hallucinating; the wings were white not gray. The port city must be near. He lay down to rest. Just for a few minutes, he told himself.

What irony, Merisi thought, if he who had been accused of being too vulgar in his exact replication of scenes should be abandoned by this play of light and shadow before him. He shook himself into partial awareness. Maybe his own destiny was to die in a state of confusion rather than the clarity he had always sought. What irony indeed. Rushing to Rome for a papal pardon, he might die unredeemed on an empty beach. He leaned forward on all fours. The sand gave way to his shadow. He forced himself to his feet. Then he fell back with his arms outstretched like one crucified.

#

Merisi awoke in darkness. He could hear nothing. Perhaps, he thought, my hearing has now failed as well. *Slowly, partial vision returned. He was in a room, a bare room. Yet it did not look like any of the prison cells he had been in before. His legs and arms moved without his intending them to move. This troubled him. His hearing returned. He heard a rustle of straw beneath him. But he could not feel the straw. Close to panic, he groaned when, suddenly, he could no longer distinguish light from shadow. It was as if a cloth had been dropped over his eyes.*

He knew the signs. He knew he was dying.

#

Startled by the strange man's first sound, Sister Catherine Boniglio lifted the cloth she had used to cool his forehead. He had been still now for eighteen hours. She lit the small candle at his bedside and studied the man. Now that some of the sand and dirt had been cleaned away, she could see an oblique scar across his temple and eye, the strange angle to the nose, the black goatee. His clothes were of silk and fine linen, tailored by a master. This was no vagrant. The old nun recognized him from her brother's description: This was the "most famous painter in Rome." This was Michelangelo da Merisi, the one they called Caravaggio.

Sister Catherine heard from her brother that the Milano was a notorious brawler. But her brother, who for twenty years had struggled to establish himself as an artist in Rome, insisted that Caravaggio was also a hero to the vagrants who filled the Eternal City. Caravaggio painted with the same passion fueling his violent eruptions, he told his sister, images so lifelike his subjects seemed to break out of their frames.

Caravaggio suddenly started tearing off his clothes.

#

Perhaps I'm already dead, Caravaggio thought. Unpardoned and dead. But I'm moving. And there's a woman. She's calm but anxious. Her nightmare eyes are studying me. And she's not wearing the plague mask of the Black Death. The feared beak mask was worn to protect doctors from infection from the plague.

"Inferno?" asked Caravaggio in his native Italian dialect.

"Non!" Sister Catherine withdrew in surprise.

"Suora?" he said, pointing to her, pausing to fight for more air. "Curato?"

The Franciscan nun nodded and placed another cold compress on his forehead. "Si, infatti sto aspettando che arrive Curato." *She hoped, however, the priest would hurry.*

"Sacremento della penitenza," he whispered through his caked lips.

"Si, si," she responded. She turned quickly and left the room.

He was comforted. He would make a good confession and be blessed before dying. He would escape this last prison, the earth. That hope led him to a new thought. Perhaps he will not die! If so, he knew he had very little time to act if he wanted to finish his pilgrimage to seek redemption. He was in territory controlled by the Spanish guards, the men Queen Isabella and King Charles had used in their harsh inquisition. Non-Christians underwent compulsory conversion or were expelled from Spanish territory. The Spanish soldiers dealt ruthlessly with foreigners. The bounty on his head would make them eager to hunt him down.

In addition to the Spanish, a Hospitaller Knight had been trailing him for weeks. Caravaggio sighed inwardly, recalling one of the many great sins he would have to confess to the priest. Years ago he'd killed a good friend in Rome over a tennis match. He'd fled Rome and kept running until he found refuge and a brief redemption in the priory on Malta. There, the painter had been inducted into the religious Order of Saint John of the Hospitallers of Jerusalem of Rhodes and of Malta, becoming Fra M, a Knight. The Knights were known for founding the first hospital for pilgrims in Jerusalem but then expanded to become the Pope's Mediterranean navy. The legend soon proliferated that they were miraculous healers of the severely ill and injured.

Despite his many sins, Michelangelo da Merisi remained determined to acquit himself as the newly annointed Fra M. However, the brawler in his soul finally burst forth again during this stay in Malta. Merisi slashed out in anger at a fellow Knight. His sword stroke mirrored the famous brush across his magnificent paintings. He had deftly sliced open his brother Knight's scrotum.

Once imprisoned for this transgression, he painted in anger the direction to the secret of the Knights' power over the Catholic Church—The Last Prophet. The Knights were celebrated for living through several generations, surviving terrible illnesses, recovering from near fatal battle injuries and curing the incurable patient—all through the spiritual force of The Last Prophet they possessed. To release the secret was to break his vow as a Knight. Would that secret be so powerful it would destroy the Church? Should he divide up the paintings to hide the secret? He wondered if he should destroy the three paintings that led to the hidden location of The Last Prophet, or was he compelled to release the secret to save the thousands of his fellow citizens suffering from the ravages of the Black Plague?

Unsure whether to hope for life or prepare for eternity, Caravaggio made a survivor's calculation: If he were pardoned by the judicial authorities in central Italy, which really meant if he were pardoned by the pope, he would be free of the papal guards who had been following him from Rome ever since he'd killed his friend. A papal pardon would buy him freedom. Who besides himself could negotiate on his behalf?

Before the latest escapade, he'd sent his last painting, David with the Head of Goliath, *to Cardinal Scipione Borghese, the nephew of Pope Paulo V. Borghese was his best path to a papal pardon. But the cardinal would undoubtedly now want more than a painting to take on the Knights Hospitaller.*

Caravaggio lifted his head from the mattress and assured himself that his quiver of canvases was nearby. Should he tell the cardinal about the riddle hidden within the series of paintings? Then receive the mercy he craved? But the cardinal and his mercy were as corrupt as Caravaggio's consciousness.

Moments later Sister Catherine reappeared with a priest.

Fighting for air, Caravaggio asked, "Societas Jesu?"

"Si," the priest answered.

Caravaggio started whispering the formal Latin rite: "Ignosce mihi, Pater, quia peccavi." His breathing was labored. He knew he could never complete the prayer with only one pause for a breath, as he had been instructed in his youth. Perhaps his act would be flawed? He longed to heal the torment in his soul. But he was now conflicted and his visions of virtue oscillated like his senses. He must try another form of contrition. He would bribe God. He believed that the power of the Knights came from God. On one hand he had seen so much suffering at the clutches of the Black Plague he felt compelled to share the Knights' secret that cured all illnesses—The Last Prophet. *On the other hand the Knights' secret power might become a terrible weapon in the hands of the common man and then unwelcome by God. He needed to make a decision. Caravaggio lifted one finger from the bed and pointed.* "There are three canvases. Burn them."

#

The Jesuit hurried to start absolution: "Dominus noster Jesus Christus te absolvat . . ." *He stopped. His eyes strayed to the rolled up canvasses extending from his leather bag. The moonlight from a small, high window reflected the glow of the paintings' landscapes upward in the darkness of the room. When the priest turned back to complete his blessing, the artist was dead.*

#

A short time later, Sister Catherine began preparing the body for burial. As she paused in her ministrations she looked around the small room. The dead man's belongings were gone.

ABOUT THE AUTHOR

Michael J. Hallisey, M.D. is a practicing Endovascular Surgeon and Interventional Radiologist from Hartford, CT, and has been a Top Doctor in America for more than 10 consecutive years. He majored in English at the College of the Holy Cross before graduating from The University of Connecticut School of Medicine. Dr. Hallisey has published extensively in the medical literature.

Author's Note:
Join the March of Dimes

The March of Dimes is the leading nonprofit organization for pregnancy and baby health. I support its mission to improve the health of babies by preventing birth defects, premature birth, and infant mortality -- and I ask my readers to do so, too.

The March of Dimes is an historic organization, founded in 1938 by President Franklin D. Roosevelt to end polio in the United States. In those days, polio was a real life medical mystery that tragically killed and paralyzed thousands of children every year until Dr. Jonas Salk, funded by the March of Dimes, developed the first safe and effective polio vaccine. Every baby born today continues to receive the polio vaccine and also benefit from many other March of Dimes-supported breakthroughs.

Today, the March of Dimes is committed to reducing the rate of premature birth, the leading cause of death among babies in the United States. The group also works with global partners to prevent prematurity and improve care for nearly 15 million babies born too soon each year worldwide.

The March of Dimes funds education and health promotion programs in local communities. For example, when a baby is born early or with a birth defect, families receive information and comfort from March of Dimes NICU Family Support® in more than 130 hospitals nationwide. The March of Dimes advocates at the federal and state level for policies that will improve maternal and infant health, including access to health care, newborn screening, and protection from toxic substances. In 2016, the March of Dimes launched #ZAPzika campaign to prevent pregnant women from becoming infected with the Zika virus, which causes serious brain damage in unborn babies.

Learn more about what you can do to help moms have healthy pregnancies and healthy babies at **marchofdimes.org** and **nacersano.org**. Please make a donation while you're there to help fund the lifesaving work of the March of Dimes. Thank you.

38048187R00198

Made in the USA
Middletown, DE
11 December 2016